PiX™

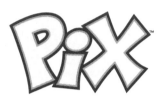

HATTER entertainment
hatterentertainment.com

Book Design by Gregg Schigiel
Color Assists by Paul Tutrone & Chris Dickey
"Schigiel" Font Design by John Green

image

IMAGE COMICS, INC.
Robert Kirkman — Chief Operating Officer
Erik Larsen — Chief Financial Officer
Todd McFarlane — President
Marc Silvestri — Chief Executive Officer
Jim Valentino — Vice-President
Eric Stephenson — Publisher
Corey Murphy — Director of Sales
Jeff Boison — Director of Publishing Planning & Book Trade Sales
Chris Ross — Director of Digital Sales
Kat Salazar — Director of PR & Marketing
Branwyn Bigglestone — Controller
Susan Korpela — Accounts Manager
Drew Gill — Art Director
Brett Warnock — Production Manager
Meredith Wallace — Print Manager
Briah Skelly — Publicist
Aly Hoffman — Conventions & Events Coordinator
Sasha Head — Sales & Marketing Production Designer
David Brothers — Branding Manager
Melissa Gifford — Content Manager
Erika Schnatz — Production Artist
Ryan Brewer — Production Artist
Shanna Matuszak — Production Artist
Tricia Ramos — Production Artist
Vincent Kukua — Production Artist
Jeff Stang — Direct Market Sales Representative
Emilio Bautista — Digital Sales Associate
Leanna Counter — Accounting Assistant
Chloe Ramos-Peterson — Library Market Sales Representative
IMAGECOMICS.COM

ONE WEIRDEST WEEKEND

Story and Art by Gregg Schigiel

pixcomic.com

image

PROLOGUE

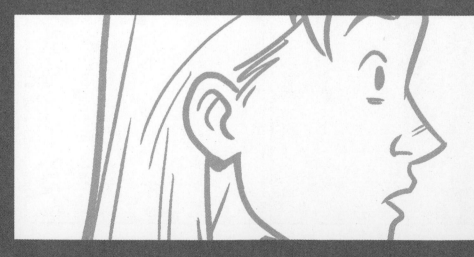

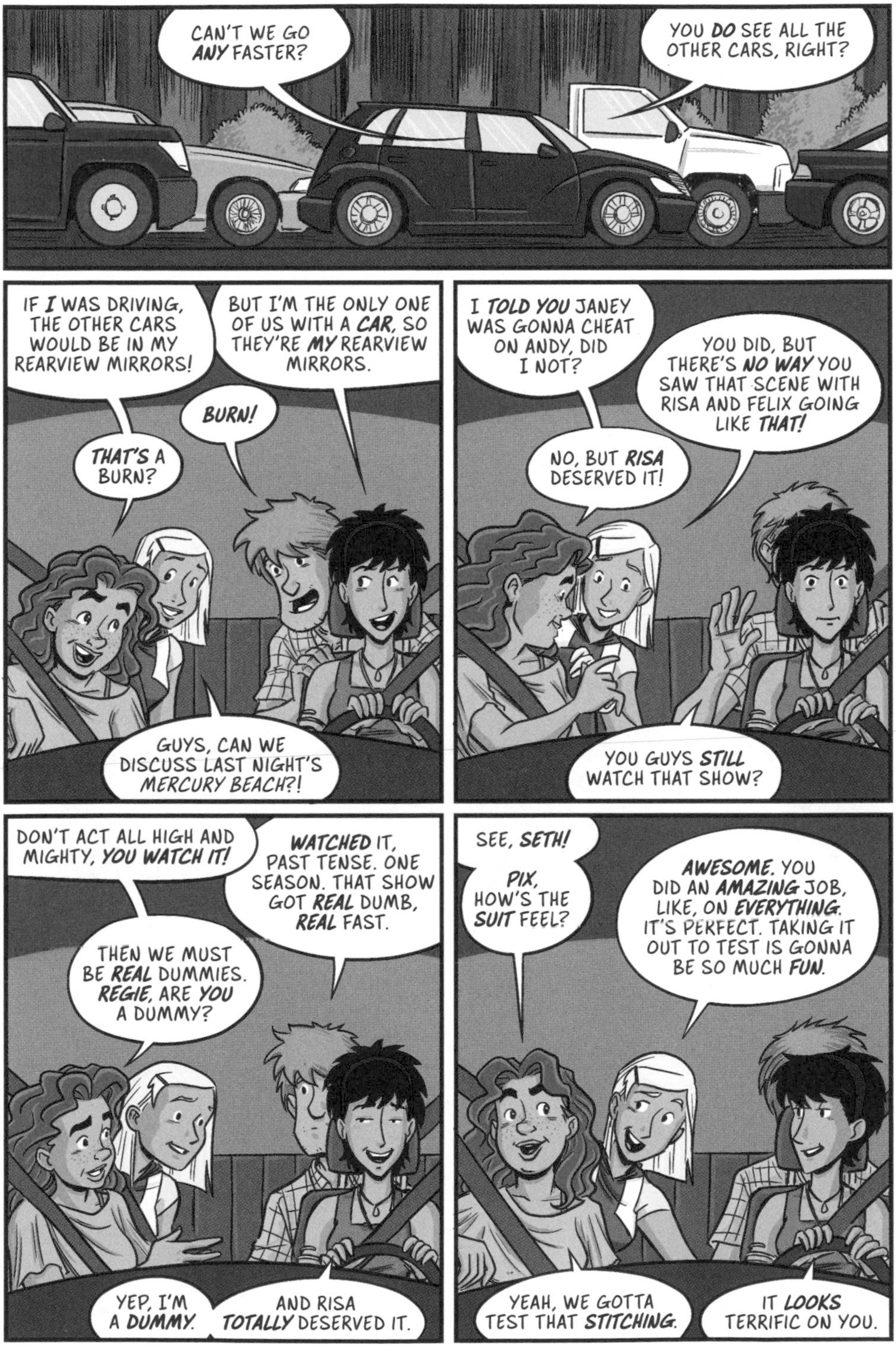

CAN'T WE GO ANY FASTER?
YOU DO SEE ALL THE OTHER CARS, RIGHT?
IF I WAS DRIVING, THE OTHER CARS WOULD BE IN MY REARVIEW MIRRORS!
BUT I'M THE ONLY ONE OF US WITH A CAR, SO THEY'RE MY REARVIEW MIRRORS.
BURN!
THAT'S A BURN?
GUYS, CAN WE DISCUSS LAST NIGHT'S MERCURY BEACH?!
I TOLD YOU JANEY WAS GONNA CHEAT ON ANDY, DID I NOT?
YOU DID, BUT THERE'S NO WAY YOU SAW THAT SCENE WITH RISA AND FELIX GOING LIKE THAT!
NO, BUT RISA DESERVED IT!
YOU GUYS STILL WATCH THAT SHOW?
DON'T ACT ALL HIGH AND MIGHTY, YOU WATCH IT!
WATCHED IT, PAST TENSE. ONE SEASON. THAT SHOW GOT REAL DUMB, REAL FAST.
THEN WE MUST BE REAL DUMMIES. REGIE, ARE YOU A DUMMY?
YEP, I'M A DUMMY.
AND RISA TOTALLY DESERVED IT.
SEE, SETH!
PIX, HOW'S THE SUIT FEEL?
AWESOME. YOU DID AN AMAZING JOB, LIKE, ON EVERYTHING. IT'S PERFECT. TAKING IT OUT TO TEST IS GONNA BE SO MUCH FUN.
YEAH, WE GOTTA TEST THAT STITCHING.
IT LOOKS TERRIFIC ON YOU.

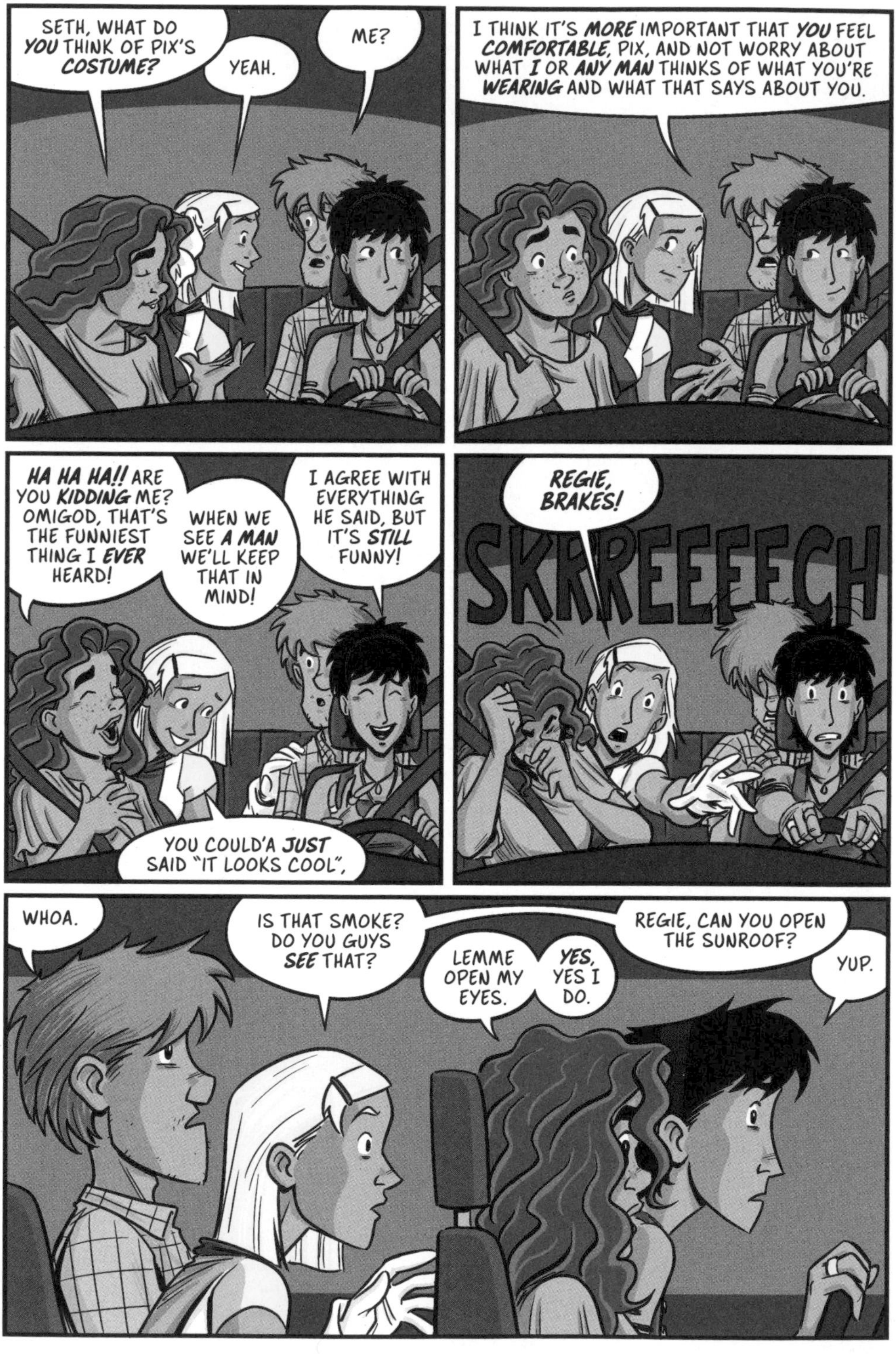
SETH, WHAT DO YOU THINK OF PIX'S COSTUME?
YEAH.
ME?
I THINK IT'S MORE IMPORTANT THAT YOU FEEL COMFORTABLE, PIX, AND NOT WORRY ABOUT WHAT I OR ANY MAN THINKS OF WHAT YOU'RE WEARING AND WHAT THAT SAYS ABOUT YOU.
HA HA HA!! ARE YOU KIDDING ME? OMIGOD, THAT'S THE FUNNIEST THING I EVER HEARD!
WHEN WE SEE A MAN WE'LL KEEP THAT IN MIND!
I AGREE WITH EVERYTHING HE SAID, BUT IT'S STILL FUNNY!
YOU COULD'A JUST SAID "IT LOOKS COOL".
REGIE, BRAKES!
SKRREEEECH
WHOA.
IS THAT SMOKE? DO YOU GUYS SEE THAT?
LEMME OPEN MY EYES.
YES, YES I DO.
REGIE, CAN YOU OPEN THE SUNROOF?
YUP.

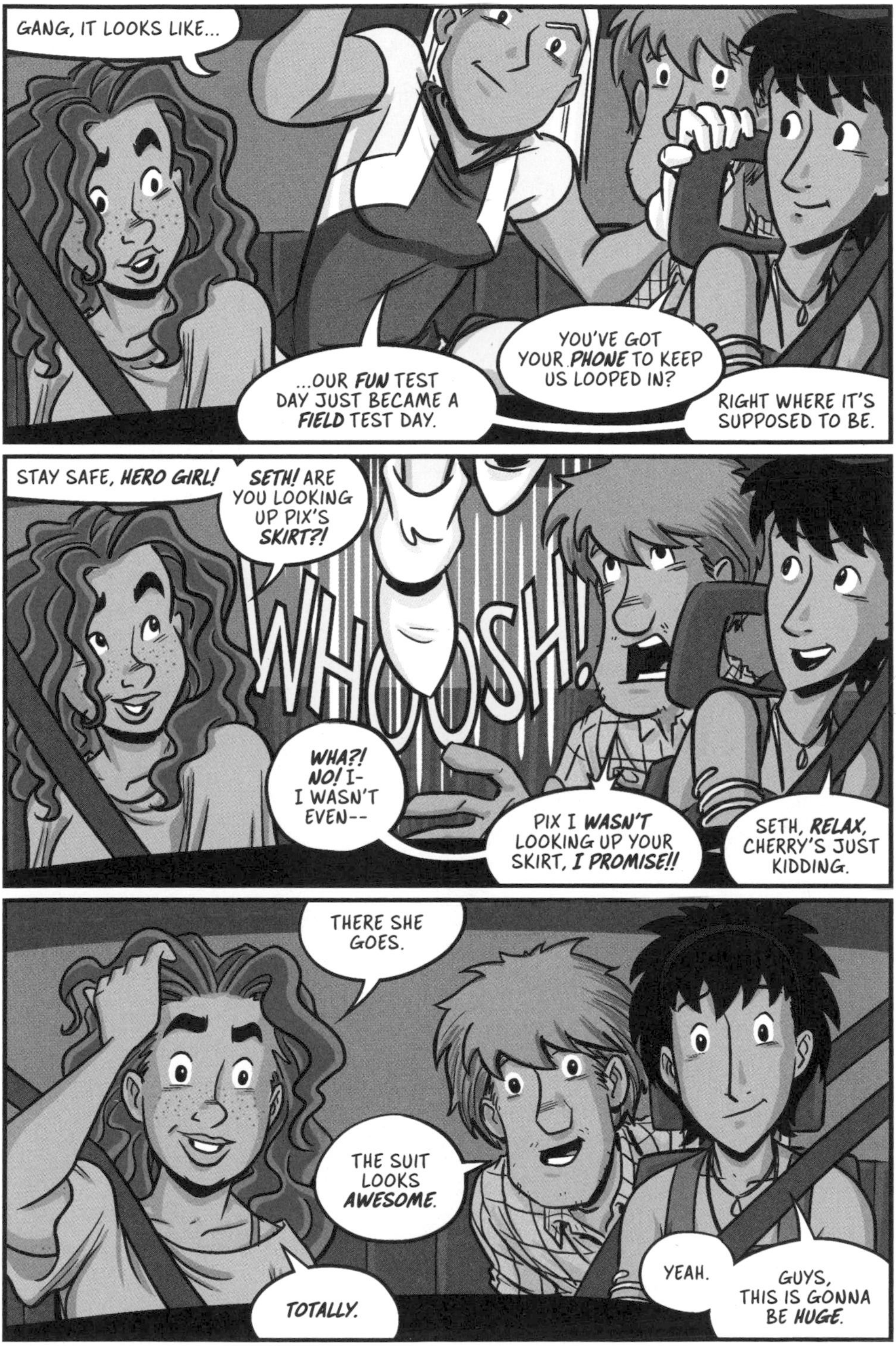
GANG, IT LOOKS LIKE...
...OUR **FUN** TEST DAY JUST BECAME A **FIELD** TEST DAY.
YOU'VE GOT YOUR **PHONE** TO KEEP US LOOPED IN?
RIGHT WHERE IT'S SUPPOSED TO BE.
STAY SAFE, **HERO GIRL!**
SETH! ARE YOU LOOKING UP PIX'S **SKIRT?!**
WHOOSH!
WHA?! NO! I- I WASN'T EVEN--
PIX I **WASN'T** LOOKING UP YOUR SKIRT, **I PROMISE!!**
SETH, **RELAX**, CHERRY'S JUST KIDDING.
THERE SHE GOES.
THE SUIT LOOKS **AWESOME**.
TOTALLY.
YEAH.
GUYS, THIS IS GONNA BE **HUGE**.

CHAPTER ONE

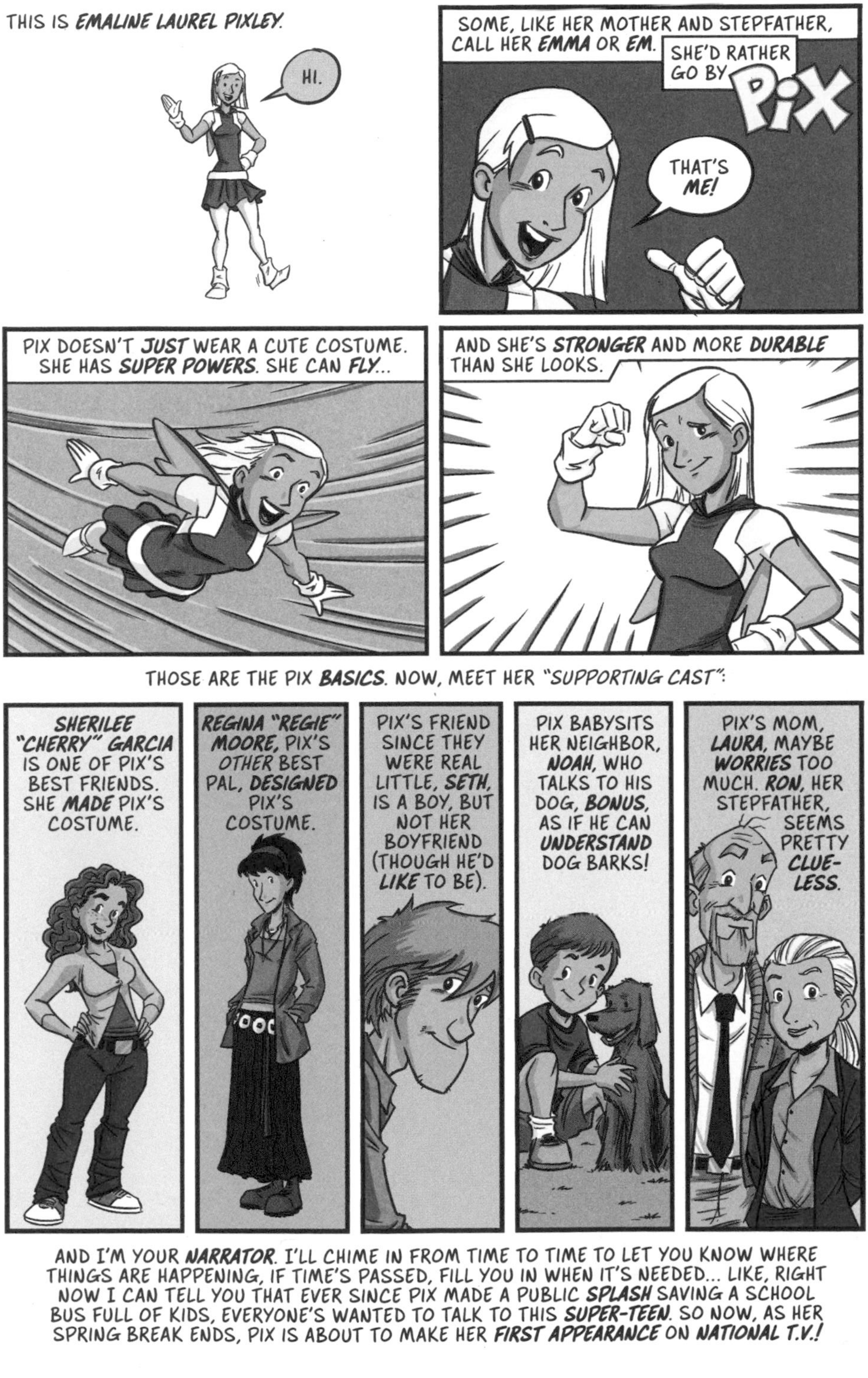
THIS IS EMALINE LAUREL PIXLEY.
HI.
SOME, LIKE HER MOTHER AND STEPFATHER, CALL HER EMMA OR EM.
SHE'D RATHER GO BY
PIX
THAT'S ME!
PIX DOESN'T JUST WEAR A CUTE COSTUME. SHE HAS SUPER POWERS. SHE CAN FLY...
AND SHE'S STRONGER AND MORE DURABLE THAN SHE LOOKS.
THOSE ARE THE PIX BASICS. NOW, MEET HER "SUPPORTING CAST":
SHERILEE "CHERRY" GARCIA IS ONE OF PIX'S BEST FRIENDS. SHE MADE PIX'S COSTUME.
REGINA "REGIE" MOORE, PIX'S OTHER BEST PAL, DESIGNED PIX'S COSTUME.
PIX'S FRIEND SINCE THEY WERE REAL LITTLE, SETH, IS A BOY, BUT NOT HER BOYFRIEND (THOUGH HE'D LIKE TO BE).
PIX BABYSITS HER NEIGHBOR, NOAH, WHO TALKS TO HIS DOG, BONUS, AS IF HE CAN UNDERSTAND DOG BARKS!
PIX'S MOM, LAURA, MAYBE WORRIES TOO MUCH. RON, HER STEPFATHER, SEEMS PRETTY CLUELESS.
AND I'M YOUR NARRATOR. I'LL CHIME IN FROM TIME TO TIME TO LET YOU KNOW WHERE THINGS ARE HAPPENING, IF TIME'S PASSED, FILL YOU IN WHEN IT'S NEEDED... LIKE, RIGHT NOW I CAN TELL YOU THAT EVER SINCE PIX MADE A PUBLIC SPLASH SAVING A SCHOOL BUS FULL OF KIDS, EVERYONE'S WANTED TO TALK TO THIS SUPER-TEEN. SO NOW, AS HER SPRING BREAK ENDS, PIX IS ABOUT TO MAKE HER FIRST APPEARANCE ON NATIONAL T.V.!

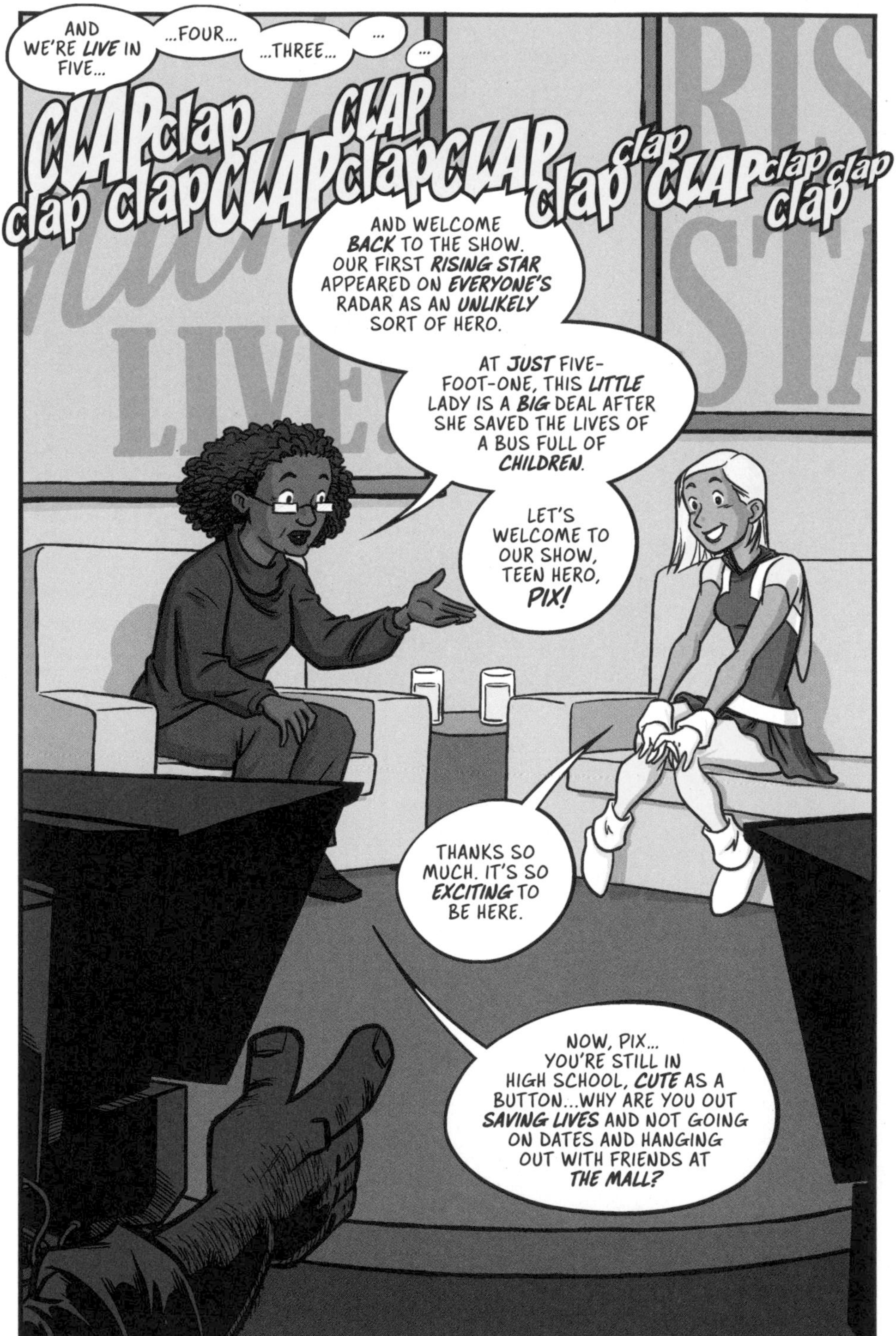
AND WE'RE LIVE IN FIVE...
...FOUR...
...THREE...
...
...
CLAP clap clap clap CLAP CLAP clap CLAP clap clap CLAP clap clap clap
AND WELCOME BACK TO THE SHOW. OUR FIRST RISING STAR APPEARED ON EVERYONE'S RADAR AS AN UNLIKELY SORT OF HERO.
AT JUST FIVE-FOOT-ONE, THIS LITTLE LADY IS A BIG DEAL AFTER SHE SAVED THE LIVES OF A BUS FULL OF CHILDREN.
LET'S WELCOME TO OUR SHOW, TEEN HERO, PIX!
THANKS SO MUCH. IT'S SO EXCITING TO BE HERE.
NOW, PIX... YOU'RE STILL IN HIGH SCHOOL, CUTE AS A BUTTON...WHY ARE YOU OUT SAVING LIVES AND NOT GOING ON DATES AND HANGING OUT WITH FRIENDS AT THE MALL?

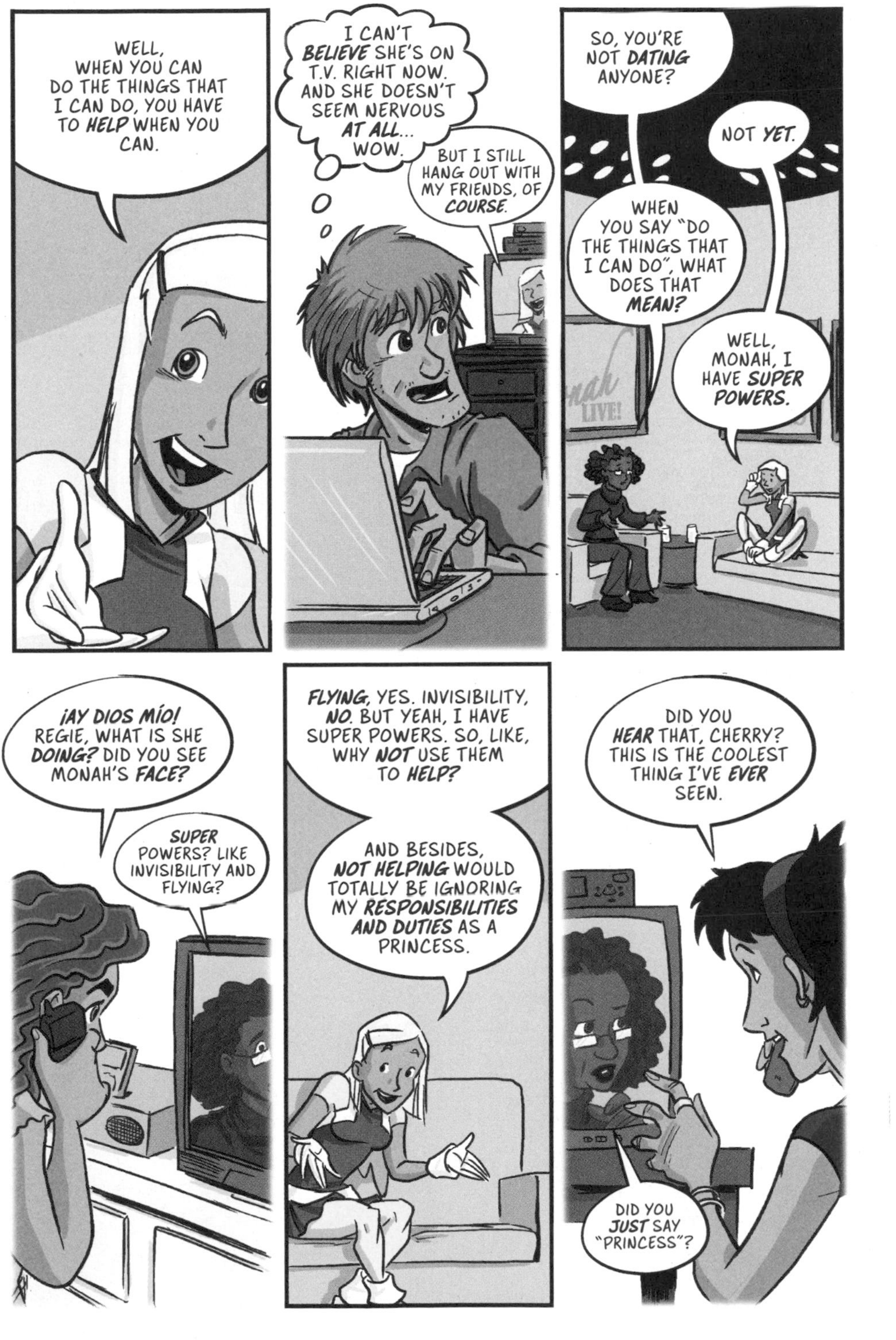

WELL, WHEN YOU CAN DO THE THINGS THAT I CAN DO, YOU HAVE TO HELP WHEN YOU CAN.
I CAN'T BELIEVE SHE'S ON T.V. RIGHT NOW. AND SHE DOESN'T SEEM NERVOUS AT ALL... WOW.
BUT I STILL HANG OUT WITH MY FRIENDS, OF COURSE.
SO, YOU'RE NOT DATING ANYONE?
NOT YET.
WHEN YOU SAY "DO THE THINGS THAT I CAN DO", WHAT DOES THAT MEAN?
WELL, MONAH, I HAVE SUPER POWERS.
¡AY DIOS MÍO! REGIE, WHAT IS SHE DOING? DID YOU SEE MONAH'S FACE?
SUPER POWERS? LIKE INVISIBILITY AND FLYING?
FLYING, YES. INVISIBILITY, NO. BUT YEAH, I HAVE SUPER POWERS. SO, LIKE, WHY NOT USE THEM TO HELP?
AND BESIDES, NOT HELPING WOULD TOTALLY BE IGNORING MY RESPONSIBILITIES AND DUTIES AS A PRINCESS.
DID YOU HEAR THAT, CHERRY? THIS IS THE COOLEST THING I'VE EVER SEEN.
DID YOU JUST SAY "PRINCESS"?

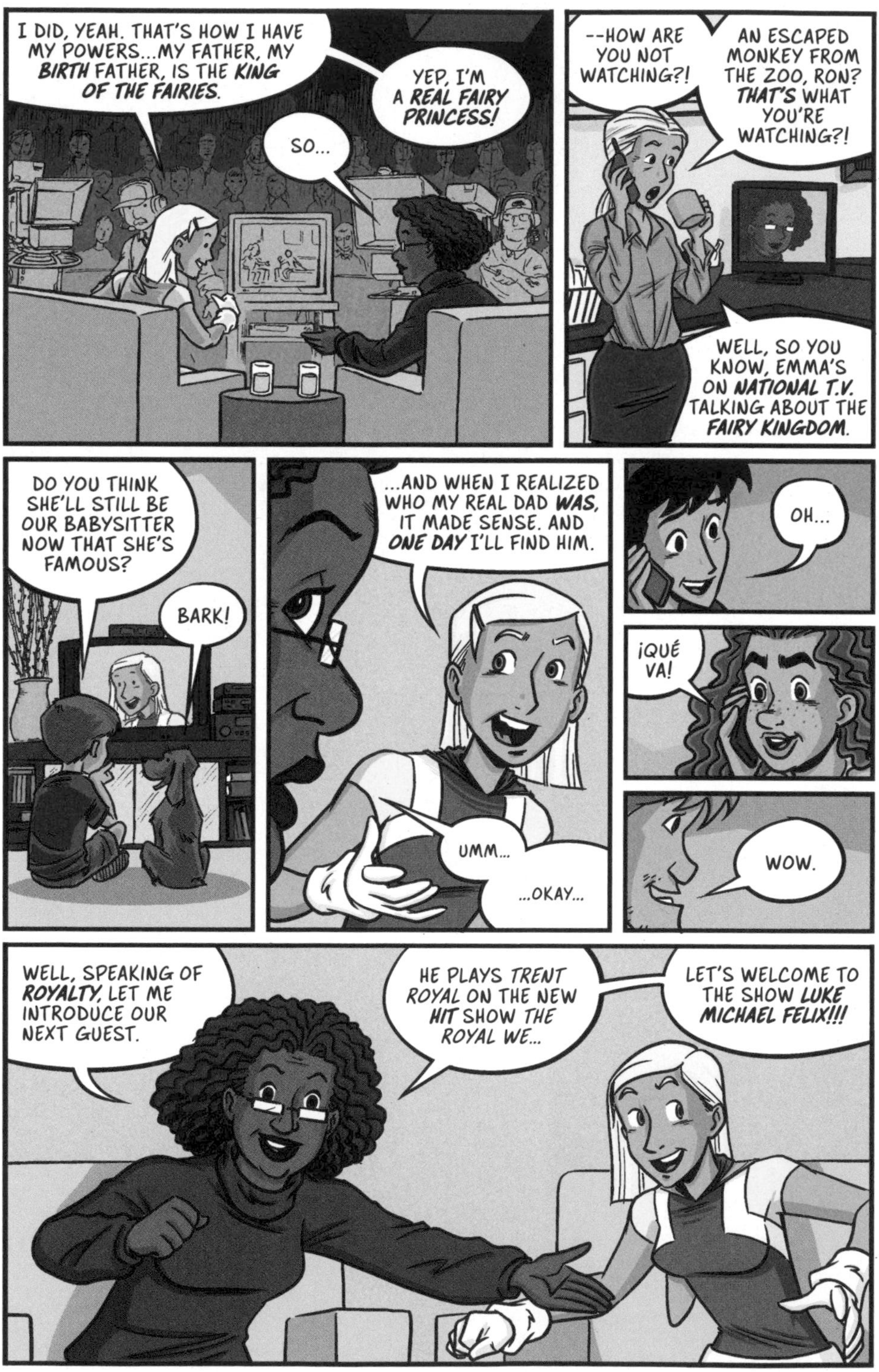

I DID, YEAH. THAT'S HOW I HAVE MY POWERS...MY FATHER, MY BIRTH FATHER, IS THE KING OF THE FAIRIES.
YEP, I'M A REAL FAIRY PRINCESS!
SO...
--HOW ARE YOU NOT WATCHING?!
AN ESCAPED MONKEY FROM THE ZOO, RON? THAT'S WHAT YOU'RE WATCHING?!
WELL, SO YOU KNOW, EMMA'S ON NATIONAL T.V. TALKING ABOUT THE FAIRY KINGDOM.
DO YOU THINK SHE'LL STILL BE OUR BABYSITTER NOW THAT SHE'S FAMOUS?
BARK!
...AND WHEN I REALIZED WHO MY REAL DAD WAS, IT MADE SENSE. AND ONE DAY I'LL FIND HIM.
UMM...
...OKAY...
OH...
¡QUÉ VA!
WOW.
WELL, SPEAKING OF ROYALTY, LET ME INTRODUCE OUR NEXT GUEST.
HE PLAYS TRENT ROYAL ON THE NEW HIT SHOW THE ROYAL WE...
LET'S WELCOME TO THE SHOW LUKE MICHAEL FELIX!!!

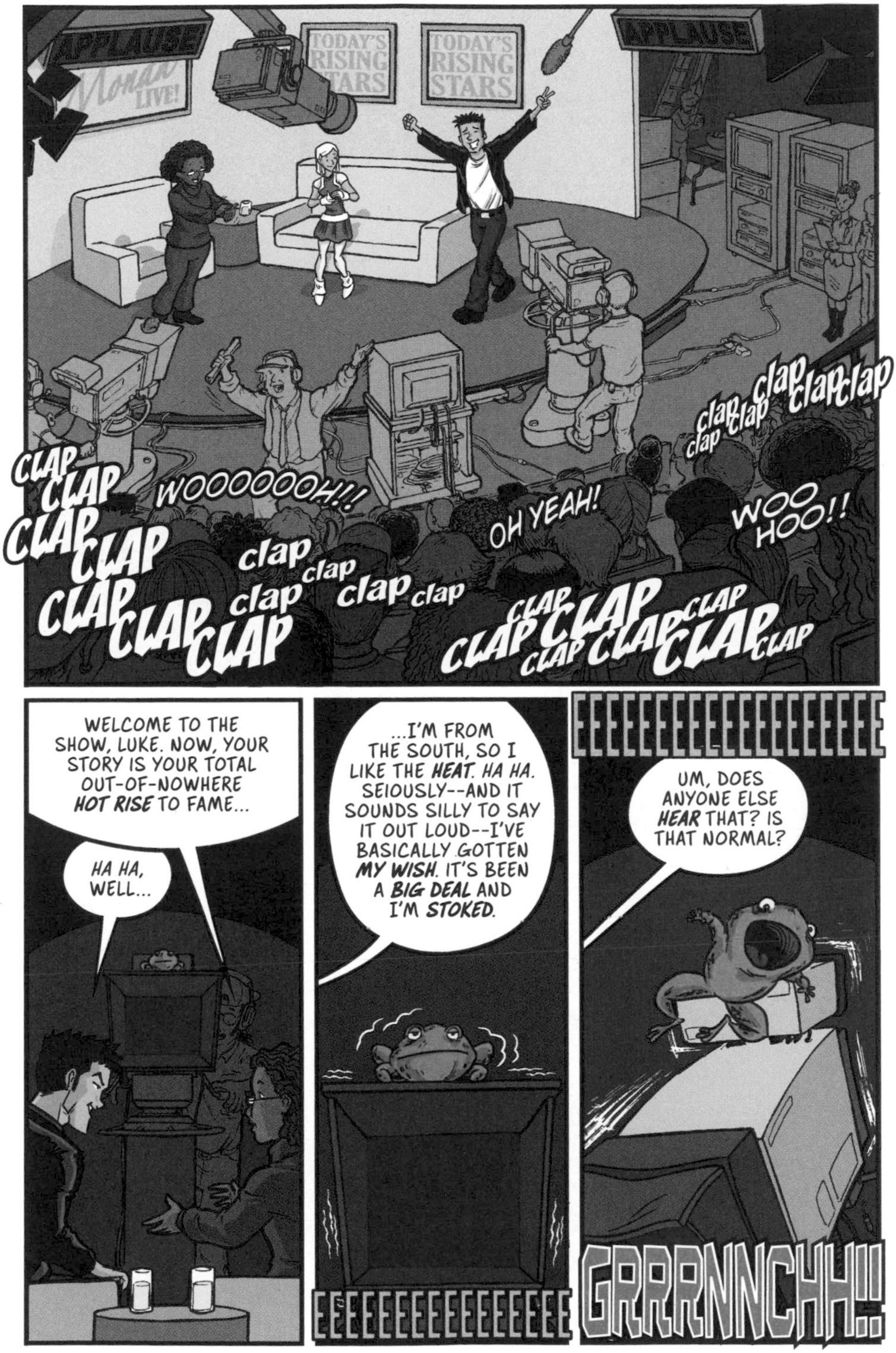
APPLAUSE
TODAY'S RISING STARS
TODAY'S RISING STARS
APPLAUSE
LIVE!
clap clap clap clap clap clap
CLAP CLAP CLAP CLAP CLAP CLAP CLAP
WOOOOOOH!!
clap clap clap clap clap
OH YEAH!
WOO HOO!!
CLAP CLAP CLAP CLAP CLAP CLAP CLAP clap
WELCOME TO THE SHOW, LUKE. NOW, YOUR STORY IS YOUR TOTAL OUT-OF-NOWHERE HOT RISE TO FAME...
HA HA, WELL...
...I'M FROM THE SOUTH, SO I LIKE THE HEAT. HA HA. SEIOUSLY--AND IT SOUNDS SILLY TO SAY IT OUT LOUD--I'VE BASICALLY GOTTEN MY WISH. IT'S BEEN A BIG DEAL AND I'M STOKED.
EEEEEEEEEEEEEEEE
EEEEEEEEEEEEEEEEEE
UM, DOES ANYONE ELSE HEAR THAT? IS THAT NORMAL?
GRRRNNCHH!!

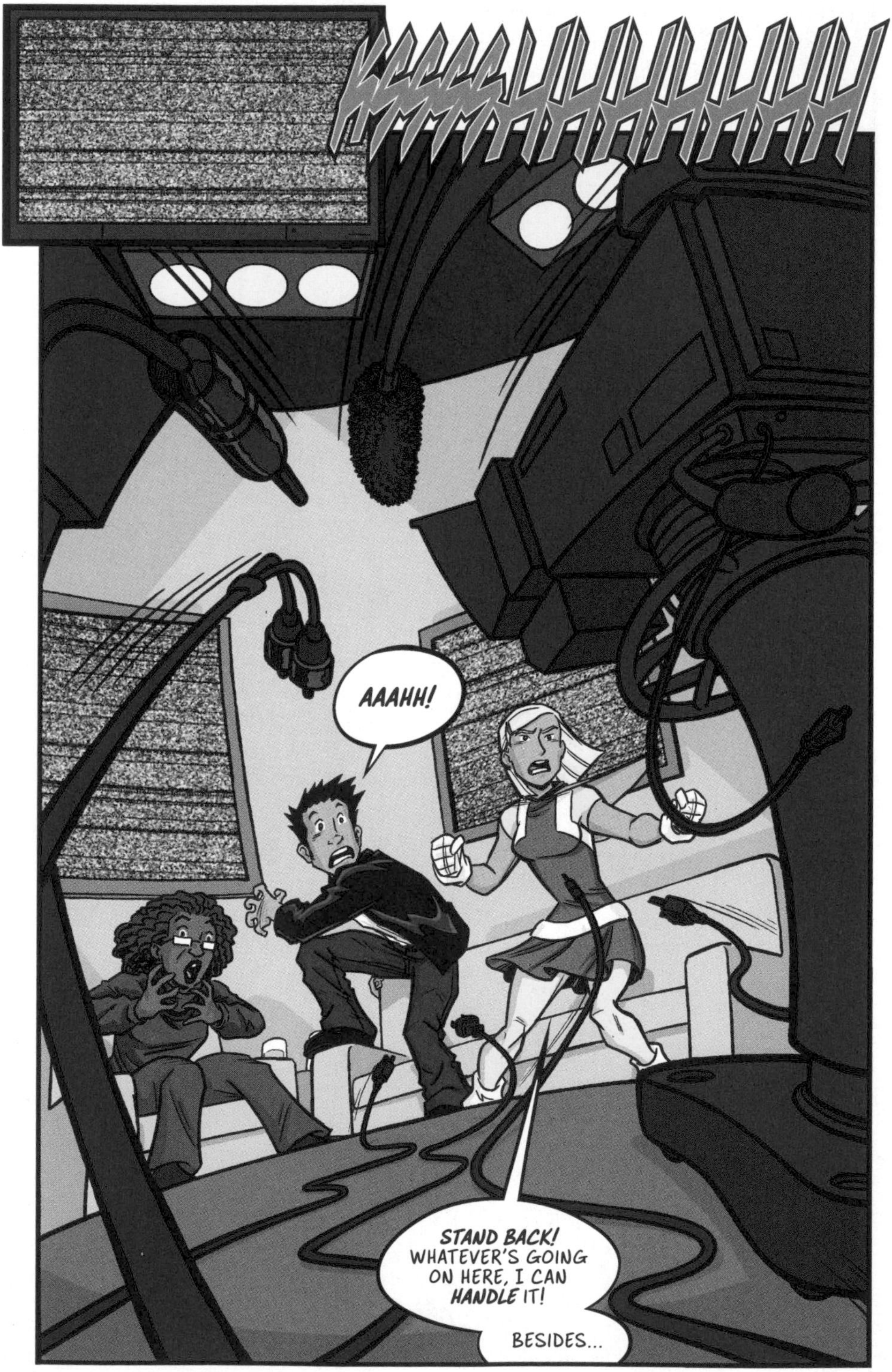
KSSSSHHHHHHHHHH
AAAHH!
STAND BACK! WHATEVER'S GOING ON HERE, I CAN HANDLE IT!
BESIDES...

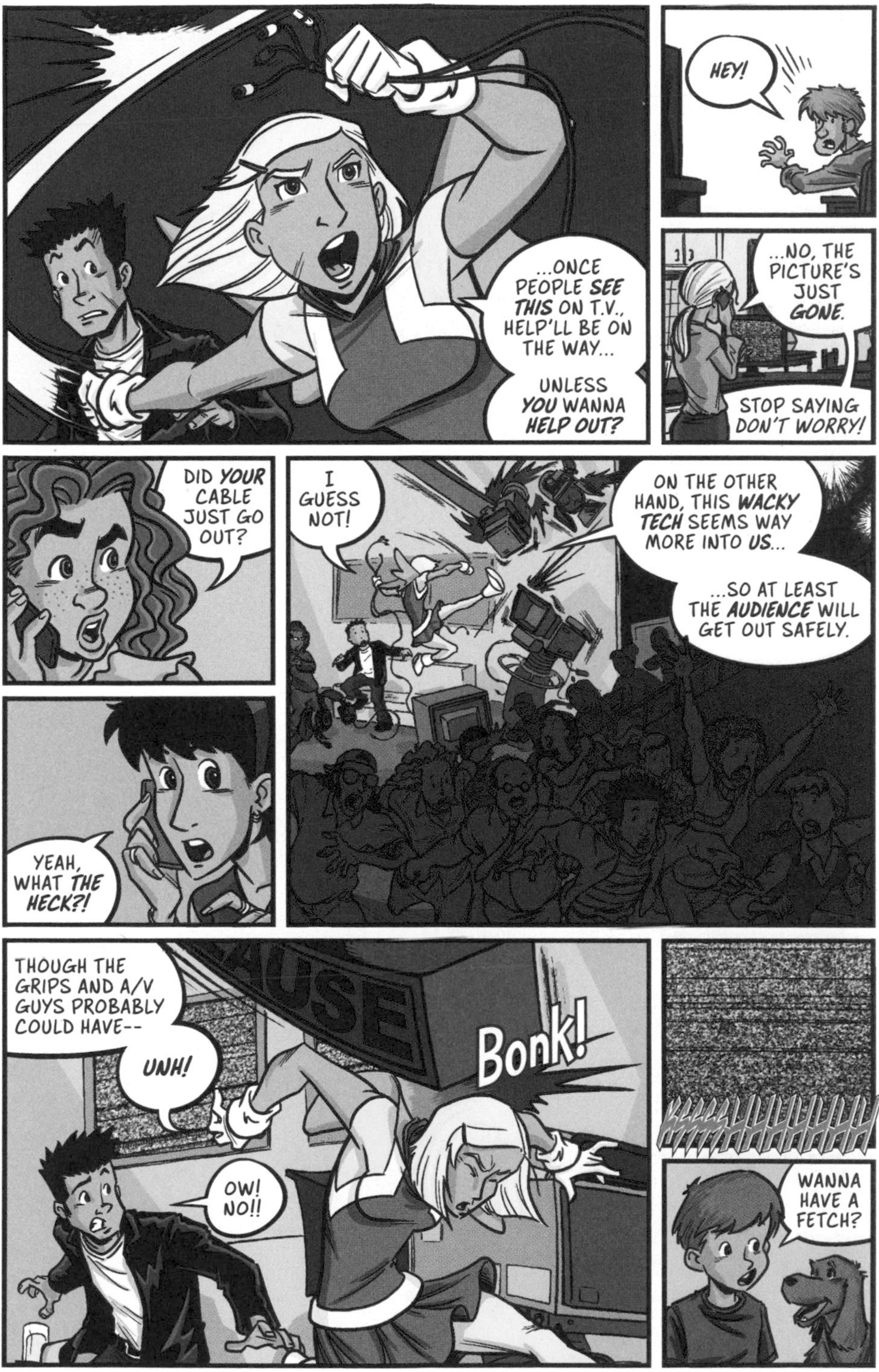
...ONCE PEOPLE SEE THIS ON T.V., HELP'LL BE ON THE WAY...
UNLESS YOU WANNA HELP OUT?
HEY!
...NO, THE PICTURE'S JUST GONE.
STOP SAYING DON'T WORRY!
DID YOUR CABLE JUST GO OUT?
YEAH, WHAT THE HECK?!
I GUESS NOT!
ON THE OTHER HAND, THIS WACKY TECH SEEMS WAY MORE INTO US...
...SO AT LEAST THE AUDIENCE WILL GET OUT SAFELY.
THOUGH THE GRIPS AND A/V GUYS PROBABLY COULD HAVE--
UNH!
Bonk!
OW! NO!!
KHHHHHHHHHHH
WANNA HAVE A FETCH?

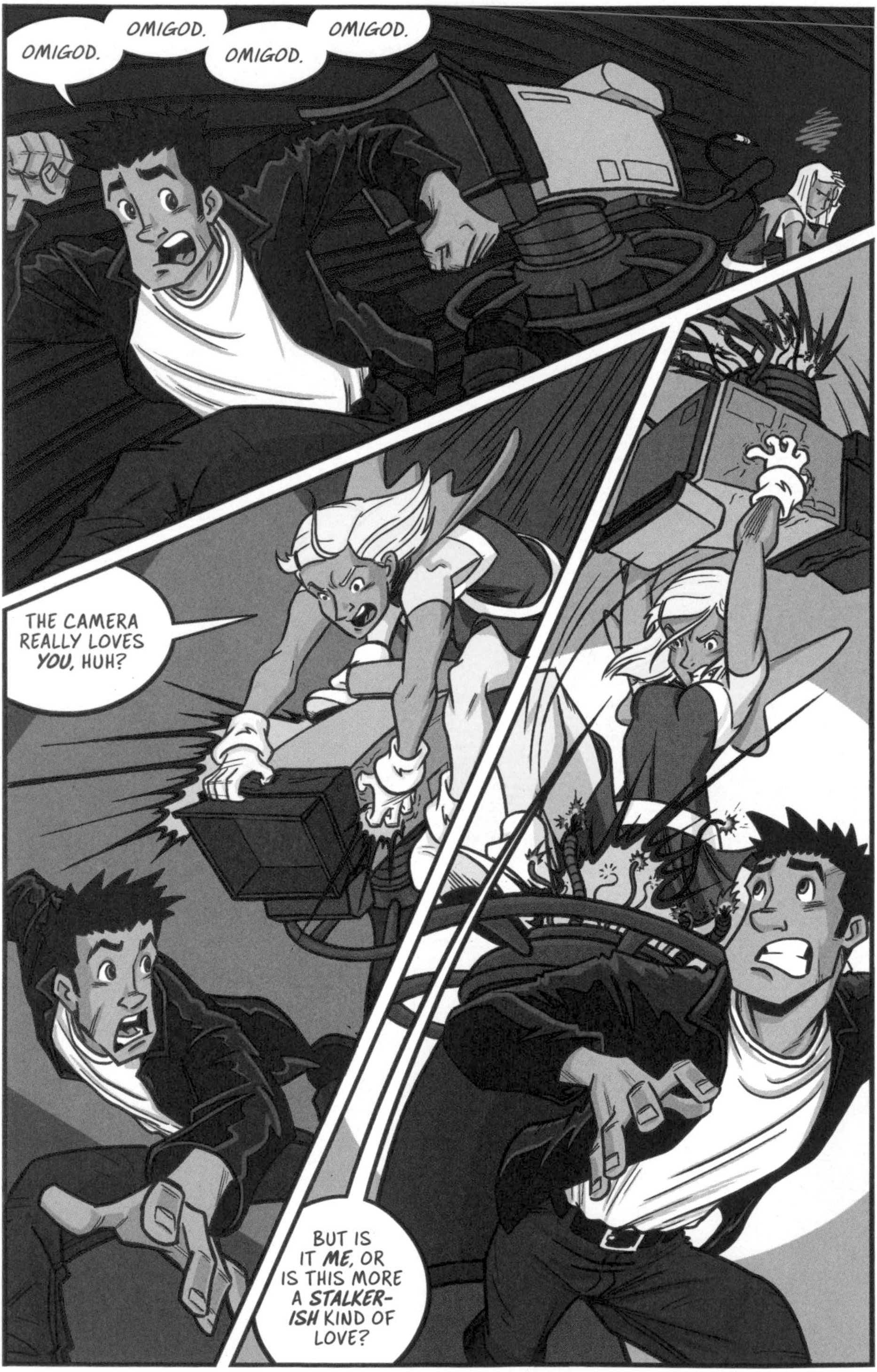
OMIGOD.
OMIGOD.
OMIGOD.
OMIGOD.
THE CAMERA REALLY LOVES *YOU,* HUH?
BUT IS IT *ME,* OR IS THIS MORE A *STALKER-ISH* KIND OF LOVE?

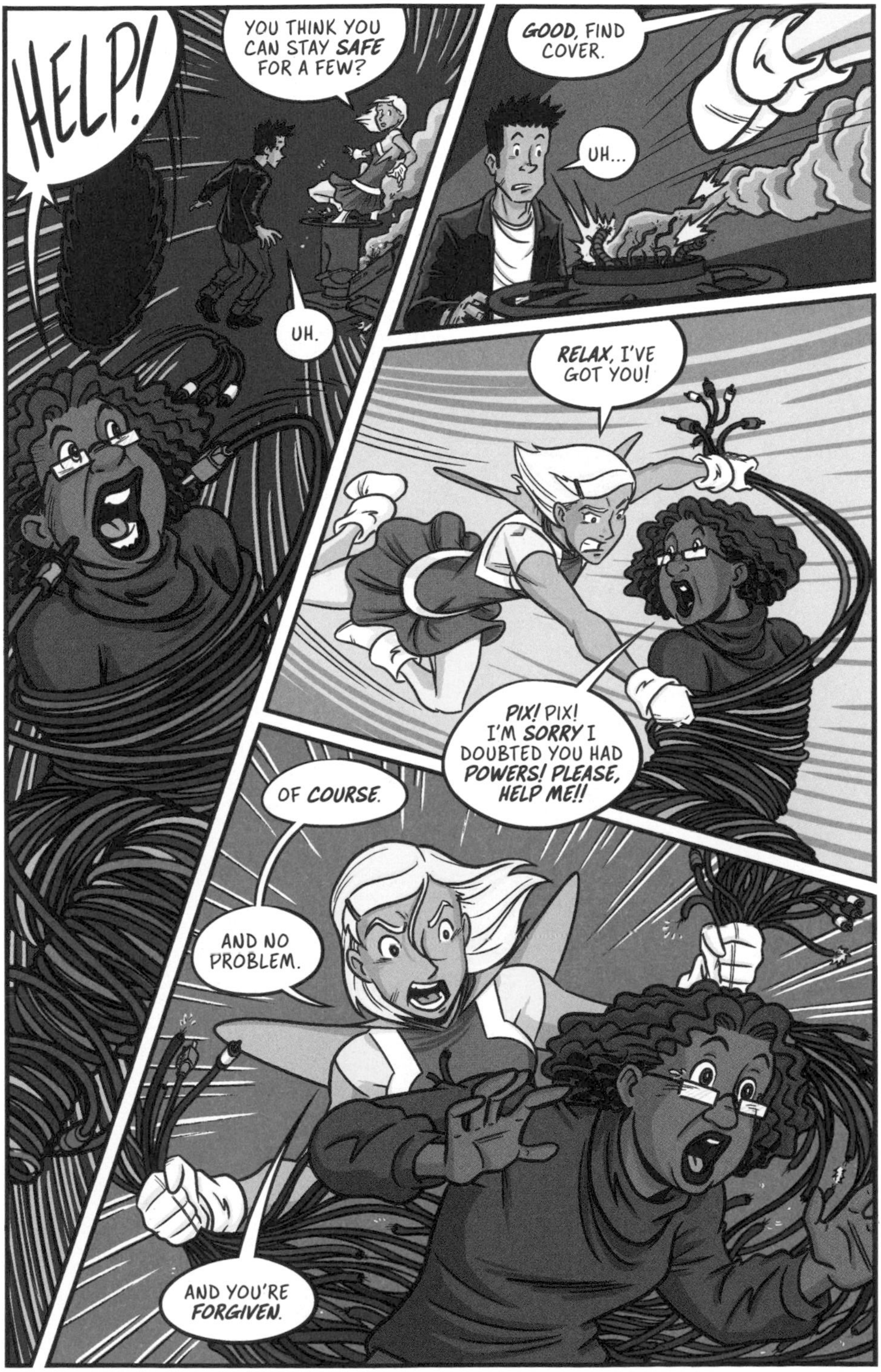
HELP!
YOU THINK YOU CAN STAY SAFE FOR A FEW?
UH.
GOOD, FIND COVER.
UH...
RELAX, I'VE GOT YOU!
PIX! PIX! I'M SORRY I DOUBTED YOU HAD POWERS! PLEASE, HELP ME!!
OF COURSE.
AND NO PROBLEM.
AND YOU'RE FORGIVEN.

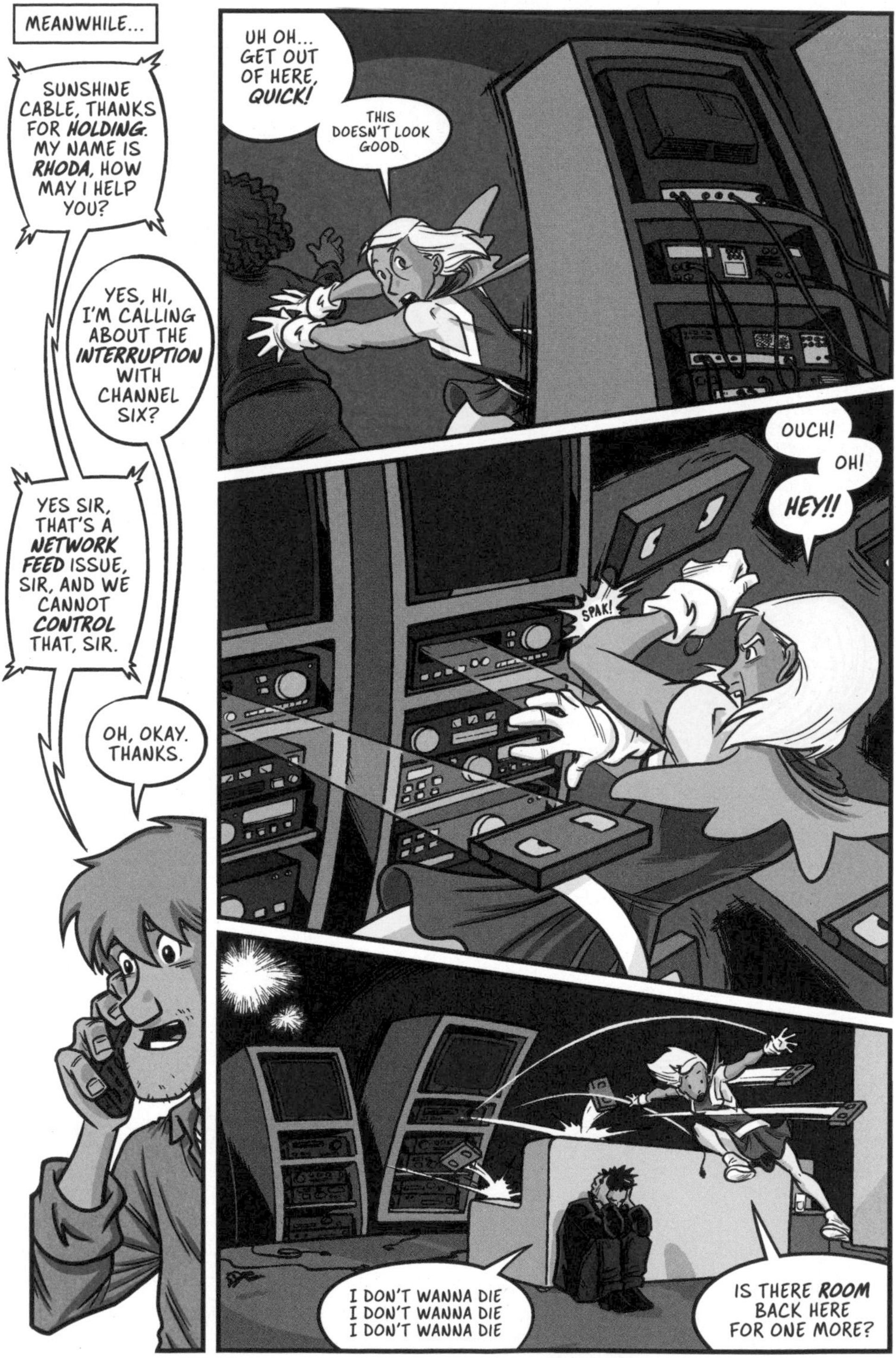
MEANWHILE...
SUNSHINE CABLE, THANKS FOR HOLDING. MY NAME IS RHODA, HOW MAY I HELP YOU?
UH OH... GET OUT OF HERE, QUICK!
THIS DOESN'T LOOK GOOD.
YES, HI, I'M CALLING ABOUT THE INTERRUPTION WITH CHANNEL SIX?
OUCH!
OH!
HEY!!
SPAK!
YES SIR, THAT'S A NETWORK FEED ISSUE, SIR, AND WE CANNOT CONTROL THAT, SIR.
OH, OKAY. THANKS.
I DON'T WANNA DIE I DON'T WANNA DIE I DON'T WANNA DIE
IS THERE ROOM BACK HERE FOR ONE MORE?

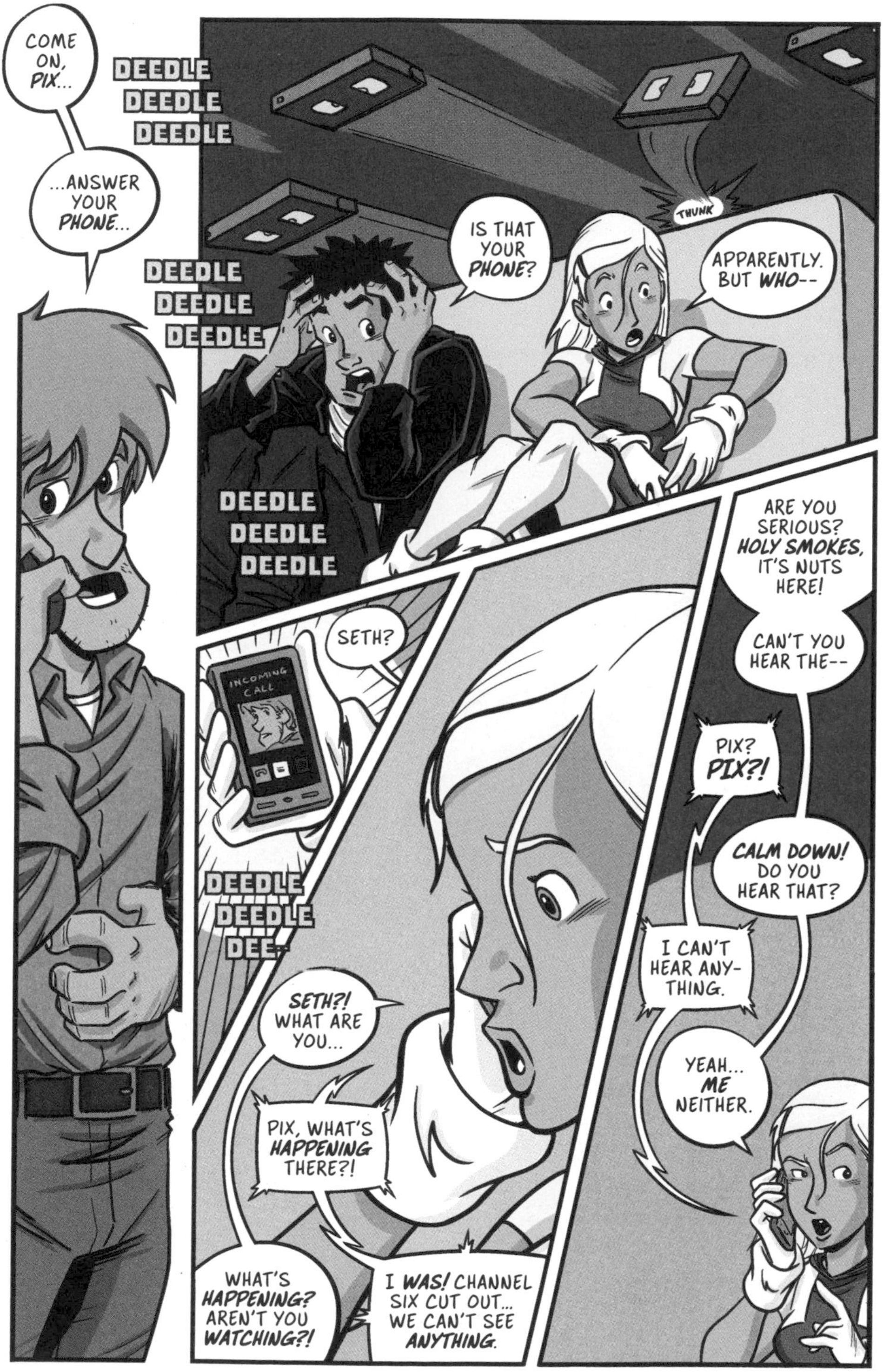
COME ON, PIX...
DEEDLE DEEDLE DEEDLE
...ANSWER YOUR PHONE...
DEEDLE DEEDLE DEEDLE
IS THAT YOUR PHONE?
THUNK
APPARENTLY. BUT WHO--
DEEDLE DEEDLE DEEDLE
INCOMING CALL
SETH?
DEEDLE DEEDLE DEE-
SETH?! WHAT ARE YOU...
PIX, WHAT'S HAPPENING THERE?!
WHAT'S HAPPENING? AREN'T YOU WATCHING?!
I WAS! CHANNEL SIX CUT OUT... WE CAN'T SEE ANYTHING.
ARE YOU SERIOUS? HOLY SMOKES, IT'S NUTS HERE!
CAN'T YOU HEAR THE--
PIX? PIX?!
CALM DOWN! DO YOU HEAR THAT?
I CAN'T HEAR ANY-THING.
YEAH... ME NEITHER.

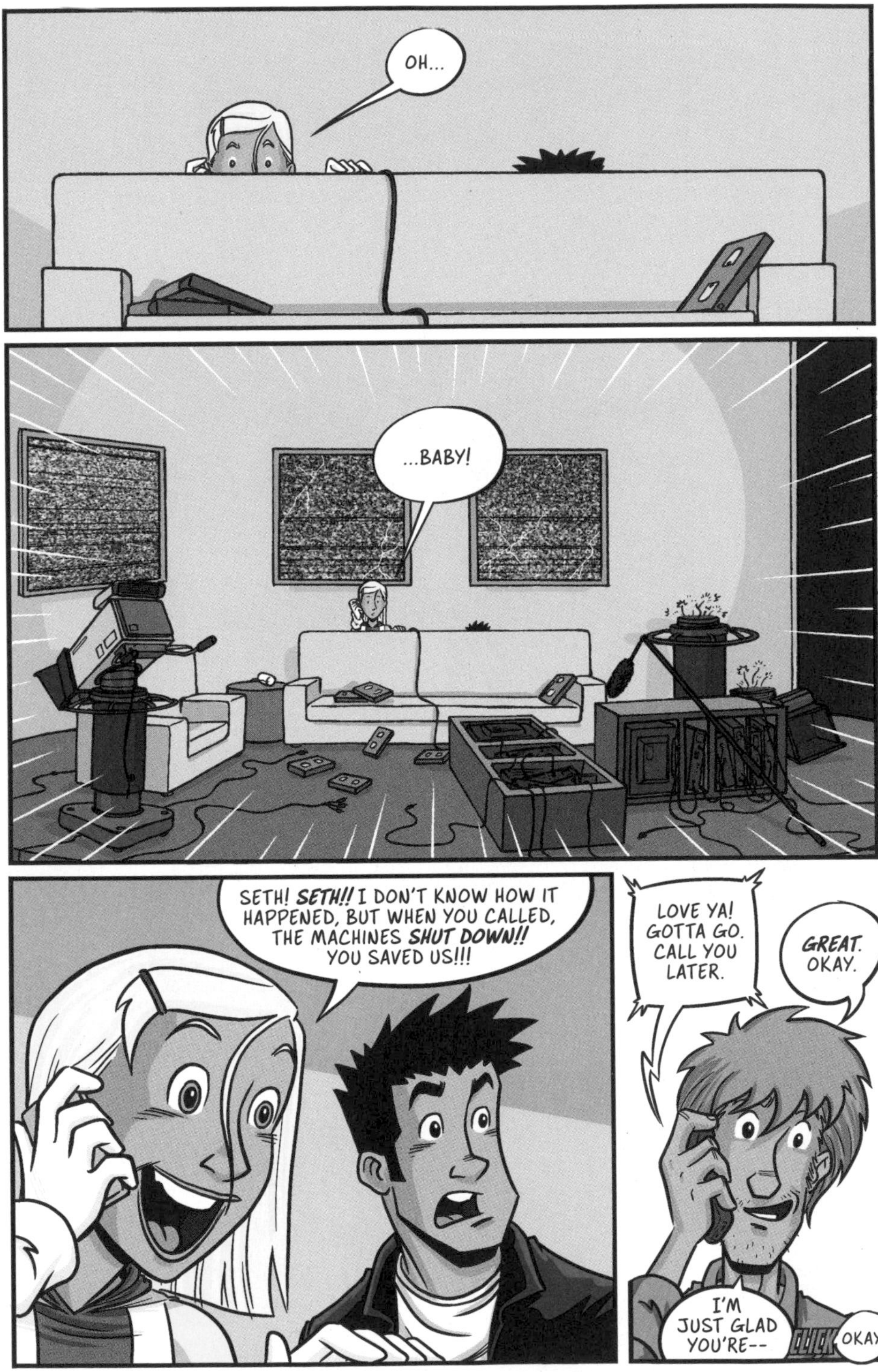
OH...
...BABY!
SETH! SETH!! I DON'T KNOW HOW IT HAPPENED, BUT WHEN YOU CALLED, THE MACHINES SHUT DOWN!! YOU SAVED US!!!
GREAT. OKAY.
LOVE YA! GOTTA GO. CALL YOU LATER.
I'M JUST GLAD YOU'RE--
CLICK
OKAY.

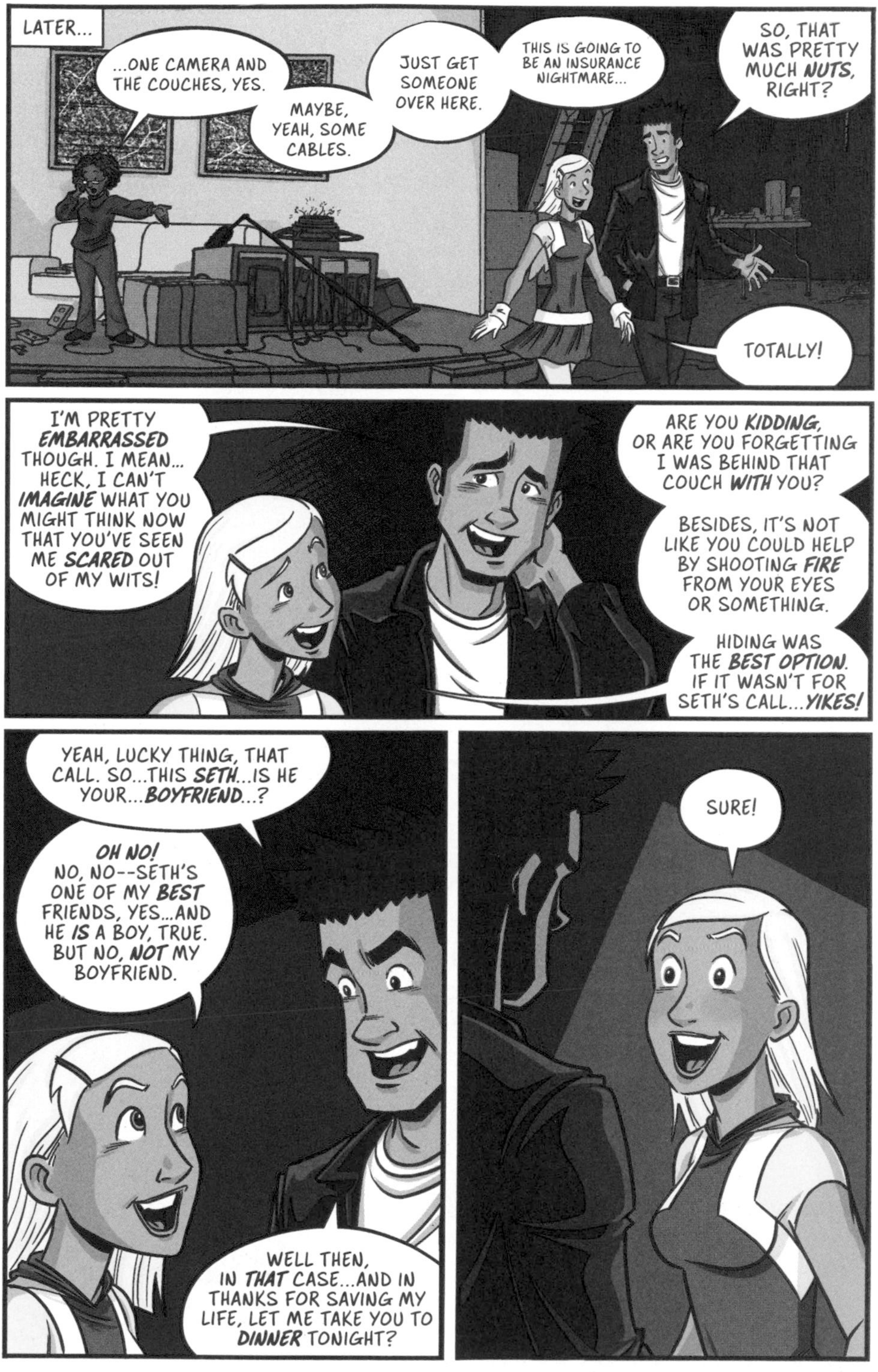
LATER...
...ONE CAMERA AND THE COUCHES, YES.
MAYBE, YEAH, SOME CABLES.
JUST GET SOMEONE OVER HERE.
THIS IS GOING TO BE AN INSURANCE NIGHTMARE...
SO, THAT WAS PRETTY MUCH NUTS, RIGHT?
TOTALLY!
I'M PRETTY EMBARRASSED THOUGH. I MEAN... HECK, I CAN'T IMAGINE WHAT YOU MIGHT THINK NOW THAT YOU'VE SEEN ME SCARED OUT OF MY WITS!
ARE YOU KIDDING, OR ARE YOU FORGETTING I WAS BEHIND THAT COUCH WITH YOU?
BESIDES, IT'S NOT LIKE YOU COULD HELP BY SHOOTING FIRE FROM YOUR EYES OR SOMETHING.
HIDING WAS THE BEST OPTION. IF IT WASN'T FOR SETH'S CALL...YIKES!
YEAH, LUCKY THING, THAT CALL. SO...THIS SETH...IS HE YOUR...BOYFRIEND...?
OH NO! NO, NO--SETH'S ONE OF MY BEST FRIENDS, YES...AND HE IS A BOY, TRUE. BUT NO, NOT MY BOYFRIEND.
WELL THEN, IN THAT CASE...AND IN THANKS FOR SAVING MY LIFE, LET ME TAKE YOU TO DINNER TONIGHT?
SURE!

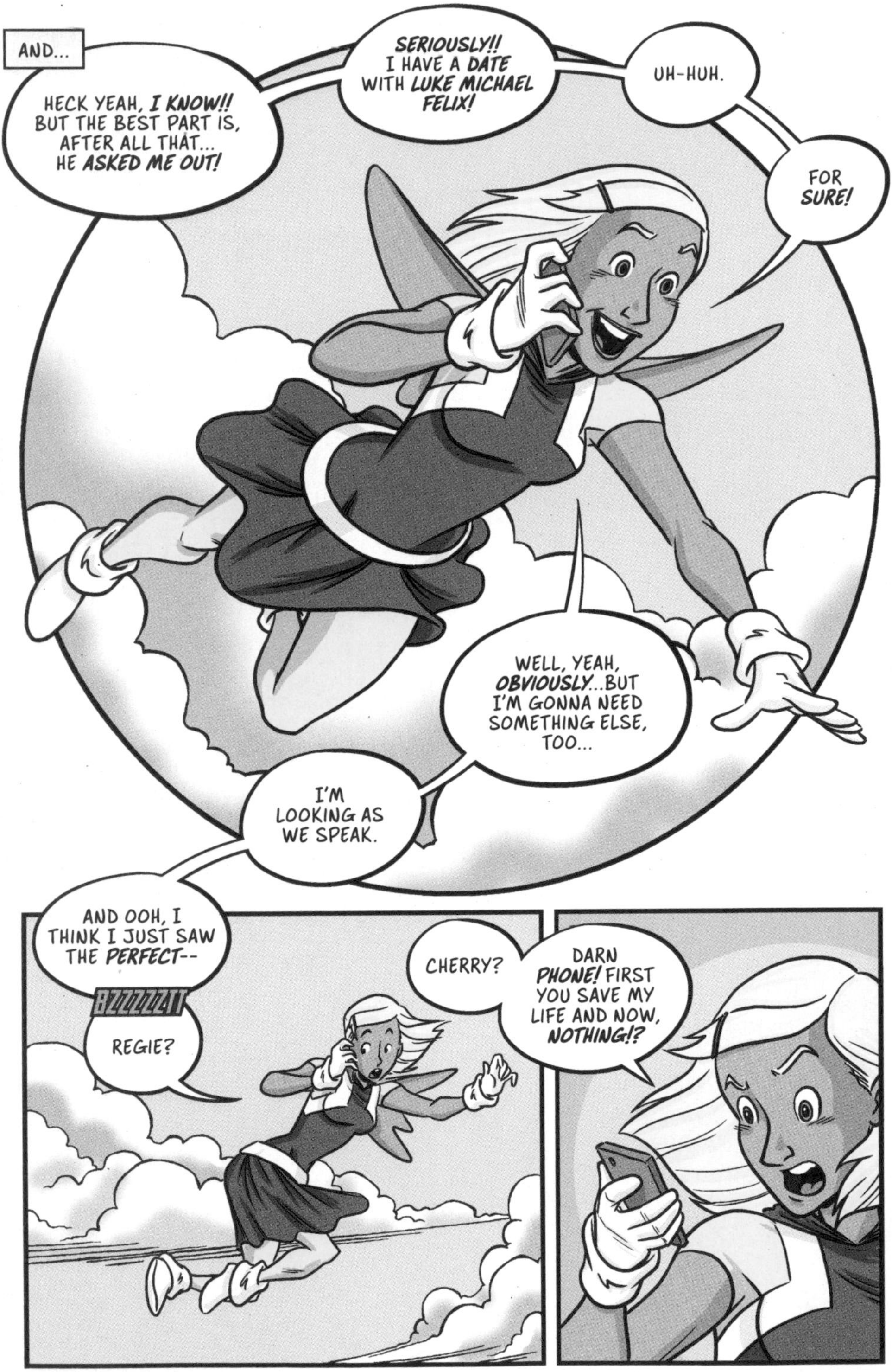
AND...
HECK YEAH, I KNOW!! BUT THE BEST PART IS, AFTER ALL THAT... HE ASKED ME OUT!
SERIOUSLY!! I HAVE A DATE WITH LUKE MICHAEL FELIX!
UH-HUH.
FOR SURE!
WELL, YEAH, OBVIOUSLY...BUT I'M GONNA NEED SOMETHING ELSE, TOO...
I'M LOOKING AS WE SPEAK.
AND OOH, I THINK I JUST SAW THE PERFECT--
BZZZZZZT
REGIE?
CHERRY?
DARN PHONE! FIRST YOU SAVE MY LIFE AND NOW, NOTHING!?

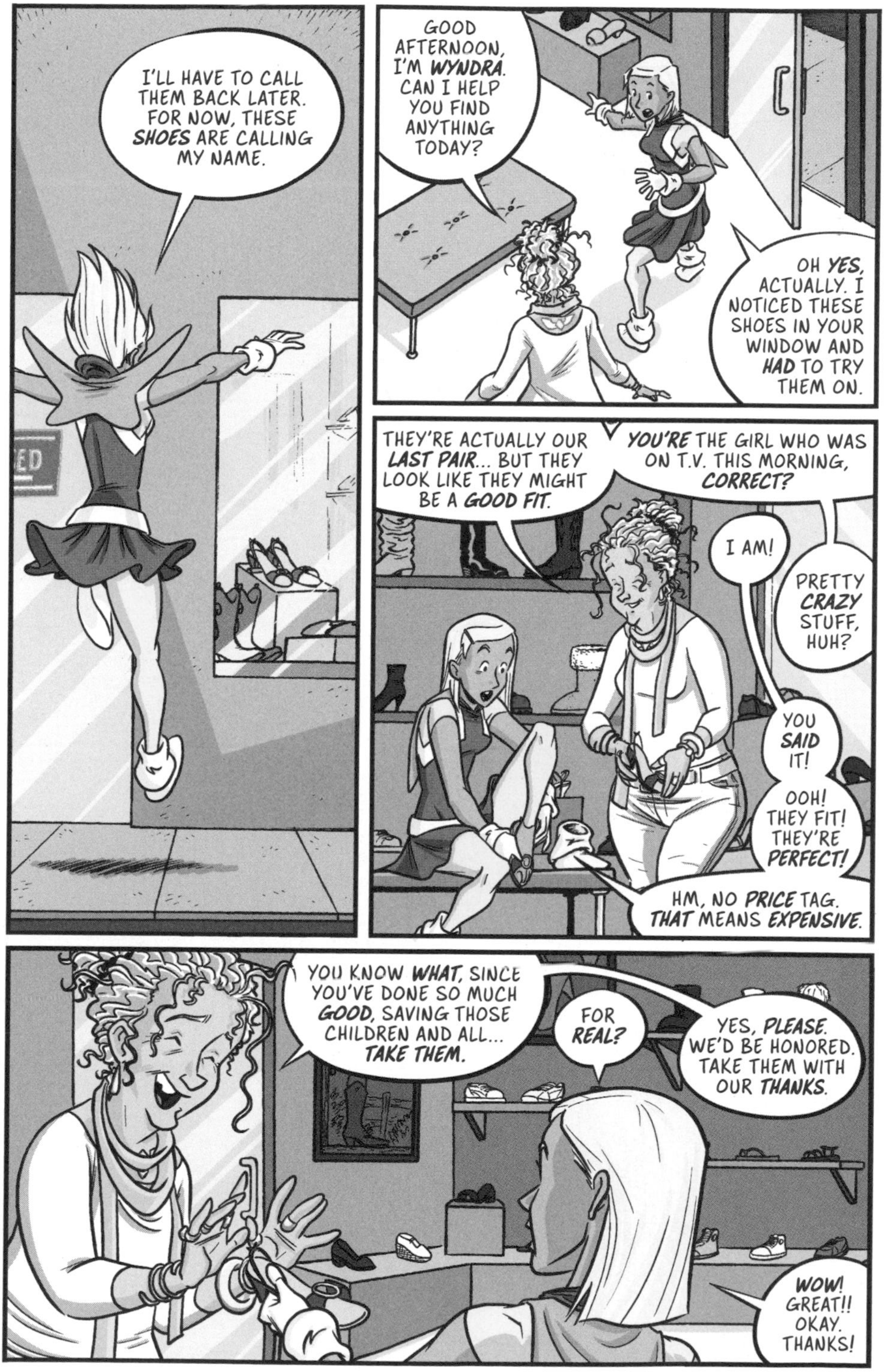
I'LL HAVE TO CALL THEM BACK LATER. FOR NOW, THESE SHOES ARE CALLING MY NAME.
GOOD AFTERNOON, I'M WYNDRA. CAN I HELP YOU FIND ANYTHING TODAY?
OH YES, ACTUALLY. I NOTICED THESE SHOES IN YOUR WINDOW AND HAD TO TRY THEM ON.
THEY'RE ACTUALLY OUR LAST PAIR... BUT THEY LOOK LIKE THEY MIGHT BE A GOOD FIT.
YOU'RE THE GIRL WHO WAS ON T.V. THIS MORNING, CORRECT?
I AM!
PRETTY CRAZY STUFF, HUH?
YOU SAID IT!
OOH! THEY FIT! THEY'RE PERFECT!
HM, NO PRICE TAG. THAT MEANS EXPENSIVE.
YOU KNOW WHAT, SINCE YOU'VE DONE SO MUCH GOOD, SAVING THOSE CHILDREN AND ALL... TAKE THEM.
FOR REAL?
YES, PLEASE. WE'D BE HONORED. TAKE THEM WITH OUR THANKS.
WOW! GREAT!! OKAY. THANKS!

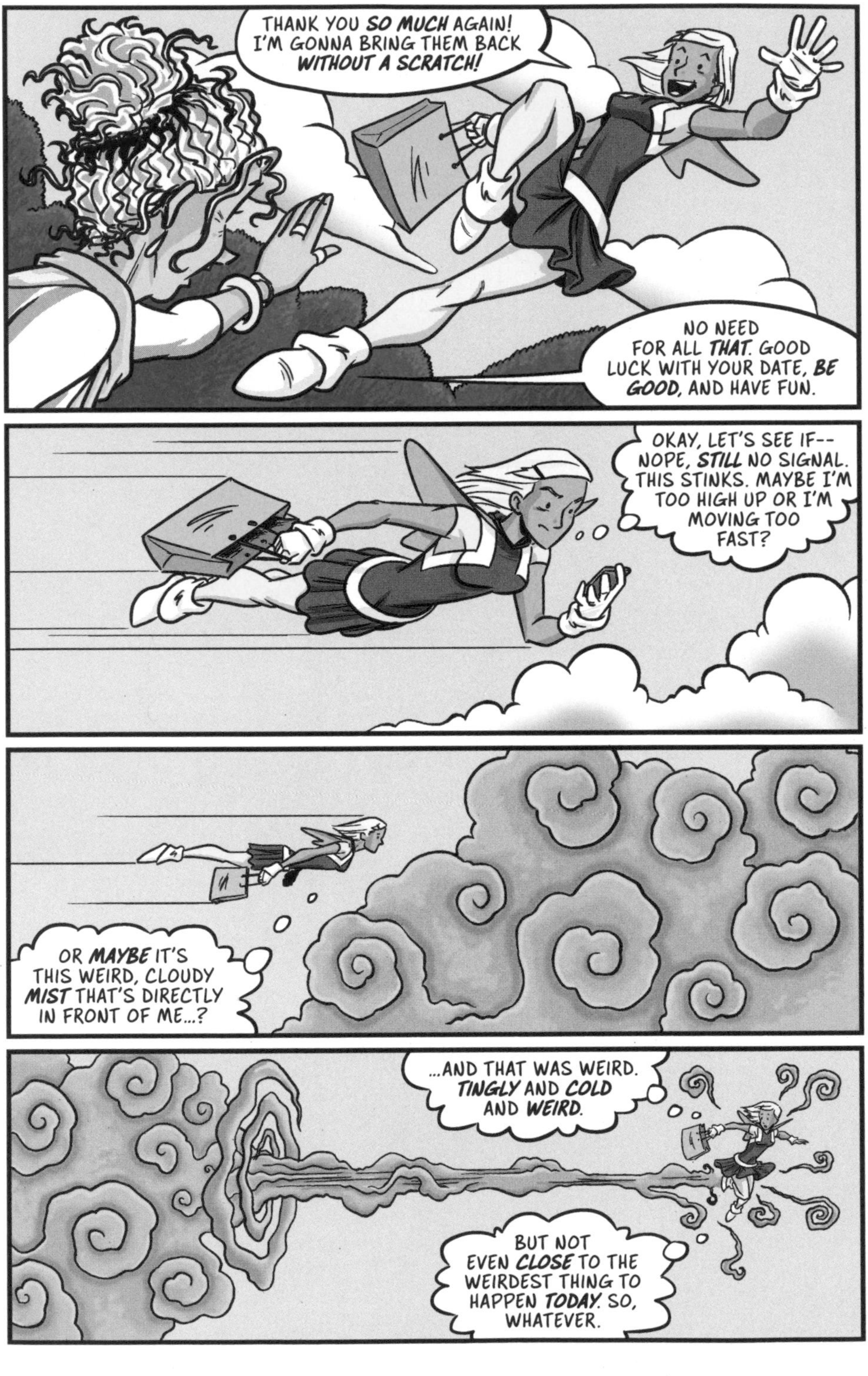
THANK YOU SO MUCH AGAIN! I'M GONNA BRING THEM BACK WITHOUT A SCRATCH!
NO NEED FOR ALL THAT. GOOD LUCK WITH YOUR DATE, BE GOOD, AND HAVE FUN.
OKAY, LET'S SEE IF-- NOPE, STILL NO SIGNAL. THIS STINKS. MAYBE I'M TOO HIGH UP OR I'M MOVING TOO FAST?
OR MAYBE IT'S THIS WEIRD, CLOUDY MIST THAT'S DIRECTLY IN FRONT OF ME...?
...AND THAT WAS WEIRD. TINGLY AND COLD AND WEIRD.
BUT NOT EVEN CLOSE TO THE WEIRDEST THING TO HAPPEN TODAY. SO, WHATEVER.

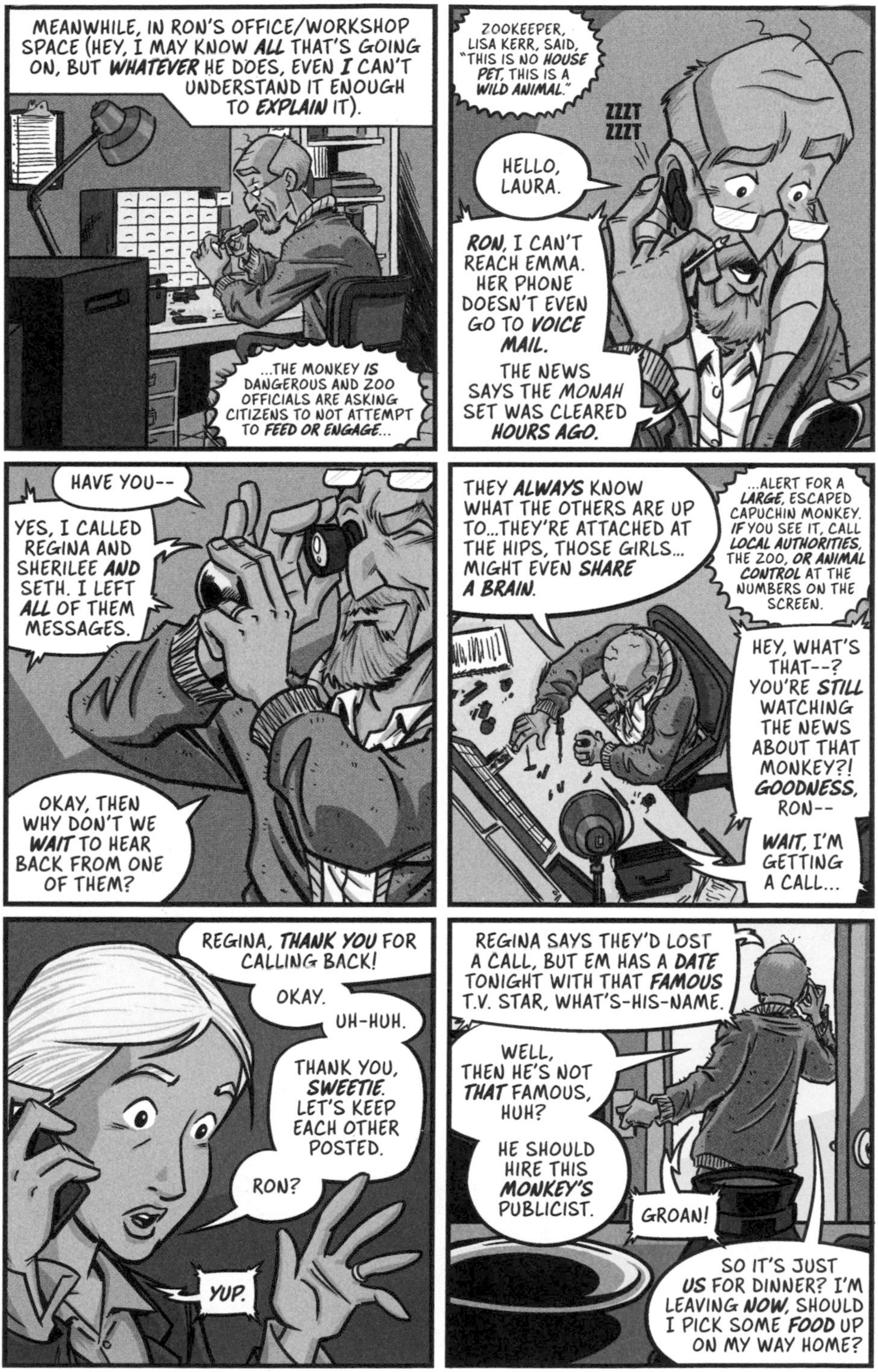

MEANWHILE, IN RON'S OFFICE/WORKSHOP SPACE (HEY, I MAY KNOW ALL THAT'S GOING ON, BUT WHATEVER HE DOES, EVEN I CAN'T UNDERSTAND IT ENOUGH TO EXPLAIN IT).
...THE MONKEY IS DANGEROUS AND ZOO OFFICIALS ARE ASKING CITIZENS TO NOT ATTEMPT TO FEED OR ENGAGE...
ZOOKEEPER, LISA KERR, SAID, "THIS IS NO HOUSE PET, THIS IS A WILD ANIMAL."
ZZZT ZZZT
HELLO, LAURA.
RON, I CAN'T REACH EMMA. HER PHONE DOESN'T EVEN GO TO VOICE MAIL.
THE NEWS SAYS THE MONAH SET WAS CLEARED HOURS AGO.
HAVE YOU--
YES, I CALLED REGINA AND SHERILEE AND SETH. I LEFT ALL OF THEM MESSAGES.
OKAY, THEN WHY DON'T WE WAIT TO HEAR BACK FROM ONE OF THEM?
THEY ALWAYS KNOW WHAT THE OTHERS ARE UP TO...THEY'RE ATTACHED AT THE HIPS, THOSE GIRLS... MIGHT EVEN SHARE A BRAIN.
...ALERT FOR A LARGE, ESCAPED CAPUCHIN MONKEY. IF YOU SEE IT, CALL LOCAL AUTHORITIES, THE ZOO, OR ANIMAL CONTROL AT THE NUMBERS ON THE SCREEN.
HEY, WHAT'S THAT--? YOU'RE STILL WATCHING THE NEWS ABOUT THAT MONKEY?! GOODNESS, RON--
WAIT, I'M GETTING A CALL...
REGINA, THANK YOU FOR CALLING BACK!
OKAY.
UH-HUH.
THANK YOU, SWEETIE. LET'S KEEP EACH OTHER POSTED.
RON?
YUP.
REGINA SAYS THEY'D LOST A CALL, BUT EM HAS A DATE TONIGHT WITH THAT FAMOUS T.V. STAR, WHAT'S-HIS-NAME.
WELL, THEN HE'S NOT THAT FAMOUS, HUH?
HE SHOULD HIRE THIS MONKEY'S PUBLICIST.
GROAN!
SO IT'S JUST US FOR DINNER? I'M LEAVING NOW, SHOULD I PICK SOME FOOD UP ON MY WAY HOME?

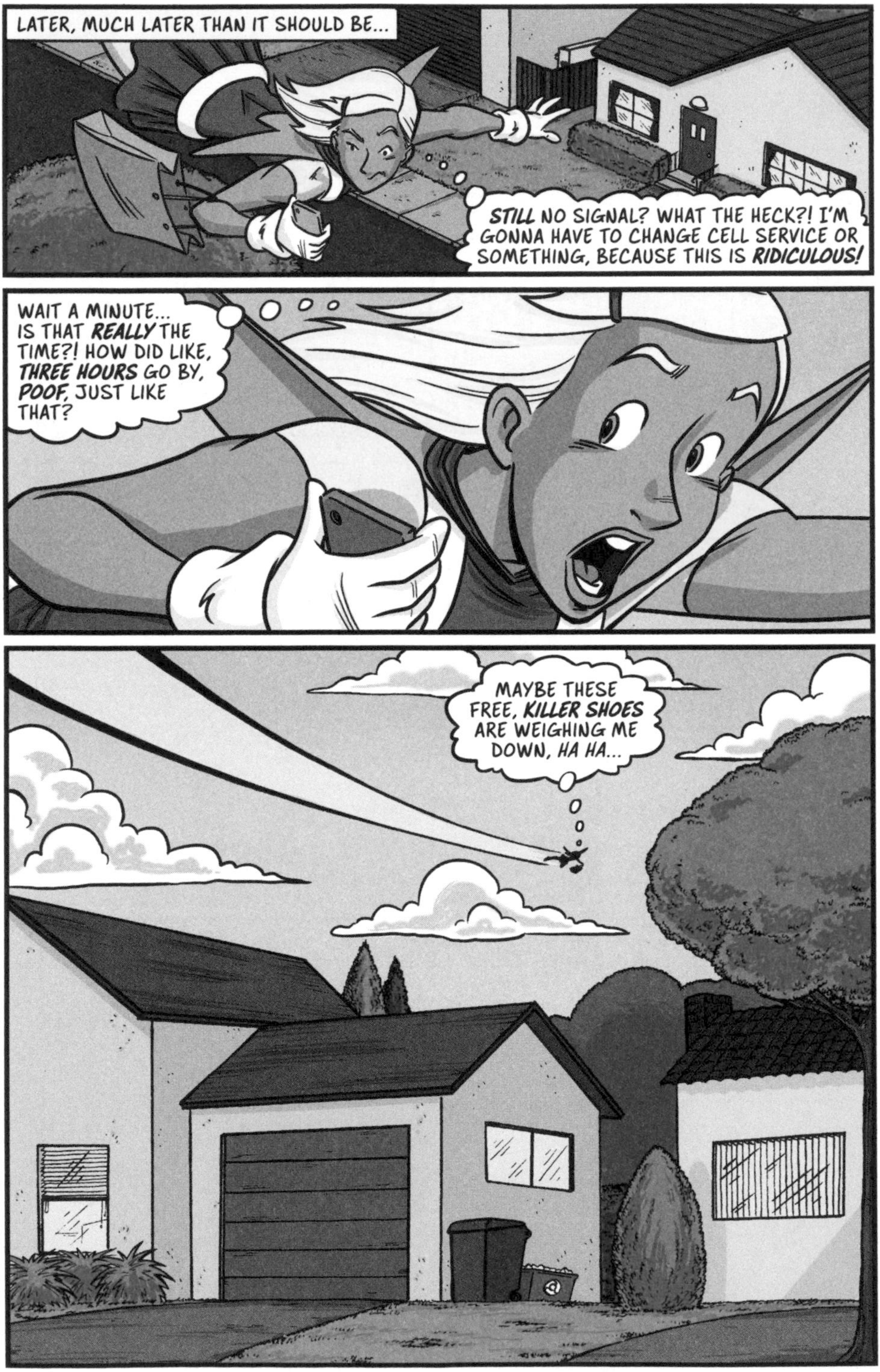
LATER, MUCH LATER THAN IT SHOULD BE...
STILL NO SIGNAL? WHAT THE HECK?! I'M GONNA HAVE TO CHANGE CELL SERVICE OR SOMETHING, BECAUSE THIS IS RIDICULOUS!
WAIT A MINUTE... IS THAT REALLY THE TIME?! HOW DID LIKE, THREE HOURS GO BY, POOF, JUST LIKE THAT?
MAYBE THESE FREE, KILLER SHOES ARE WEIGHING ME DOWN, HA HA...

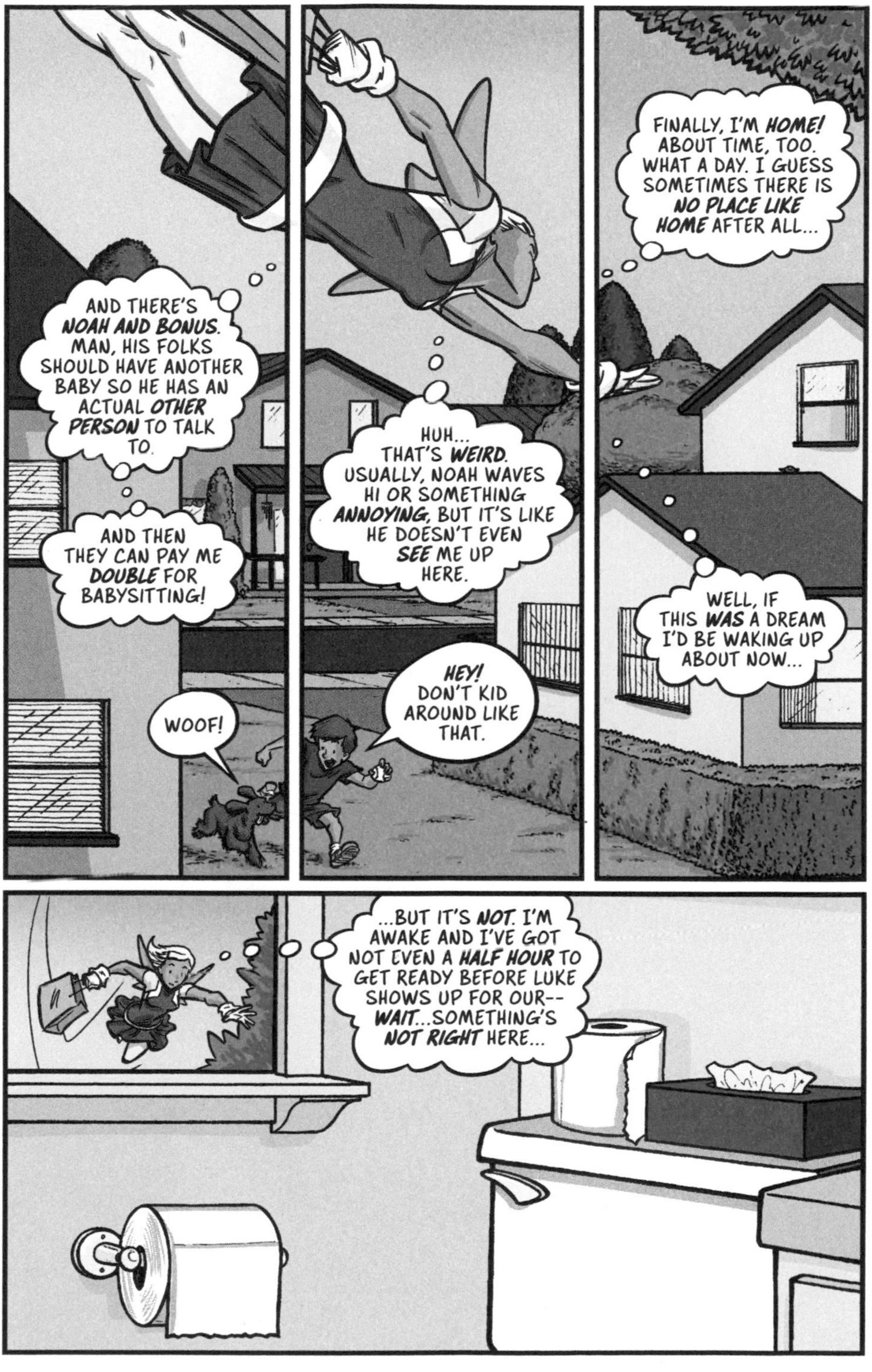
AND THERE'S NOAH AND BONUS. MAN, HIS FOLKS SHOULD HAVE ANOTHER BABY SO HE HAS AN ACTUAL OTHER PERSON TO TALK TO.
AND THEN THEY CAN PAY ME DOUBLE FOR BABYSITTING!
WOOF!
HUH... THAT'S WEIRD. USUALLY, NOAH WAVES HI OR SOMETHING ANNOYING, BUT IT'S LIKE HE DOESN'T EVEN SEE ME UP HERE.
HEY! DON'T KID AROUND LIKE THAT.
FINALLY, I'M HOME! ABOUT TIME, TOO. WHAT A DAY. I GUESS SOMETIMES THERE IS NO PLACE LIKE HOME AFTER ALL...
WELL, IF THIS WAS A DREAM I'D BE WAKING UP ABOUT NOW...
...BUT IT'S NOT. I'M AWAKE AND I'VE GOT NOT EVEN A HALF HOUR TO GET READY BEFORE LUKE SHOWS UP FOR OUR-- WAIT...SOMETHING'S NOT RIGHT HERE...

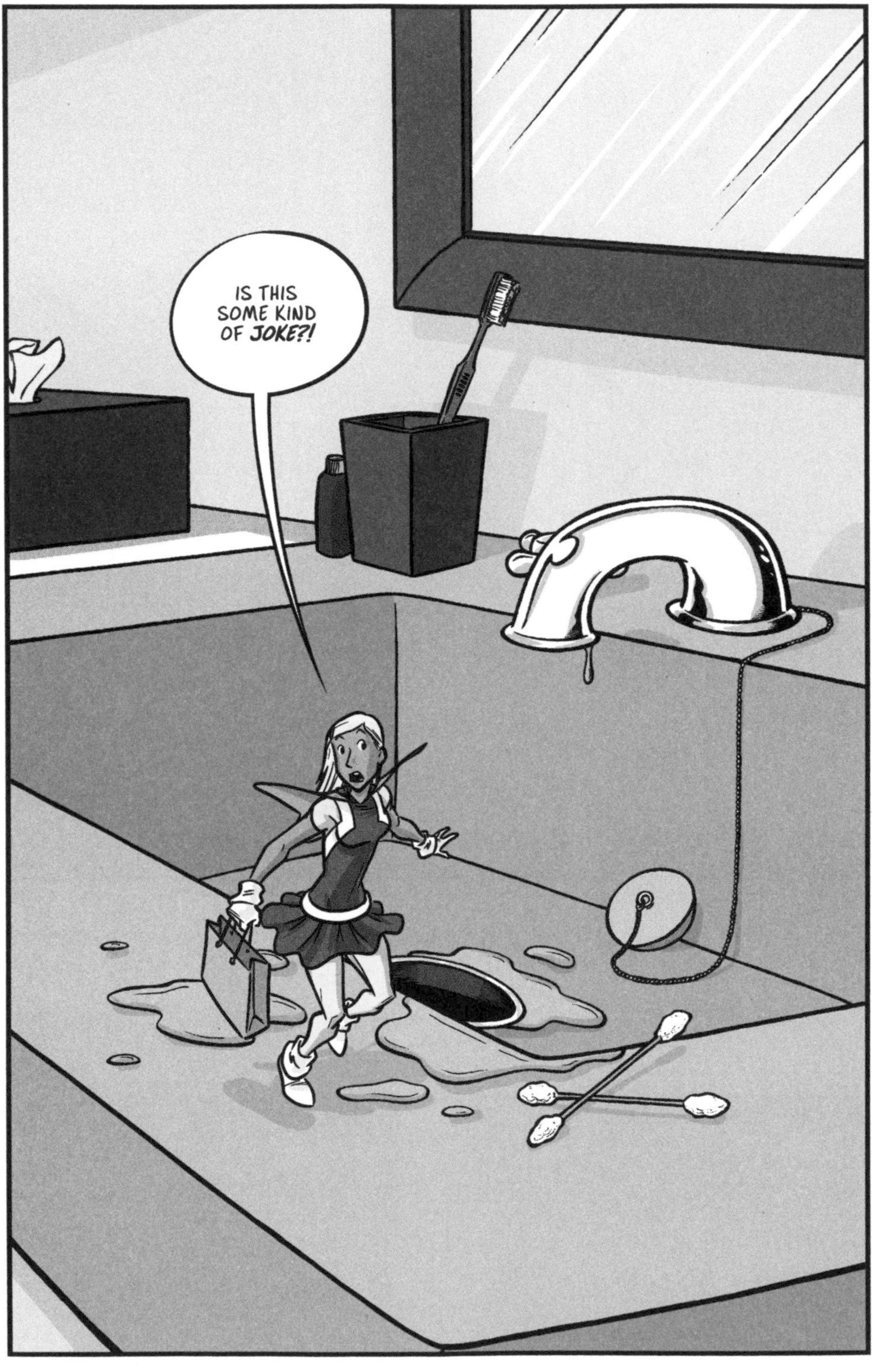
IS THIS SOME KIND OF JOKE?!

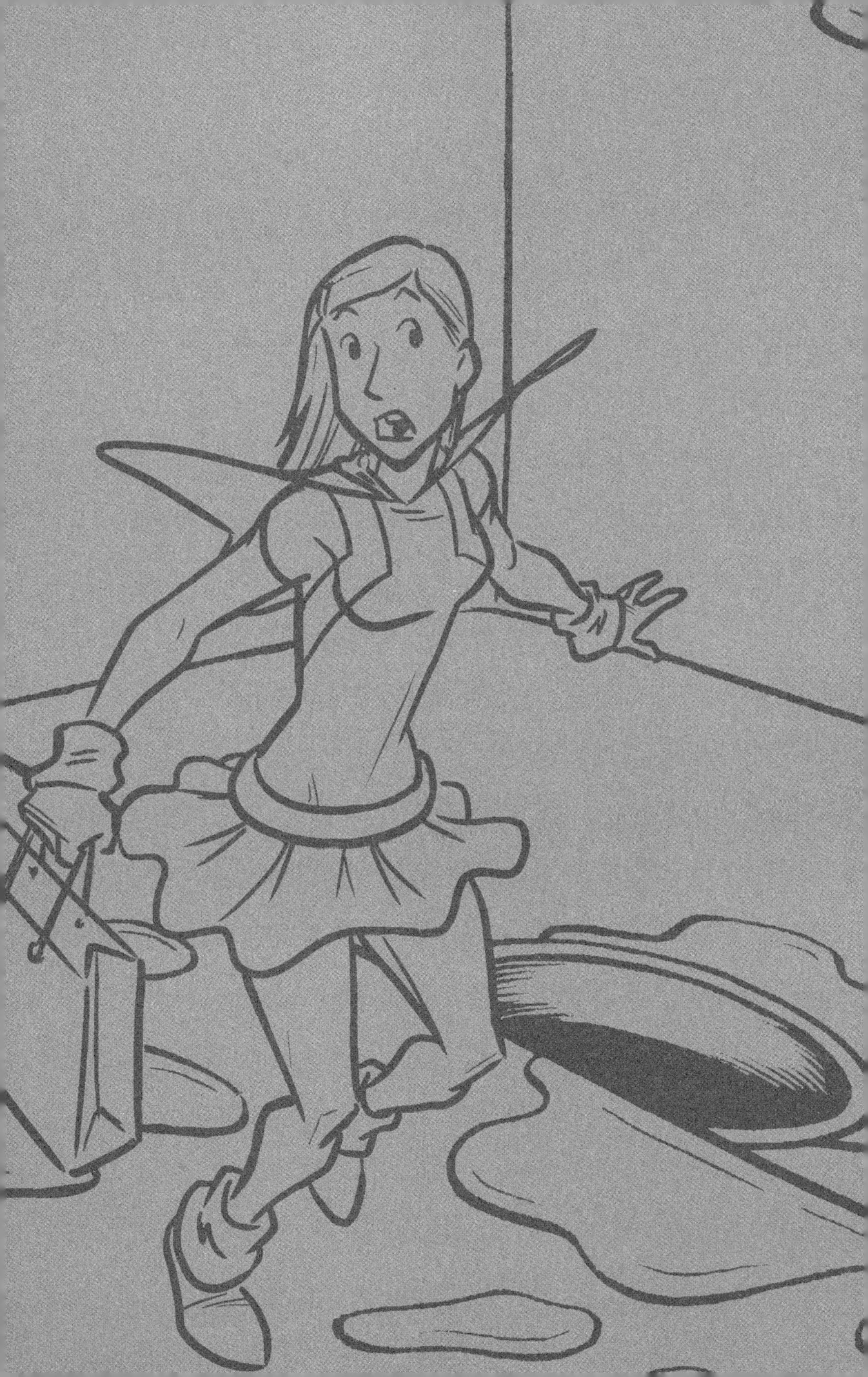

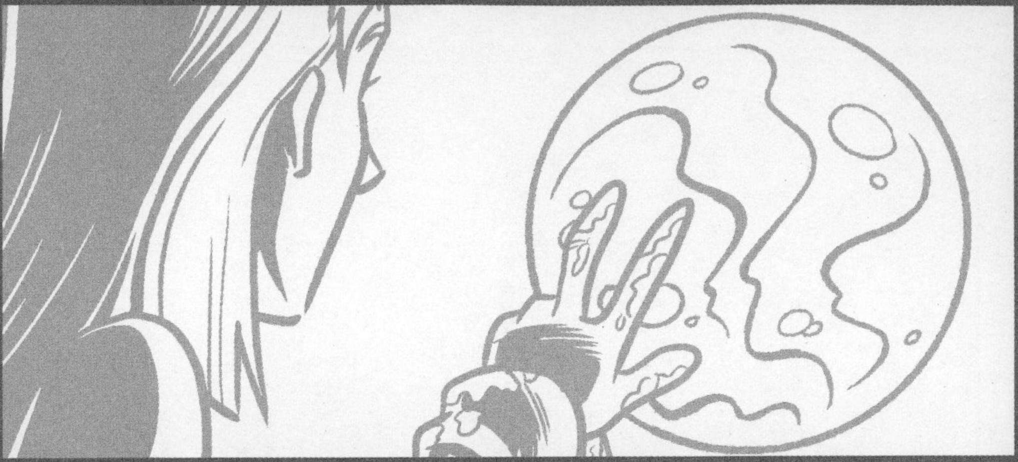

CHAPTER TWO

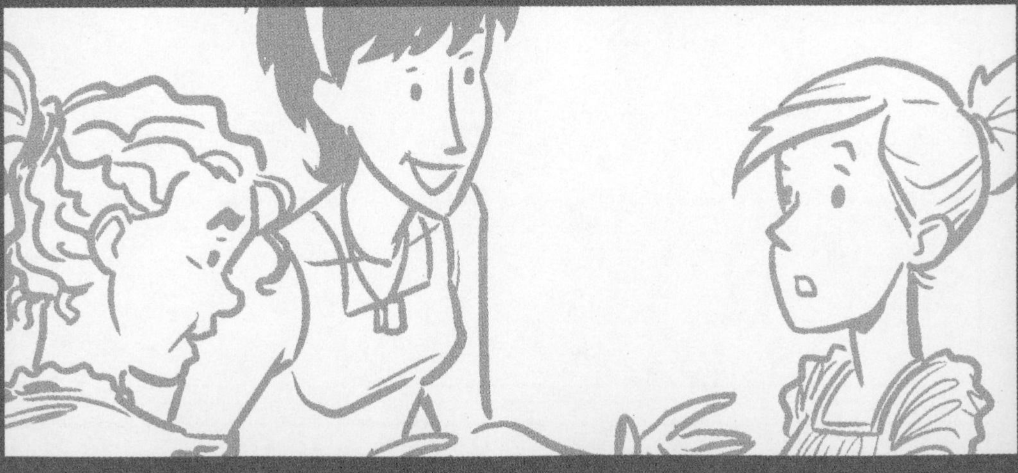

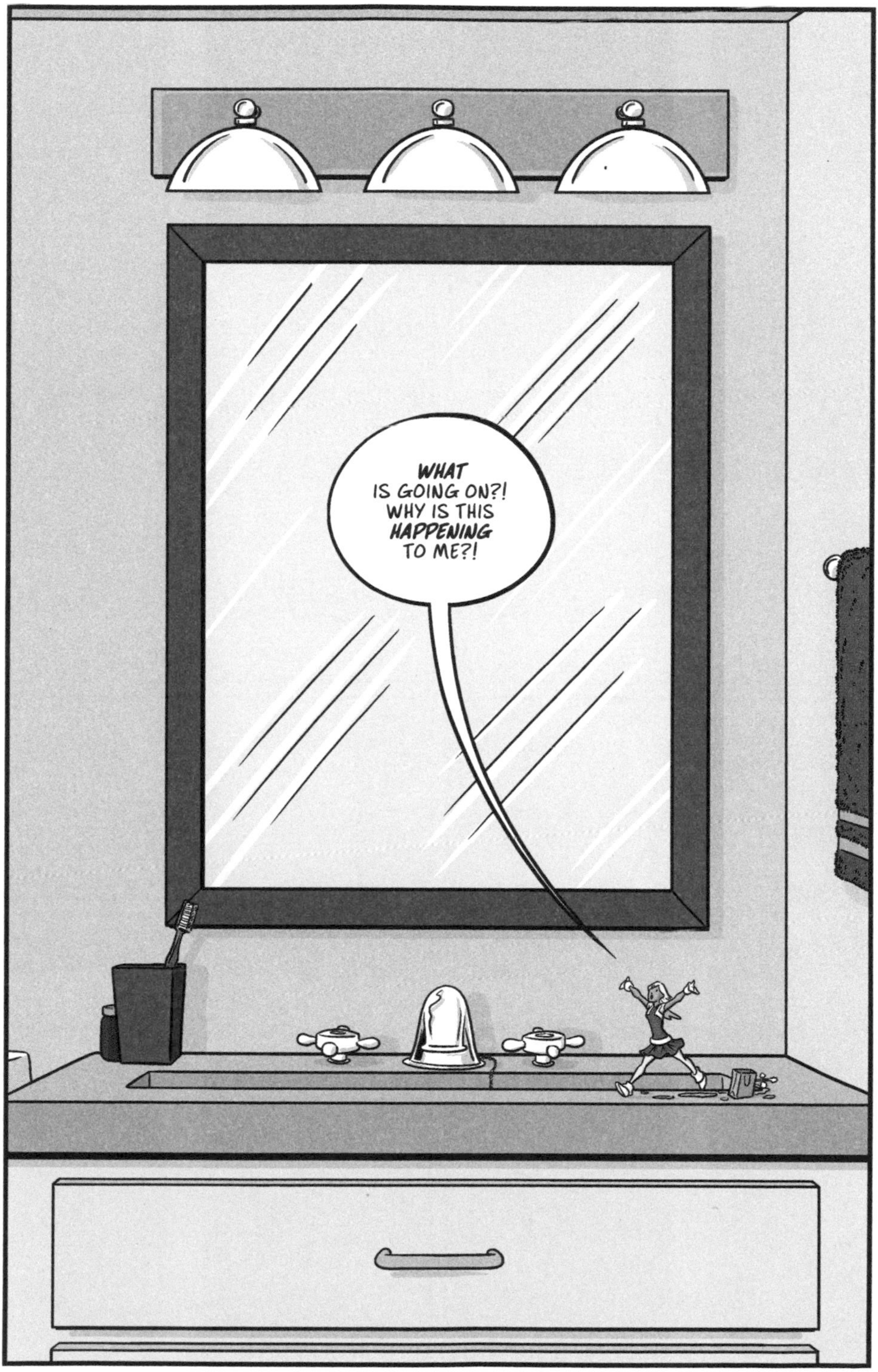
WHAT IS GOING ON?! WHY IS THIS HAPPENING TO ME?!

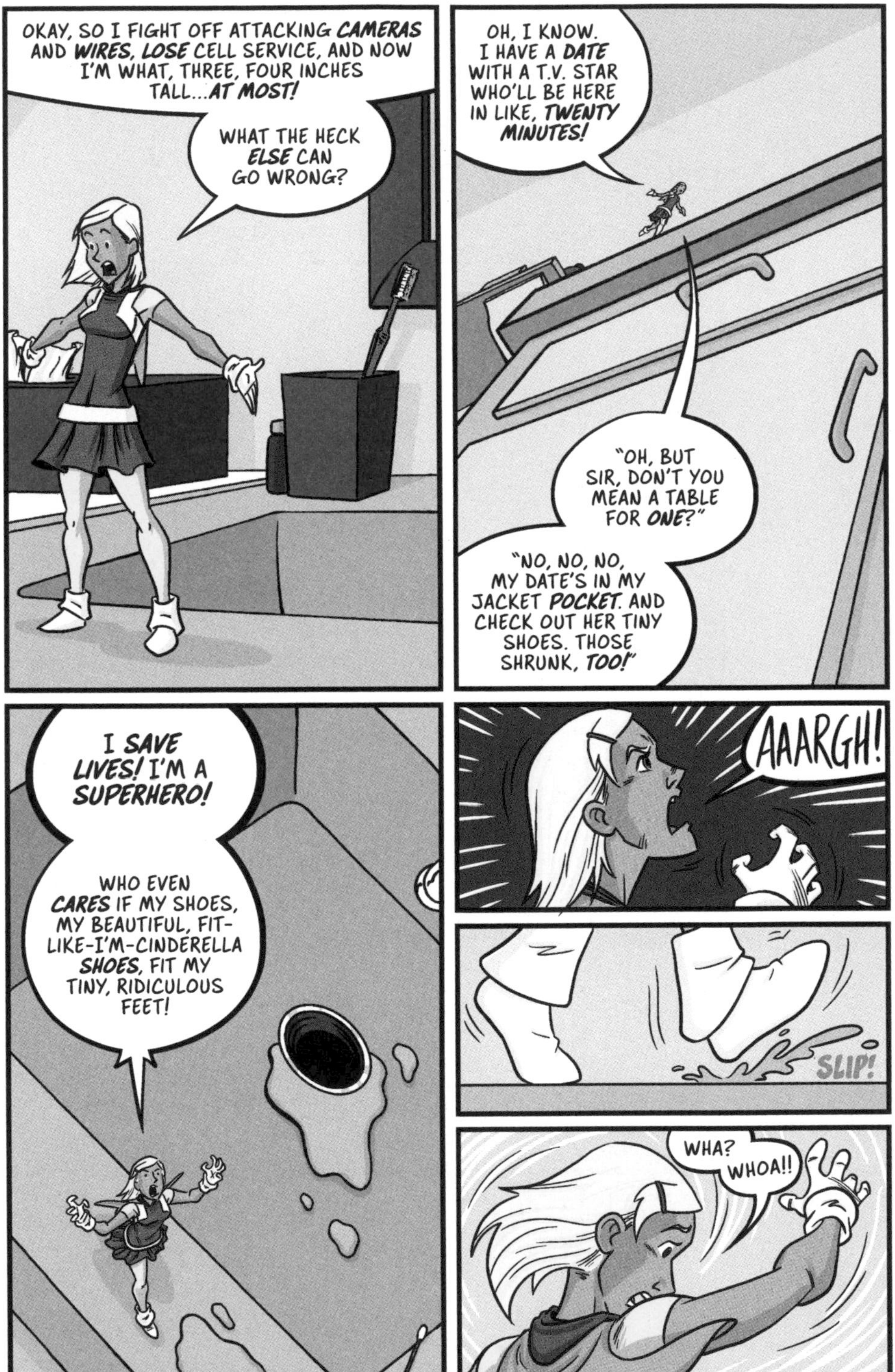
OKAY, SO I FIGHT OFF ATTACKING CAMERAS AND WIRES, LOSE CELL SERVICE, AND NOW I'M WHAT, THREE, FOUR INCHES TALL...AT MOST!
WHAT THE HECK ELSE CAN GO WRONG?
OH, I KNOW. I HAVE A DATE WITH A T.V. STAR WHO'LL BE HERE IN LIKE, TWENTY MINUTES!
"OH, BUT SIR, DON'T YOU MEAN A TABLE FOR ONE?"
"NO, NO, NO, MY DATE'S IN MY JACKET POCKET. AND CHECK OUT HER TINY SHOES. THOSE SHRUNK, TOO!"
I SAVE LIVES! I'M A SUPERHERO!
WHO EVEN CARES IF MY SHOES, MY BEAUTIFUL, FIT-LIKE-I'M-CINDERELLA SHOES, FIT MY TINY, RIDICULOUS FEET!
AAARGH!
SLIP!
WHA?
WHOA!!

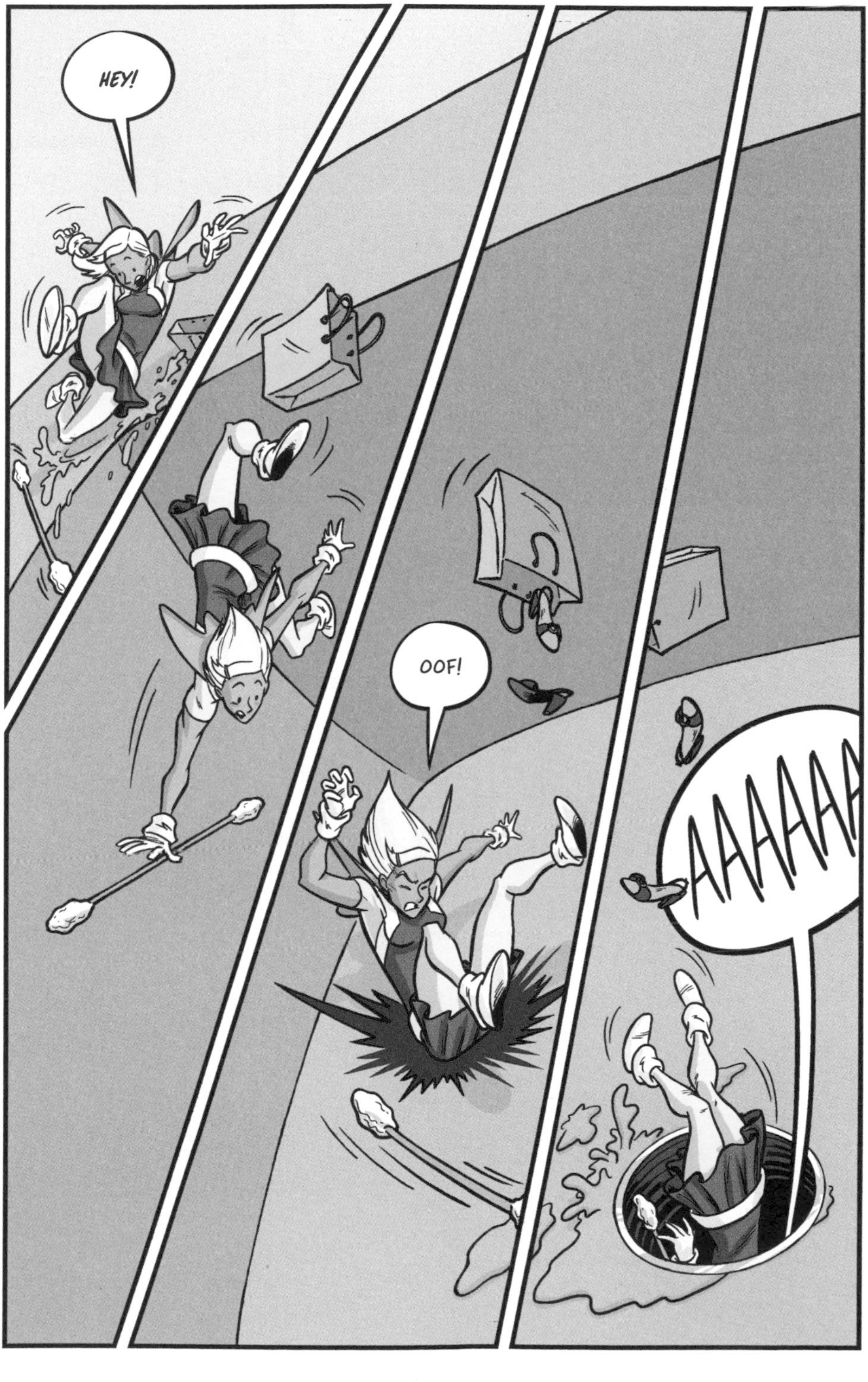
HEY!
OOF!
AAAAAA

MEANWHILE...

AAAH!! I DON'T LIKE THIS! THERE HAS TO BE AN ANSWER... AN *EXPLANATION.*

BUT IS IT *POSSIBLE?*

COULD PIX LIKE ME *MORE* THAN AS A FRIEND?

ON THE *ONE HAND*, WE'VE BEEN FRIENDS SINCE WE WERE KIDS AND SHE ACTS AROUND ME LIKE SHE DOES AROUND REGIE AND CHERRY. SO THAT TELLS ME I'M "JUST A FRIEND".

ON THE *OTHER* HAND, SHE SAID "I LOVE YOU" ON THE PHONE...AND SHE'S NEVER SAID IT *BEFORE...*

...WITHOUT THEN *ADDING* "AS A FRIEND" OR "LIKE A BROTHER".

MAYBE SHE REALIZED *I* LIKED HER AND THAT TRIGGERED SOMETHING IN HER BRAIN AND SHE SAW IT *TOO.*

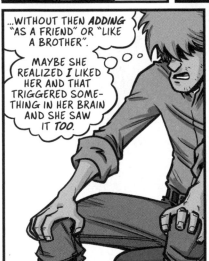

OH, MAN, I'M NERVOUS JUST *THINKING* OF CALLING HER.

BUT I *HAVE* TO KNOW! I'M GONNA CALL AND ASK AND KNOW *FOR SURE.*

RIGHT AFTER I GO TO THE *BATHROOM.*

MUST BE MY NERVOUS STOMACH.

SPEAKING OF BATHROOMS, LOOKS LIKE PIX HAS A *VISITOR...*

BUT AS *WE* KNOW, PIX IS OTHERWISE *ENGAGED...*

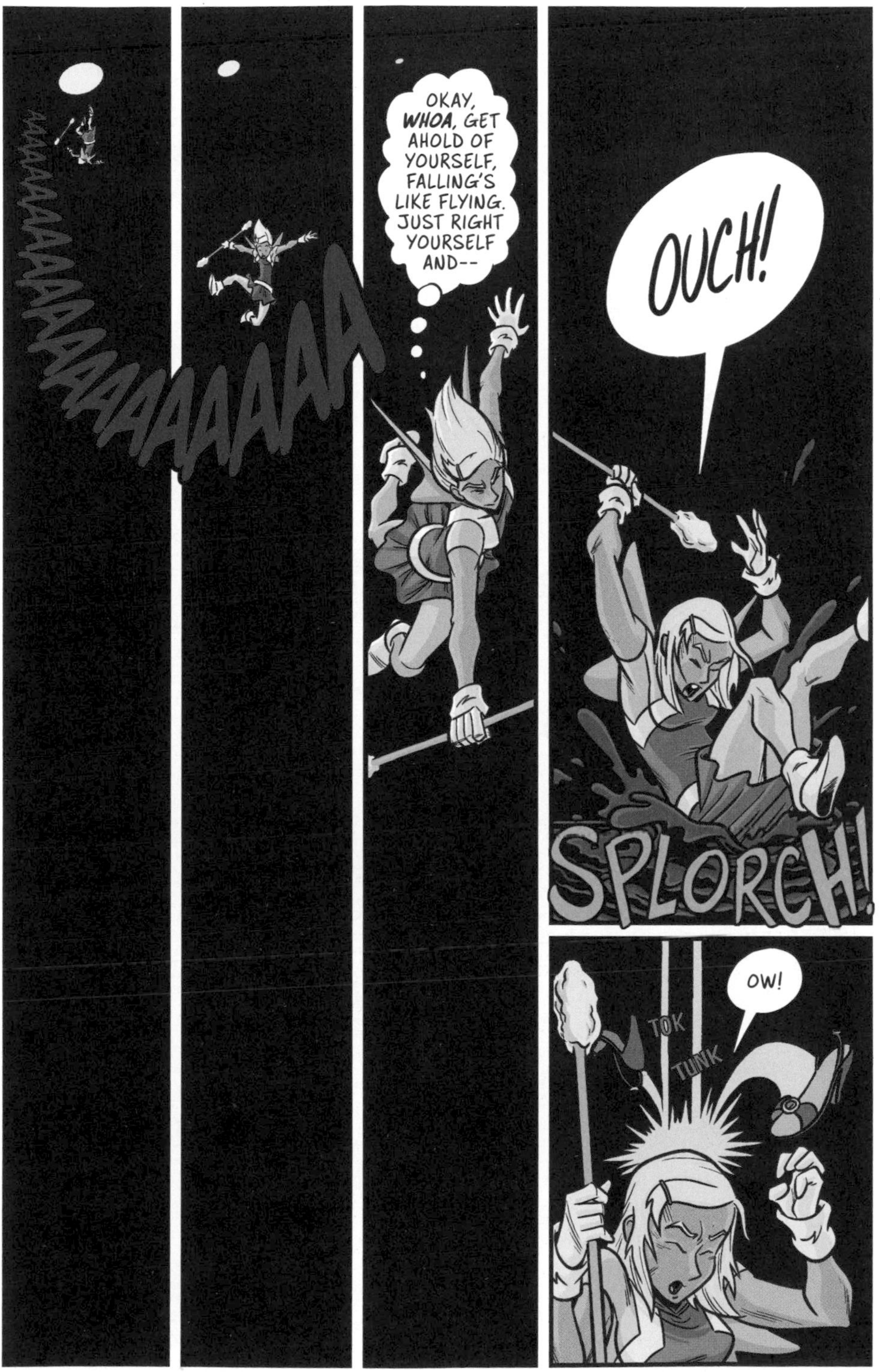
AAAAAAAAAAAAAAAAAAAAAAA
OKAY, WHOA, GET AHOLD OF YOURSELF, FALLING'S LIKE FLYING. JUST RIGHT YOURSELF AND--
OUCH!
SPLORCH!
TOK
TUNK
OW!

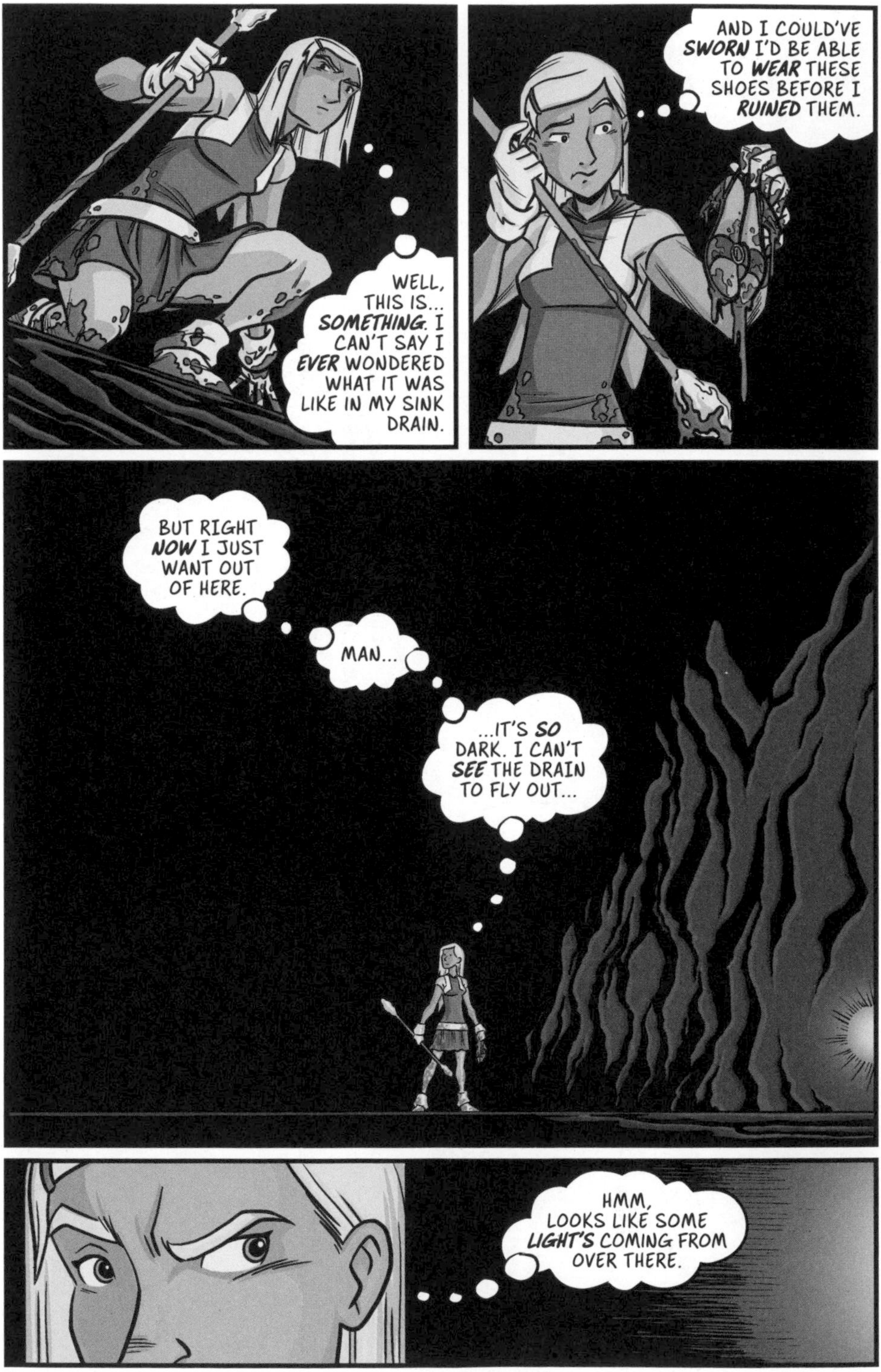
WELL, THIS IS... SOMETHING. I CAN'T SAY I EVER WONDERED WHAT IT WAS LIKE IN MY SINK DRAIN.
AND I COULD'VE SWORN I'D BE ABLE TO WEAR THESE SHOES BEFORE I RUINED THEM.
BUT RIGHT NOW I JUST WANT OUT OF HERE.
MAN...
...IT'S SO DARK. I CAN'T SEE THE DRAIN TO FLY OUT...
HMM, LOOKS LIKE SOME LIGHT'S COMING FROM OVER THERE.

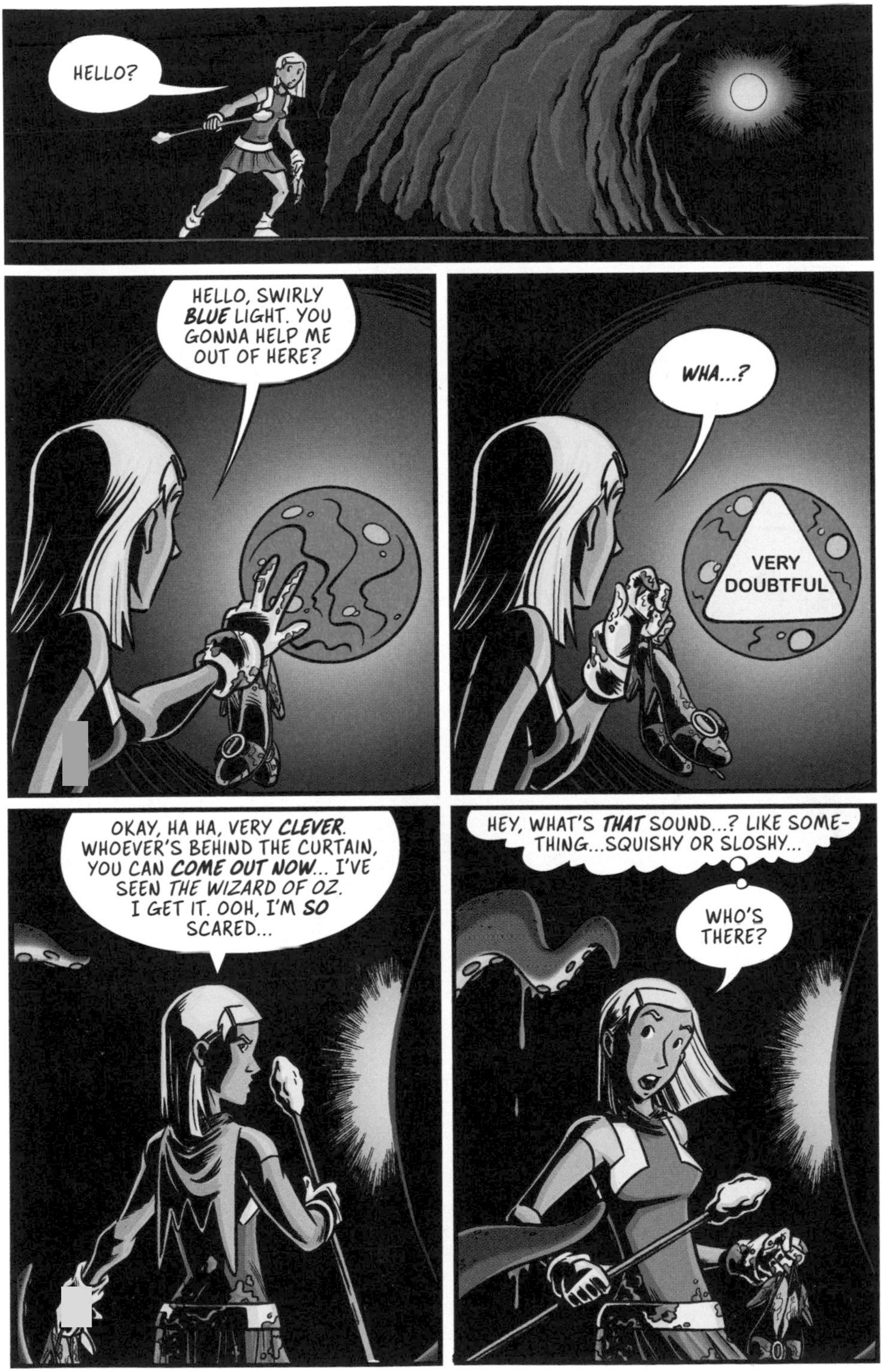
HELLO?
HELLO, SWIRLY BLUE LIGHT. YOU GONNA HELP ME OUT OF HERE?
WHA...?
VERY DOUBTFUL
OKAY, HA HA, VERY CLEVER. WHOEVER'S BEHIND THE CURTAIN, YOU CAN COME OUT NOW... I'VE SEEN THE WIZARD OF OZ. I GET IT. OOH, I'M SO SCARED...
HEY, WHAT'S THAT SOUND...? LIKE SOME-THING...SQUISHY OR SLOSHY...
WHO'S THERE?

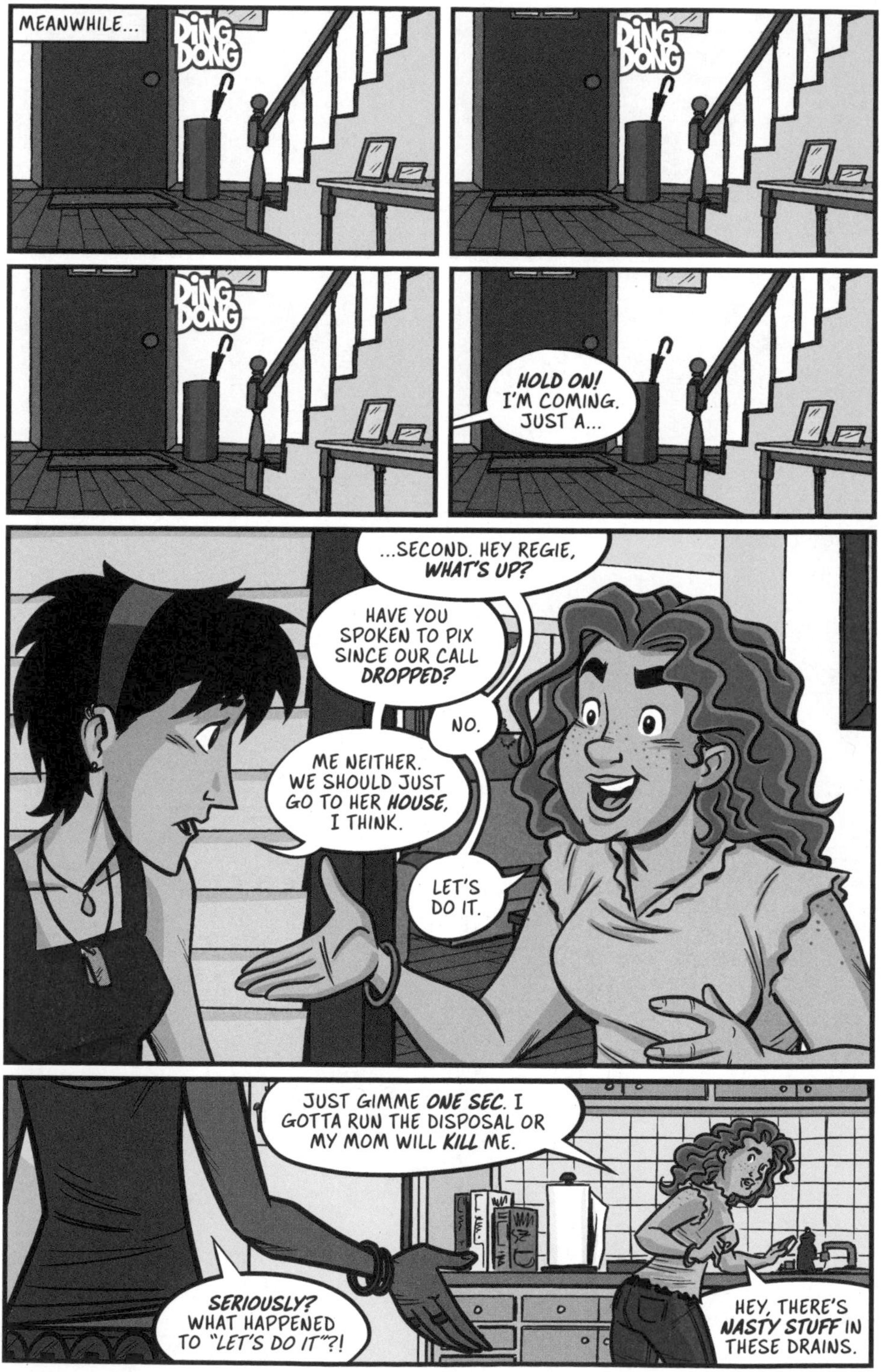
MEANWHILE...
DING DONG
DING DONG
DING DONG
HOLD ON! I'M COMING. JUST A...
...SECOND. HEY REGIE, WHAT'S UP?
HAVE YOU SPOKEN TO PIX SINCE OUR CALL DROPPED?
NO.
ME NEITHER. WE SHOULD JUST GO TO HER HOUSE, I THINK.
LET'S DO IT.
JUST GIMME ONE SEC. I GOTTA RUN THE DISPOSAL OR MY MOM WILL KILL ME.
SERIOUSLY? WHAT HAPPENED TO "LET'S DO IT"?!
HEY, THERE'S NASTY STUFF IN THESE DRAINS.

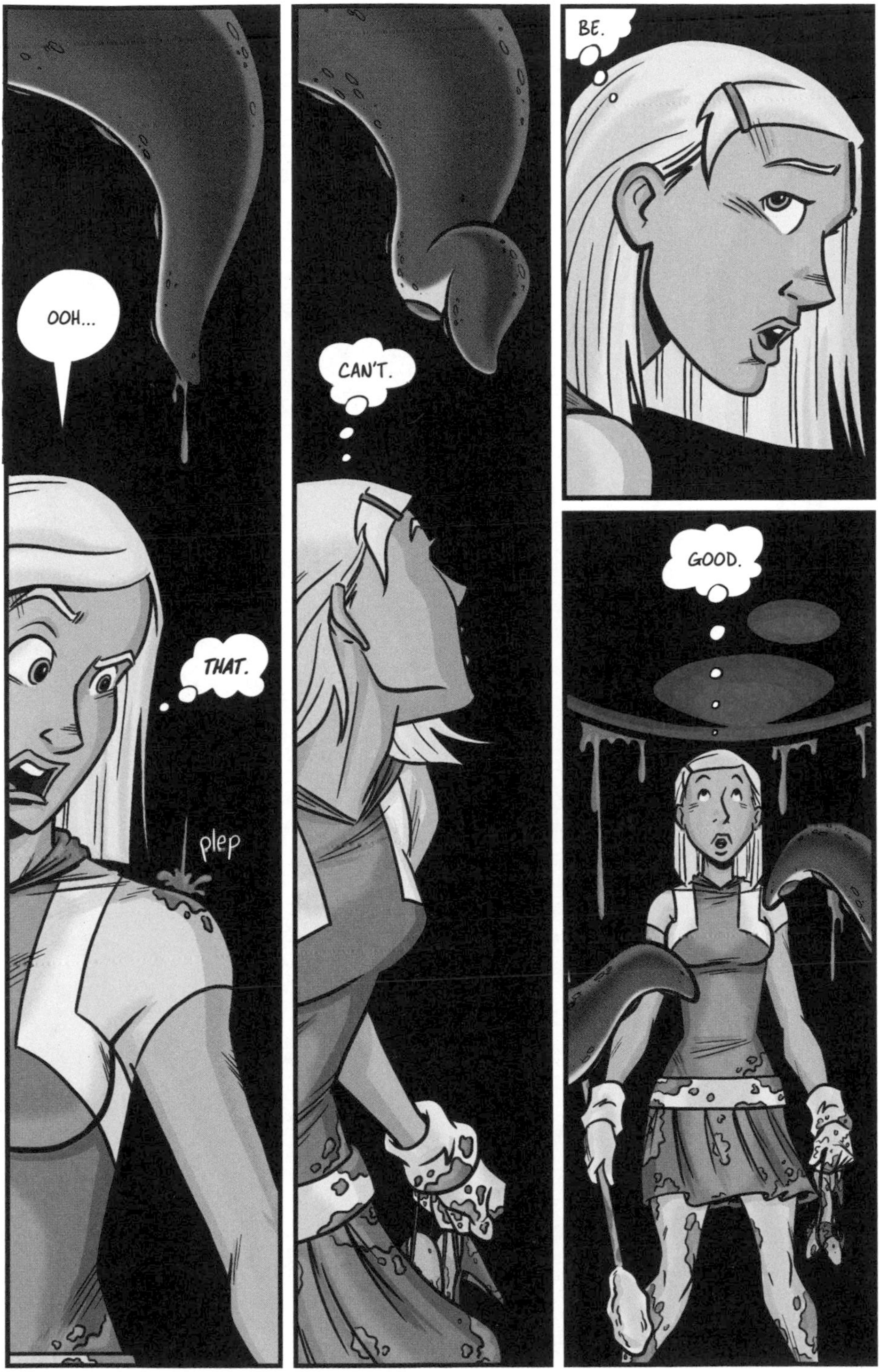
OOH...
THAT.
plep
CAN'T.
BE.
GOOD.

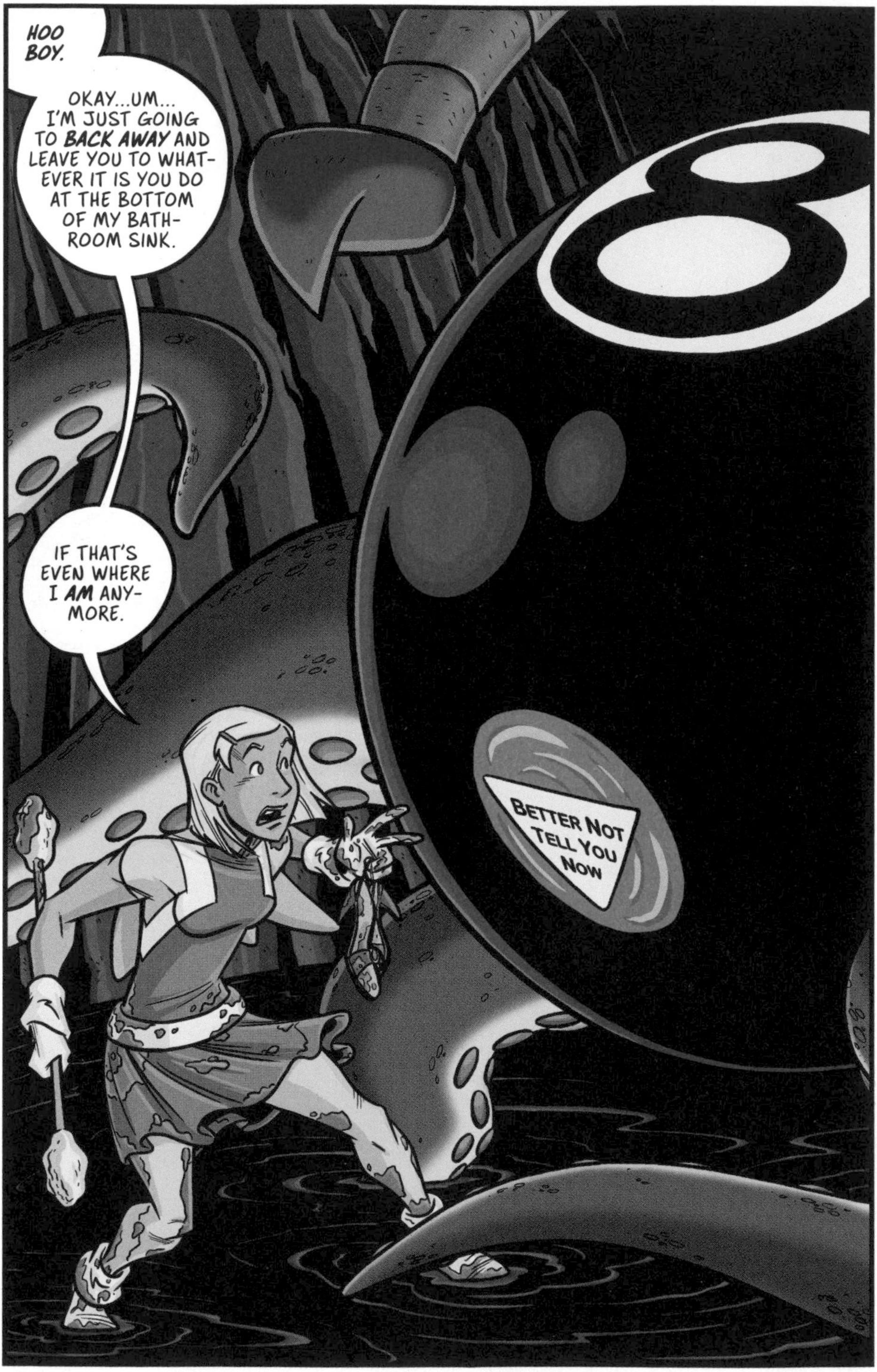
HOO BOY.
OKAY...UM... I'M JUST GOING TO BACK AWAY AND LEAVE YOU TO WHATEVER IT IS YOU DO AT THE BOTTOM OF MY BATHROOM SINK.
IF THAT'S EVEN WHERE I AM ANYMORE.
BETTER NOT TELL YOU NOW

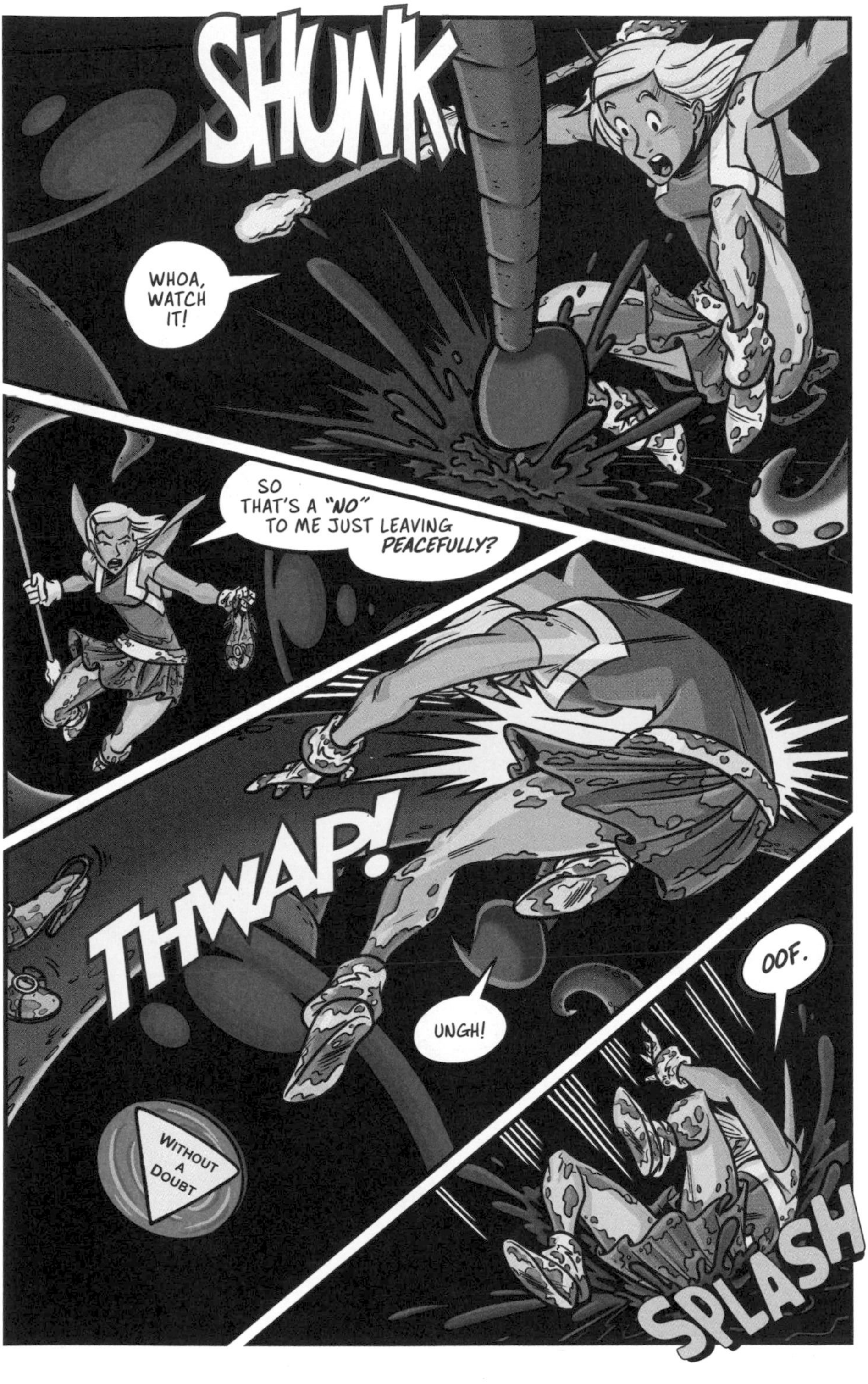
SHUNK
WHOA, WATCH IT!
SO THAT'S A "NO" TO ME JUST LEAVING PEACEFULLY?
THWAP!
UNGH!
WITHOUT A DOUBT
OOF.
SPLASH

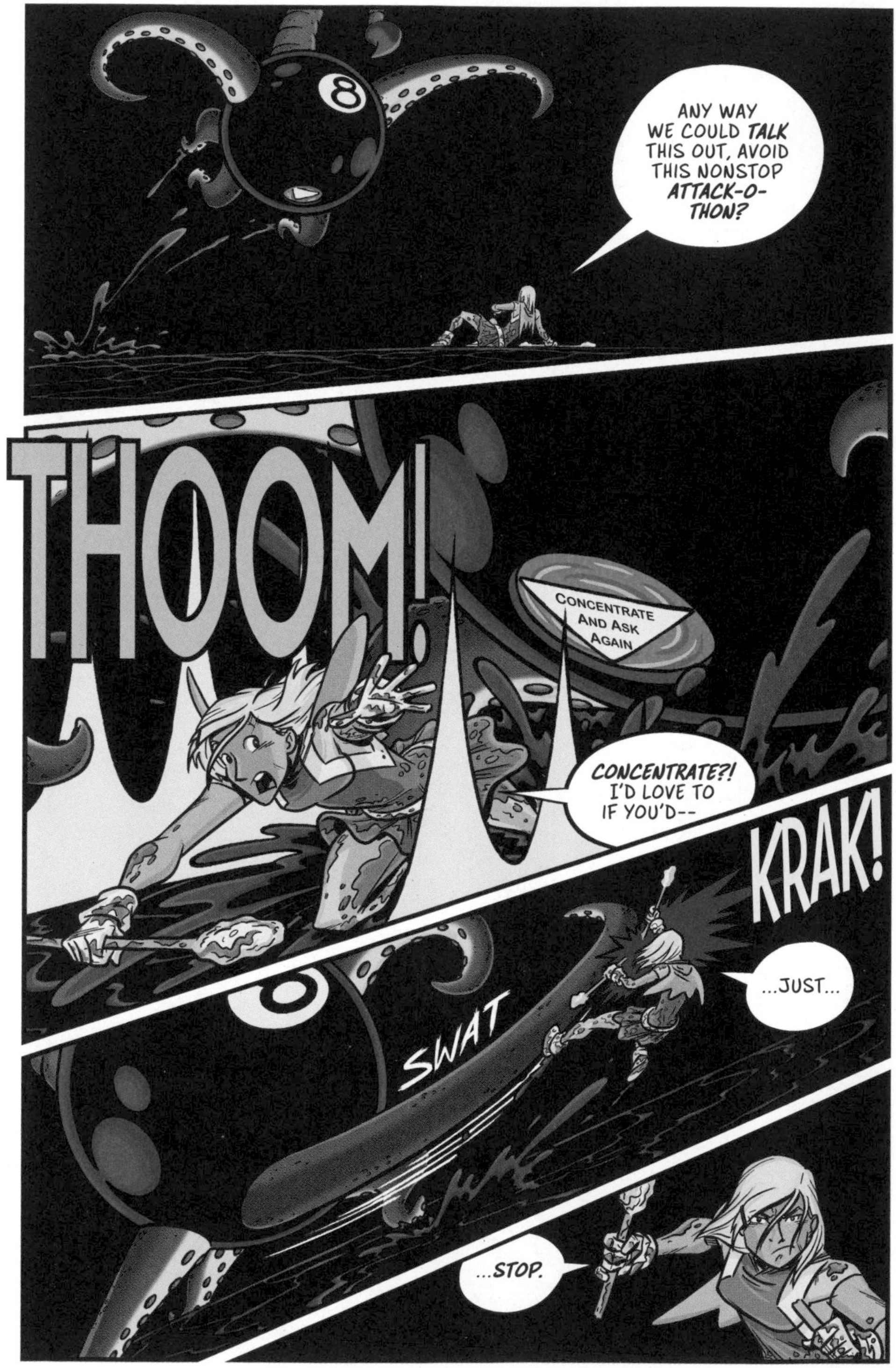
ANY WAY WE COULD TALK THIS OUT, AVOID THIS NONSTOP ATTACK-O-THON?
THOOM!
CONCENTRATE AND ASK AGAIN
CONCENTRATE?! I'D LOVE TO IF YOU'D--
KRAK!
...JUST...
SWAT
...STOP.

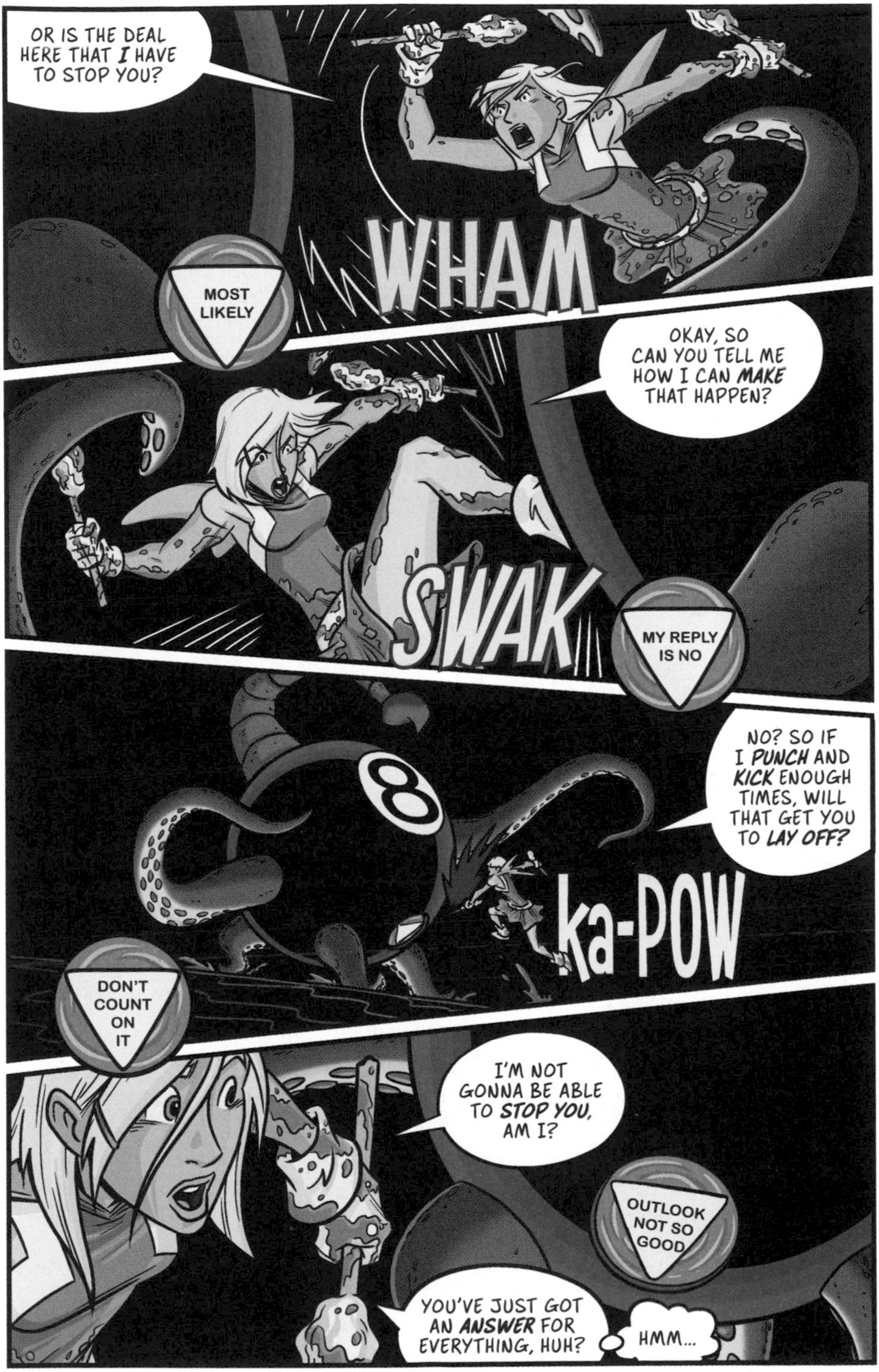

OR IS THE DEAL HERE THAT I HAVE TO STOP YOU?
WHAM
MOST LIKELY
OKAY, SO CAN YOU TELL ME HOW I CAN MAKE THAT HAPPEN?
SWAK
MY REPLY IS NO
NO? SO IF I PUNCH AND KICK ENOUGH TIMES, WILL THAT GET YOU TO LAY OFF?
8
ka-POW
DON'T COUNT ON IT
I'M NOT GONNA BE ABLE TO STOP YOU, AM I?
OUTLOOK NOT SO GOOD
YOU'VE JUST GOT AN ANSWER FOR EVERYTHING, HUH?
HMM...

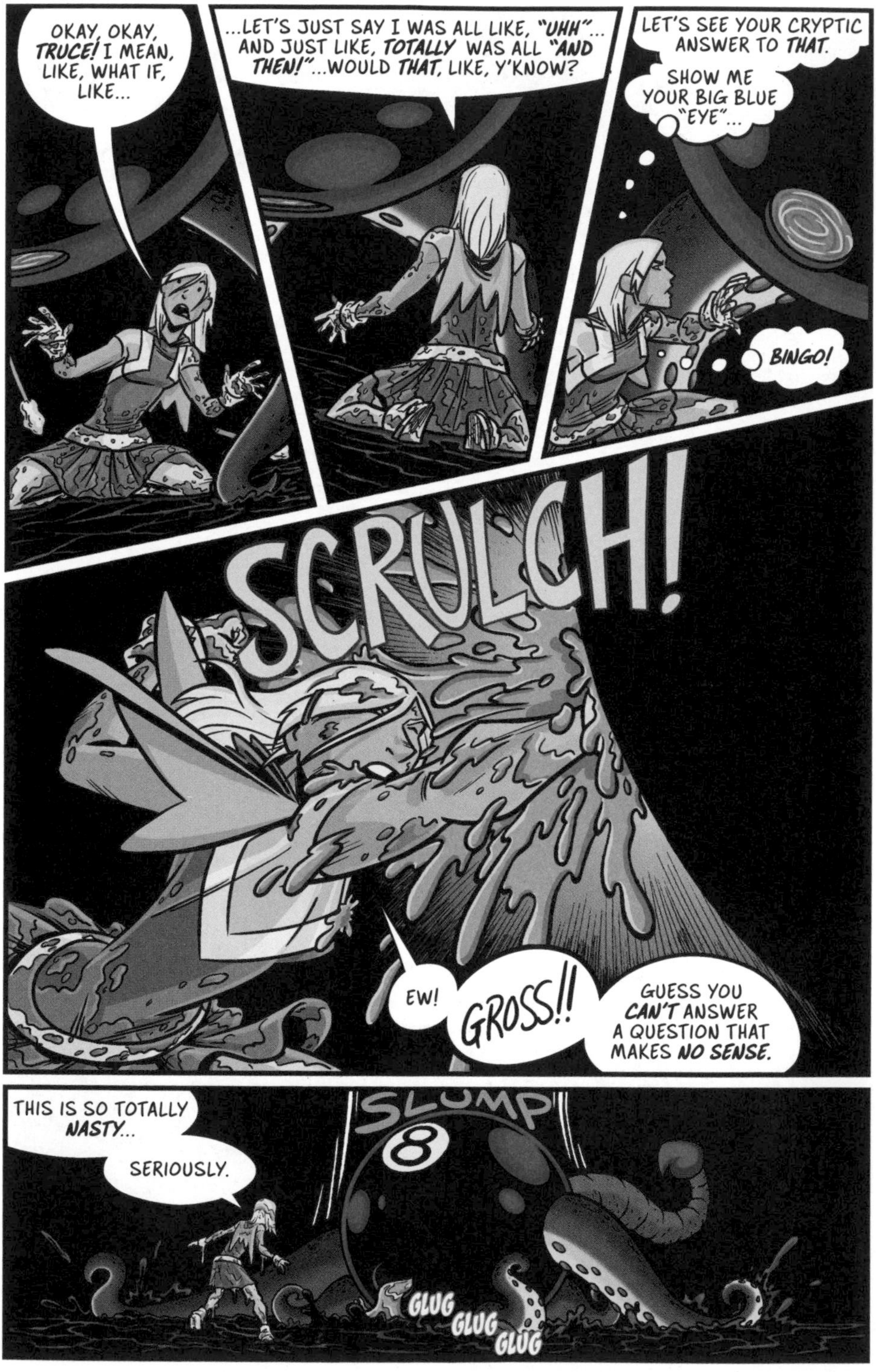
OKAY, OKAY, TRUCE! I MEAN, LIKE, WHAT IF, LIKE...
...LET'S JUST SAY I WAS ALL LIKE, "UHH"... AND JUST LIKE, TOTALLY WAS ALL "AND THEN!"...WOULD THAT, LIKE, Y'KNOW?
LET'S SEE YOUR CRYPTIC ANSWER TO THAT.
SHOW ME YOUR BIG BLUE "EYE"...
BINGO!
SCRULCH!
EW!
GROSS!!
GUESS YOU CAN'T ANSWER A QUESTION THAT MAKES NO SENSE.
THIS IS SO TOTALLY NASTY...
SERIOUSLY.
SLUMP
8
GLUG
GLUG
GLUG

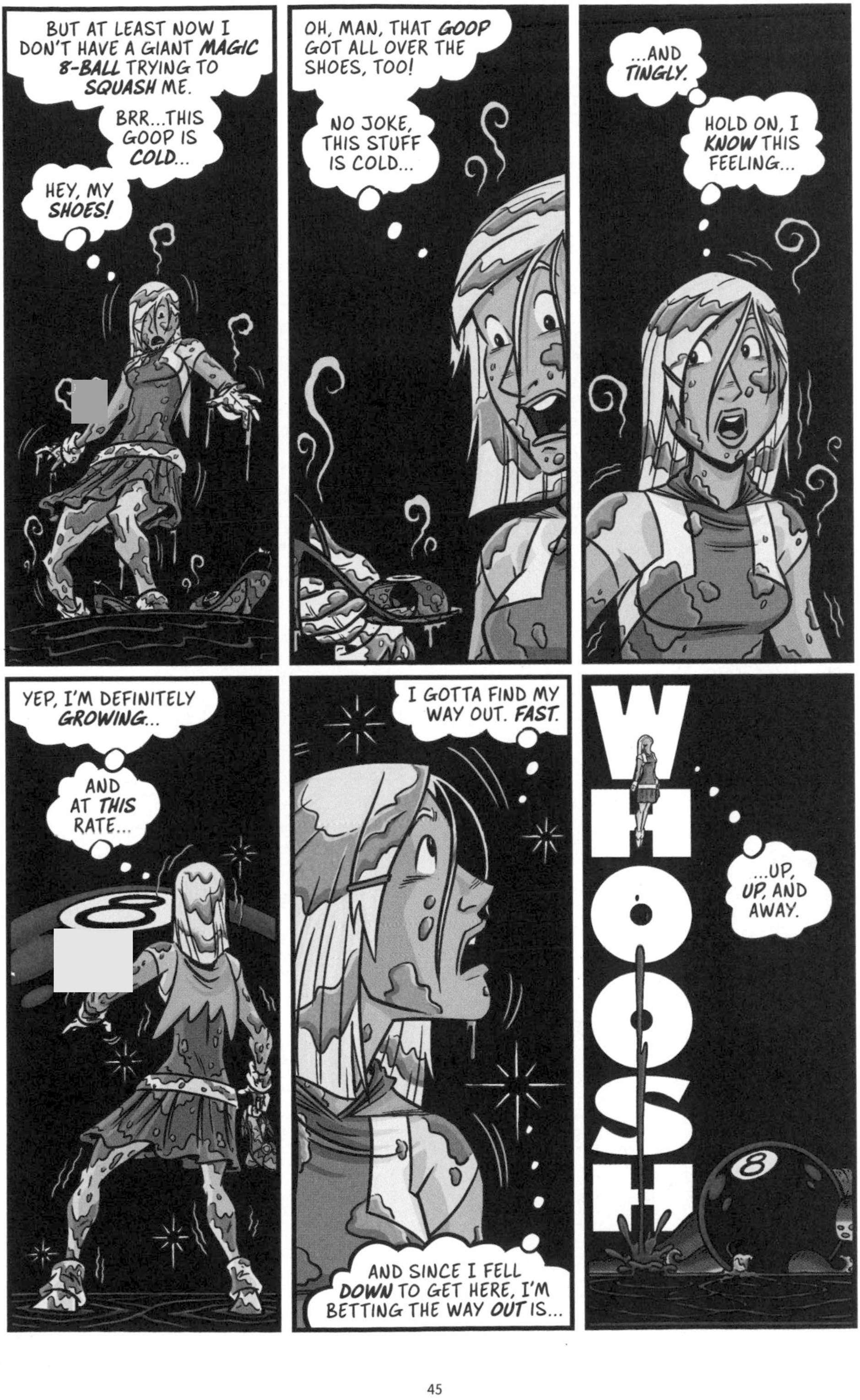
BUT AT LEAST NOW I DON'T HAVE A GIANT MAGIC 8-BALL TRYING TO SQUASH ME.
BRR...THIS GOOP IS COLD...
HEY, MY SHOES!
OH, MAN, THAT GOOP GOT ALL OVER THE SHOES, TOO!
NO JOKE, THIS STUFF IS COLD...
...AND TINGLY.
HOLD ON, I KNOW THIS FEELING...
YEP, I'M DEFINITELY GROWING...
AND AT THIS RATE...
I GOTTA FIND MY WAY OUT. FAST.
AND SINCE I FELL DOWN TO GET HERE, I'M BETTING THE WAY OUT IS...
WHOOSH
...UP, UP, AND AWAY.

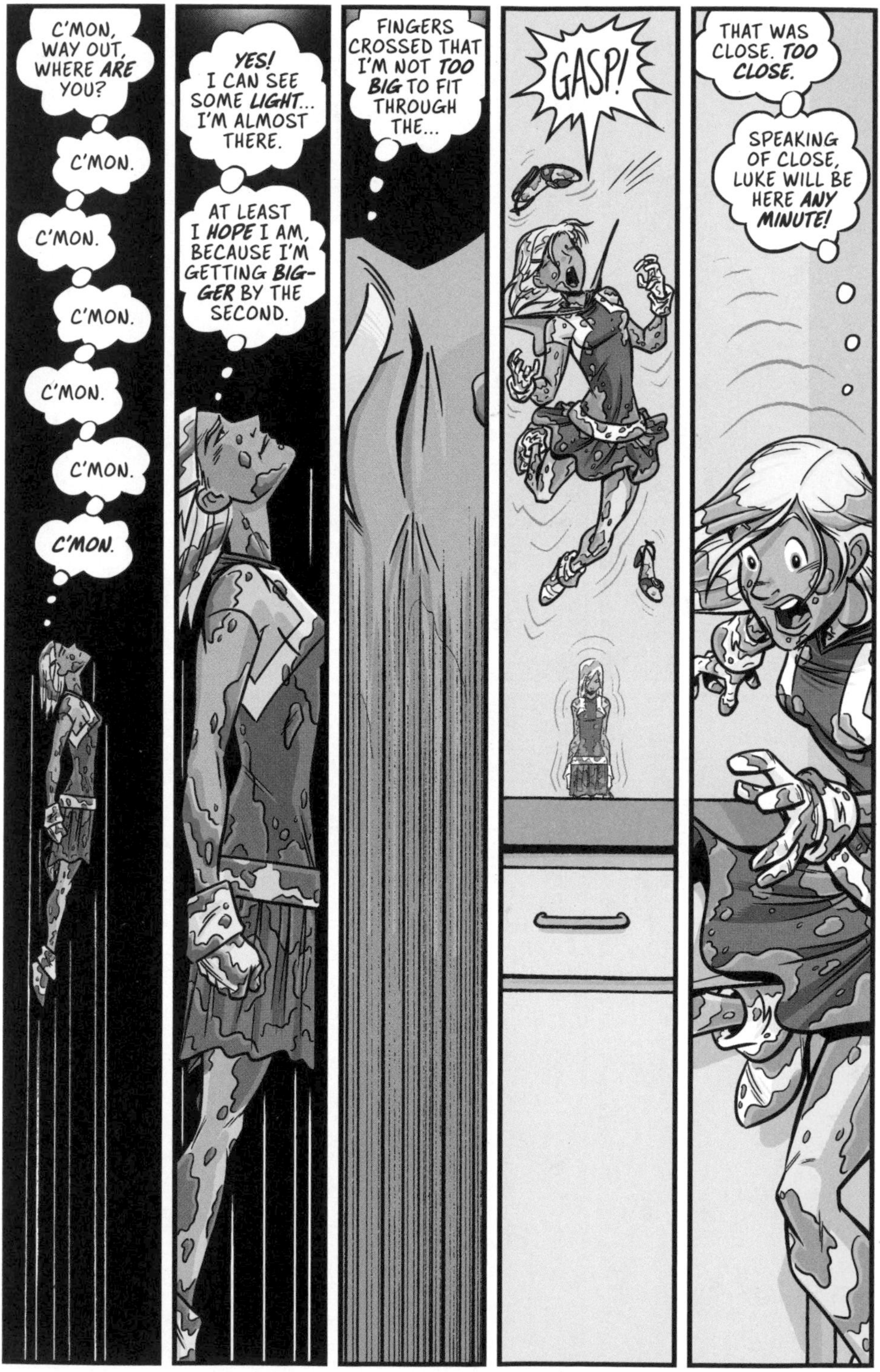

C'MON, WAY OUT, WHERE ARE YOU?
C'MON.
C'MON.
C'MON.
C'MON.
C'MON.
C'MON.
YES! I CAN SEE SOME LIGHT... I'M ALMOST THERE.
AT LEAST I HOPE I AM, BECAUSE I'M GETTING BIG-GER BY THE SECOND.
FINGERS CROSSED THAT I'M NOT TOO BIG TO FIT THROUGH THE...
GASP!
THAT WAS CLOSE. TOO CLOSE.
SPEAKING OF CLOSE, LUKE WILL BE HERE ANY MINUTE!

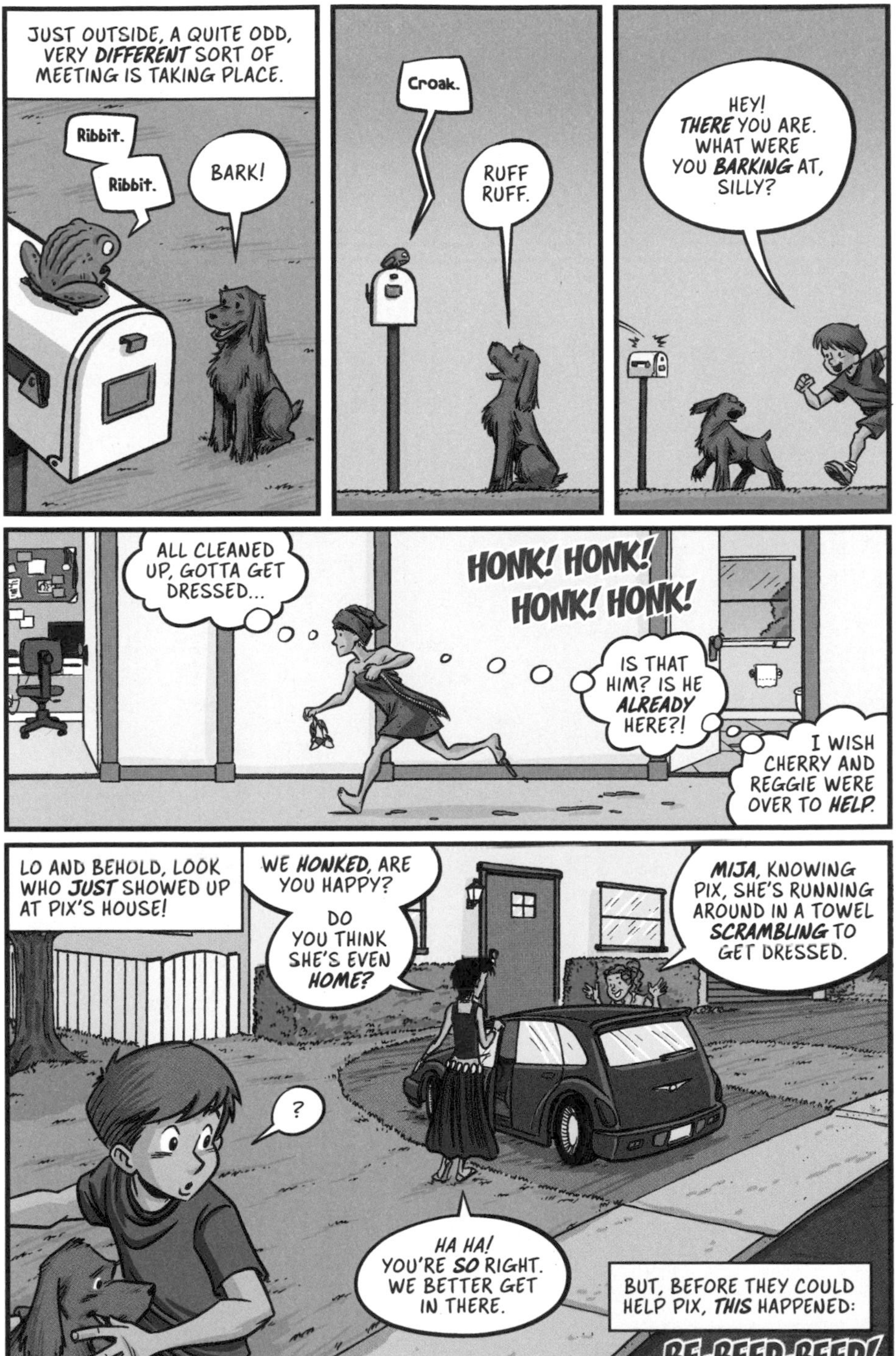
JUST OUTSIDE, A QUITE ODD, VERY DIFFERENT SORT OF MEETING IS TAKING PLACE.
Ribbit.
Ribbit.
BARK!
Croak.
RUFF RUFF.
HEY! THERE YOU ARE. WHAT WERE YOU BARKING AT, SILLY?
ALL CLEANED UP, GOTTA GET DRESSED...
HONK! HONK! HONK! HONK!
IS THAT HIM? IS HE ALREADY HERE?!
I WISH CHERRY AND REGGIE WERE OVER TO HELP.
LO AND BEHOLD, LOOK WHO JUST SHOWED UP AT PIX'S HOUSE!
WE HONKED, ARE YOU HAPPY?
DO YOU THINK SHE'S EVEN HOME?
MIJA, KNOWING PIX, SHE'S RUNNING AROUND IN A TOWEL SCRAMBLING TO GET DRESSED.
?
HA HA! YOU'RE SO RIGHT. WE BETTER GET IN THERE.
BUT, BEFORE THEY COULD HELP PIX, THIS HAPPENED:
BE-BEEP-BEEP!

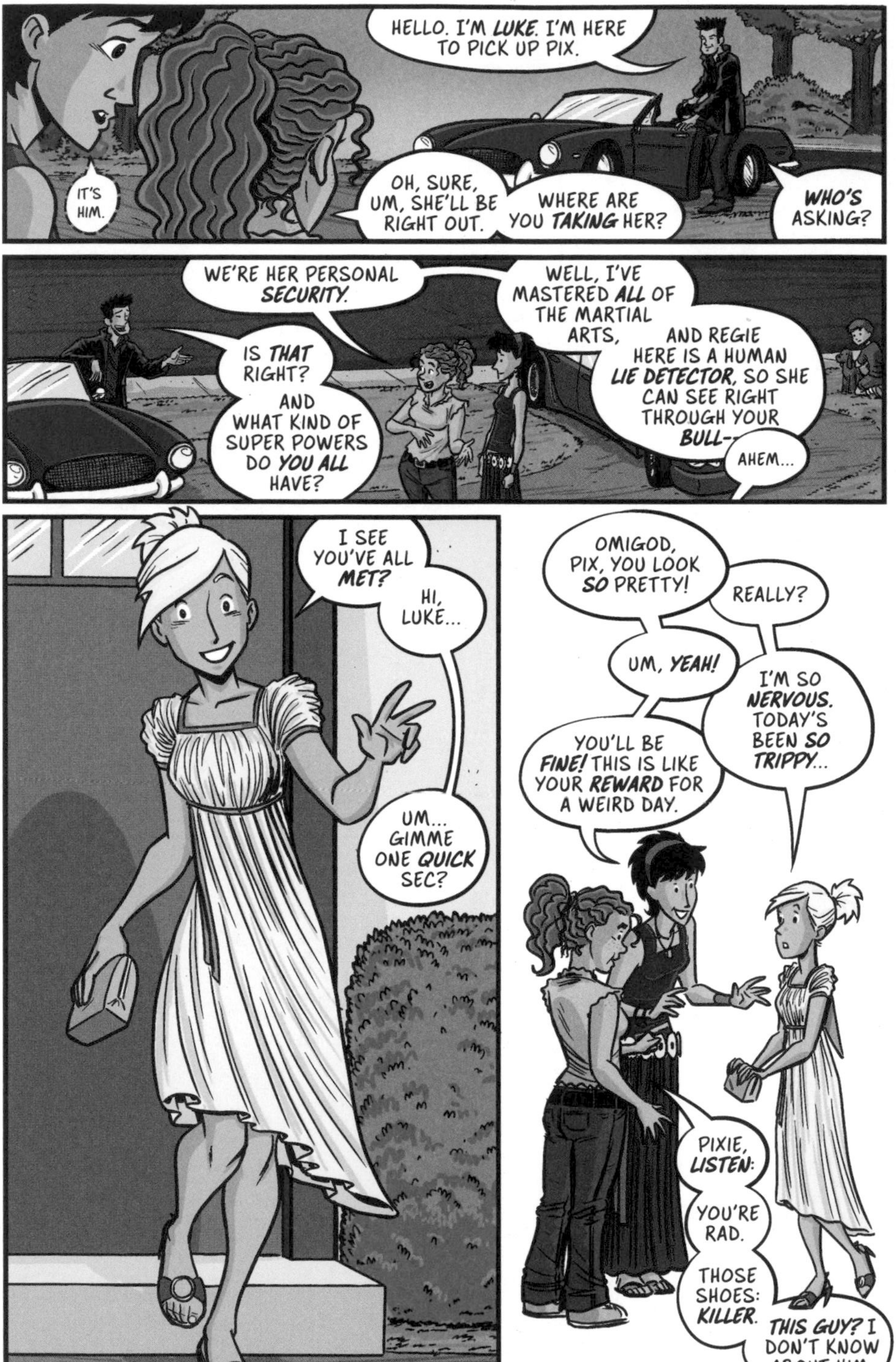
HELLO. I'M LUKE. I'M HERE TO PICK UP PIX.
IT'S HIM.
OH, SURE, UM, SHE'LL BE RIGHT OUT.
WHERE ARE YOU TAKING HER?
WHO'S ASKING?
WE'RE HER PERSONAL SECURITY.
IS THAT RIGHT?
AND WHAT KIND OF SUPER POWERS DO YOU ALL HAVE?
WELL, I'VE MASTERED ALL OF THE MARTIAL ARTS,
AND REGIE HERE IS A HUMAN LIE DETECTOR, SO SHE CAN SEE RIGHT THROUGH YOUR BULL--
AHEM...
I SEE YOU'VE ALL MET?
HI, LUKE...
UM... GIMME ONE QUICK SEC?
OMIGOD, PIX, YOU LOOK SO PRETTY!
REALLY?
UM, YEAH!
I'M SO NERVOUS. TODAY'S BEEN SO TRIPPY...
YOU'LL BE FINE! THIS IS LIKE YOUR REWARD FOR A WEIRD DAY.
PIXIE, LISTEN:
YOU'RE RAD.
THOSE SHOES: KILLER.
THIS GUY? I DON'T KNOW ABOUT HIM.

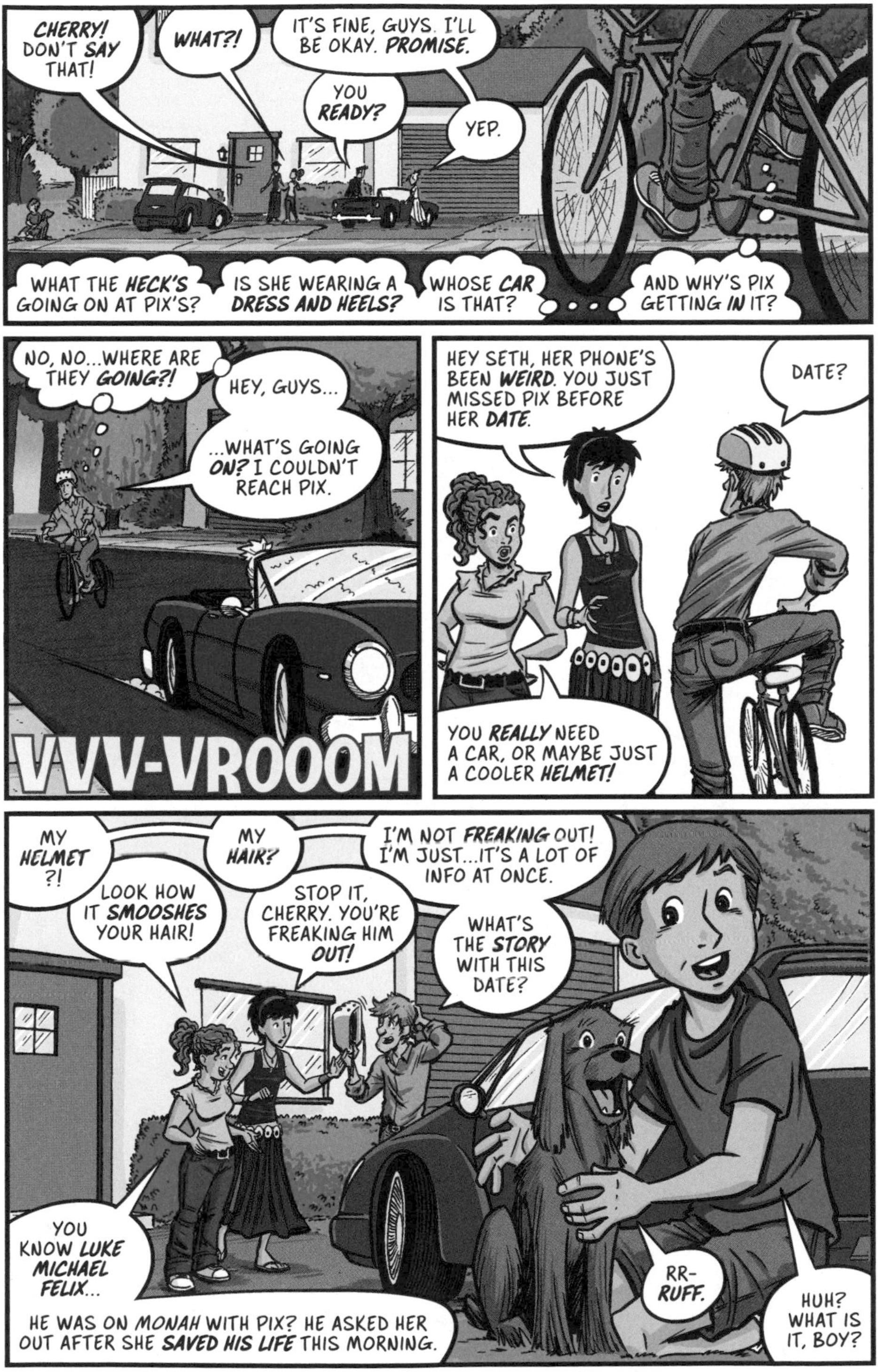
CHERRY! DON'T SAY THAT!
WHAT?!
IT'S FINE, GUYS. I'LL BE OKAY. PROMISE.
YOU READY?
YEP.
WHAT THE HECK'S GOING ON AT PIX'S?
IS SHE WEARING A DRESS AND HEELS?
WHOSE CAR IS THAT?
AND WHY'S PIX GETTING IN IT?
NO, NO...WHERE ARE THEY GOING?!
HEY, GUYS...
...WHAT'S GOING ON? I COULDN'T REACH PIX.
VVV-VROOOM
HEY SETH, HER PHONE'S BEEN WEIRD. YOU JUST MISSED PIX BEFORE HER DATE.
DATE?
YOU REALLY NEED A CAR, OR MAYBE JUST A COOLER HELMET!
MY HELMET?!
LOOK HOW IT SMOOSHES YOUR HAIR!
MY HAIR?
STOP IT, CHERRY. YOU'RE FREAKING HIM OUT!
I'M NOT FREAKING OUT! I'M JUST...IT'S A LOT OF INFO AT ONCE.
WHAT'S THE STORY WITH THIS DATE?
YOU KNOW LUKE MICHAEL FELIX...
HE WAS ON MONAH WITH PIX? HE ASKED HER OUT AFTER SHE SAVED HIS LIFE THIS MORNING.
RR-RUFF.
HUH? WHAT IS IT, BOY?

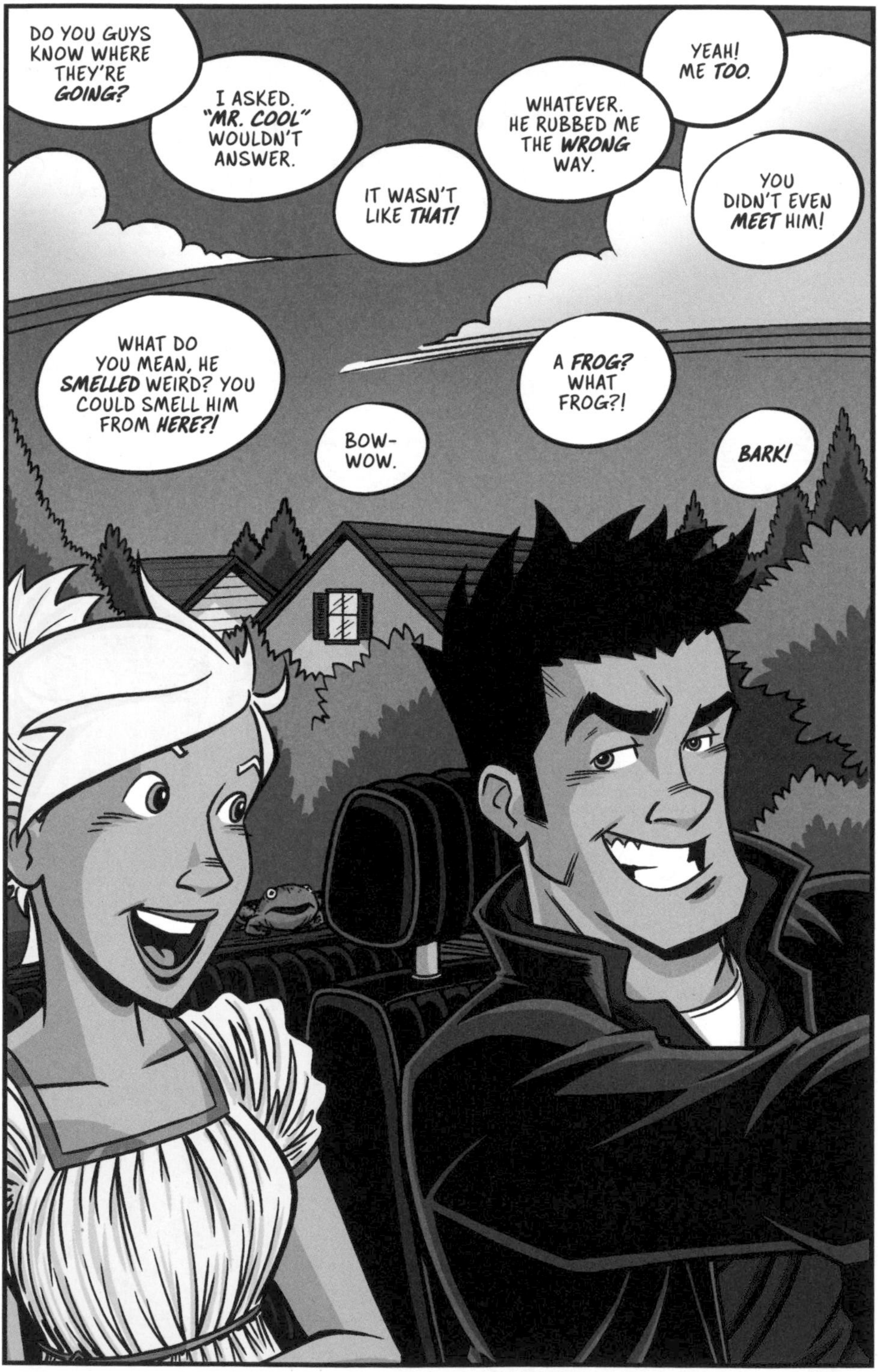
DO YOU GUYS KNOW WHERE THEY'RE GOING?
I ASKED. "MR. COOL" WOULDN'T ANSWER.
IT WASN'T LIKE THAT!
WHATEVER. HE RUBBED ME THE WRONG WAY.
YEAH! ME TOO.
YOU DIDN'T EVEN MEET HIM!
WHAT DO YOU MEAN, HE SMELLED WEIRD? YOU COULD SMELL HIM FROM HERE?!
BOW-WOW.
A FROG? WHAT FROG?!
BARK!

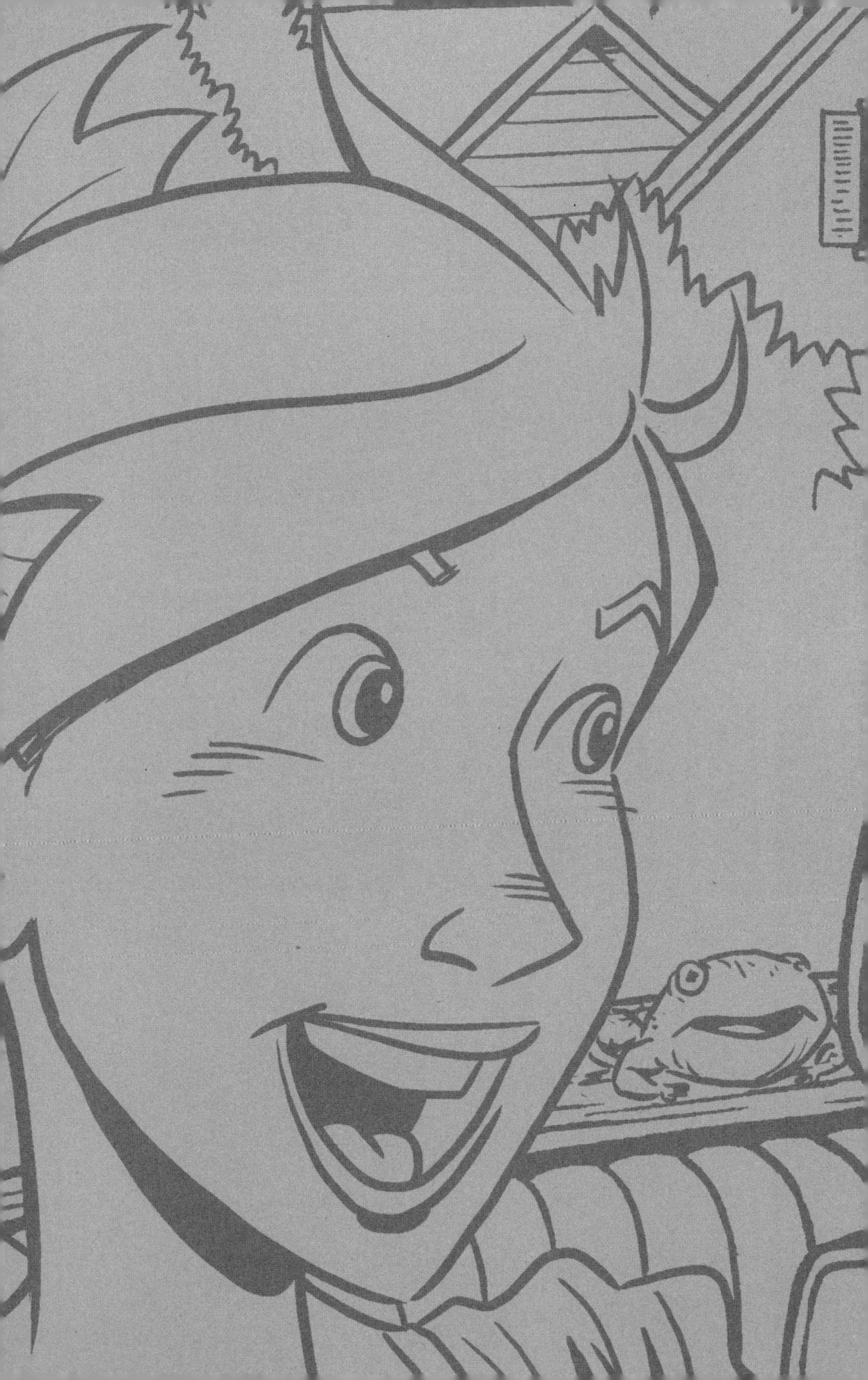

CHAPTER THREE

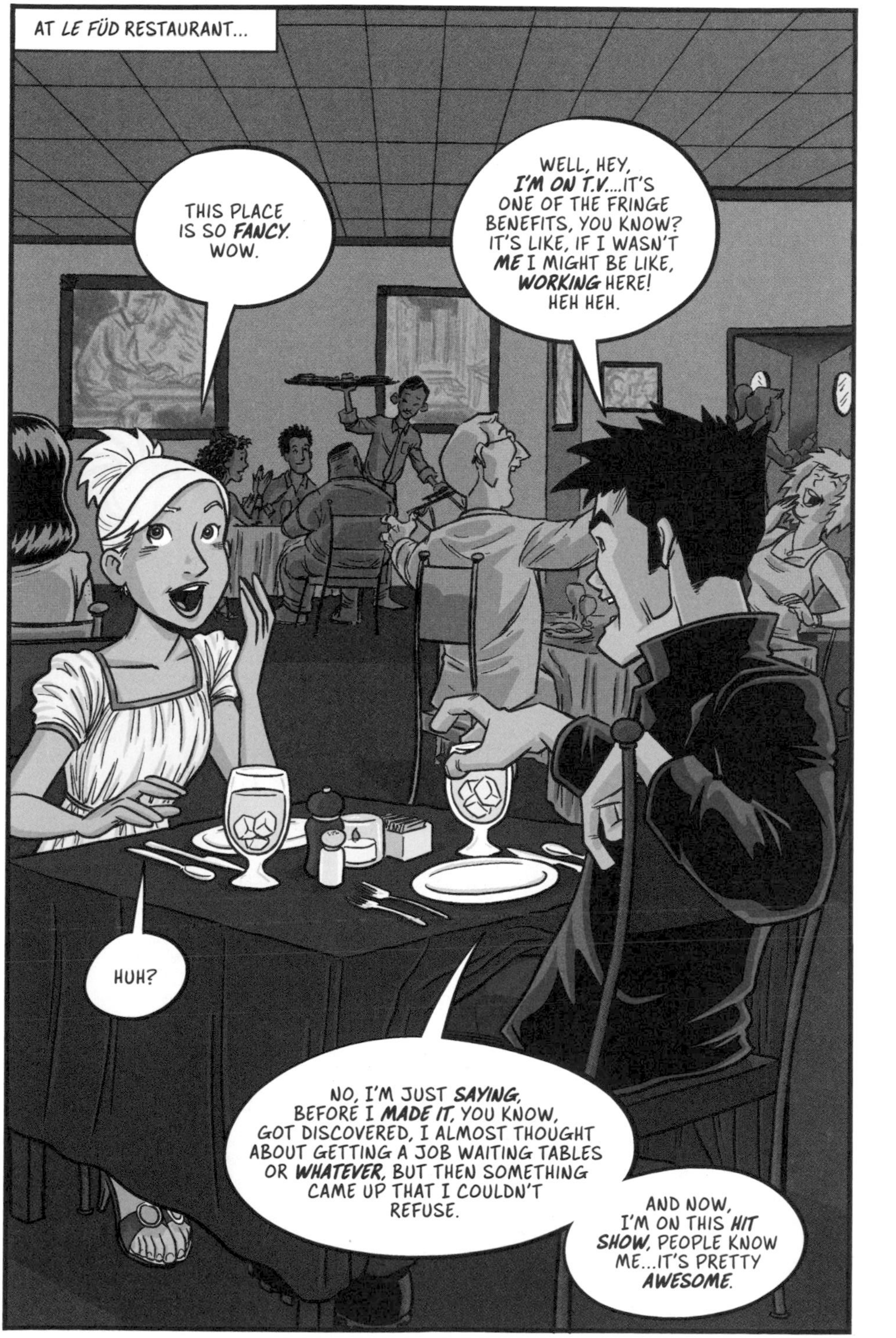
AT LE FÜD RESTAURANT...
THIS PLACE IS SO FANCY. WOW.
WELL, HEY, I'M ON T.V....IT'S ONE OF THE FRINGE BENEFITS, YOU KNOW? IT'S LIKE, IF I WASN'T ME I MIGHT BE LIKE, WORKING HERE! HEH HEH.
HUH?
NO, I'M JUST SAYING, BEFORE I MADE IT, YOU KNOW, GOT DISCOVERED, I ALMOST THOUGHT ABOUT GETTING A JOB WAITING TABLES OR WHATEVER, BUT THEN SOMETHING CAME UP THAT I COULDN'T REFUSE.
AND NOW, I'M ON THIS HIT SHOW, PEOPLE KNOW ME...IT'S PRETTY AWESOME.

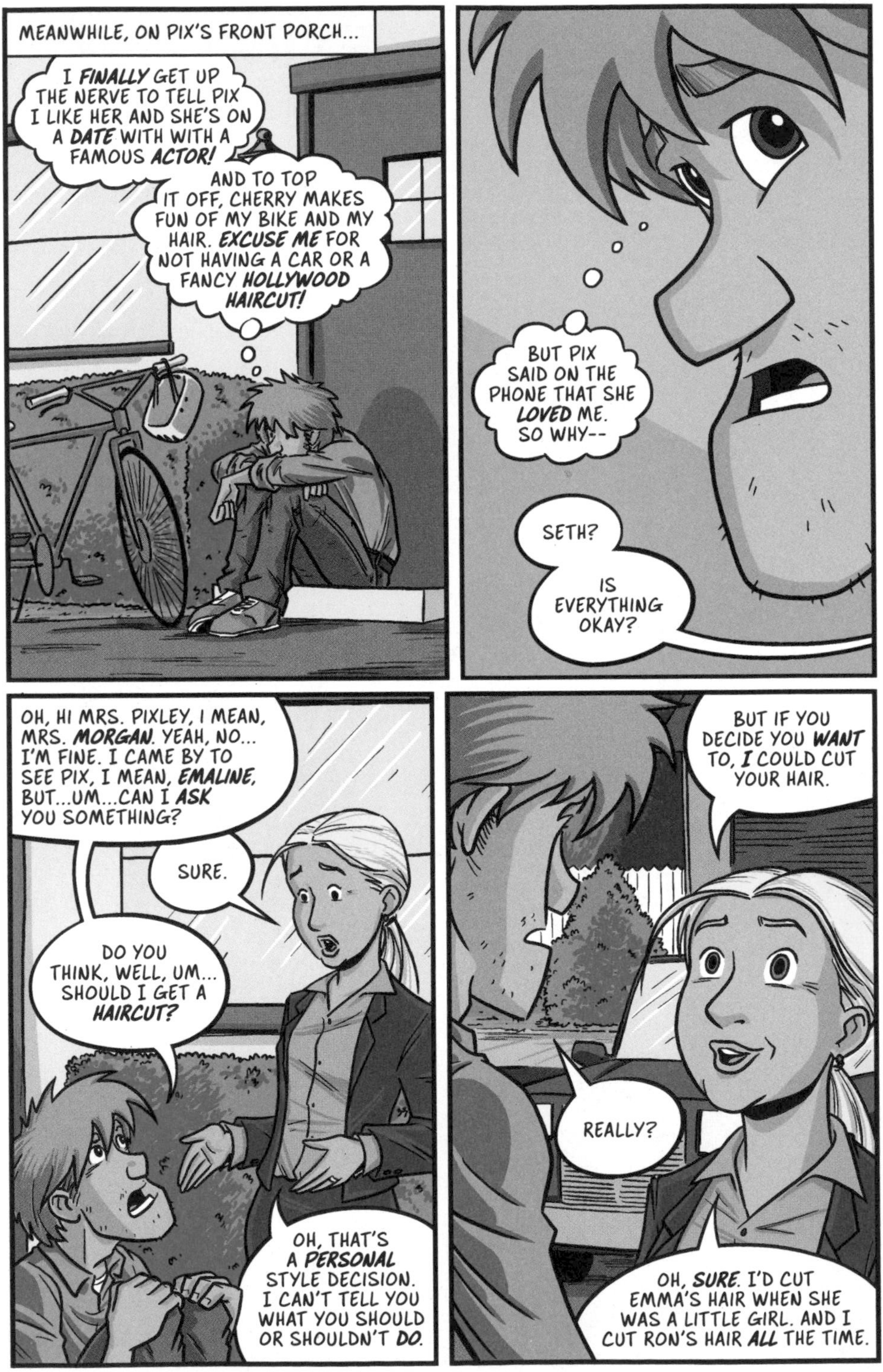
MEANWHILE, ON PIX'S FRONT PORCH...
I FINALLY GET UP THE NERVE TO TELL PIX I LIKE HER AND SHE'S ON A DATE WITH WITH A FAMOUS ACTOR!
AND TO TOP IT OFF, CHERRY MAKES FUN OF MY BIKE AND MY HAIR. EXCUSE ME FOR NOT HAVING A CAR OR A FANCY HOLLYWOOD HAIRCUT!
BUT PIX SAID ON THE PHONE THAT SHE LOVED ME. SO WHY--
SETH?
IS EVERYTHING OKAY?
OH, HI MRS. PIXLEY, I MEAN, MRS. MORGAN. YEAH, NO... I'M FINE. I CAME BY TO SEE PIX, I MEAN, EMALINE, BUT...UM...CAN I ASK YOU SOMETHING?
SURE.
DO YOU THINK, WELL, UM... SHOULD I GET A HAIRCUT?
OH, THAT'S A PERSONAL STYLE DECISION. I CAN'T TELL YOU WHAT YOU SHOULD OR SHOULDN'T DO.
BUT IF YOU DECIDE YOU WANT TO, I COULD CUT YOUR HAIR.
REALLY?
OH, SURE. I'D CUT EMMA'S HAIR WHEN SHE WAS A LITTLE GIRL. AND I CUT RON'S HAIR ALL THE TIME.

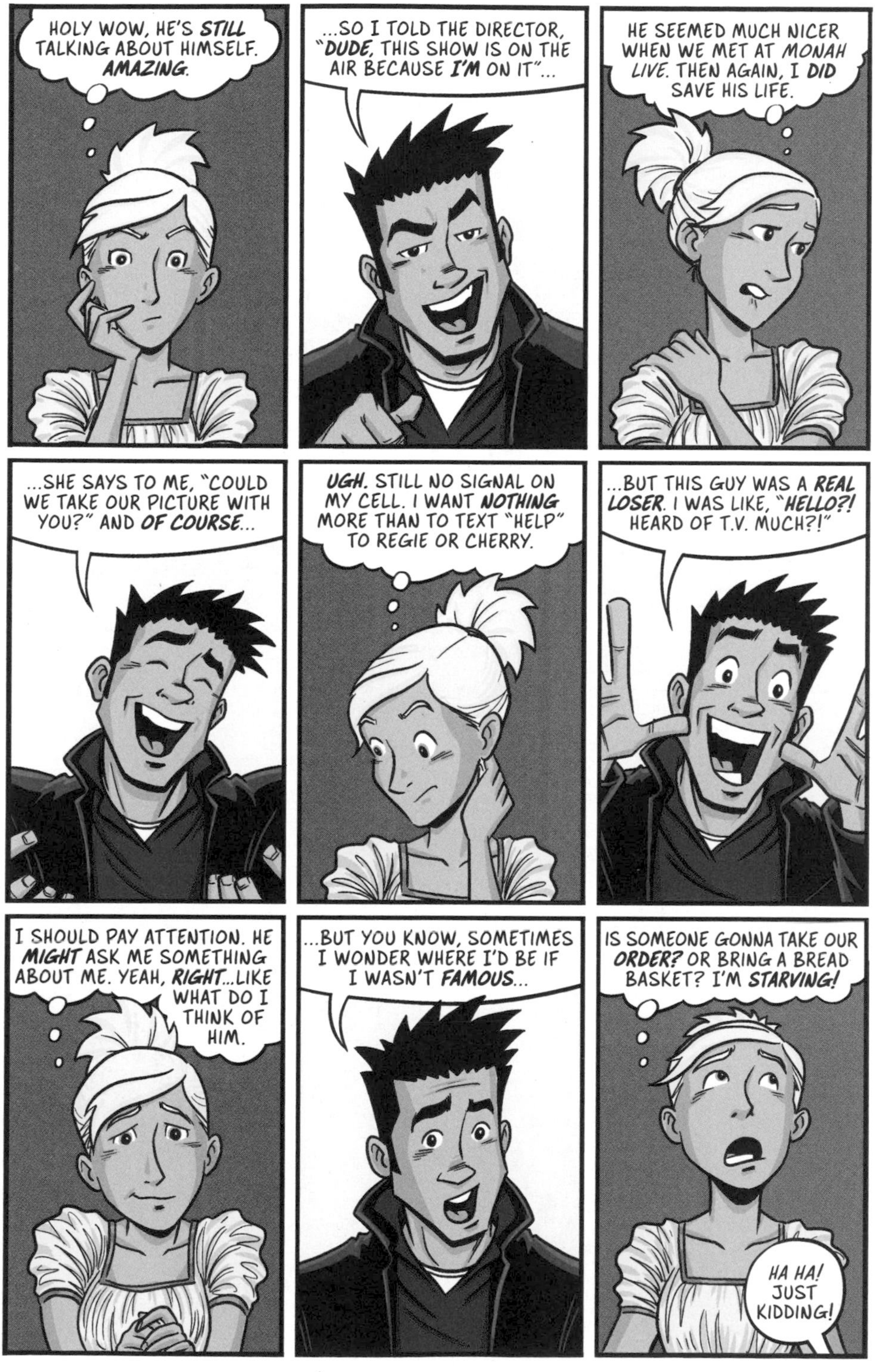
HOLY WOW, HE'S STILL TALKING ABOUT HIMSELF. AMAZING.
...SO I TOLD THE DIRECTOR, "DUDE, THIS SHOW IS ON THE AIR BECAUSE I'M ON IT"...
HE SEEMED MUCH NICER WHEN WE MET AT MONAH LIVE. THEN AGAIN, I DID SAVE HIS LIFE.
...SHE SAYS TO ME, "COULD WE TAKE OUR PICTURE WITH YOU?" AND OF COURSE...
UGH. STILL NO SIGNAL ON MY CELL. I WANT NOTHING MORE THAN TO TEXT "HELP" TO REGIE OR CHERRY.
...BUT THIS GUY WAS A REAL LOSER. I WAS LIKE, "HELLO?! HEARD OF T.V. MUCH?!"
I SHOULD PAY ATTENTION. HE MIGHT ASK ME SOMETHING ABOUT ME. YEAH, RIGHT...LIKE WHAT DO I THINK OF HIM.
...BUT YOU KNOW, SOMETIMES I WONDER WHERE I'D BE IF I WASN'T FAMOUS...
IS SOMEONE GONNA TAKE OUR ORDER? OR BRING A BREAD BASKET? I'M STARVING!
HA HA! JUST KIDDING!

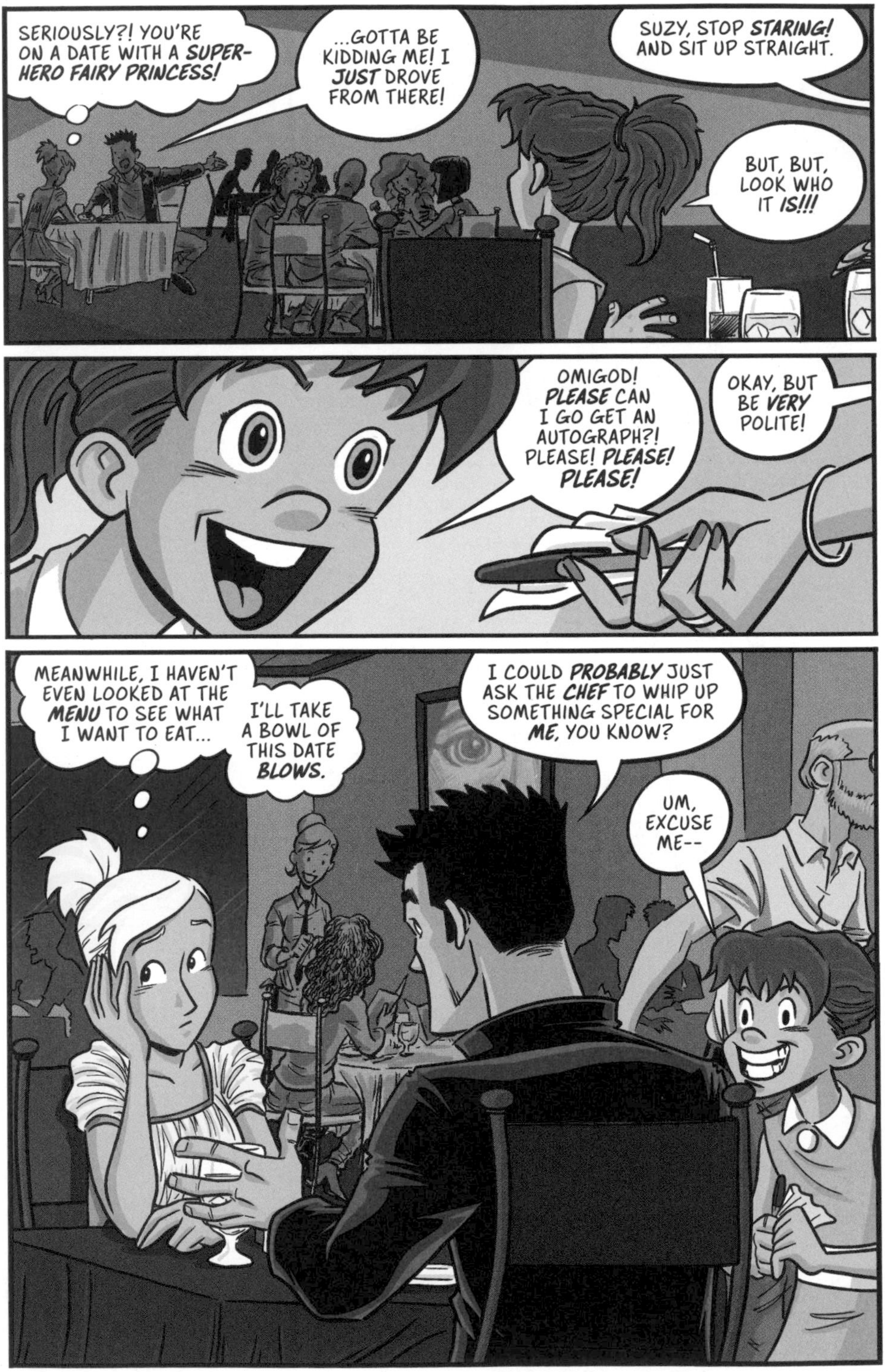
SERIOUSLY?! YOU'RE ON A DATE WITH A SUPER-HERO FAIRY PRINCESS!
...GOTTA BE KIDDING ME! I JUST DROVE FROM THERE!
SUZY, STOP STARING! AND SIT UP STRAIGHT.
BUT, BUT, LOOK WHO IT IS!!!
OMIGOD! PLEASE CAN I GO GET AN AUTOGRAPH?! PLEASE! PLEASE! PLEASE!
OKAY, BUT BE VERY POLITE!
MEANWHILE, I HAVEN'T EVEN LOOKED AT THE MENU TO SEE WHAT I WANT TO EAT...
I'LL TAKE A BOWL OF THIS DATE BLOWS.
I COULD PROBABLY JUST ASK THE CHEF TO WHIP UP SOMETHING SPECIAL FOR ME, YOU KNOW?
UM, EXCUSE ME--

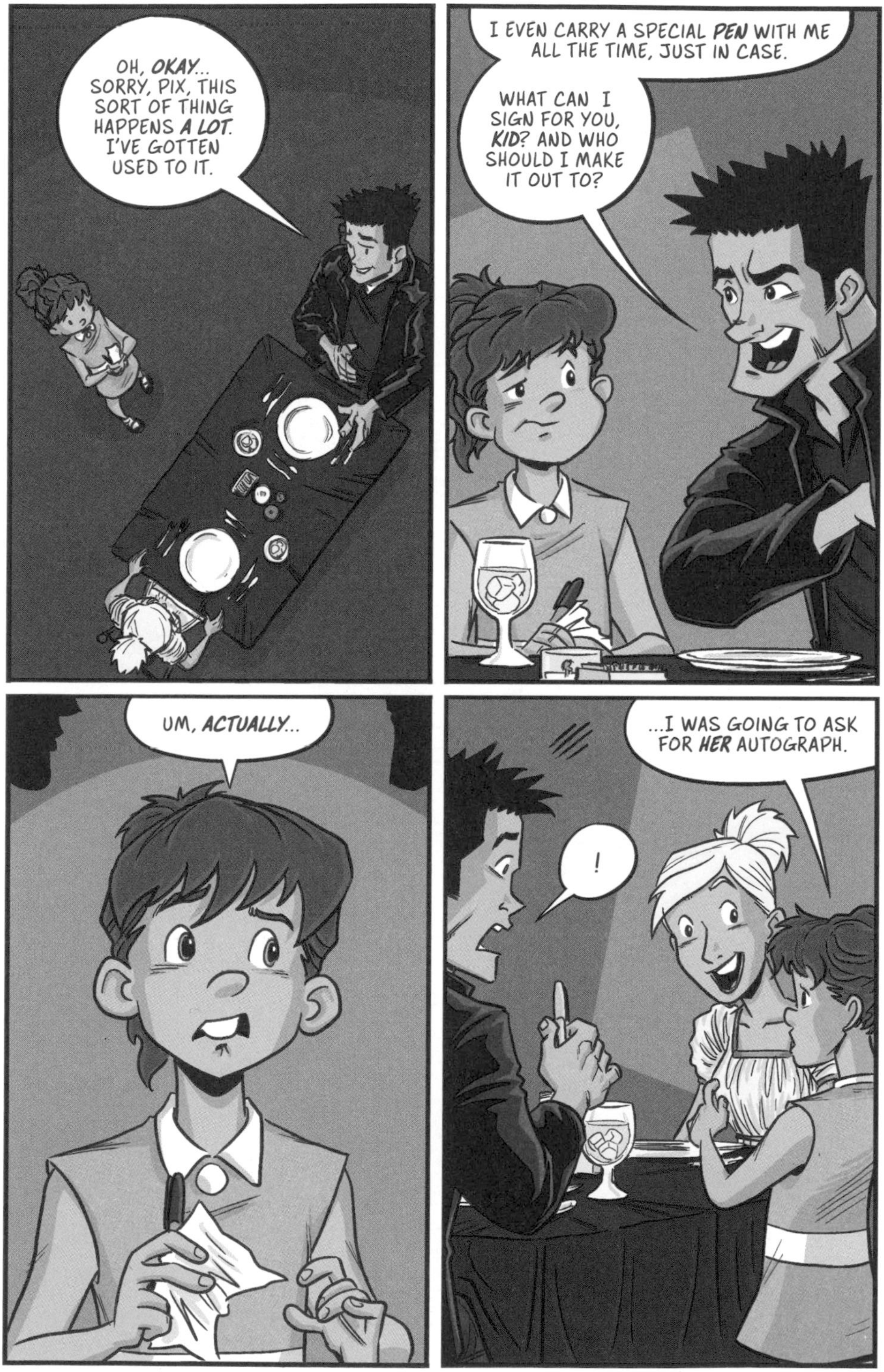
OH, OKAY... SORRY, PIX, THIS SORT OF THING HAPPENS A LOT. I'VE GOTTEN USED TO IT.
I EVEN CARRY A SPECIAL PEN WITH ME ALL THE TIME, JUST IN CASE.
WHAT CAN I SIGN FOR YOU, KID? AND WHO SHOULD I MAKE IT OUT TO?
UM, ACTUALLY...
...I WAS GOING TO ASK FOR HER AUTOGRAPH.
!

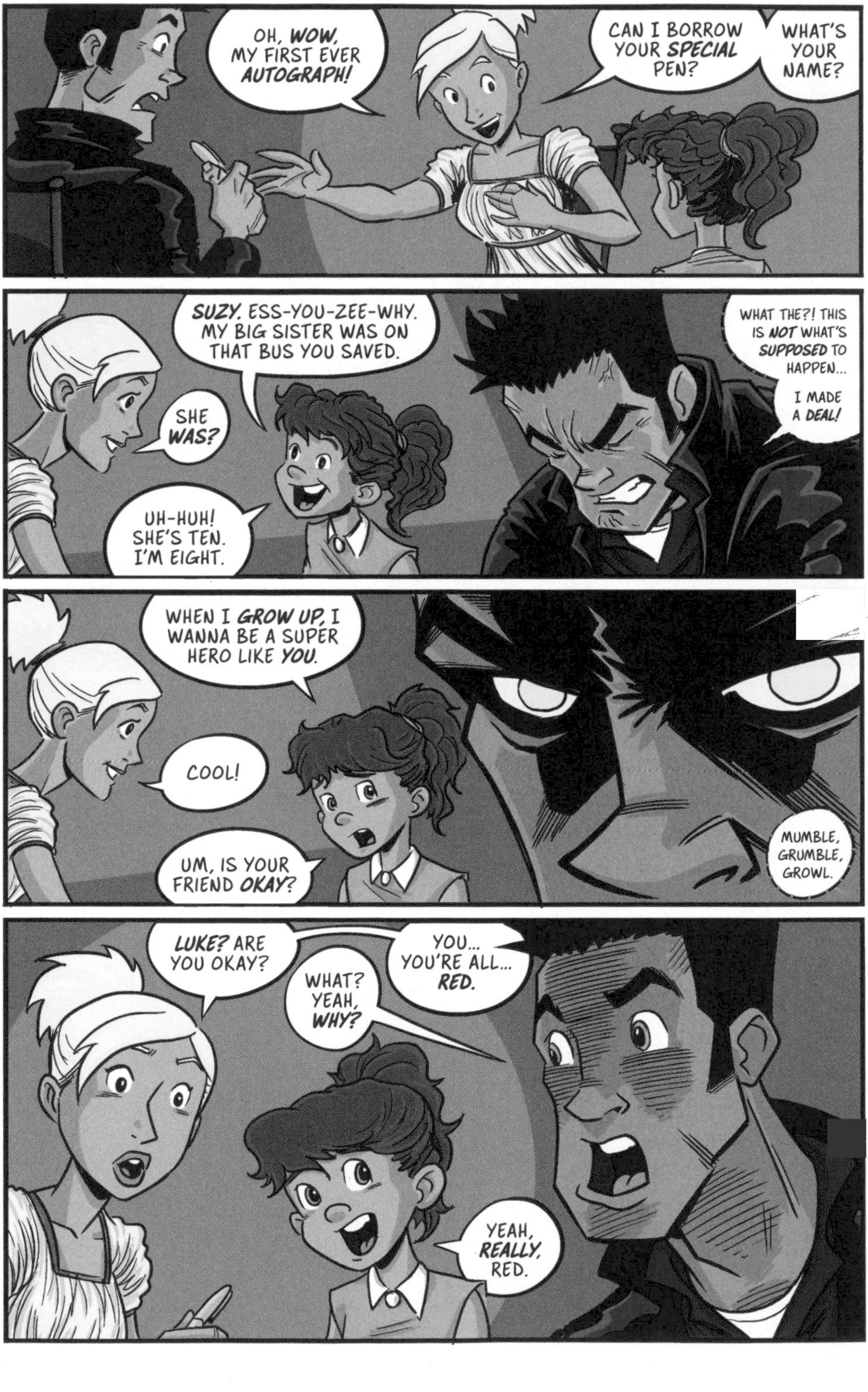
OH, WOW, MY FIRST EVER AUTOGRAPH!
CAN I BORROW YOUR SPECIAL PEN?
WHAT'S YOUR NAME?
SUZY. ESS-YOU-ZEE-WHY. MY BIG SISTER WAS ON THAT BUS YOU SAVED.
SHE WAS?
UH-HUH! SHE'S TEN. I'M EIGHT.
WHAT THE?! THIS IS NOT WHAT'S SUPPOSED TO HAPPEN...
I MADE A DEAL!
WHEN I GROW UP, I WANNA BE A SUPER HERO LIKE YOU.
COOL!
UM, IS YOUR FRIEND OKAY?
MUMBLE, GRUMBLE, GROWL.
LUKE? ARE YOU OKAY?
WHAT? YEAH, WHY?
YOU... YOU'RE ALL... RED.
YEAH, REALLY, RED.

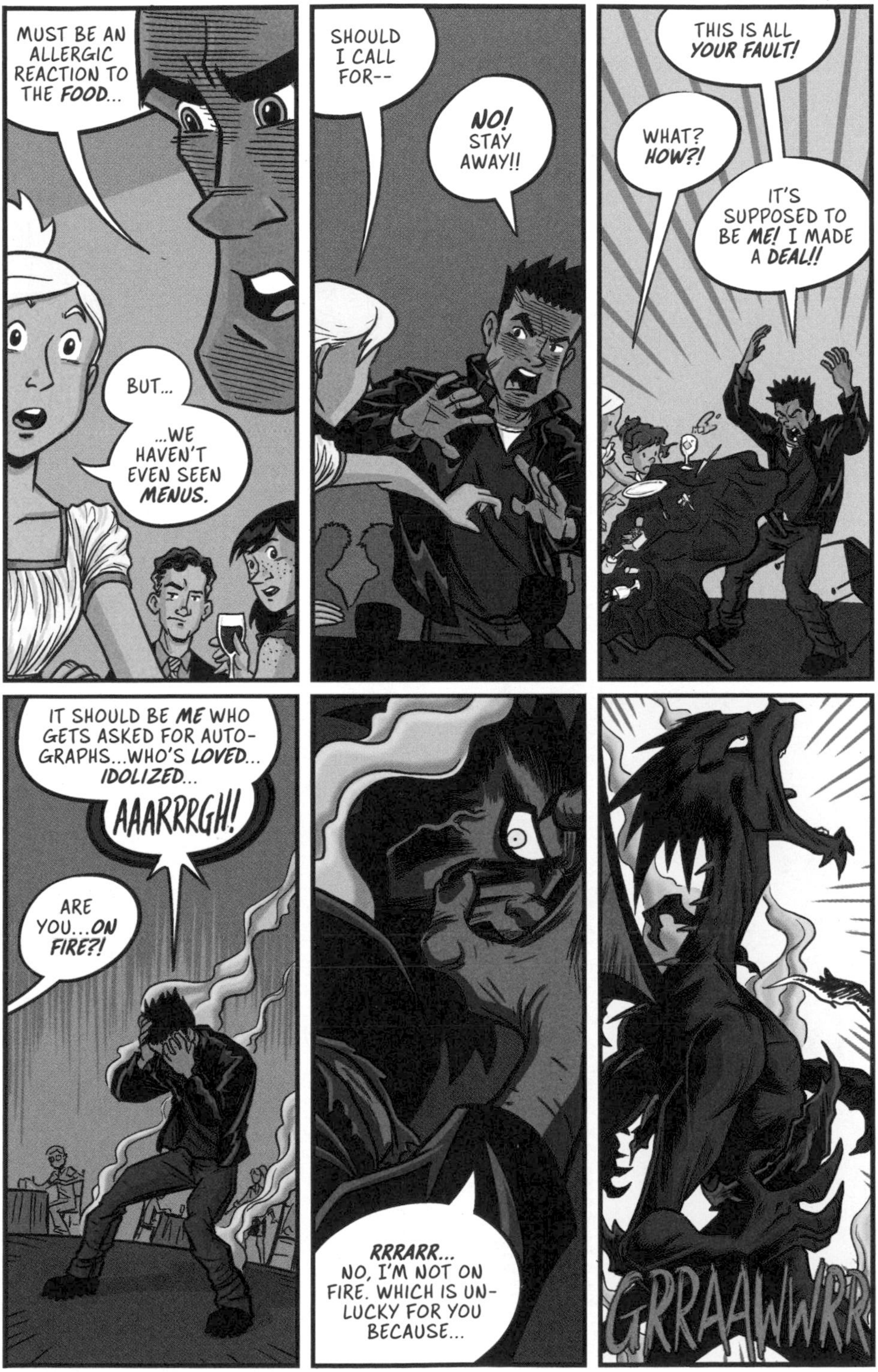
MUST BE AN ALLERGIC REACTION TO THE FOOD...
BUT...
...WE HAVEN'T EVEN SEEN MENUS.
SHOULD I CALL FOR--
NO! STAY AWAY!!
THIS IS ALL YOUR FAULT!
WHAT? HOW?!
IT'S SUPPOSED TO BE ME! I MADE A DEAL!!
IT SHOULD BE ME WHO GETS ASKED FOR AUTO-GRAPHS...WHO'S LOVED... IDOLIZED...
AAARRRGH!
ARE YOU...ON FIRE?!
RRRARR... NO, I'M NOT ON FIRE. WHICH IS UN-LUCKY FOR YOU BECAUSE...
GRRAAWWRR

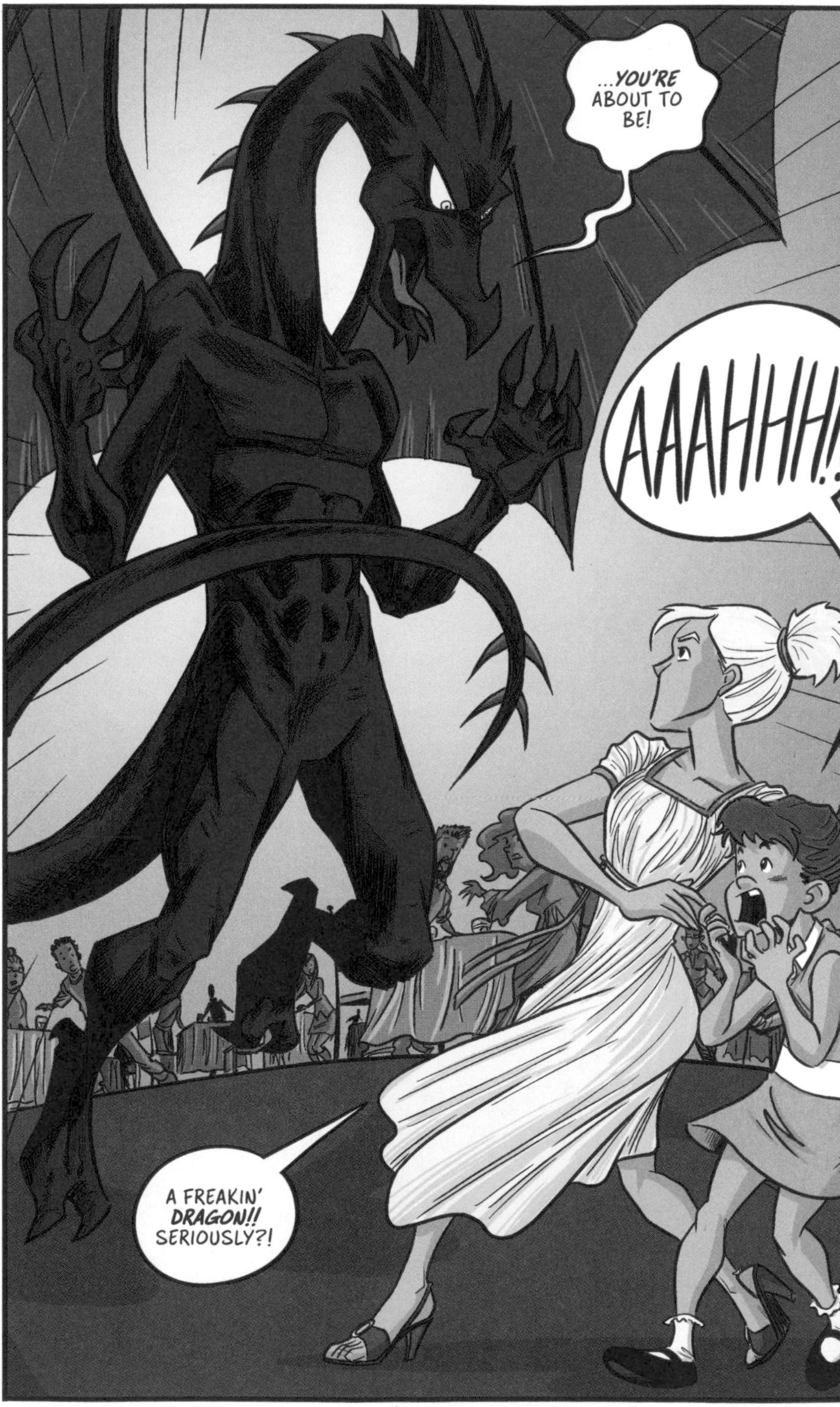
...YOU'RE ABOUT TO BE!
AAAHHH!!
A FREAKIN' DRAGON!! SERIOUSLY?!

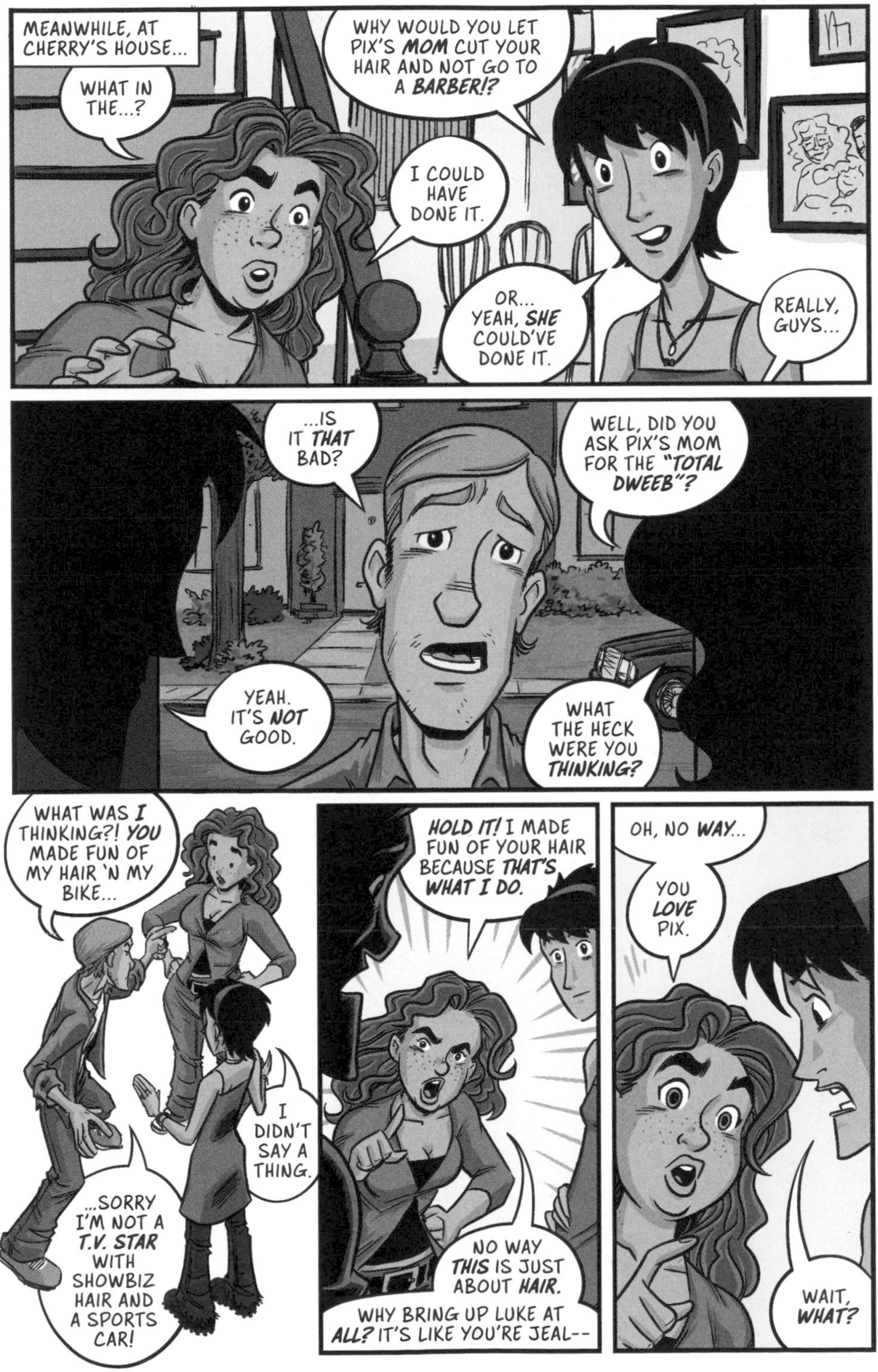

MEANWHILE, AT CHERRY'S HOUSE...
WHAT IN THE...?
WHY WOULD YOU LET PIX'S MOM CUT YOUR HAIR AND NOT GO TO A BARBER!?
I COULD HAVE DONE IT.
OR... YEAH, SHE COULD'VE DONE IT.
REALLY, GUYS...
...IS IT THAT BAD?
WELL, DID YOU ASK PIX'S MOM FOR THE "TOTAL DWEEB"?
YEAH. IT'S NOT GOOD.
WHAT THE HECK WERE YOU THINKING?
WHAT WAS I THINKING?! YOU MADE FUN OF MY HAIR 'N MY BIKE...
I DIDN'T SAY A THING.
...SORRY I'M NOT A T.V. STAR WITH SHOWBIZ HAIR AND A SPORTS CAR!
HOLD IT! I MADE FUN OF YOUR HAIR BECAUSE THAT'S WHAT I DO.
NO WAY THIS IS JUST ABOUT HAIR.
WHY BRING UP LUKE AT ALL? IT'S LIKE YOU'RE JEAL--
OH, NO WAY...
YOU LOVE PIX.
WAIT, WHAT?

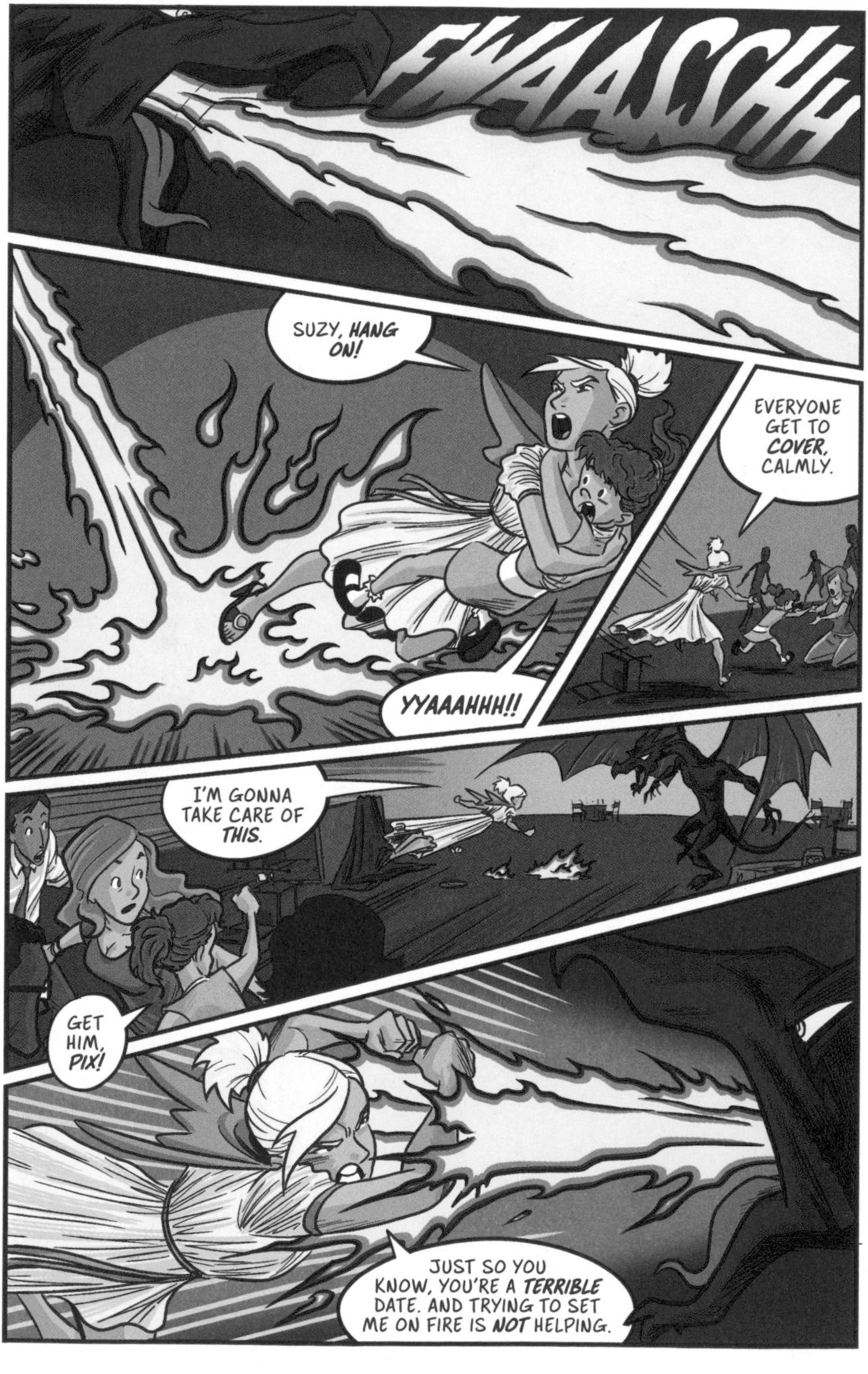
FWAASCH
SUZY, HANG ON!
YYAAAHHH!!
EVERYONE GET TO COVER, CALMLY.
I'M GONNA TAKE CARE OF THIS.
GET HIM, PIX!
JUST SO YOU KNOW, YOU'RE A TERRIBLE DATE. AND TRYING TO SET ME ON FIRE IS NOT HELPING.

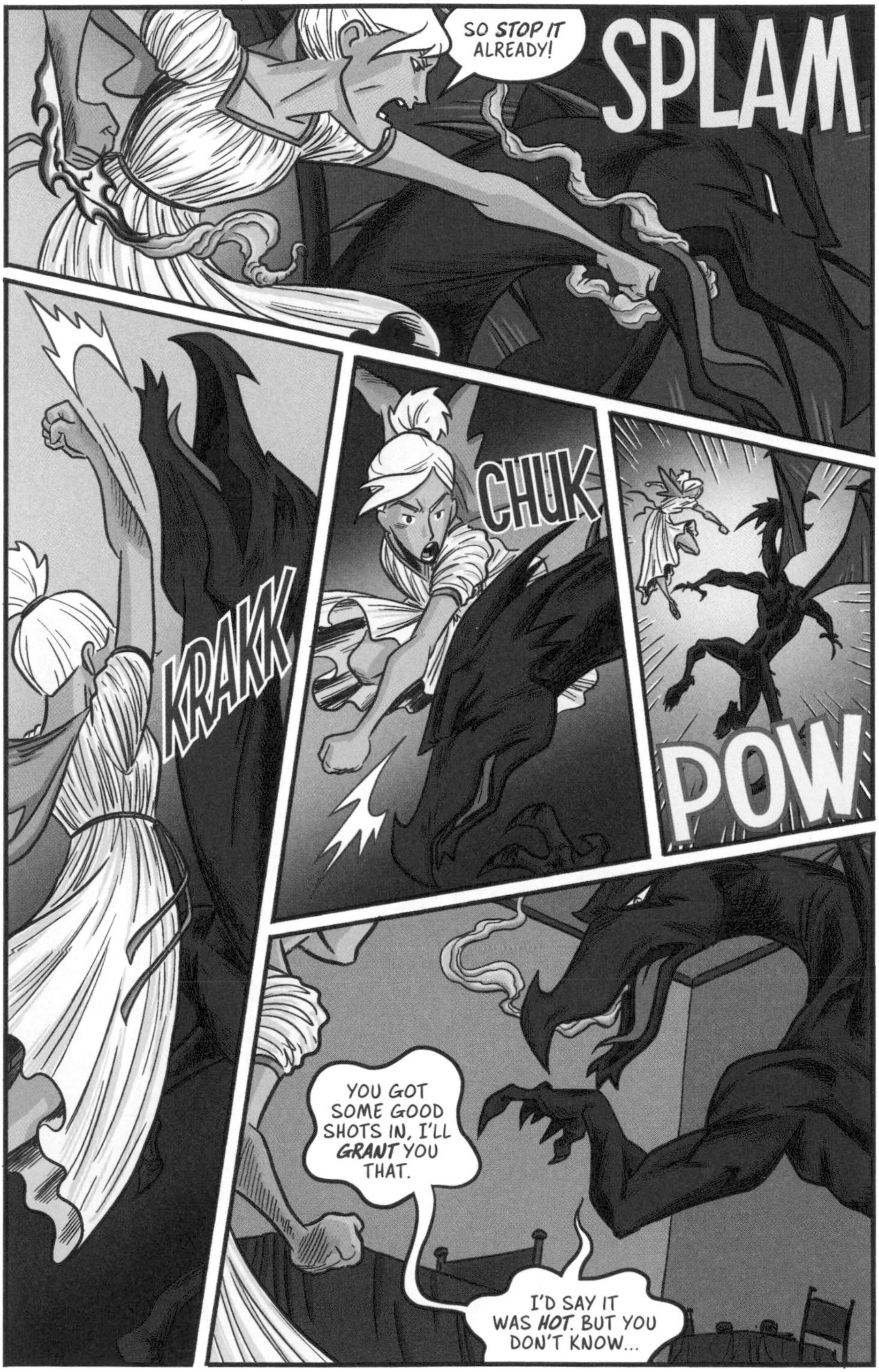
SO **STOP IT** ALREADY!
SPLAM
KRAKK
CHUK
POW
YOU GOT SOME GOOD SHOTS IN, I'LL **GRANT** YOU THAT.
I'D SAY IT WAS **HOT**. BUT YOU DON'T KNOW...

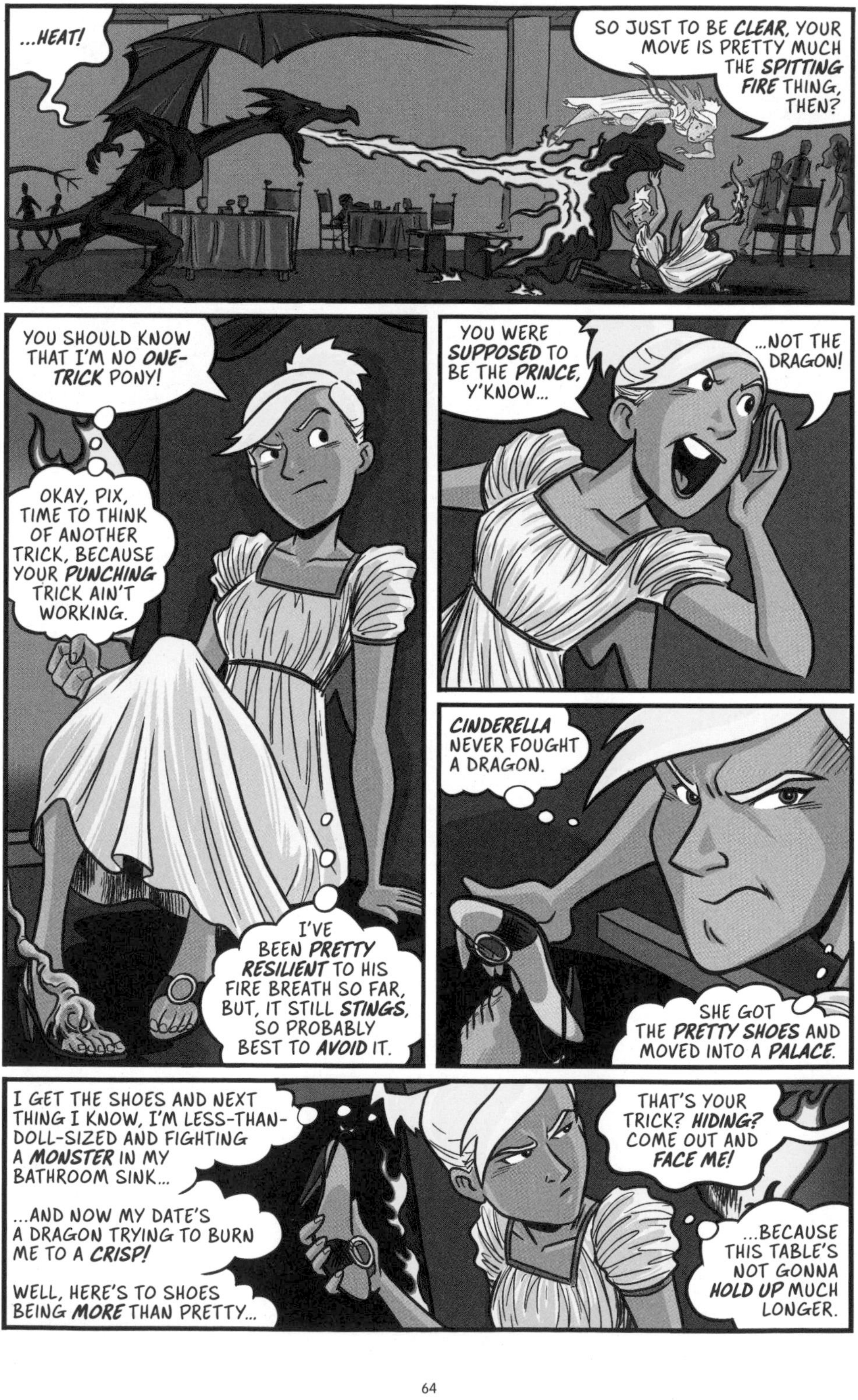
...HEAT!
SO JUST TO BE CLEAR, YOUR MOVE IS PRETTY MUCH THE SPITTING FIRE THING, THEN?
YOU SHOULD KNOW THAT I'M NO ONE-TRICK PONY!
OKAY, PIX, TIME TO THINK OF ANOTHER TRICK, BECAUSE YOUR PUNCHING TRICK AIN'T WORKING.
I'VE BEEN PRETTY RESILIENT TO HIS FIRE BREATH SO FAR, BUT, IT STILL STINGS, SO PROBABLY BEST TO AVOID IT.
YOU WERE SUPPOSED TO BE THE PRINCE, Y'KNOW...
...NOT THE DRAGON!
CINDERELLA NEVER FOUGHT A DRAGON.
SHE GOT THE PRETTY SHOES AND MOVED INTO A PALACE.
I GET THE SHOES AND NEXT THING I KNOW, I'M LESS-THAN-DOLL-SIZED AND FIGHTING A MONSTER IN MY BATHROOM SINK...
...AND NOW MY DATE'S A DRAGON TRYING TO BURN ME TO A CRISP!
WELL, HERE'S TO SHOES BEING MORE THAN PRETTY...
THAT'S YOUR TRICK? HIDING? COME OUT AND FACE ME!
...BECAUSE THIS TABLE'S NOT GONNA HOLD UP MUCH LONGER.

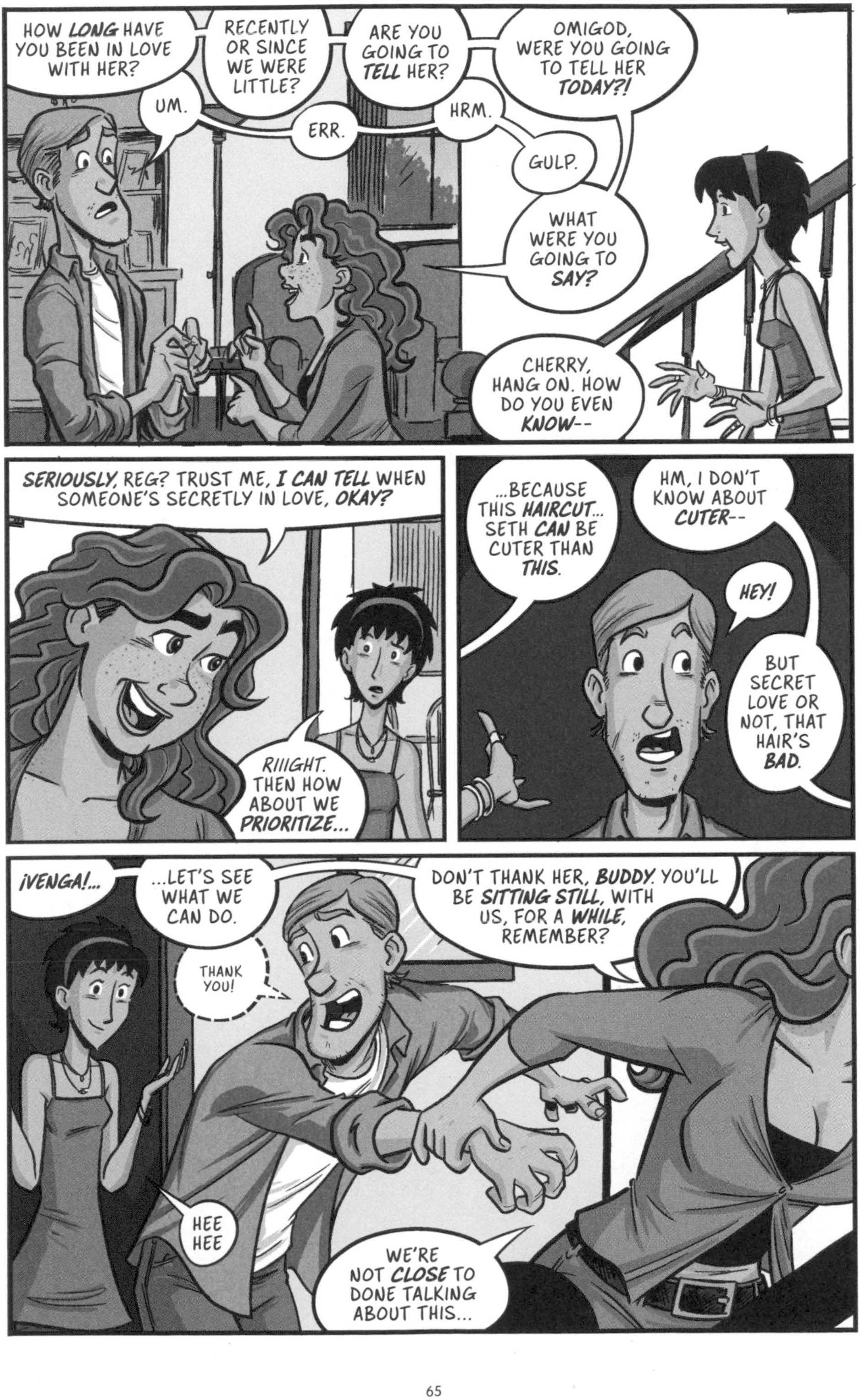
HOW LONG HAVE YOU BEEN IN LOVE WITH HER?
UM.
RECENTLY OR SINCE WE WERE LITTLE?
ERR.
ARE YOU GOING TO TELL HER?
HRM.
OMIGOD, WERE YOU GOING TO TELL HER TODAY?!
GULP.
WHAT WERE YOU GOING TO SAY?
CHERRY, HANG ON. HOW DO YOU EVEN KNOW--
SERIOUSLY, REG? TRUST ME, I CAN TELL WHEN SOMEONE'S SECRETLY IN LOVE, OKAY?
RIIIGHT. THEN HOW ABOUT WE PRIORITIZE...
...BECAUSE THIS HAIRCUT... SETH CAN BE CUTER THAN THIS.
HM, I DON'T KNOW ABOUT CUTER--
HEY!
BUT SECRET LOVE OR NOT, THAT HAIR'S BAD.
¡VENGA!...
...LET'S SEE WHAT WE CAN DO.
THANK YOU!
DON'T THANK HER, BUDDY. YOU'LL BE SITTING STILL, WITH US, FOR A WHILE, REMEMBER?
HEE HEE
WE'RE NOT CLOSE TO DONE TALKING ABOUT THIS...

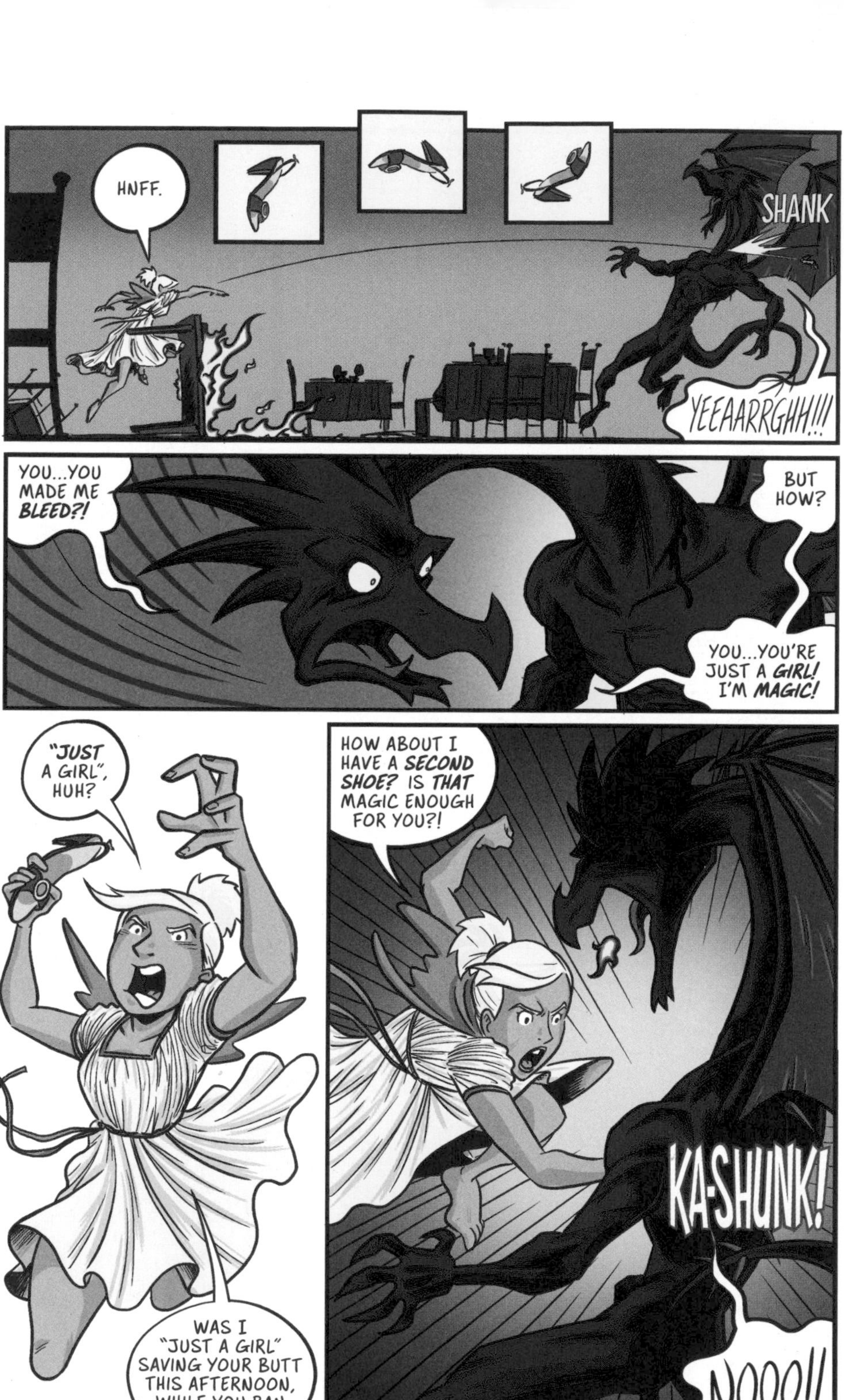
HNFF.
SHANK
YEEAARRGHH!!!
YOU...YOU MADE ME BLEED?!
BUT HOW?
YOU...YOU'RE JUST A GIRL! I'M MAGIC!
"JUST A GIRL", HUH?
WAS I "JUST A GIRL" SAVING YOUR BUTT THIS AFTERNOON, WHILE YOU RAN AND HID?!
HOW ABOUT I HAVE A SECOND SHOE? IS THAT MAGIC ENOUGH FOR YOU?!
KA-SHUNK!
NOOO!!

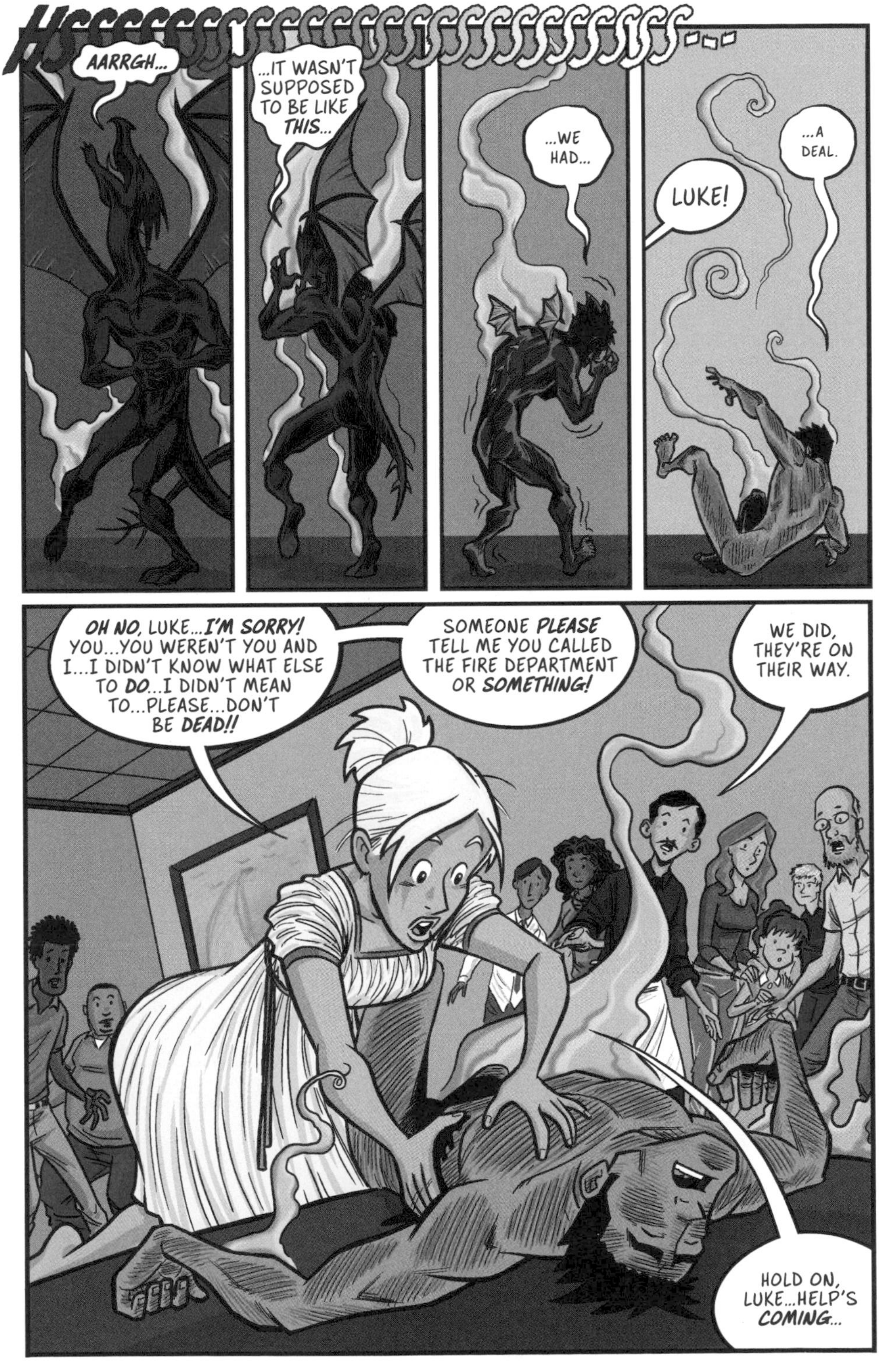
HSSSSSSSSSSSSSSSSSSSSSSSSSS...
AARRGH...
...IT WASN'T SUPPOSED TO BE LIKE THIS...
...WE HAD...
LUKE!
...A DEAL.
OH NO, LUKE...I'M SORRY! YOU...YOU WEREN'T YOU AND I...I DIDN'T KNOW WHAT ELSE TO DO...I DIDN'T MEAN TO...PLEASE...DON'T BE DEAD!!
SOMEONE PLEASE TELL ME YOU CALLED THE FIRE DEPARTMENT OR SOMETHING!
WE DID, THEY'RE ON THEIR WAY.
HOLD ON, LUKE...HELP'S COMING...

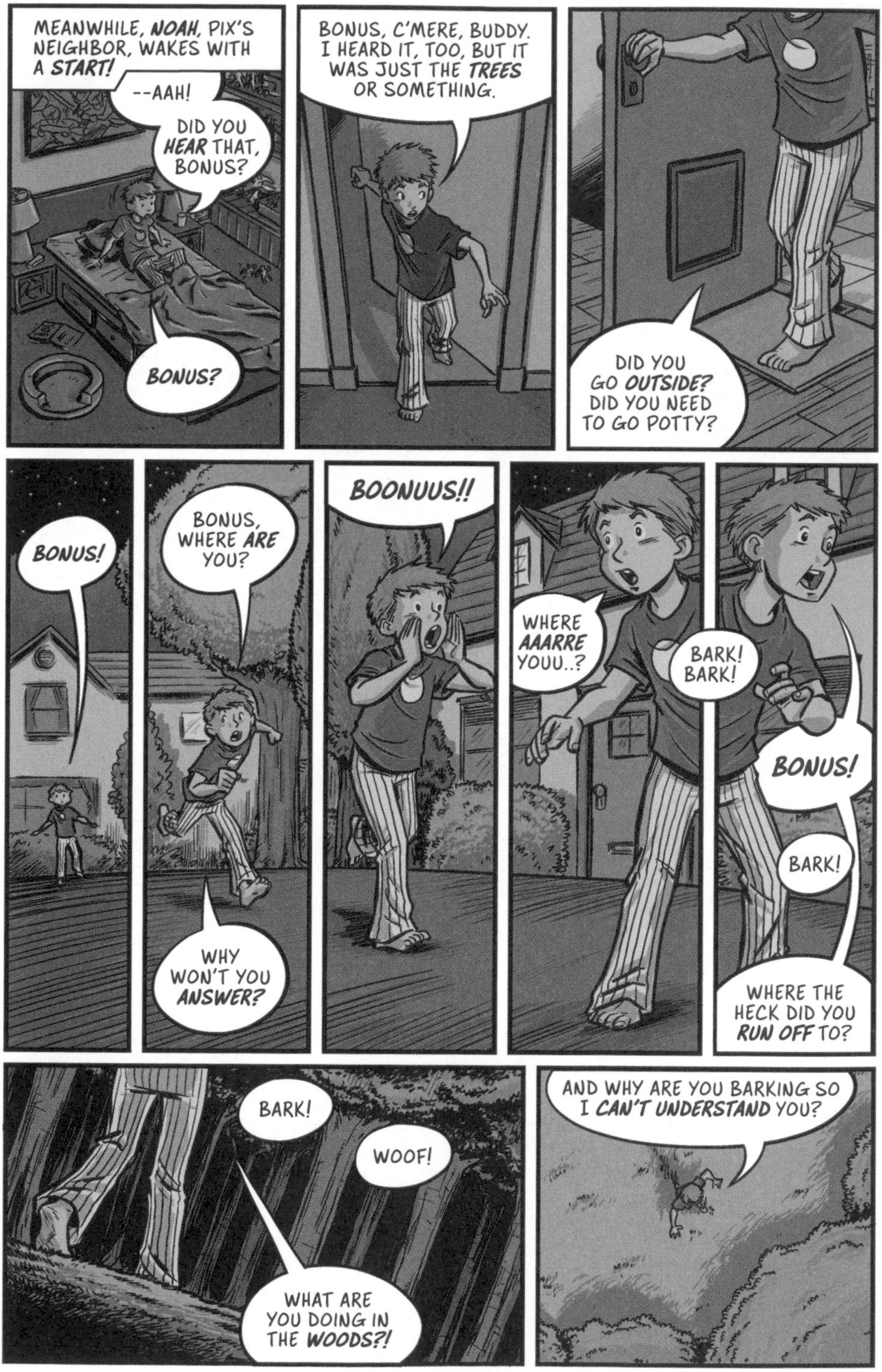
MEANWHILE, **NOAH**, PIX'S NEIGHBOR, WAKES WITH A **START!**
--AAH!
DID YOU **HEAR** THAT, BONUS?
BONUS?
BONUS, C'MERE, BUDDY. I HEARD IT, TOO, BUT IT WAS JUST THE **TREES** OR SOMETHING.
DID YOU GO **OUTSIDE?** DID YOU NEED TO GO POTTY?
BONUS!
BONUS, WHERE **ARE** YOU?
WHY WON'T YOU **ANSWER?**
BOONUUS!!
WHERE **AAARRE** YOUU..?
BARK! BARK!
BONUS!
BARK!
WHERE THE HECK DID YOU **RUN OFF** TO?
BARK!
WOOF!
WHAT ARE YOU DOING IN THE **WOODS?!**
AND WHY ARE YOU BARKING SO I **CAN'T UNDERSTAND** YOU?

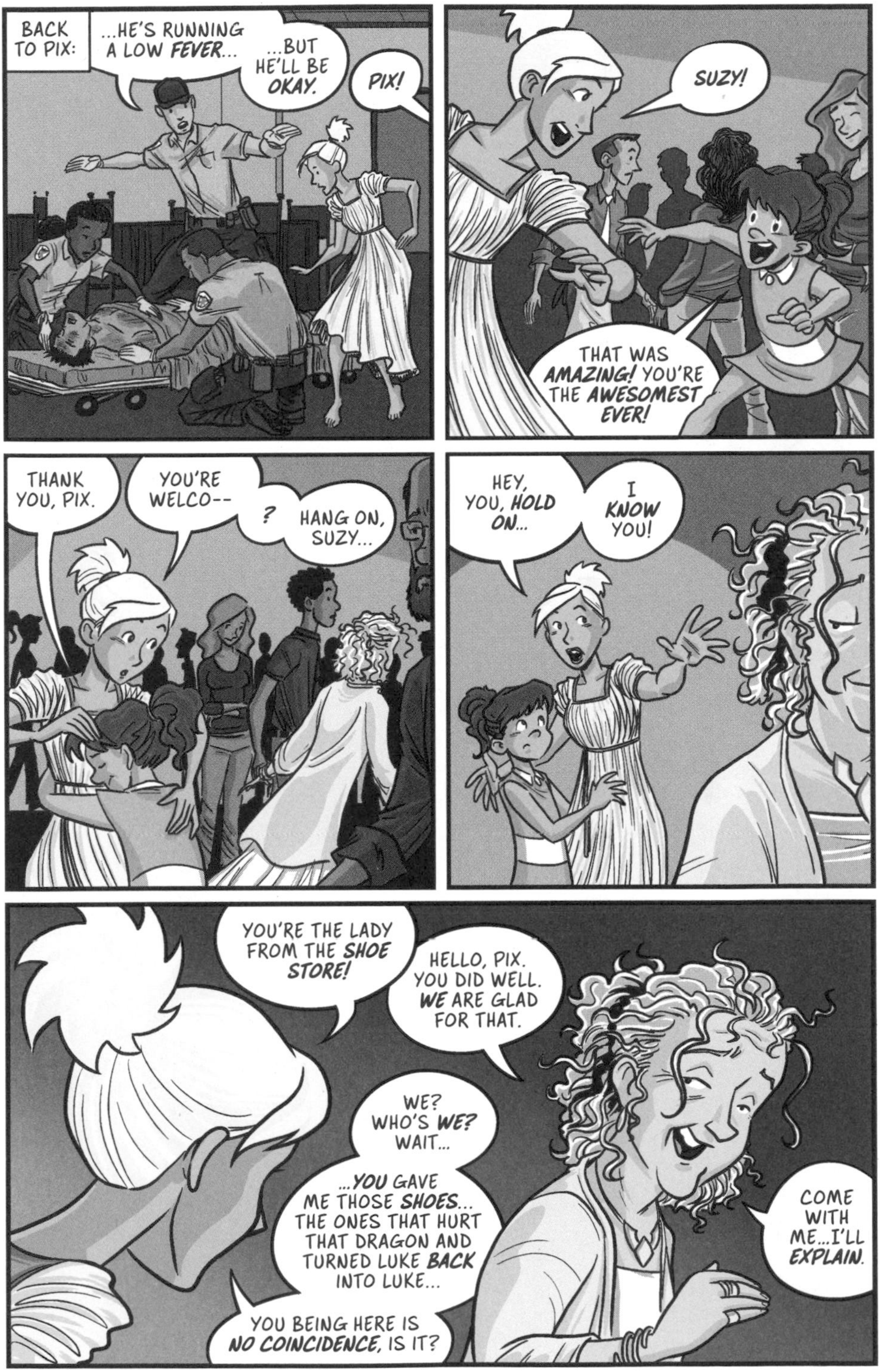
BACK TO PIX:
...HE'S RUNNING A LOW FEVER...
...BUT HE'LL BE OKAY.
PIX!
SUZY!
THAT WAS AMAZING! YOU'RE THE AWESOMEST EVER!
THANK YOU, PIX.
YOU'RE WELCO--
?
HANG ON, SUZY...
HEY, YOU, HOLD ON...
I KNOW YOU!
YOU'RE THE LADY FROM THE SHOE STORE!
HELLO, PIX. YOU DID WELL. WE ARE GLAD FOR THAT.
WE? WHO'S WE? WAIT...
...YOU GAVE ME THOSE SHOES... THE ONES THAT HURT THAT DRAGON AND TURNED LUKE BACK INTO LUKE...
YOU BEING HERE IS NO COINCIDENCE, IS IT?
COME WITH ME...I'LL EXPLAIN.

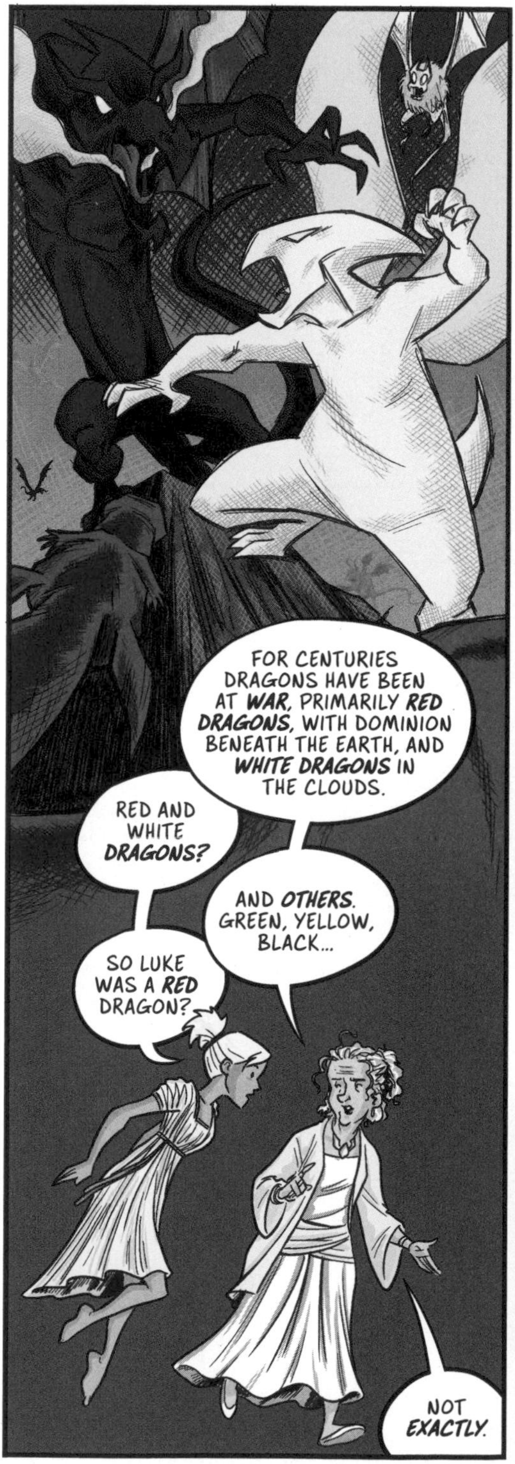

FOR CENTURIES DRAGONS HAVE BEEN AT **WAR**, PRIMARILY **RED DRAGONS**, WITH DOMINION BENEATH THE EARTH, AND **WHITE DRAGONS** IN THE CLOUDS.
RED AND WHITE **DRAGONS?**
AND **OTHERS**. GREEN, YELLOW, BLACK...
SO LUKE WAS A **RED** DRAGON?
NOT **EXACTLY**.

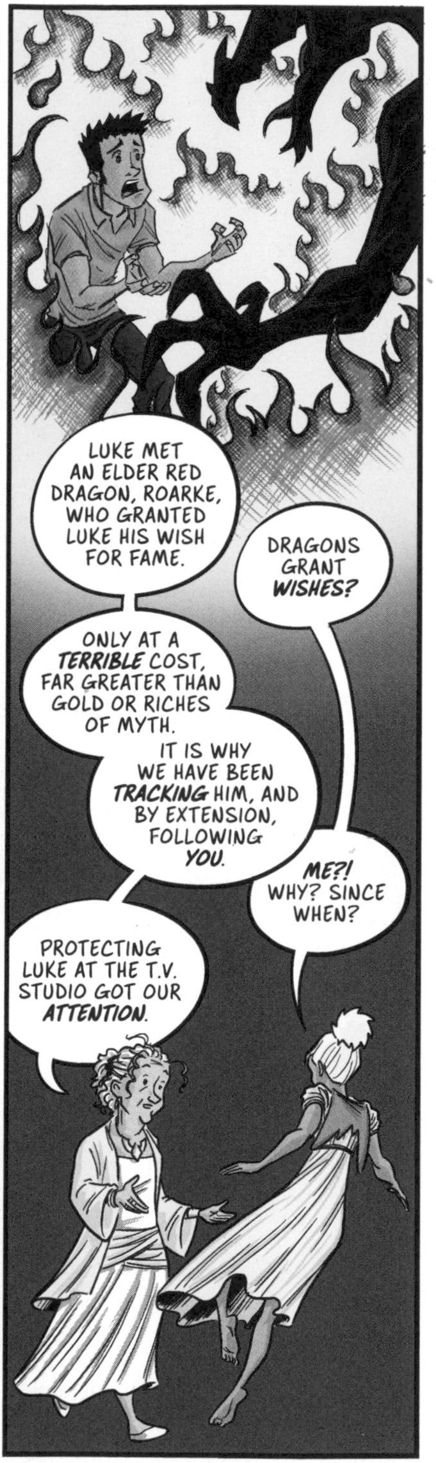

LUKE MET AN ELDER RED DRAGON, ROARKE, WHO GRANTED LUKE HIS WISH FOR FAME.
DRAGONS GRANT **WISHES?**
ONLY AT A **TERRIBLE** COST, FAR GREATER THAN GOLD OR RICHES OF MYTH.
IT IS WHY WE HAVE BEEN **TRACKING** HIM, AND BY EXTENSION, FOLLOWING **YOU**.
ME?! WHY? SINCE WHEN?
PROTECTING LUKE AT THE T.V. STUDIO GOT OUR **ATTENTION**.

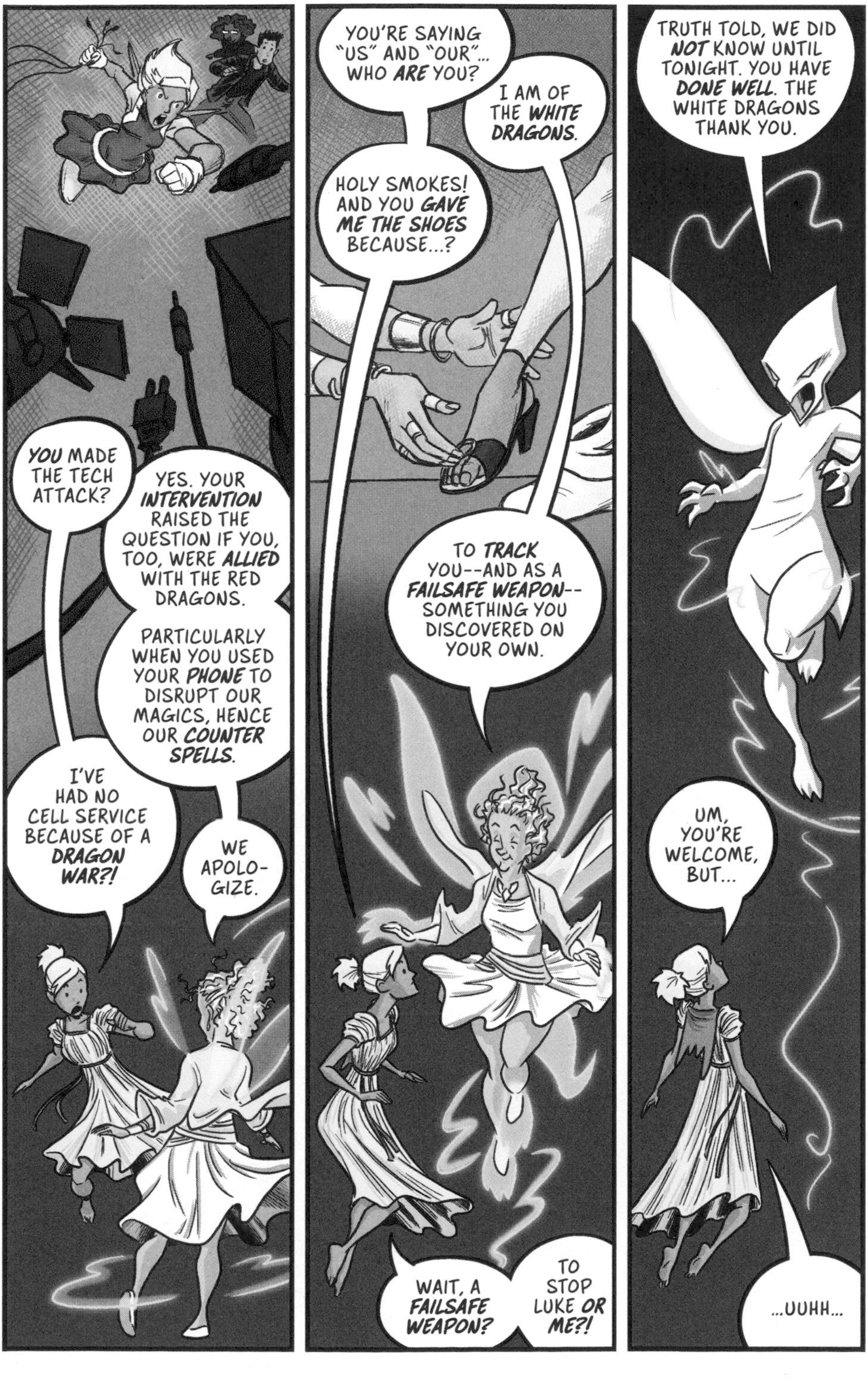
YOU MADE THE TECH ATTACK?
YES. YOUR INTERVENTION RAISED THE QUESTION IF YOU, TOO, WERE ALLIED WITH THE RED DRAGONS.
PARTICULARLY WHEN YOU USED YOUR PHONE TO DISRUPT OUR MAGICS, HENCE OUR COUNTER SPELLS.
I'VE HAD NO CELL SERVICE BECAUSE OF A DRAGON WAR?!
WE APOLOGIZE.
YOU'RE SAYING "US" AND "OUR"... WHO ARE YOU?
I AM OF THE WHITE DRAGONS.
HOLY SMOKES! AND YOU GAVE ME THE SHOES BECAUSE...?
TO TRACK YOU--AND AS A FAILSAFE WEAPON--SOMETHING YOU DISCOVERED ON YOUR OWN.
WAIT, A FAILSAFE WEAPON?
TO STOP LUKE OR ME?!
TRUTH TOLD, WE DID NOT KNOW UNTIL TONIGHT. YOU HAVE DONE WELL. THE WHITE DRAGONS THANK YOU.
UM, YOU'RE WELCOME, BUT...
...UUHH...

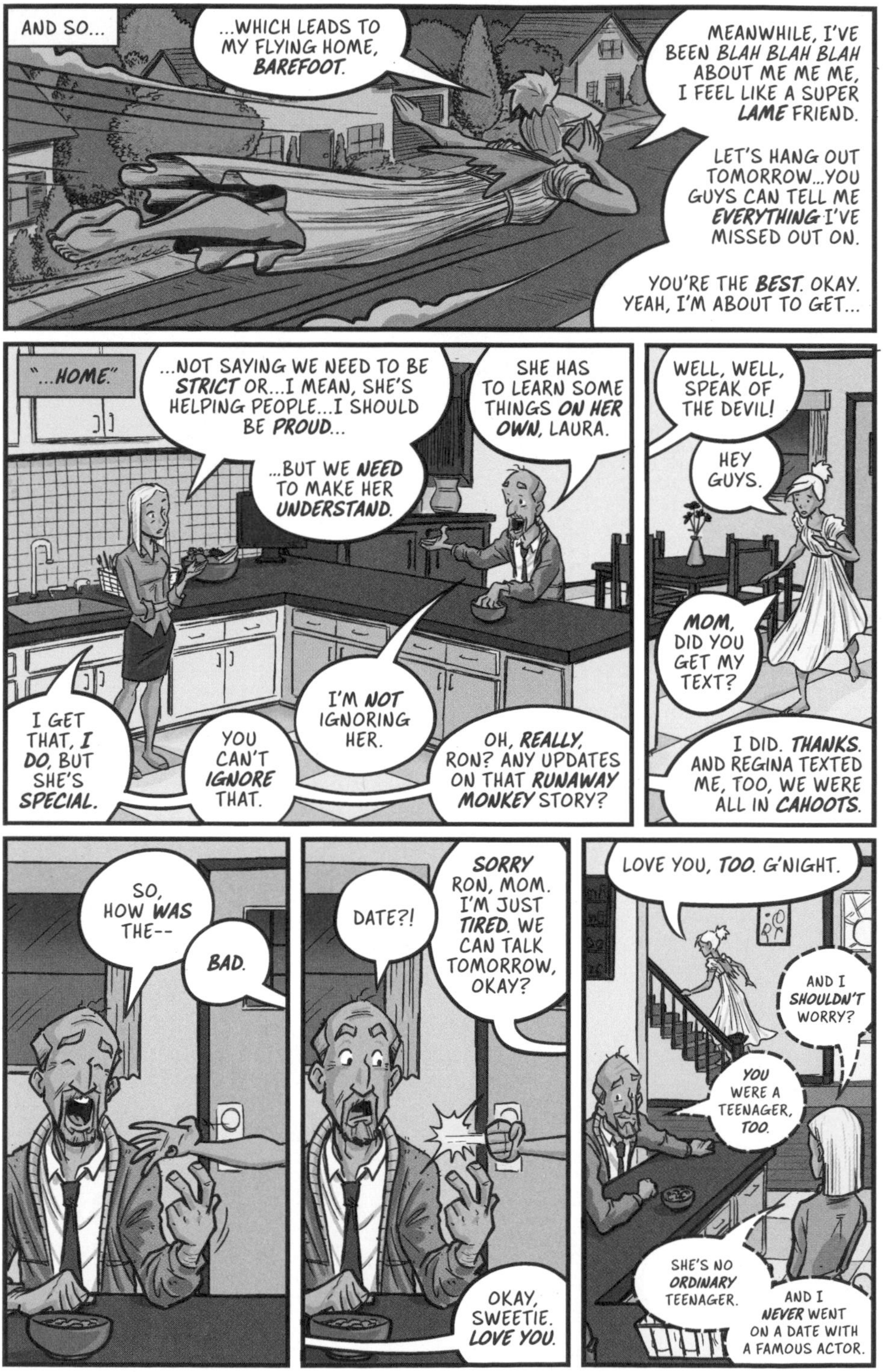
AND SO...
...WHICH LEADS TO MY FLYING HOME, BAREFOOT.
MEANWHILE, I'VE BEEN BLAH BLAH BLAH ABOUT ME ME ME, I FEEL LIKE A SUPER LAME FRIEND.
LET'S HANG OUT TOMORROW...YOU GUYS CAN TELL ME EVERYTHING I'VE MISSED OUT ON.
YOU'RE THE BEST. OKAY. YEAH, I'M ABOUT TO GET...
"...HOME."
...NOT SAYING WE NEED TO BE STRICT OR...I MEAN, SHE'S HELPING PEOPLE...I SHOULD BE PROUD...
...BUT WE NEED TO MAKE HER UNDERSTAND.
SHE HAS TO LEARN SOME THINGS ON HER OWN, LAURA.
I GET THAT, I DO, BUT SHE'S SPECIAL.
YOU CAN'T IGNORE THAT.
I'M NOT IGNORING HER.
OH, REALLY, RON? ANY UPDATES ON THAT RUNAWAY MONKEY STORY?
WELL, WELL, SPEAK OF THE DEVIL!
HEY GUYS.
MOM, DID YOU GET MY TEXT?
I DID. THANKS. AND REGINA TEXTED ME, TOO, WE WERE ALL IN CAHOOTS.
SO, HOW WAS THE--
BAD.
DATE?!
SORRY RON, MOM. I'M JUST TIRED. WE CAN TALK TOMORROW, OKAY?
OKAY, SWEETIE. LOVE YOU.
LOVE YOU, TOO. G'NIGHT.
AND I SHOULDN'T WORRY?
YOU WERE A TEENAGER, TOO.
SHE'S NO ORDINARY TEENAGER.
AND I NEVER WENT ON A DATE WITH A FAMOUS ACTOR.

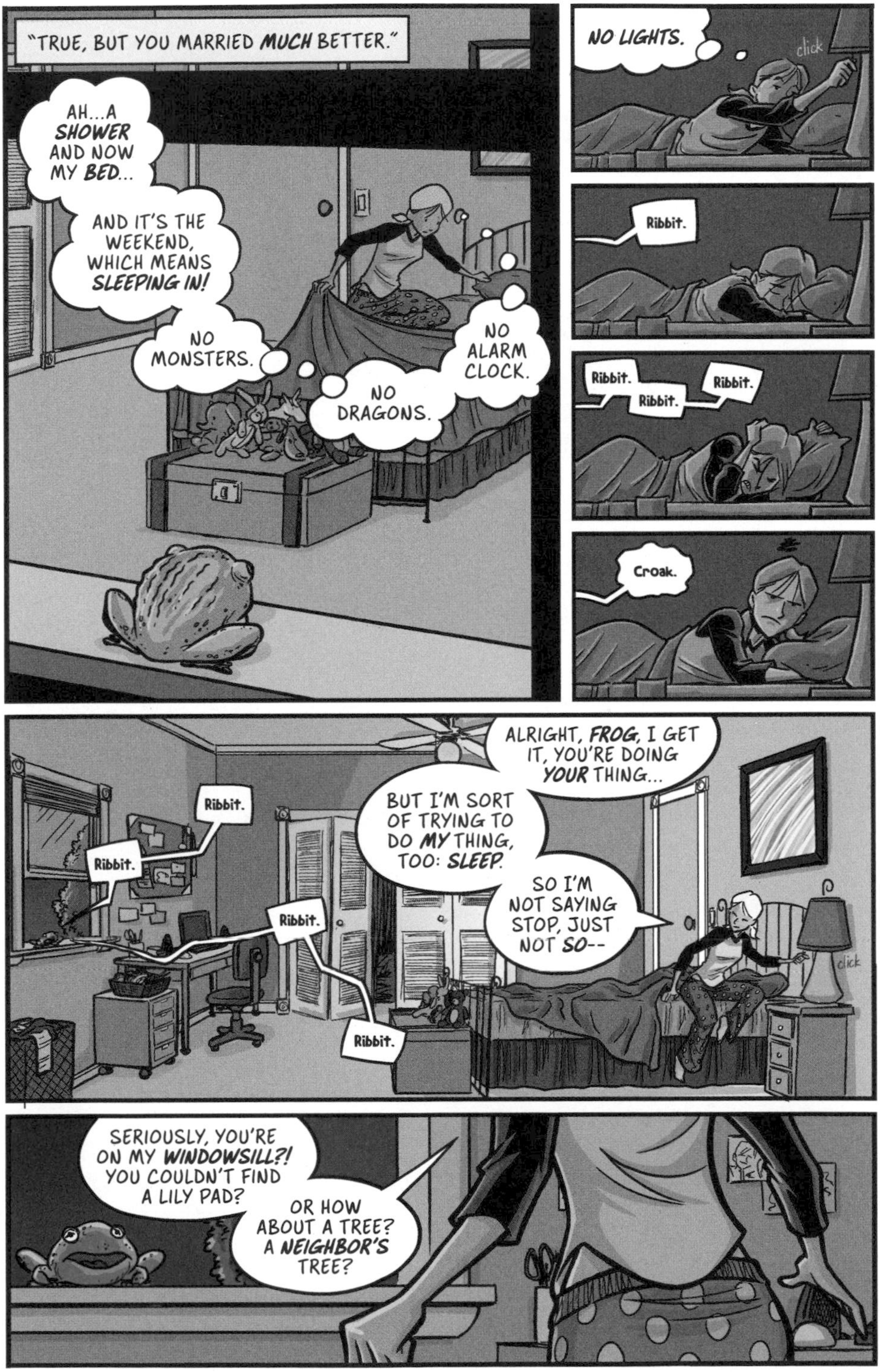

"TRUE, BUT YOU MARRIED MUCH BETTER."
AH...A SHOWER AND NOW MY BED...
AND IT'S THE WEEKEND, WHICH MEANS SLEEPING IN!
NO MONSTERS.
NO DRAGONS.
NO ALARM CLOCK.
NO LIGHTS.
click
Ribbit.
Ribbit.
Ribbit.
Ribbit.
Croak.
ALRIGHT, FROG, I GET IT, YOU'RE DOING YOUR THING...
BUT I'M SORT OF TRYING TO DO MY THING, TOO: SLEEP.
SO I'M NOT SAYING STOP, JUST NOT SO--
Ribbit.
Ribbit.
Ribbit.
Ribbit.
click
SERIOUSLY, YOU'RE ON MY WINDOWSILL?! YOU COULDN'T FIND A LILY PAD?
OR HOW ABOUT A TREE? A NEIGHBOR'S TREE?

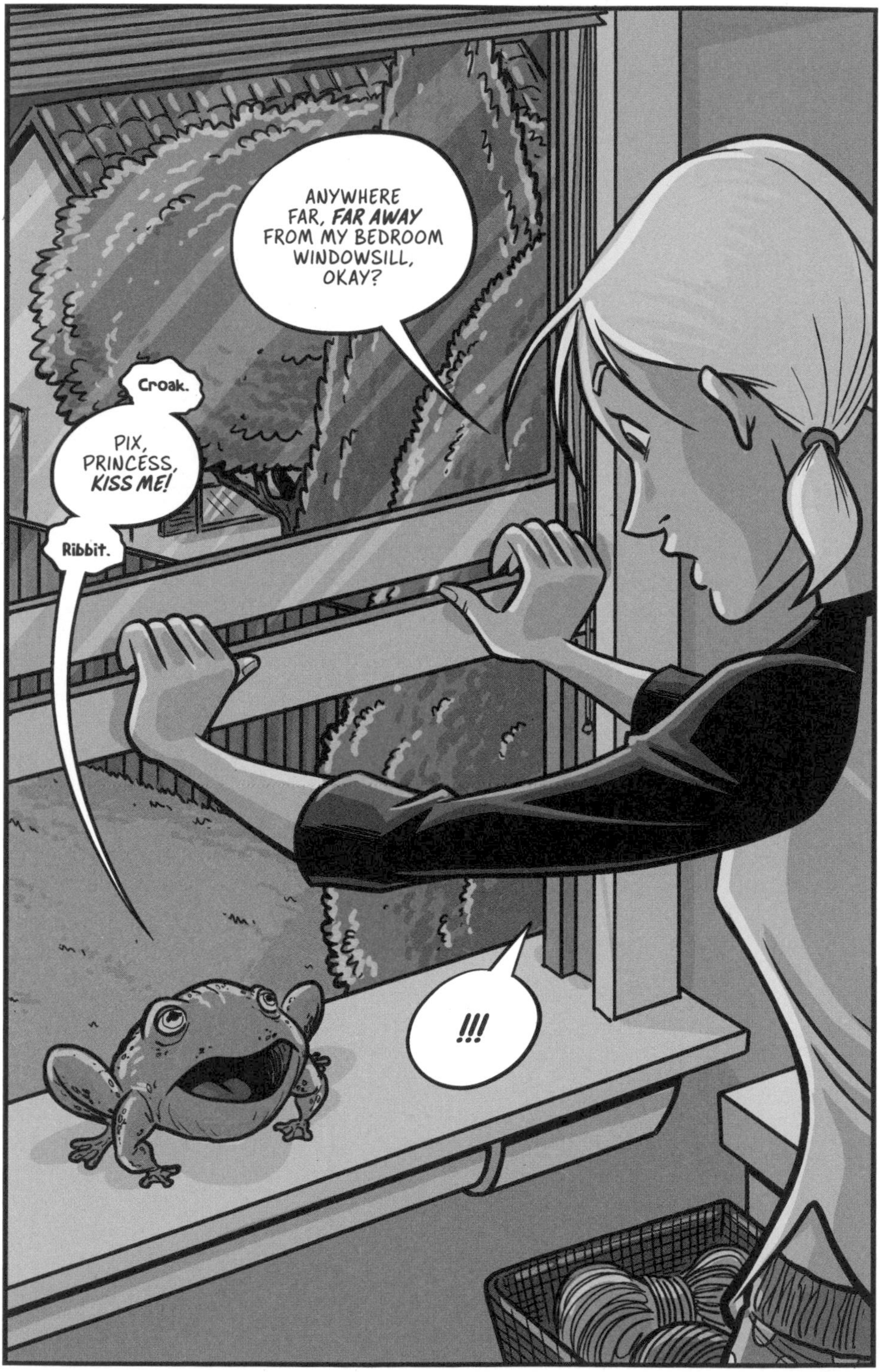
ANYWHERE FAR, **FAR AWAY** FROM MY BEDROOM WINDOWSILL, OKAY?
Croak.
PIX, PRINCESS, **KISS ME!**
Ribbit.
!!!

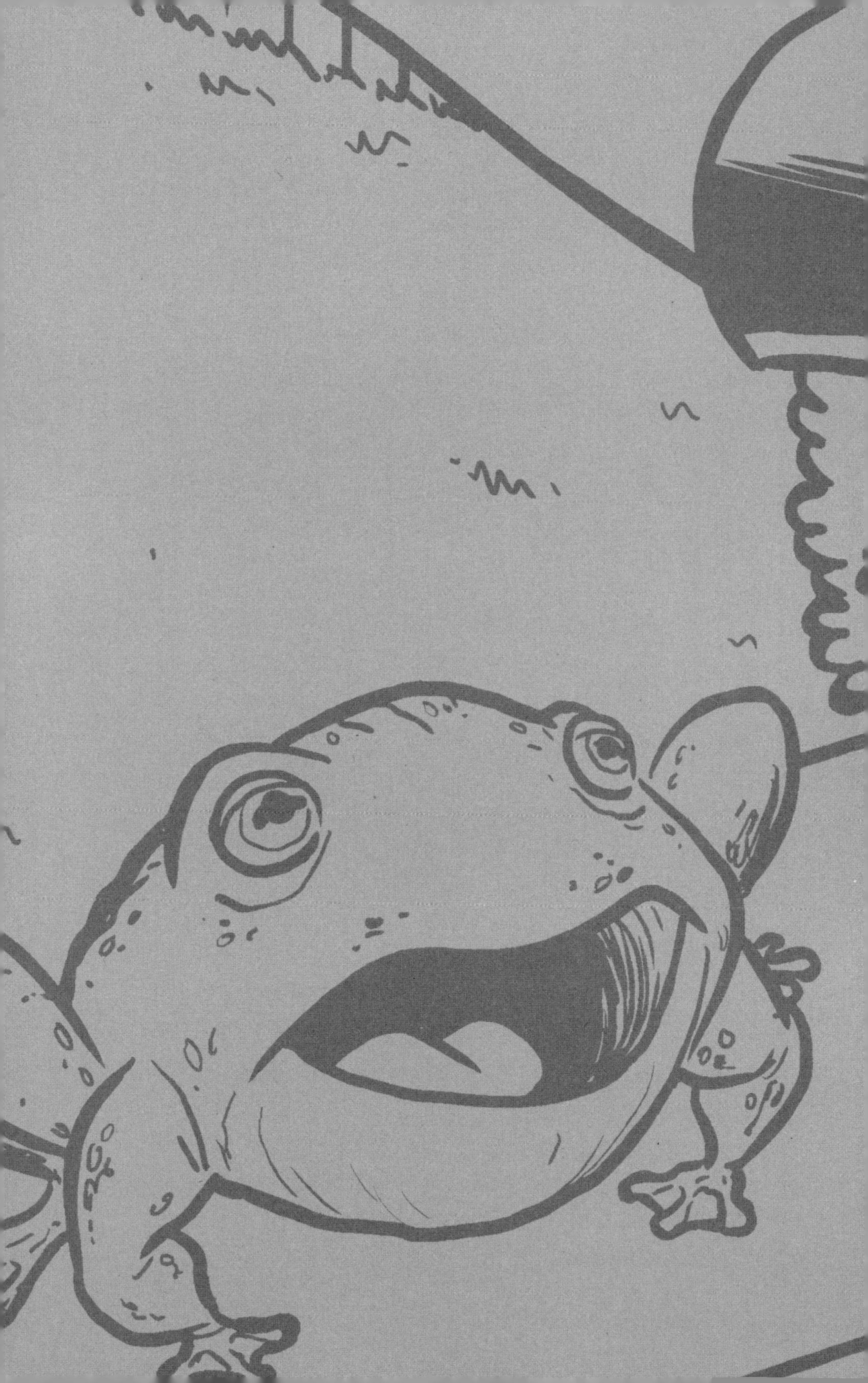

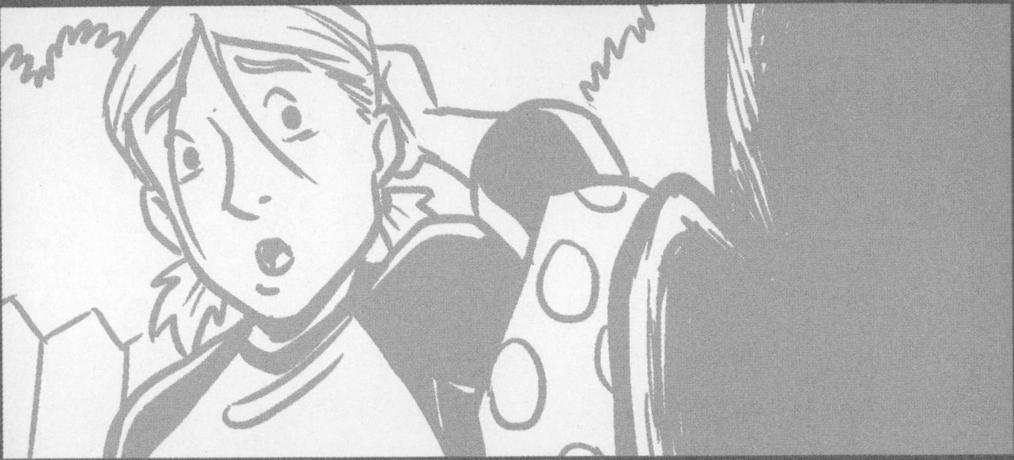

CHAPTER FOUR

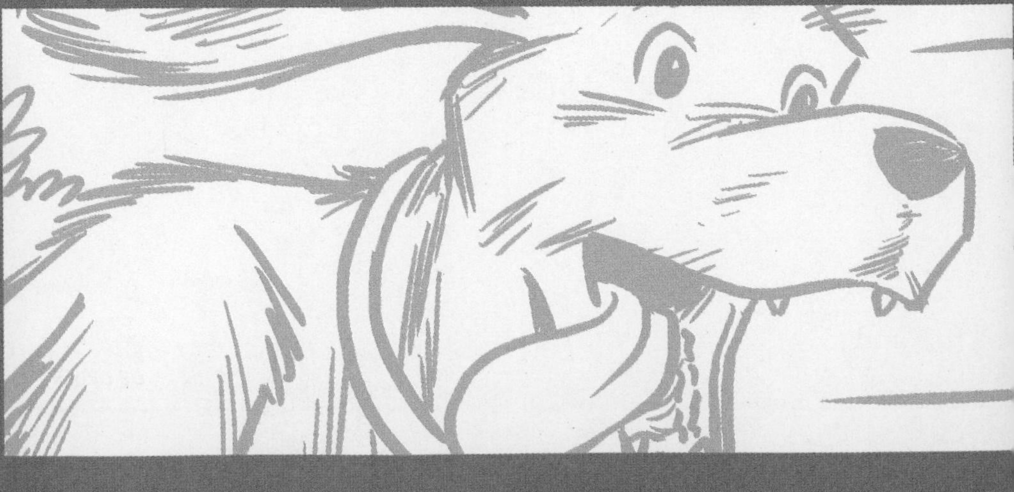

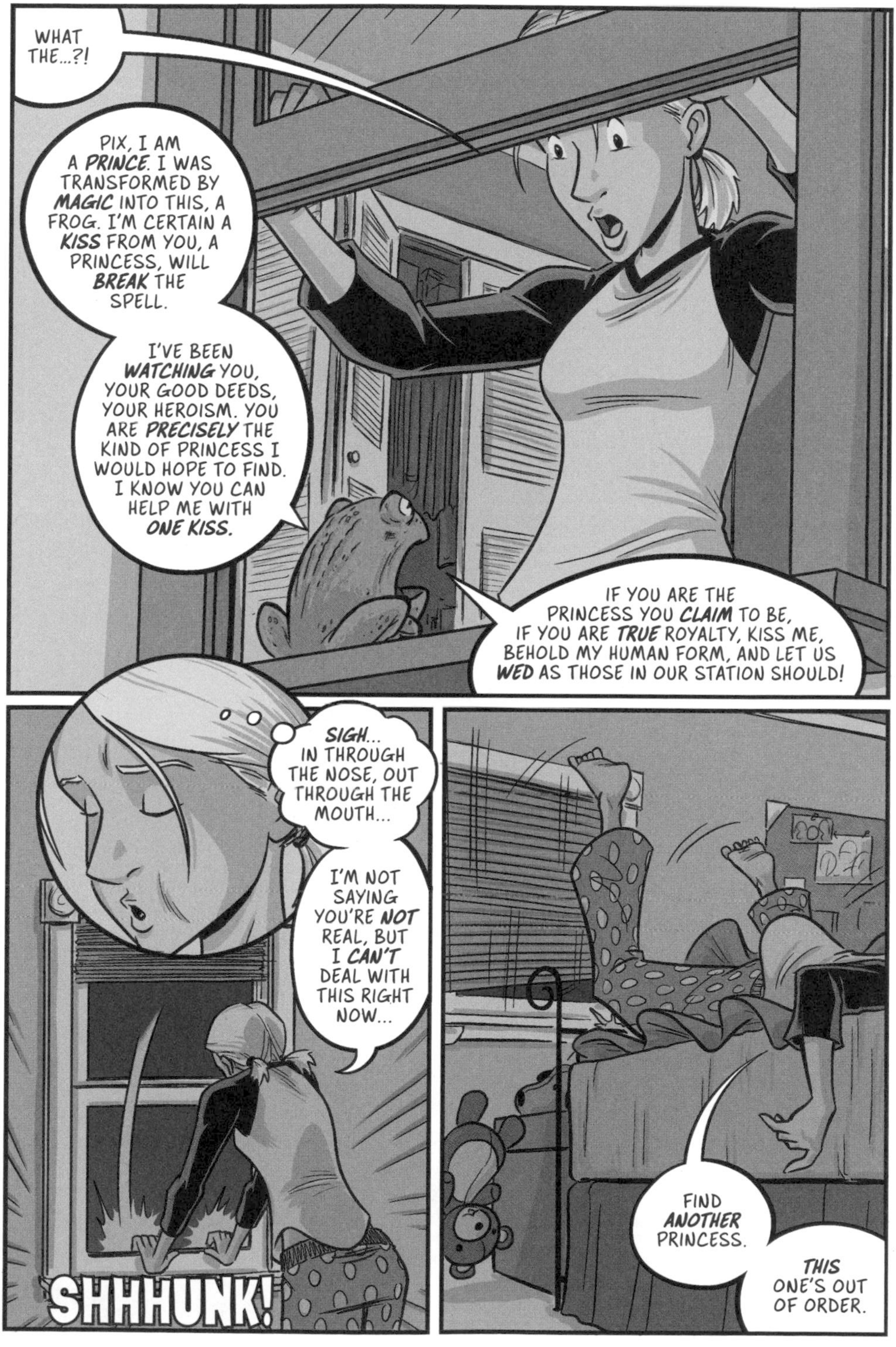
WHAT THE...?!
PIX, I AM A PRINCE. I WAS TRANSFORMED BY MAGIC INTO THIS, A FROG. I'M CERTAIN A KISS FROM YOU, A PRINCESS, WILL BREAK THE SPELL.
I'VE BEEN WATCHING YOU, YOUR GOOD DEEDS, YOUR HEROISM. YOU ARE PRECISELY THE KIND OF PRINCESS I WOULD HOPE TO FIND. I KNOW YOU CAN HELP ME WITH ONE KISS.
IF YOU ARE THE PRINCESS YOU CLAIM TO BE, IF YOU ARE TRUE ROYALTY, KISS ME, BEHOLD MY HUMAN FORM, AND LET US WED AS THOSE IN OUR STATION SHOULD!
SIGH... IN THROUGH THE NOSE, OUT THROUGH THE MOUTH...
I'M NOT SAYING YOU'RE NOT REAL, BUT I CAN'T DEAL WITH THIS RIGHT NOW...
SHHHUNK!
FIND ANOTHER PRINCESS.
THIS ONE'S OUT OF ORDER.

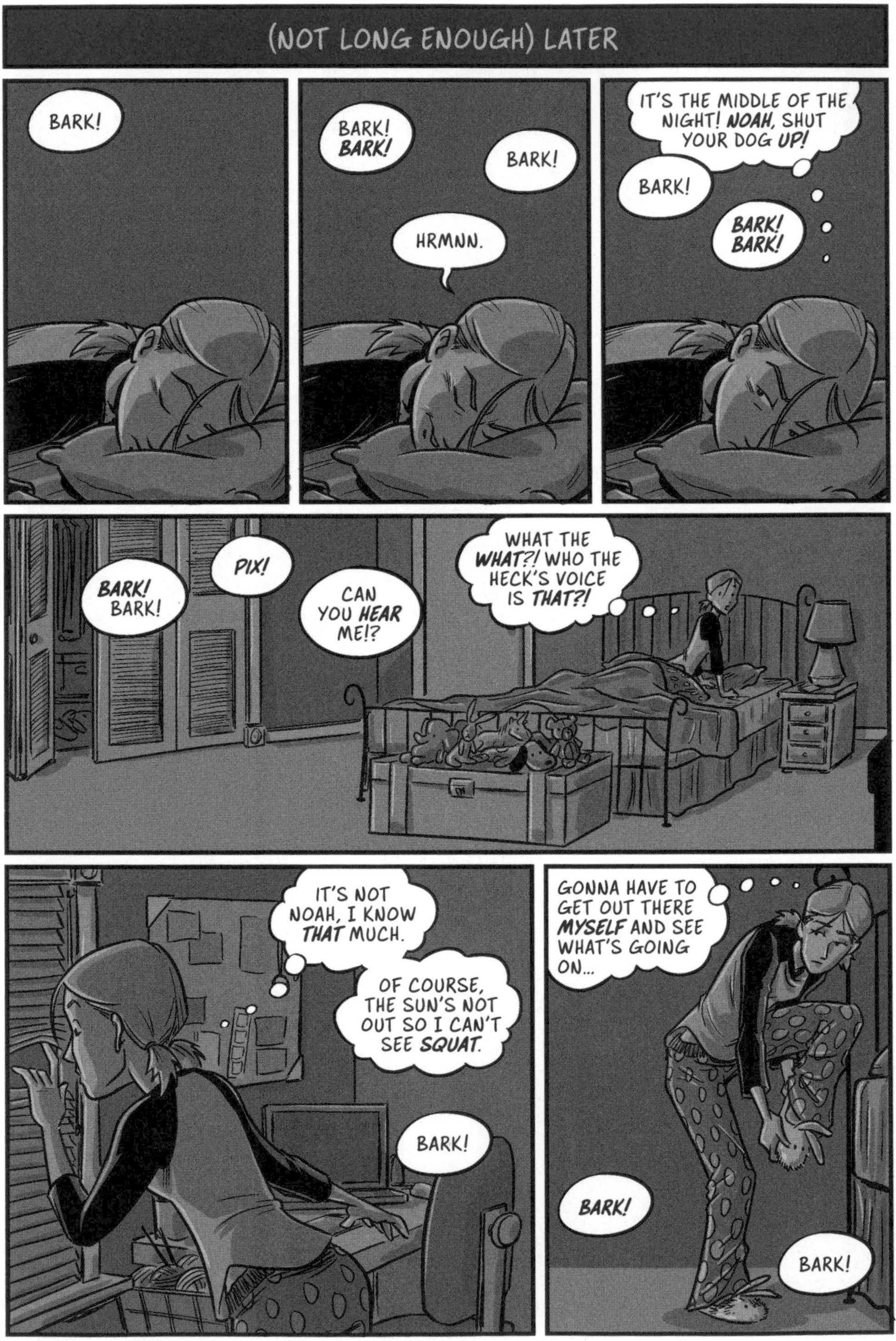
(NOT LONG ENOUGH) LATER
BARK!
BARK! BARK!
BARK!
HRMNN.
IT'S THE MIDDLE OF THE NIGHT! NOAH, SHUT YOUR DOG UP!
BARK!
BARK! BARK!
BARK! BARK!
PIX!
CAN YOU HEAR ME!?
WHAT THE WHAT?! WHO THE HECK'S VOICE IS THAT?!
IT'S NOT NOAH, I KNOW THAT MUCH.
OF COURSE, THE SUN'S NOT OUT SO I CAN'T SEE SQUAT.
BARK!
GONNA HAVE TO GET OUT THERE MYSELF AND SEE WHAT'S GOING ON...
BARK!
BARK!

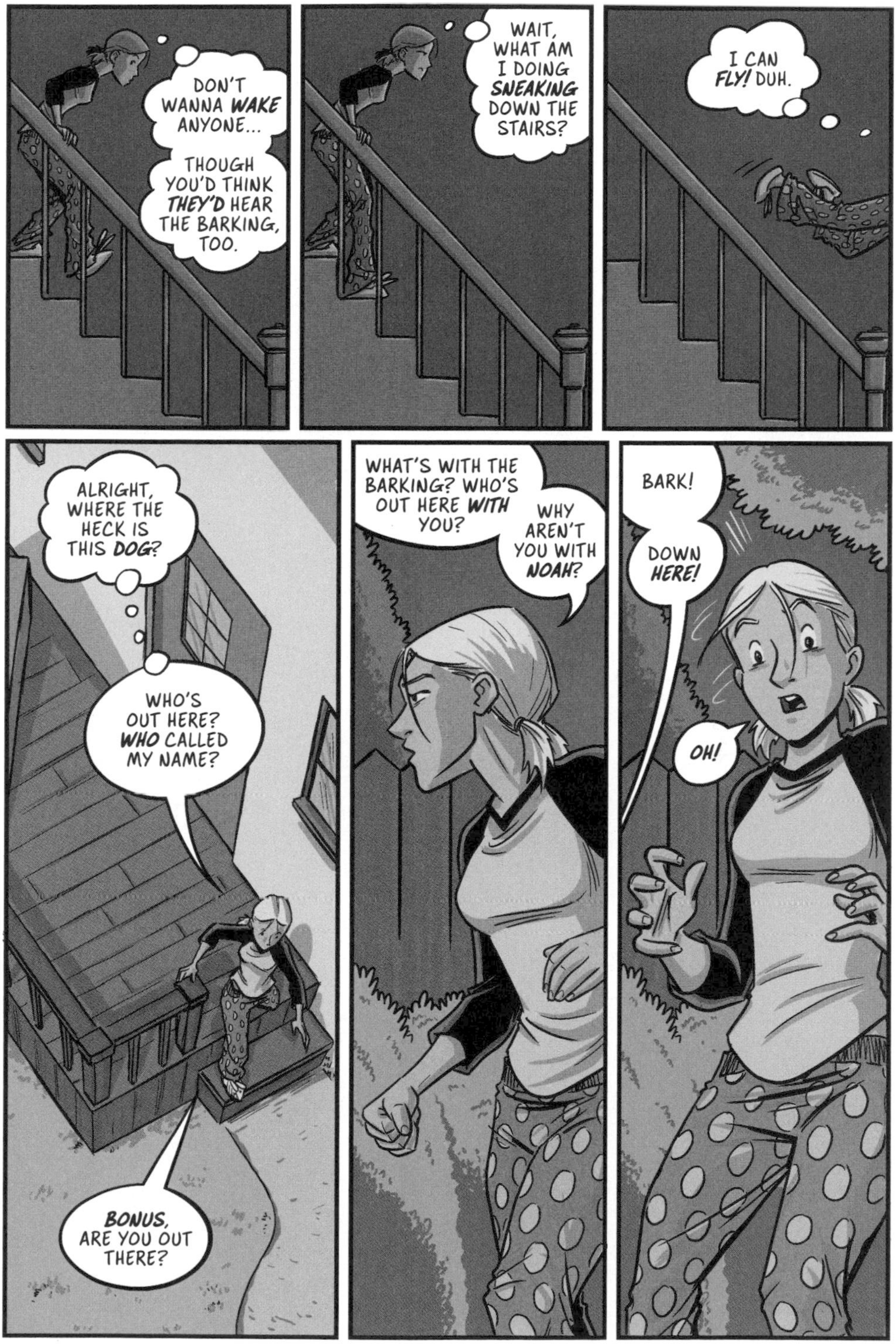
DON'T WANNA WAKE ANYONE...
THOUGH YOU'D THINK THEY'D HEAR THE BARKING, TOO.
WAIT, WHAT AM I DOING SNEAKING DOWN THE STAIRS?
I CAN FLY! DUH.
ALRIGHT, WHERE THE HECK IS THIS DOG?
WHO'S OUT HERE? WHO CALLED MY NAME?
BONUS, ARE YOU OUT THERE?
WHAT'S WITH THE BARKING? WHO'S OUT HERE WITH YOU?
WHY AREN'T YOU WITH NOAH?
BARK!
DOWN HERE!
OH!

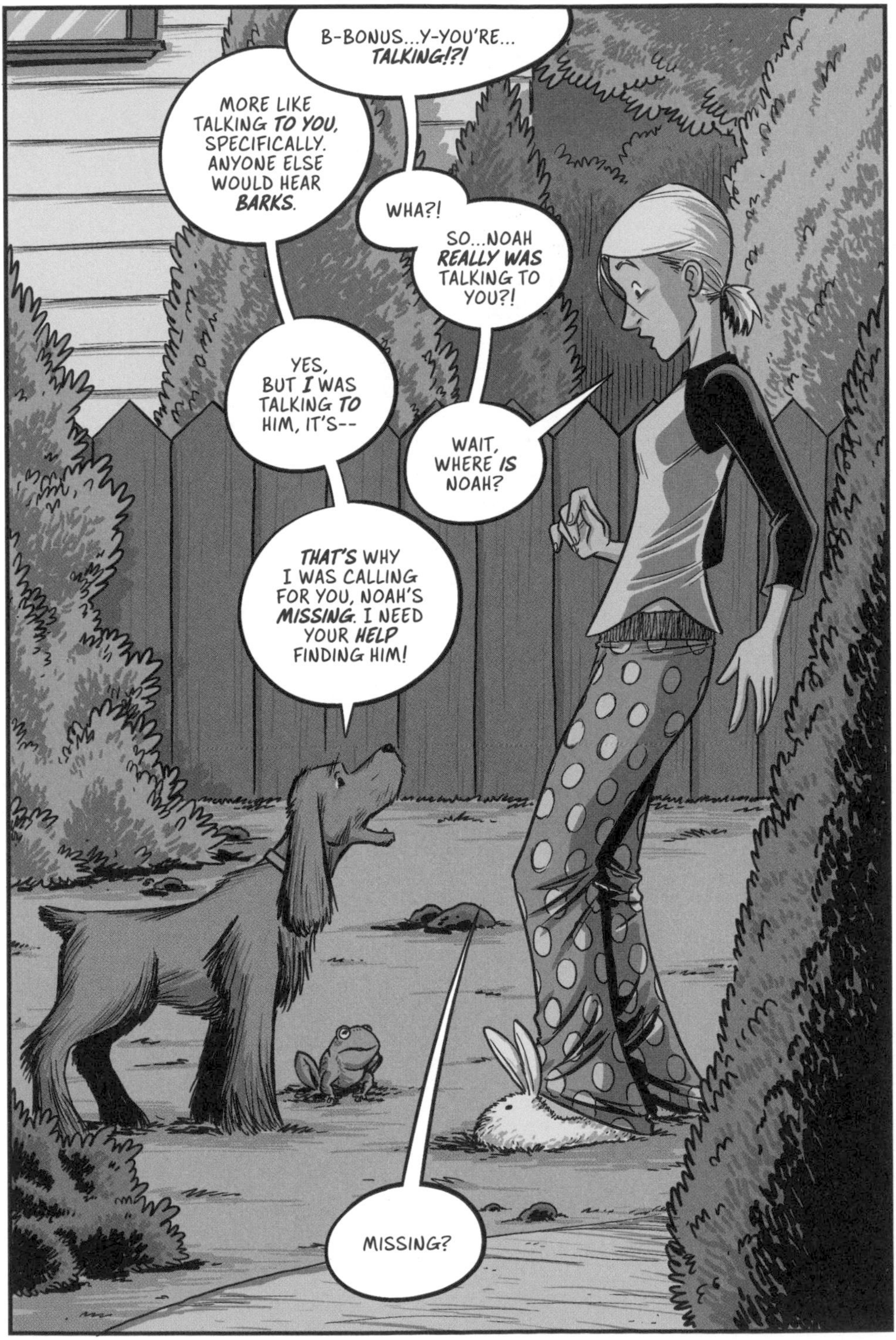
B-BONUS...Y-YOU'RE... TALKING!?!
MORE LIKE TALKING TO YOU, SPECIFICALLY. ANYONE ELSE WOULD HEAR BARKS.
WHA?!
SO...NOAH REALLY WAS TALKING TO YOU?!
YES, BUT I WAS TALKING TO HIM, IT'S--
WAIT, WHERE IS NOAH?
THAT'S WHY I WAS CALLING FOR YOU, NOAH'S MISSING. I NEED YOUR HELP FINDING HIM!
MISSING?

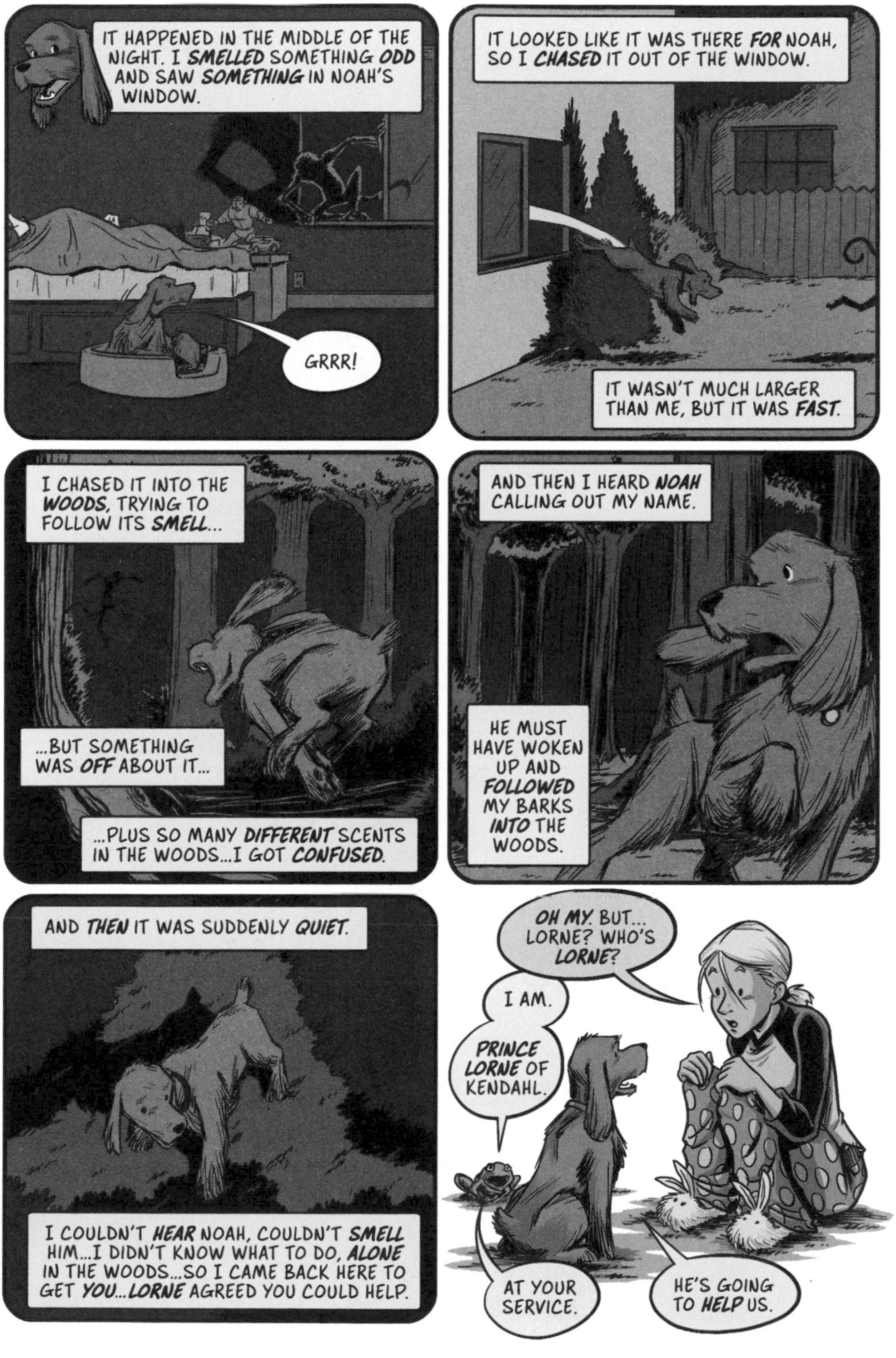
IT HAPPENED IN THE MIDDLE OF THE NIGHT. I SMELLED SOMETHING ODD AND SAW SOMETHING IN NOAH'S WINDOW.
GRRR!
IT LOOKED LIKE IT WAS THERE FOR NOAH, SO I CHASED IT OUT OF THE WINDOW.
IT WASN'T MUCH LARGER THAN ME, BUT IT WAS FAST.
I CHASED IT INTO THE WOODS, TRYING TO FOLLOW ITS SMELL...
...BUT SOMETHING WAS OFF ABOUT IT...
...PLUS SO MANY DIFFERENT SCENTS IN THE WOODS...I GOT CONFUSED.
AND THEN I HEARD NOAH CALLING OUT MY NAME.
HE MUST HAVE WOKEN UP AND FOLLOWED MY BARKS INTO THE WOODS.
AND THEN IT WAS SUDDENLY QUIET.
I COULDN'T HEAR NOAH, COULDN'T SMELL HIM...I DIDN'T KNOW WHAT TO DO, ALONE IN THE WOODS...SO I CAME BACK HERE TO GET YOU...LORNE AGREED YOU COULD HELP.
OH MY. BUT... LORNE? WHO'S LORNE?
I AM.
PRINCE LORNE OF KENDAHL.
AT YOUR SERVICE.
HE'S GOING TO HELP US.

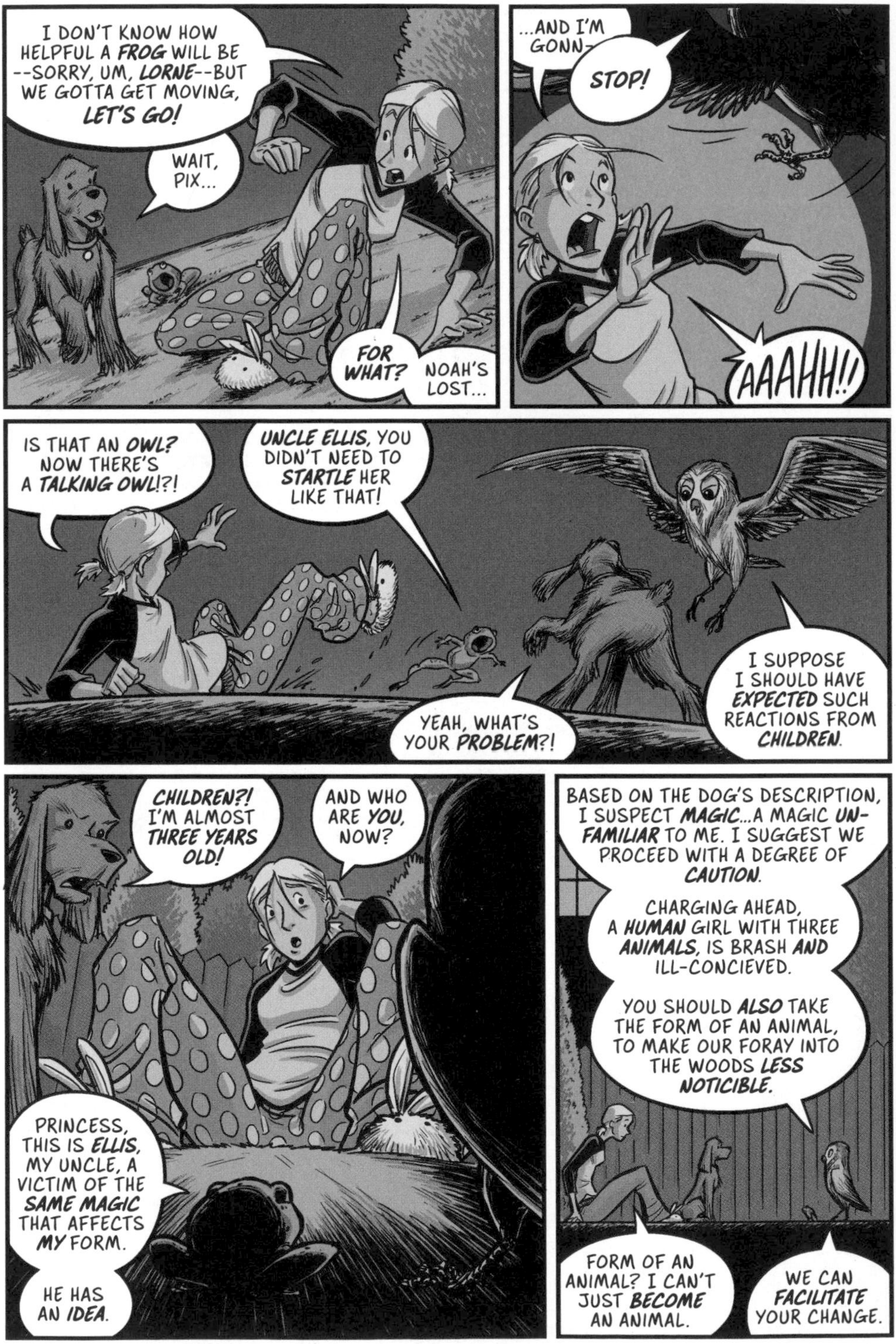
I DON'T KNOW HOW HELPFUL A FROG WILL BE --SORRY, UM, LORNE--BUT WE GOTTA GET MOVING, LET'S GO!
WAIT, PIX...
FOR WHAT?
NOAH'S LOST...
...AND I'M GONN-
STOP!
AAAHH!!
IS THAT AN OWL? NOW THERE'S A TALKING OWL!?!
UNCLE ELLIS, YOU DIDN'T NEED TO STARTLE HER LIKE THAT!
YEAH, WHAT'S YOUR PROBLEM?!
I SUPPOSE I SHOULD HAVE EXPECTED SUCH REACTIONS FROM CHILDREN.
CHILDREN?! I'M ALMOST THREE YEARS OLD!
AND WHO ARE YOU, NOW?
PRINCESS, THIS IS ELLIS, MY UNCLE, A VICTIM OF THE SAME MAGIC THAT AFFECTS MY FORM.
HE HAS AN IDEA.
BASED ON THE DOG'S DESCRIPTION, I SUSPECT MAGIC...A MAGIC UNFAMILIAR TO ME. I SUGGEST WE PROCEED WITH A DEGREE OF CAUTION.
CHARGING AHEAD, A HUMAN GIRL WITH THREE ANIMALS, IS BRASH AND ILL-CONCIEVED.
YOU SHOULD ALSO TAKE THE FORM OF AN ANIMAL, TO MAKE OUR FORAY INTO THE WOODS LESS NOTICIBLE.
FORM OF AN ANIMAL? I CAN'T JUST BECOME AN ANIMAL.
WE CAN FACILITATE YOUR CHANGE.

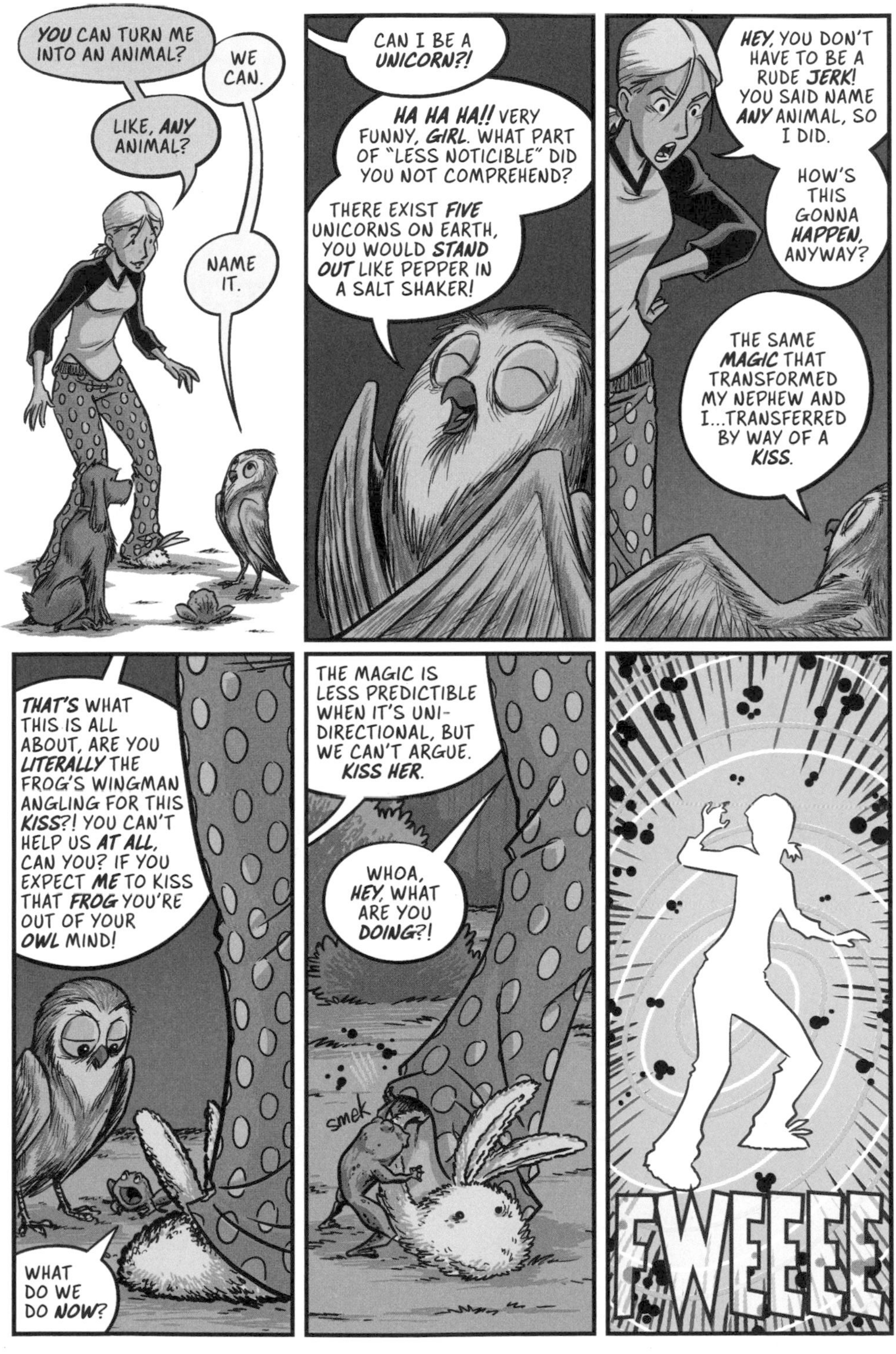
YOU CAN TURN ME INTO AN ANIMAL?
WE CAN.
LIKE, ANY ANIMAL?
NAME IT.
CAN I BE A UNICORN?!
HA HA HA!! VERY FUNNY, GIRL. WHAT PART OF "LESS NOTICIBLE" DID YOU NOT COMPREHEND?
THERE EXIST FIVE UNICORNS ON EARTH, YOU WOULD STAND OUT LIKE PEPPER IN A SALT SHAKER!
HEY, YOU DON'T HAVE TO BE A RUDE JERK! YOU SAID NAME ANY ANIMAL, SO I DID.
HOW'S THIS GONNA HAPPEN, ANYWAY?
THE SAME MAGIC THAT TRANSFORMED MY NEPHEW AND I...TRANSFERRED BY WAY OF A KISS.
THAT'S WHAT THIS IS ALL ABOUT, ARE YOU LITERALLY THE FROG'S WINGMAN ANGLING FOR THIS KISS?! YOU CAN'T HELP US AT ALL, CAN YOU? IF YOU EXPECT ME TO KISS THAT FROG YOU'RE OUT OF YOUR OWL MIND!
WHAT DO WE DO NOW?
THE MAGIC IS LESS PREDICTIBLE WHEN IT'S UNI-DIRECTIONAL, BUT WE CAN'T ARGUE. KISS HER.
WHOA, HEY, WHAT ARE YOU DOING?!
smek
FWEEEE

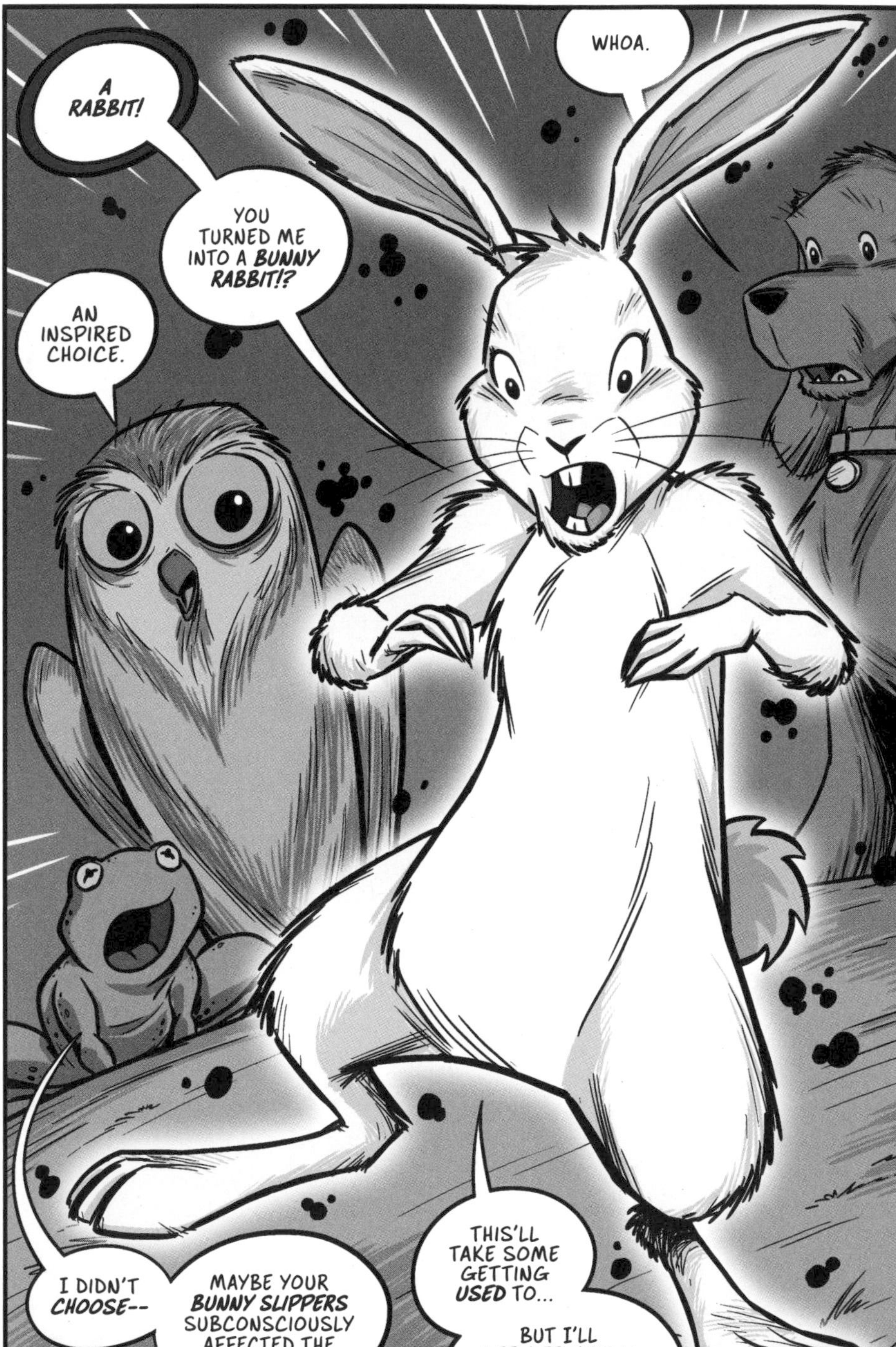

A RABBIT!
WHOA.
YOU TURNED ME INTO A BUNNY RABBIT!?
AN INSPIRED CHOICE.
I DIDN'T CHOOSE--
MAYBE YOUR BUNNY SLIPPERS SUBCONSCIOUSLY AFFECTED THE MAGIC?
THIS'LL TAKE SOME GETTING USED TO...
BUT I'LL DEFINITELY FIT IN WITH THE WOODS LOOKING LIKE THIS!

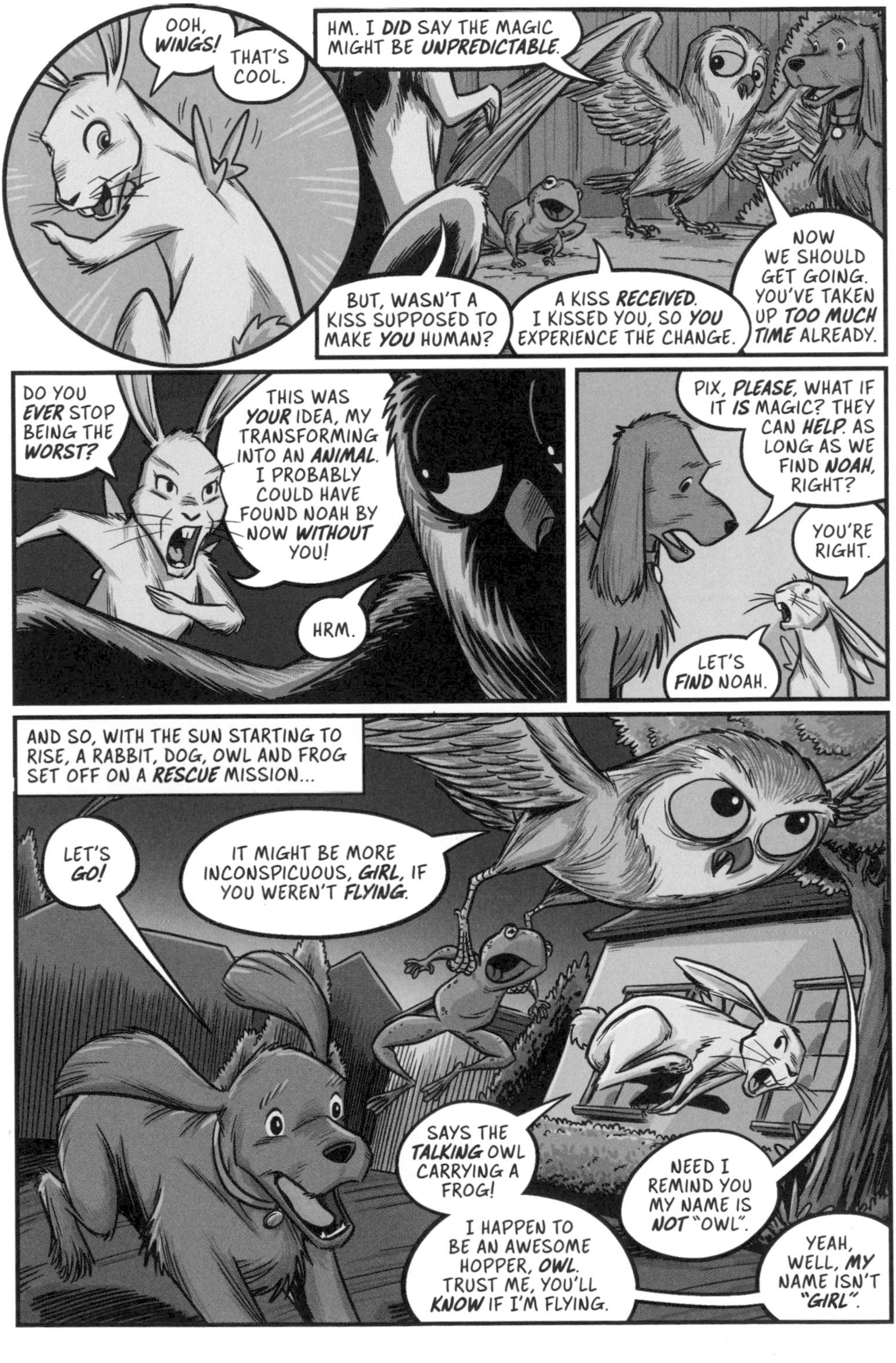

OOH, WINGS!
THAT'S COOL.
HM. I DID SAY THE MAGIC MIGHT BE UNPREDICTABLE.
BUT, WASN'T A KISS SUPPOSED TO MAKE YOU HUMAN?
A KISS RECEIVED. I KISSED YOU, SO YOU EXPERIENCE THE CHANGE.
NOW WE SHOULD GET GOING. YOU'VE TAKEN UP TOO MUCH TIME ALREADY.
DO YOU EVER STOP BEING THE WORST?
THIS WAS YOUR IDEA, MY TRANSFORMING INTO AN ANIMAL. I PROBABLY COULD HAVE FOUND NOAH BY NOW WITHOUT YOU!
HRM.
PIX, PLEASE, WHAT IF IT IS MAGIC? THEY CAN HELP. AS LONG AS WE FIND NOAH, RIGHT?
YOU'RE RIGHT.
LET'S FIND NOAH.
AND SO, WITH THE SUN STARTING TO RISE, A RABBIT, DOG, OWL AND FROG SET OFF ON A RESCUE MISSION...
LET'S GO!
IT MIGHT BE MORE INCONSPICUOUS, GIRL, IF YOU WEREN'T FLYING.
SAYS THE TALKING OWL CARRYING A FROG!
I HAPPEN TO BE AN AWESOME HOPPER, OWL. TRUST ME, YOU'LL KNOW IF I'M FLYING.
NEED I REMIND YOU MY NAME IS NOT "OWL".
YEAH, WELL, MY NAME ISN'T "GIRL".

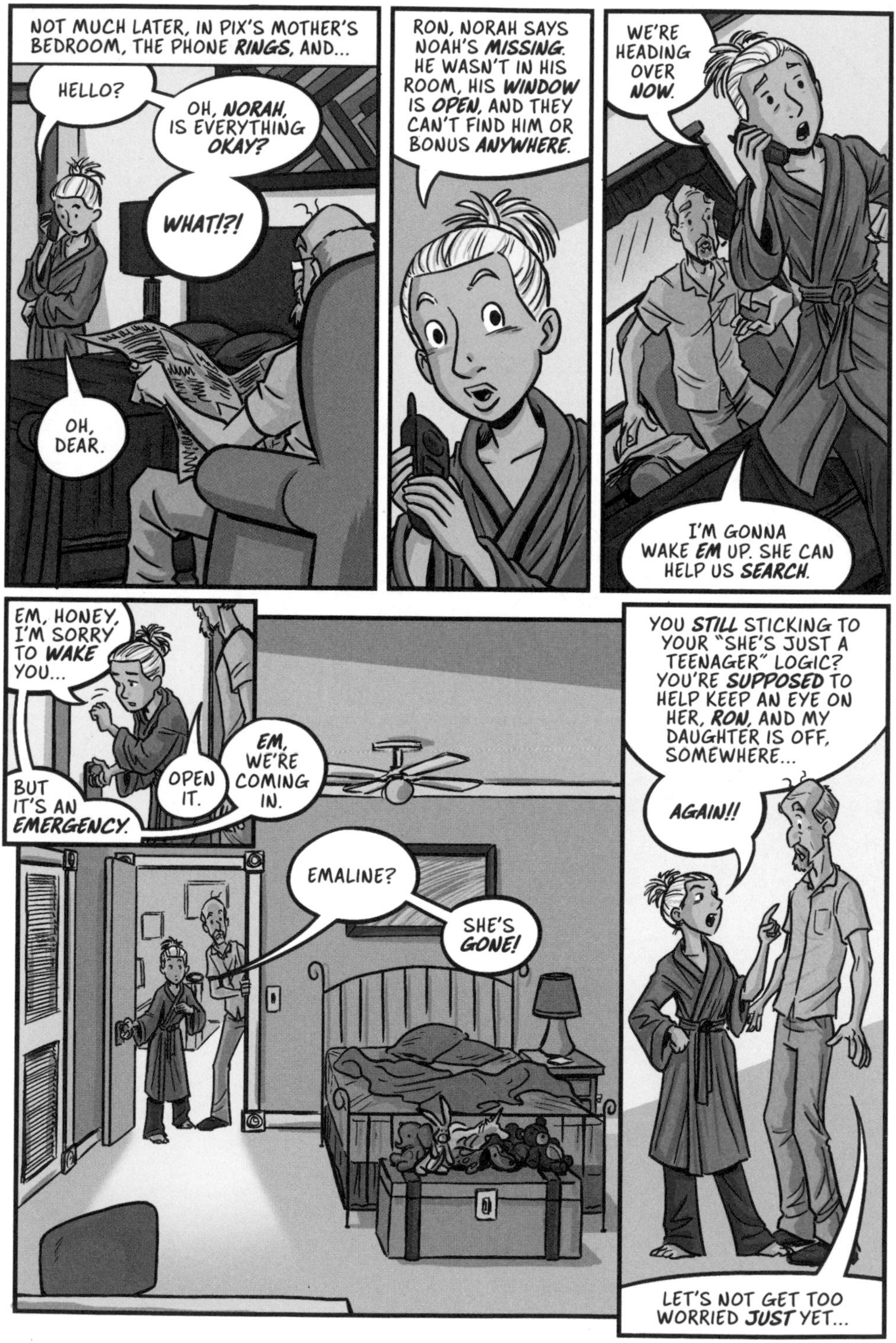
NOT MUCH LATER, IN PIX'S MOTHER'S BEDROOM, THE PHONE RINGS, AND...
HELLO?
OH, NORAH, IS EVERYTHING OKAY?
WHAT!?!
OH, DEAR.
RON, NORAH SAYS NOAH'S MISSING. HE WASN'T IN HIS ROOM, HIS WINDOW IS OPEN, AND THEY CAN'T FIND HIM OR BONUS ANYWHERE.
WE'RE HEADING OVER NOW.
I'M GONNA WAKE EM UP. SHE CAN HELP US SEARCH.
EM, HONEY, I'M SORRY TO WAKE YOU...
BUT IT'S AN EMERGENCY.
OPEN IT.
EM, WE'RE COMING IN.
EMALINE?
SHE'S GONE!
YOU STILL STICKING TO YOUR "SHE'S JUST A TEENAGER" LOGIC? YOU'RE SUPPOSED TO HELP KEEP AN EYE ON HER, RON, AND MY DAUGHTER IS OFF, SOMEWHERE...
AGAIN!!
LET'S NOT GET TOO WORRIED JUST YET...

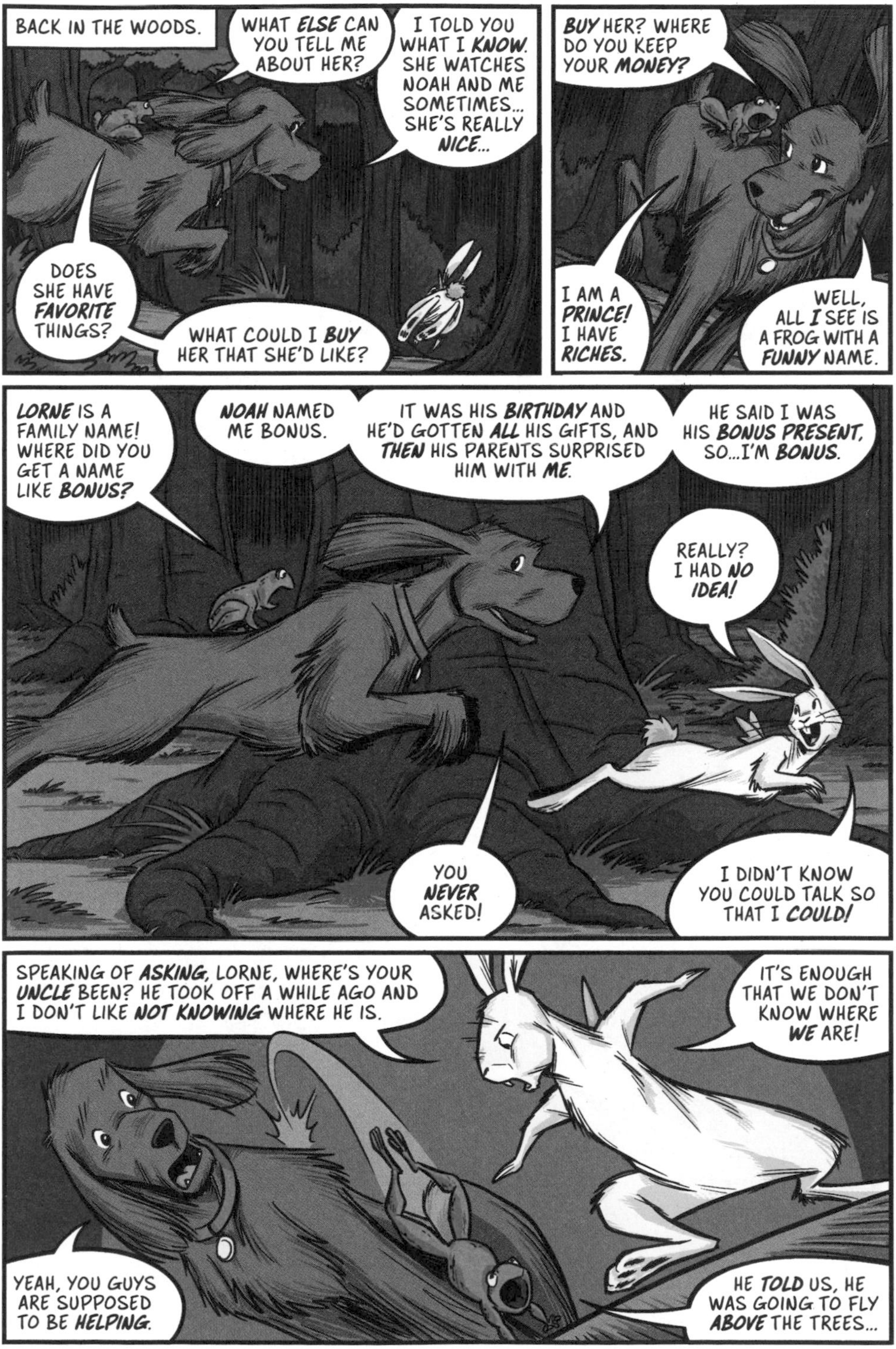
BACK IN THE WOODS.
WHAT ELSE CAN YOU TELL ME ABOUT HER?
I TOLD YOU WHAT I KNOW. SHE WATCHES NOAH AND ME SOMETIMES... SHE'S REALLY NICE...
DOES SHE HAVE FAVORITE THINGS?
WHAT COULD I BUY HER THAT SHE'D LIKE?
BUY HER? WHERE DO YOU KEEP YOUR MONEY?
I AM A PRINCE! I HAVE RICHES.
WELL, ALL I SEE IS A FROG WITH A FUNNY NAME.
LORNE IS A FAMILY NAME! WHERE DID YOU GET A NAME LIKE BONUS?
NOAH NAMED ME BONUS.
IT WAS HIS BIRTHDAY AND HE'D GOTTEN ALL HIS GIFTS, AND THEN HIS PARENTS SURPRISED HIM WITH ME.
HE SAID I WAS HIS BONUS PRESENT, SO...I'M BONUS.
REALLY? I HAD NO IDEA!
YOU NEVER ASKED!
I DIDN'T KNOW YOU COULD TALK SO THAT I COULD!
SPEAKING OF ASKING, LORNE, WHERE'S YOUR UNCLE BEEN? HE TOOK OFF A WHILE AGO AND I DON'T LIKE NOT KNOWING WHERE HE IS.
IT'S ENOUGH THAT WE DON'T KNOW WHERE WE ARE!
YEAH, YOU GUYS ARE SUPPOSED TO BE HELPING.
HE TOLD US, HE WAS GOING TO FLY ABOVE THE TREES...

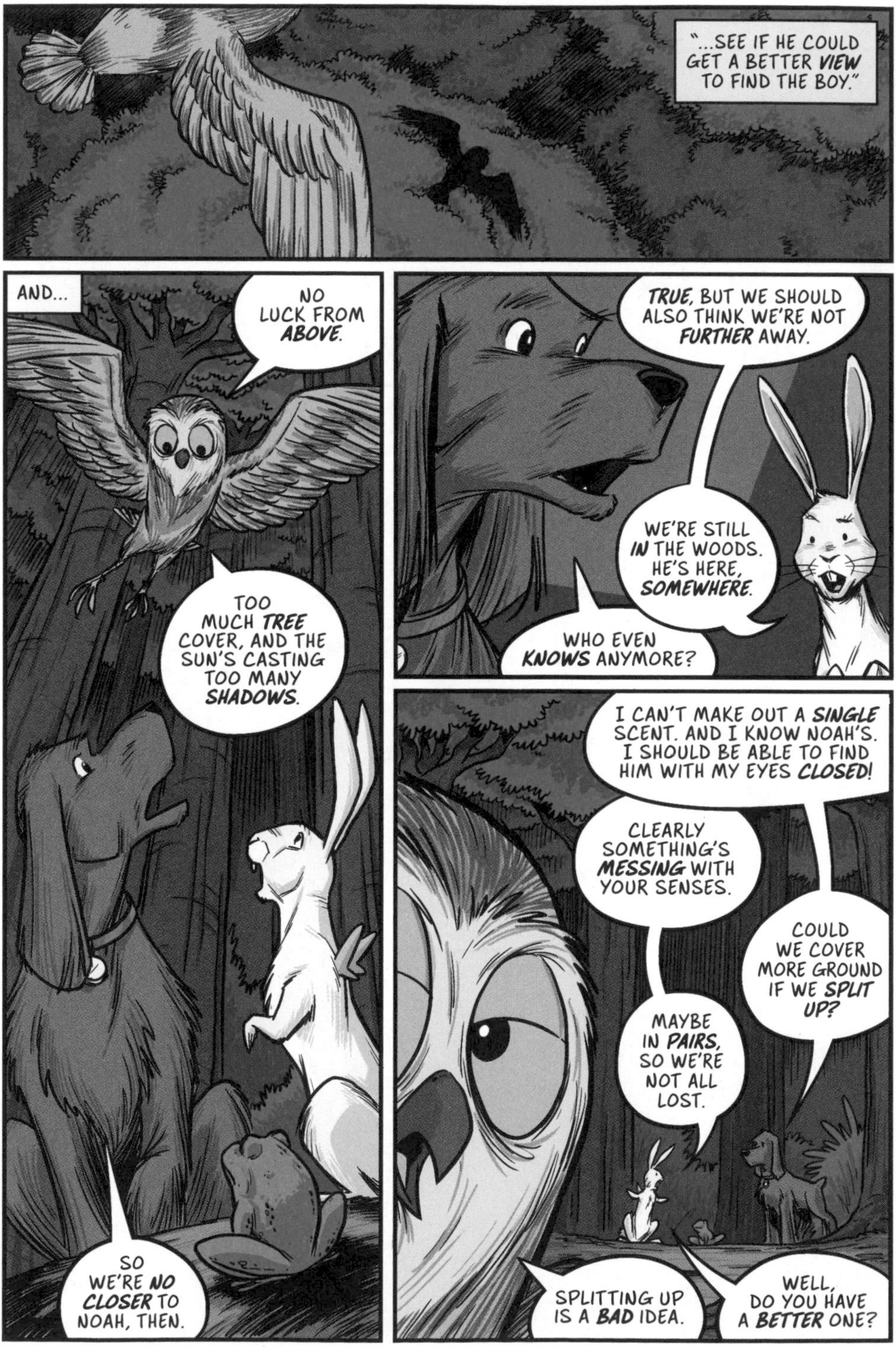
"...SEE IF HE COULD GET A BETTER VIEW TO FIND THE BOY."
AND...
NO LUCK FROM ABOVE.
TOO MUCH TREE COVER, AND THE SUN'S CASTING TOO MANY SHADOWS.
SO WE'RE NO CLOSER TO NOAH, THEN.
TRUE, BUT WE SHOULD ALSO THINK WE'RE NOT FURTHER AWAY.
WE'RE STILL IN THE WOODS. HE'S HERE, SOMEWHERE.
WHO EVEN KNOWS ANYMORE?
I CAN'T MAKE OUT A SINGLE SCENT. AND I KNOW NOAH'S. I SHOULD BE ABLE TO FIND HIM WITH MY EYES CLOSED!
CLEARLY SOMETHING'S MESSING WITH YOUR SENSES.
COULD WE COVER MORE GROUND IF WE SPLIT UP?
MAYBE IN PAIRS, SO WE'RE NOT ALL LOST.
SPLITTING UP IS A BAD IDEA.
WELL, DO YOU HAVE A BETTER ONE?

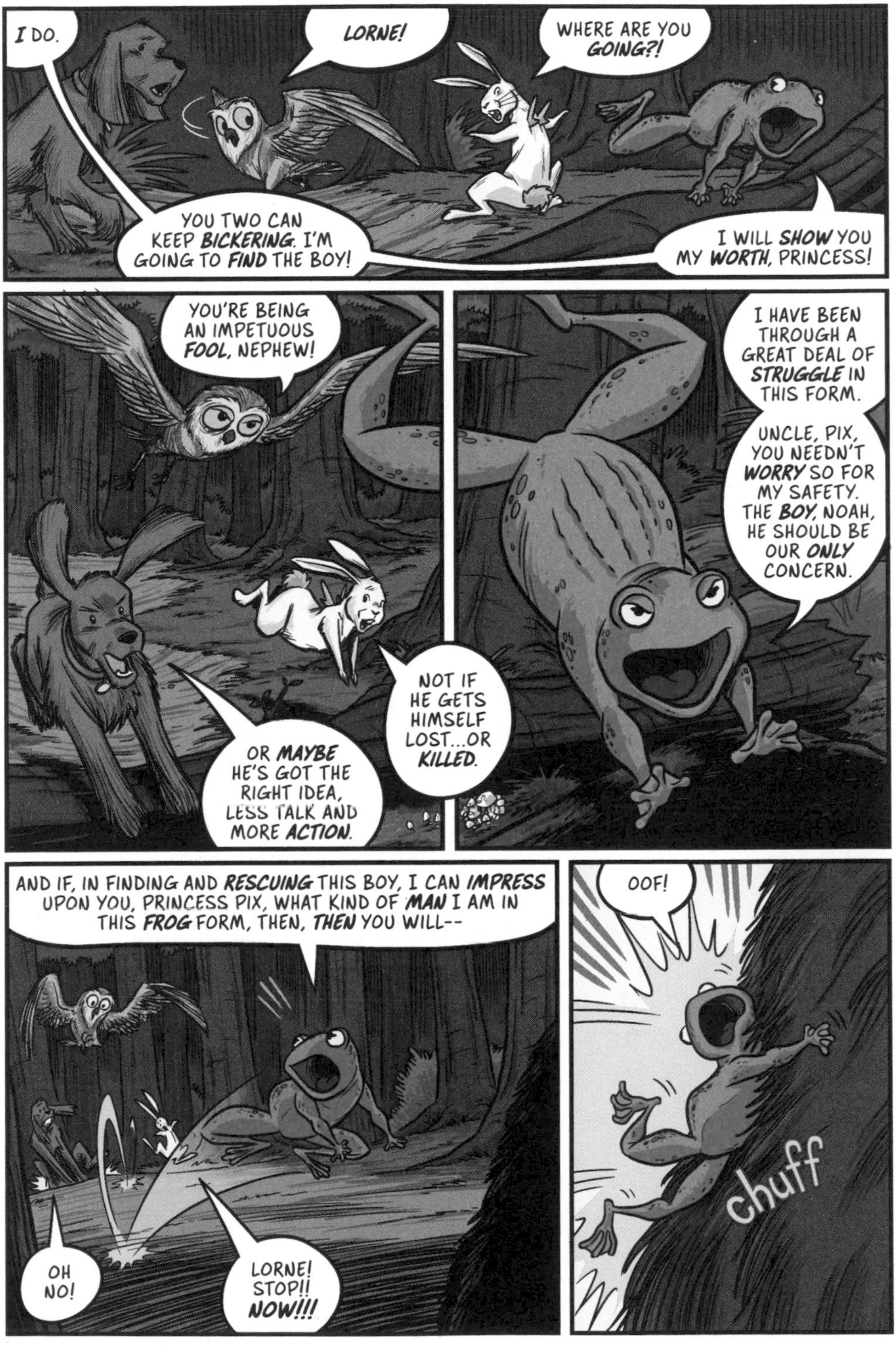
I DO.
LORNE!
WHERE ARE YOU GOING?!
YOU TWO CAN KEEP BICKERING. I'M GOING TO FIND THE BOY!
I WILL SHOW YOU MY WORTH, PRINCESS!
YOU'RE BEING AN IMPETUOUS FOOL, NEPHEW!
NOT IF HE GETS HIMSELF LOST...OR KILLED.
OR MAYBE HE'S GOT THE RIGHT IDEA, LESS TALK AND MORE ACTION.
I HAVE BEEN THROUGH A GREAT DEAL OF STRUGGLE IN THIS FORM.
UNCLE, PIX, YOU NEEDN'T WORRY SO FOR MY SAFETY. THE BOY, NOAH, HE SHOULD BE OUR ONLY CONCERN.
AND IF, IN FINDING AND RESCUING THIS BOY, I CAN IMPRESS UPON YOU, PRINCESS PIX, WHAT KIND OF MAN I AM IN THIS FROG FORM, THEN, THEN YOU WILL--
OH NO!
LORNE! STOP!! NOW!!!
OOF!
chuff

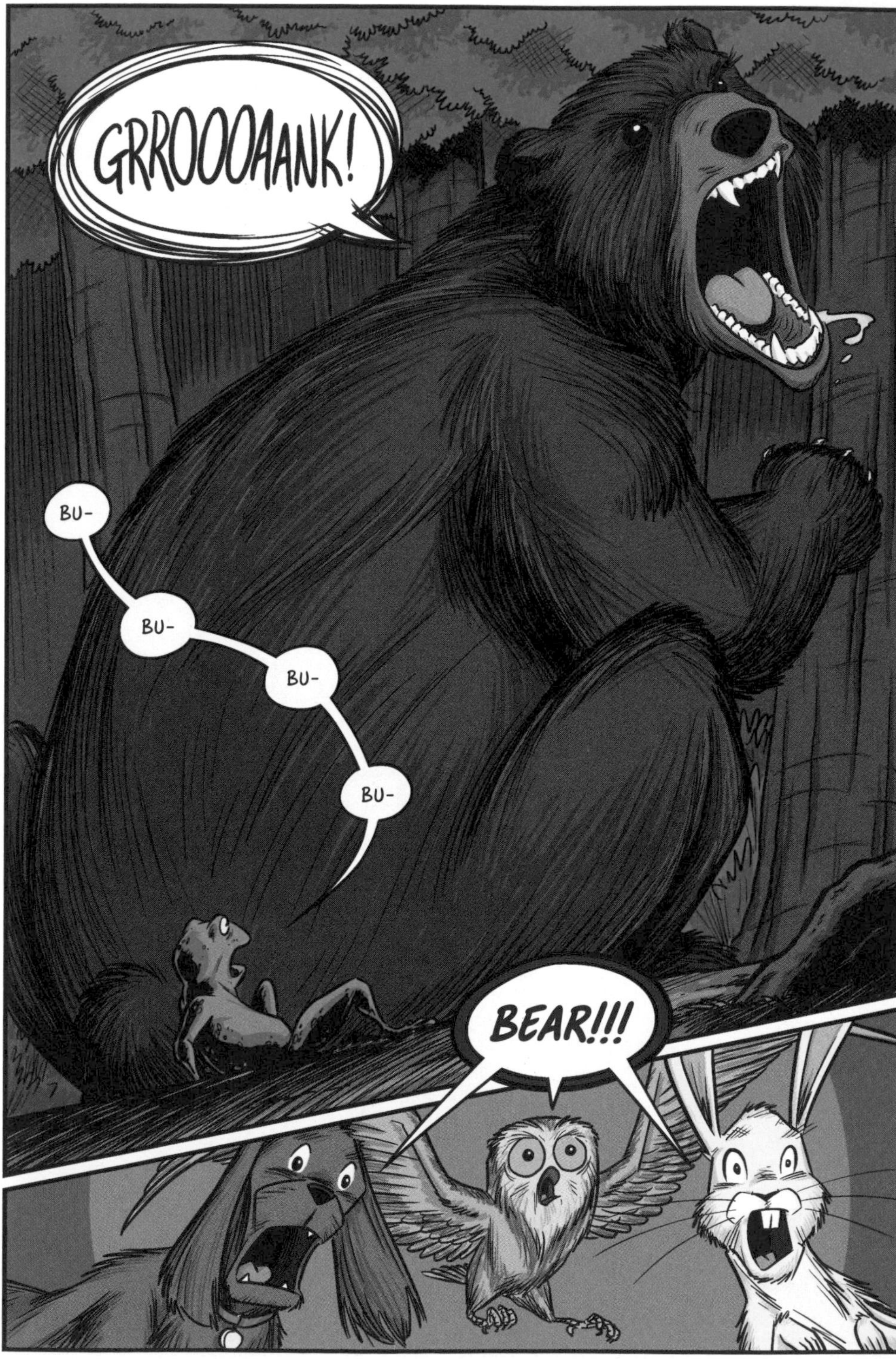
GRROOOAANK!
BU-
BU-
BU-
BU-
BEAR!!!

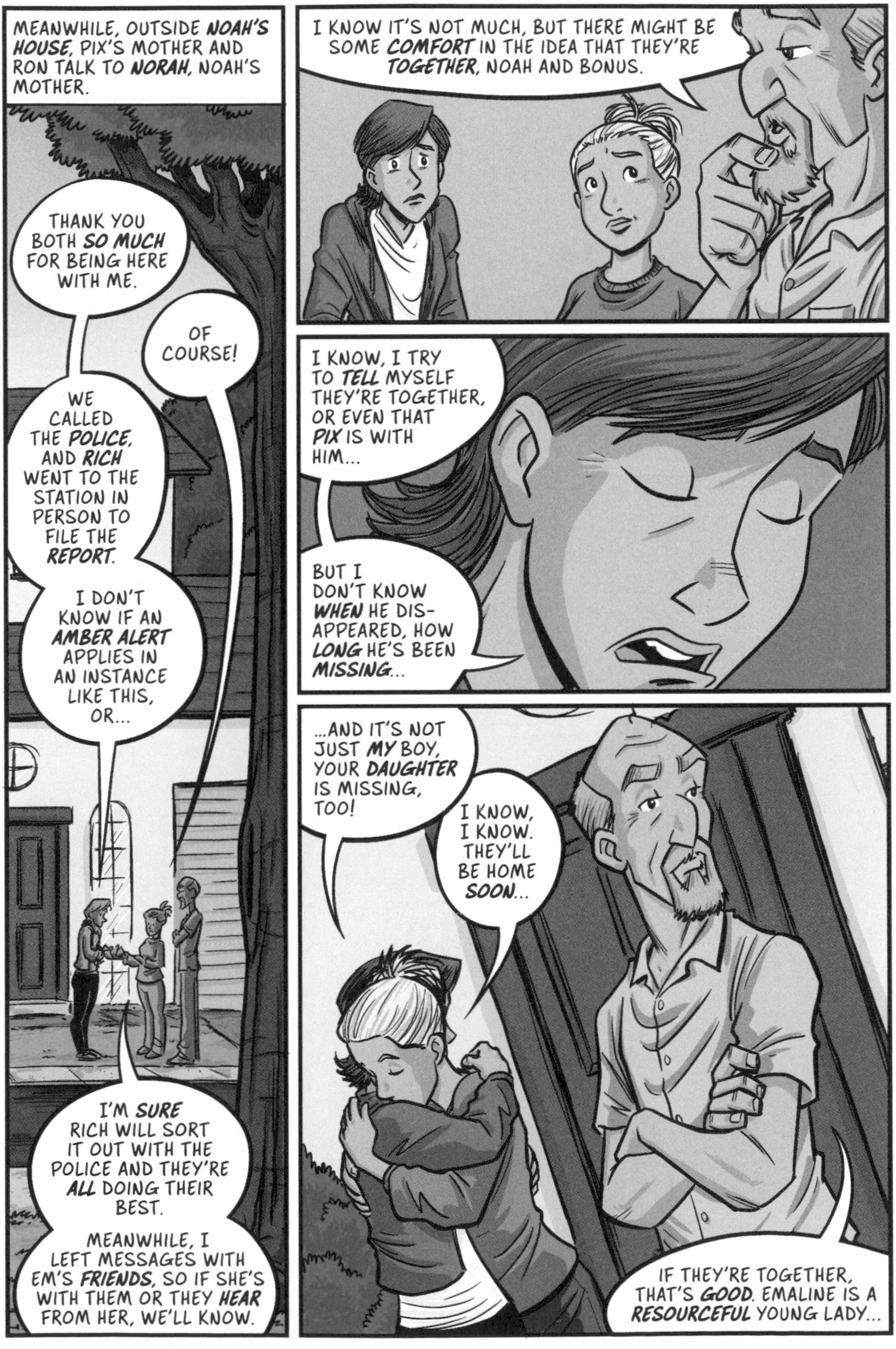
MEANWHILE, OUTSIDE NOAH'S HOUSE, PIX'S MOTHER AND RON TALK TO NORAH, NOAH'S MOTHER.
THANK YOU BOTH SO MUCH FOR BEING HERE WITH ME.
OF COURSE!
WE CALLED THE POLICE, AND RICH WENT TO THE STATION IN PERSON TO FILE THE REPORT.
I DON'T KNOW IF AN AMBER ALERT APPLIES IN AN INSTANCE LIKE THIS, OR...
I'M SURE RICH WILL SORT IT OUT WITH THE POLICE AND THEY'RE ALL DOING THEIR BEST.
MEANWHILE, I LEFT MESSAGES WITH EM'S FRIENDS, SO IF SHE'S WITH THEM OR THEY HEAR FROM HER, WE'LL KNOW.
I KNOW IT'S NOT MUCH, BUT THERE MIGHT BE SOME COMFORT IN THE IDEA THAT THEY'RE TOGETHER, NOAH AND BONUS.
I KNOW, I TRY TO TELL MYSELF THEY'RE TOGETHER, OR EVEN THAT PIX IS WITH HIM...
BUT I DON'T KNOW WHEN HE DIS-APPEARED, HOW LONG HE'S BEEN MISSING...
...AND IT'S NOT JUST MY BOY, YOUR DAUGHTER IS MISSING, TOO!
I KNOW, I KNOW. THEY'LL BE HOME SOON...
IF THEY'RE TOGETHER, THAT'S GOOD. EMALINE IS A RESOURCEFUL YOUNG LADY...

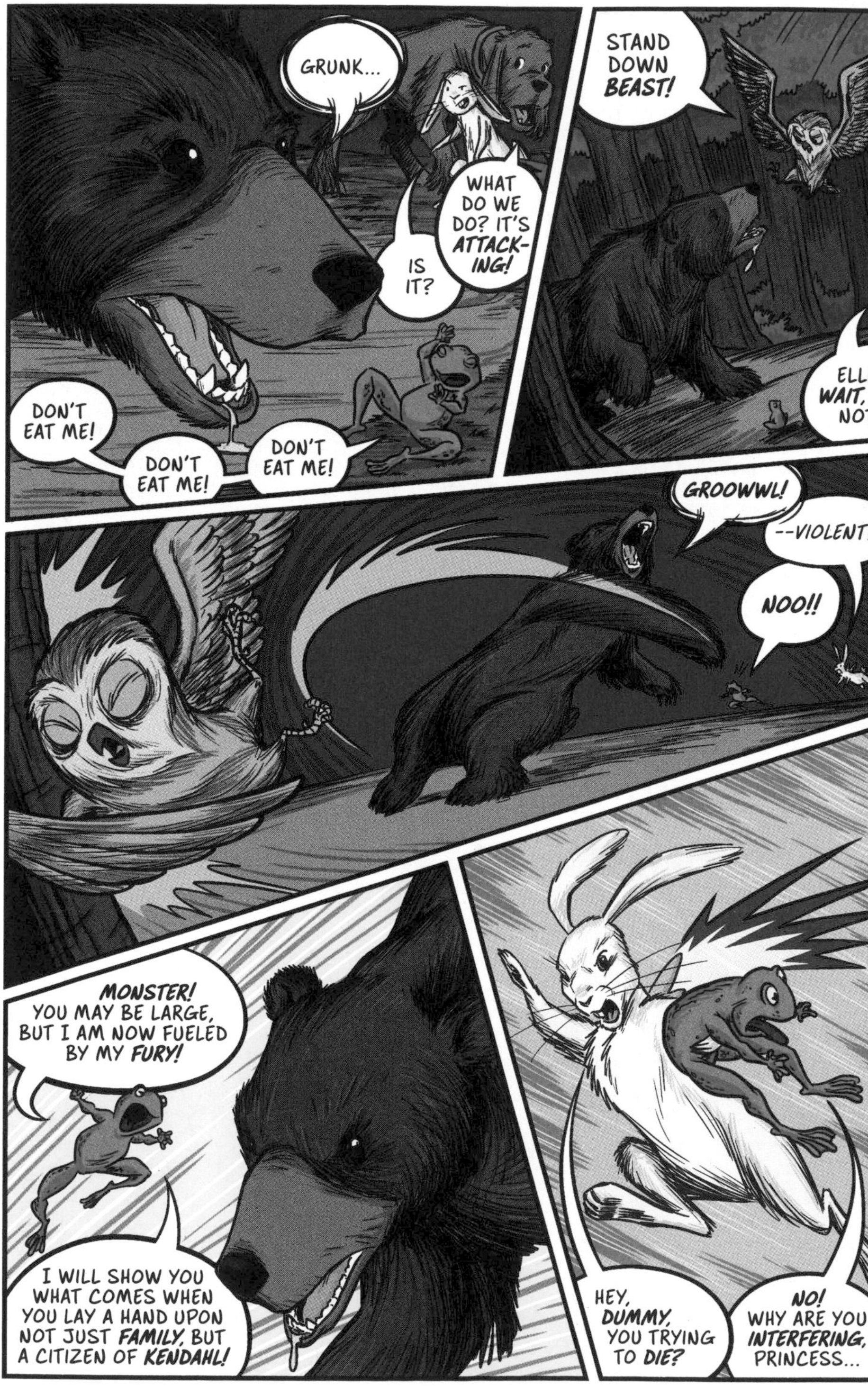
GRUNK...
WHAT DO WE DO? IT'S ATTACKING!
IS IT?
DON'T EAT ME!
DON'T EAT ME!
DON'T EAT ME!
STAND DOWN BEAST!
ELLIS, WAIT, HE'S NOT--
GROOWWL!
--VIOLENT?!
NOO!!
MONSTER! YOU MAY BE LARGE, BUT I AM NOW FUELED BY MY FURY!
I WILL SHOW YOU WHAT COMES WHEN YOU LAY A HAND UPON NOT JUST FAMILY, BUT A CITIZEN OF KENDAHL!
HEY, DUMMY, YOU TRYING TO DIE?
NO! WHY ARE YOU INTERFERING, PRINCESS...

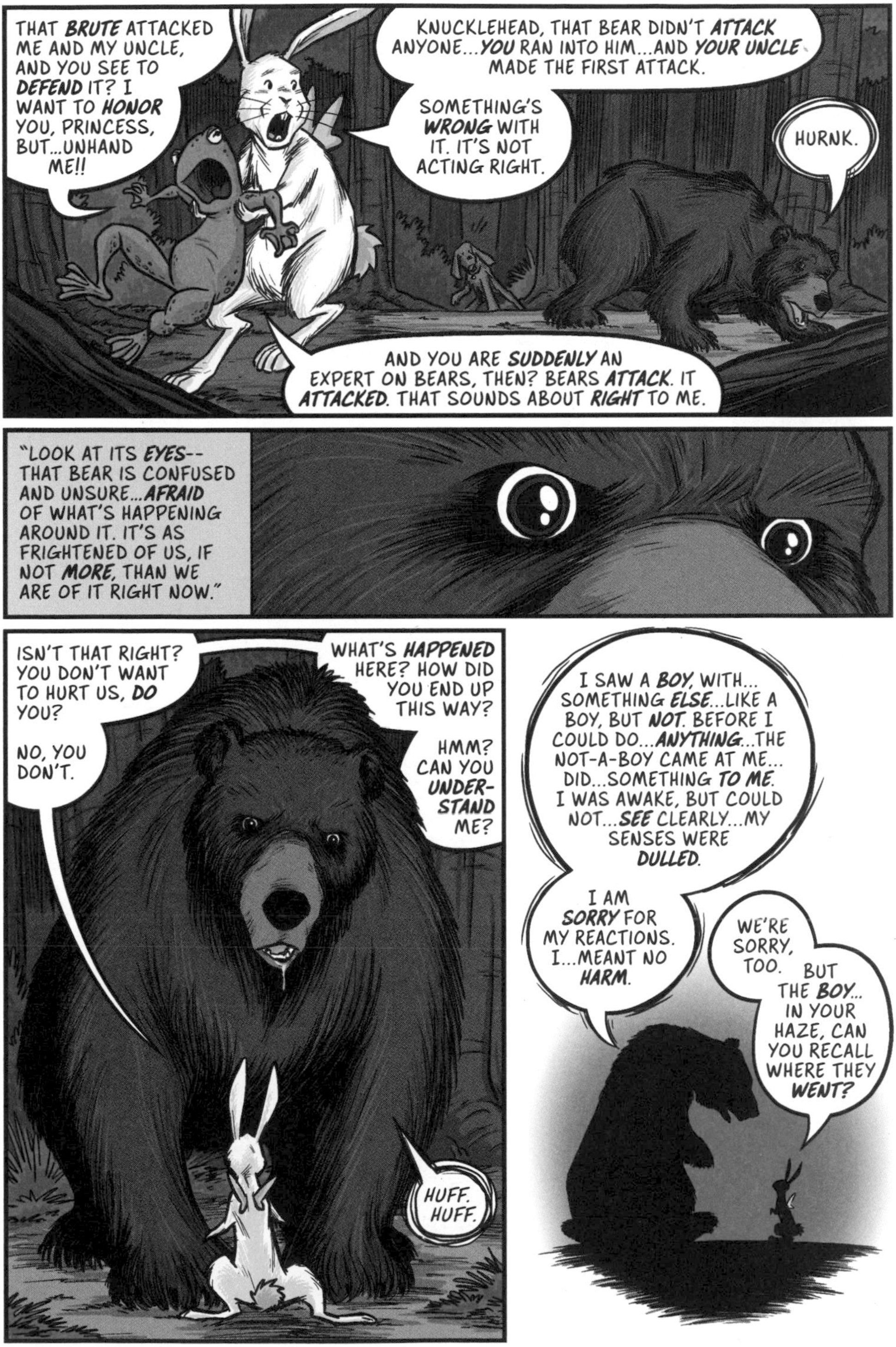
THAT BRUTE ATTACKED ME AND MY UNCLE, AND YOU SEE TO DEFEND IT? I WANT TO HONOR YOU, PRINCESS, BUT...UNHAND ME!!
KNUCKLEHEAD, THAT BEAR DIDN'T ATTACK ANYONE...YOU RAN INTO HIM...AND YOUR UNCLE MADE THE FIRST ATTACK.
SOMETHING'S WRONG WITH IT. IT'S NOT ACTING RIGHT.
HURNK.
AND YOU ARE SUDDENLY AN EXPERT ON BEARS, THEN? BEARS ATTACK. IT ATTACKED. THAT SOUNDS ABOUT RIGHT TO ME.
"LOOK AT ITS EYES--THAT BEAR IS CONFUSED AND UNSURE...AFRAID OF WHAT'S HAPPENING AROUND IT. IT'S AS FRIGHTENED OF US, IF NOT MORE, THAN WE ARE OF IT RIGHT NOW."
ISN'T THAT RIGHT? YOU DON'T WANT TO HURT US, DO YOU?
NO, YOU DON'T.
WHAT'S HAPPENED HERE? HOW DID YOU END UP THIS WAY?
HMM? CAN YOU UNDER-STAND ME?
HUFF. HUFF.
I SAW A BOY, WITH... SOMETHING ELSE...LIKE A BOY, BUT NOT. BEFORE I COULD DO...ANYTHING...THE NOT-A-BOY CAME AT ME... DID...SOMETHING TO ME. I WAS AWAKE, BUT COULD NOT...SEE CLEARLY...MY SENSES WERE DULLED.
I AM SORRY FOR MY REACTIONS. I...MEANT NO HARM.
WE'RE SORRY, TOO.
BUT THE BOY... IN YOUR HAZE, CAN YOU RECALL WHERE THEY WENT?

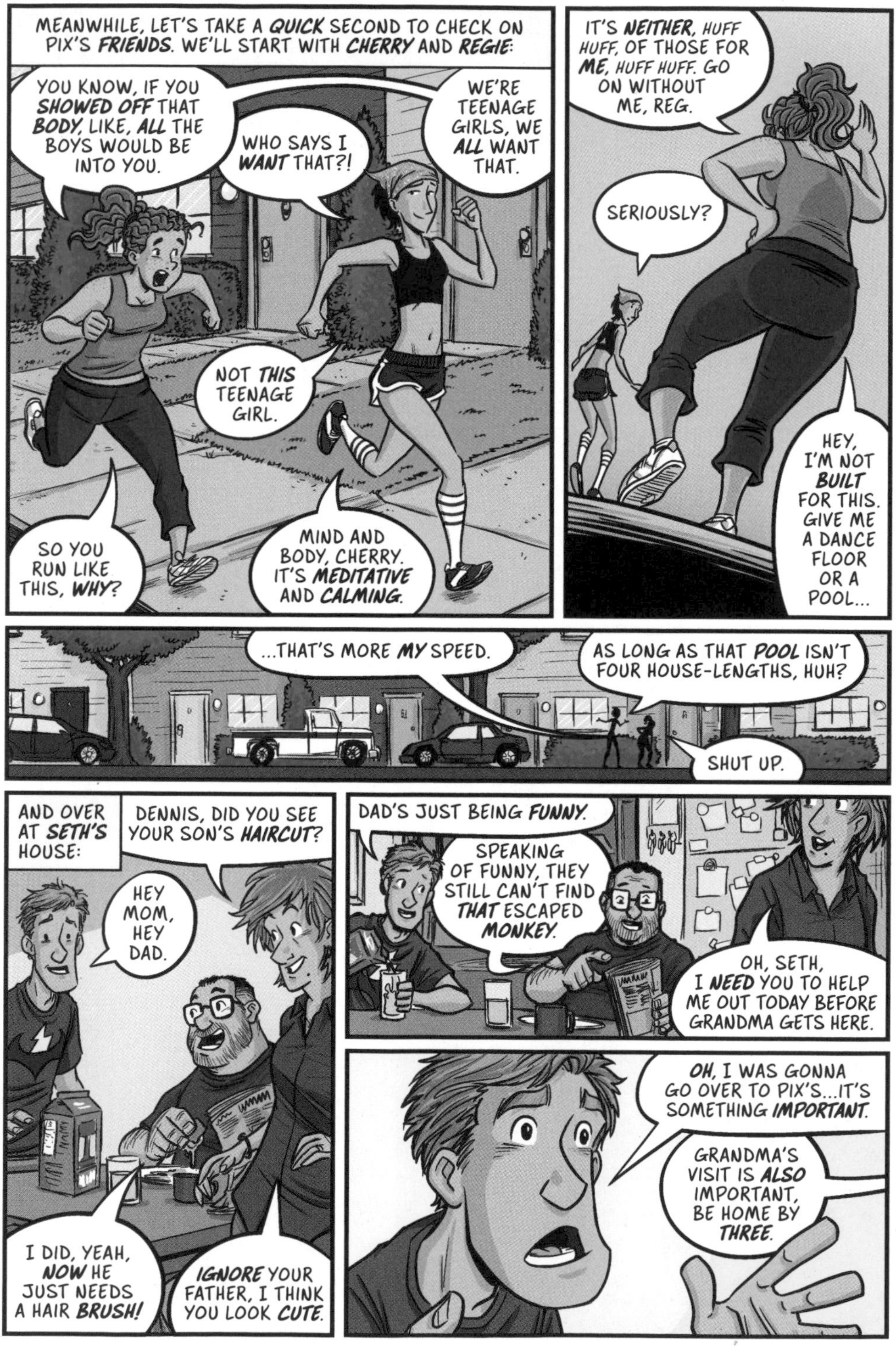
MEANWHILE, LET'S TAKE A QUICK SECOND TO CHECK ON PIX'S FRIENDS. WE'LL START WITH CHERRY AND REGIE:
YOU KNOW, IF YOU SHOWED OFF THAT BODY, LIKE, ALL THE BOYS WOULD BE INTO YOU.
WHO SAYS I WANT THAT?!
WE'RE TEENAGE GIRLS, WE ALL WANT THAT.
NOT THIS TEENAGE GIRL.
SO YOU RUN LIKE THIS, WHY?
MIND AND BODY, CHERRY. IT'S MEDITATIVE AND CALMING.
IT'S NEITHER, HUFF HUFF, OF THOSE FOR ME, HUFF HUFF. GO ON WITHOUT ME, REG.
SERIOUSLY?
HEY, I'M NOT BUILT FOR THIS. GIVE ME A DANCE FLOOR OR A POOL...
...THAT'S MORE MY SPEED.
AS LONG AS THAT POOL ISN'T FOUR HOUSE-LENGTHS, HUH?
SHUT UP.
AND OVER AT SETH'S HOUSE:
DENNIS, DID YOU SEE YOUR SON'S HAIRCUT?
HEY MOM, HEY DAD.
I DID, YEAH, NOW HE JUST NEEDS A HAIR BRUSH!
IGNORE YOUR FATHER, I THINK YOU LOOK CUTE.
DAD'S JUST BEING FUNNY.
SPEAKING OF FUNNY, THEY STILL CAN'T FIND THAT ESCAPED MONKEY.
OH, SETH, I NEED YOU TO HELP ME OUT TODAY BEFORE GRANDMA GETS HERE.
OH, I WAS GONNA GO OVER TO PIX'S...IT'S SOMETHING IMPORTANT.
GRANDMA'S VISIT IS ALSO IMPORTANT, BE HOME BY THREE.

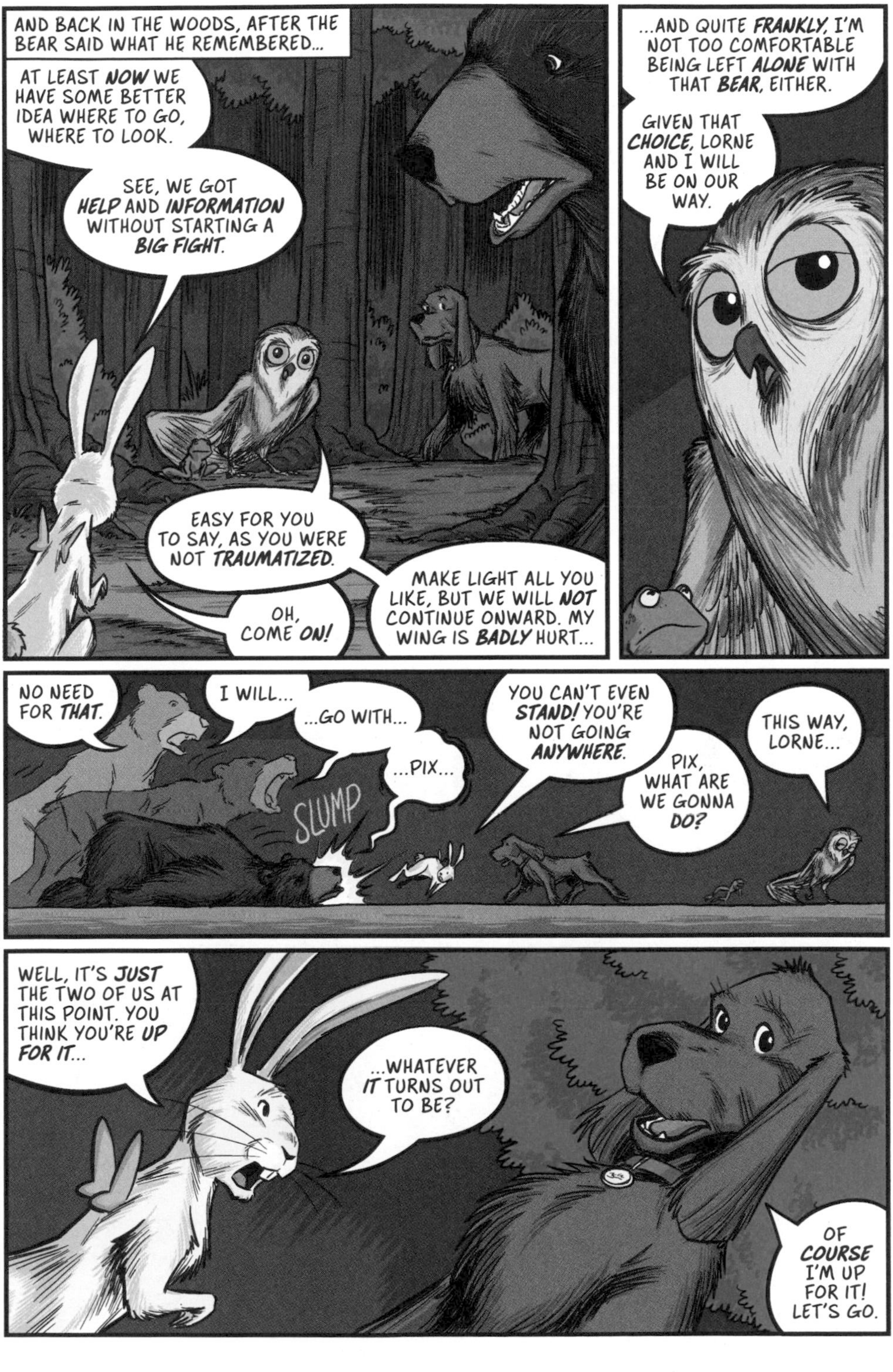
AND BACK IN THE WOODS, AFTER THE BEAR SAID WHAT HE REMEMBERED...
AT LEAST NOW WE HAVE SOME BETTER IDEA WHERE TO GO, WHERE TO LOOK.
SEE, WE GOT HELP AND INFORMATION WITHOUT STARTING A BIG FIGHT.
EASY FOR YOU TO SAY, AS YOU WERE NOT TRAUMATIZED.
OH, COME ON!
MAKE LIGHT ALL YOU LIKE, BUT WE WILL NOT CONTINUE ONWARD. MY WING IS BADLY HURT...
...AND QUITE FRANKLY, I'M NOT TOO COMFORTABLE BEING LEFT ALONE WITH THAT BEAR, EITHER.
GIVEN THAT CHOICE, LORNE AND I WILL BE ON OUR WAY.
NO NEED FOR THAT.
I WILL...
...GO WITH...
...PIX...
SLUMP
YOU CAN'T EVEN STAND! YOU'RE NOT GOING ANYWHERE.
PIX, WHAT ARE WE GONNA DO?
THIS WAY, LORNE...
WELL, IT'S JUST THE TWO OF US AT THIS POINT. YOU THINK YOU'RE UP FOR IT...
...WHATEVER IT TURNS OUT TO BE?
OF COURSE I'M UP FOR IT! LET'S GO.

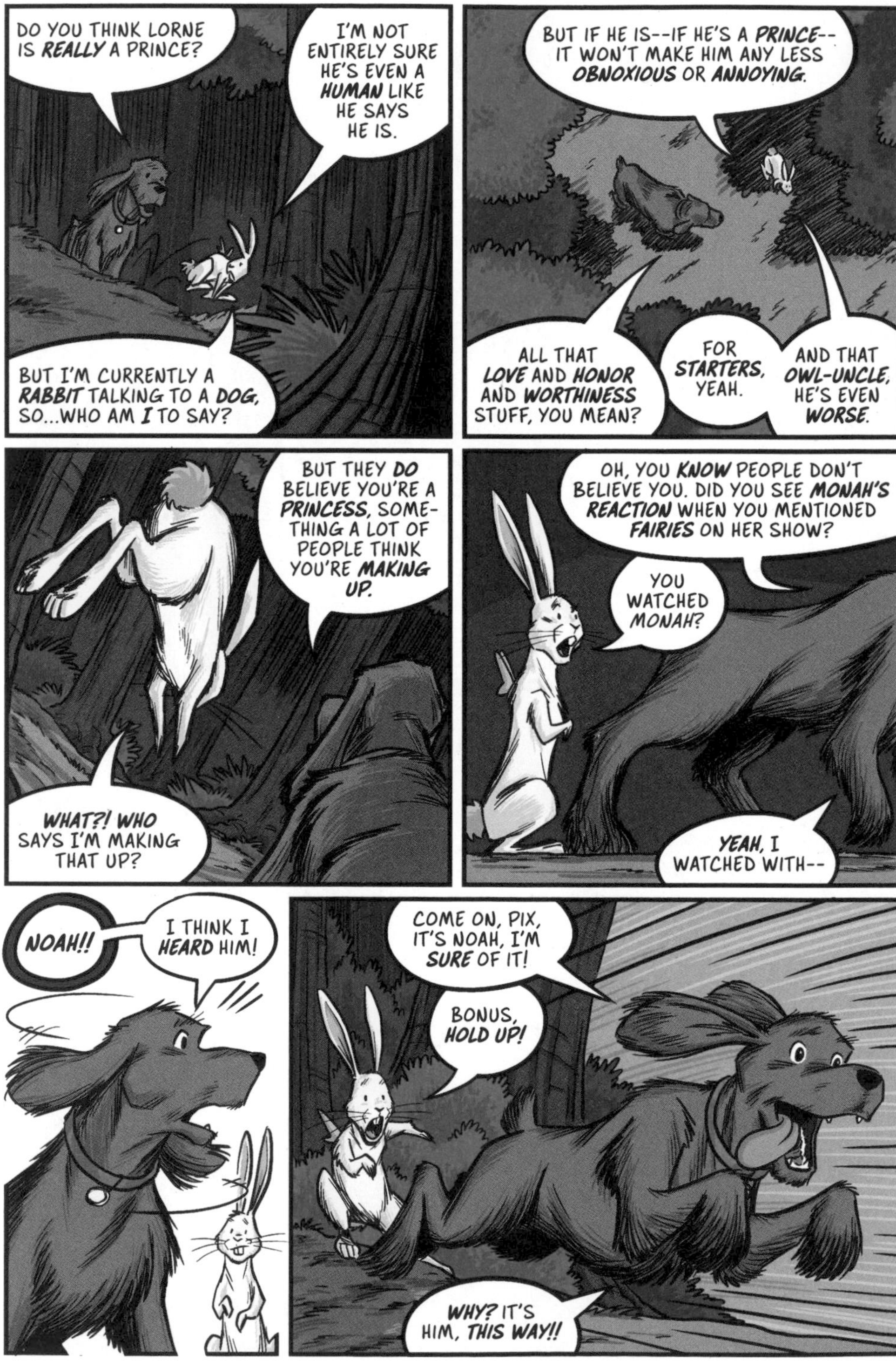
DO YOU THINK LORNE IS REALLY A PRINCE?
I'M NOT ENTIRELY SURE HE'S EVEN A HUMAN LIKE HE SAYS HE IS.
BUT I'M CURRENTLY A RABBIT TALKING TO A DOG, SO...WHO AM I TO SAY?
BUT IF HE IS--IF HE'S A PRINCE--IT WON'T MAKE HIM ANY LESS OBNOXIOUS OR ANNOYING.
ALL THAT LOVE AND HONOR AND WORTHINESS STUFF, YOU MEAN?
FOR STARTERS, YEAH.
AND THAT OWL-UNCLE, HE'S EVEN WORSE.
BUT THEY DO BELIEVE YOU'RE A PRINCESS, SOMETHING A LOT OF PEOPLE THINK YOU'RE MAKING UP.
WHAT?! WHO SAYS I'M MAKING THAT UP?
OH, YOU KNOW PEOPLE DON'T BELIEVE YOU. DID YOU SEE MONAH'S REACTION WHEN YOU MENTIONED FAIRIES ON HER SHOW?
YOU WATCHED MONAH?
YEAH, I WATCHED WITH--
NOAH!!
I THINK I HEARD HIM!
COME ON, PIX, IT'S NOAH, I'M SURE OF IT!
BONUS, HOLD UP!
WHY? IT'S HIM, THIS WAY!!

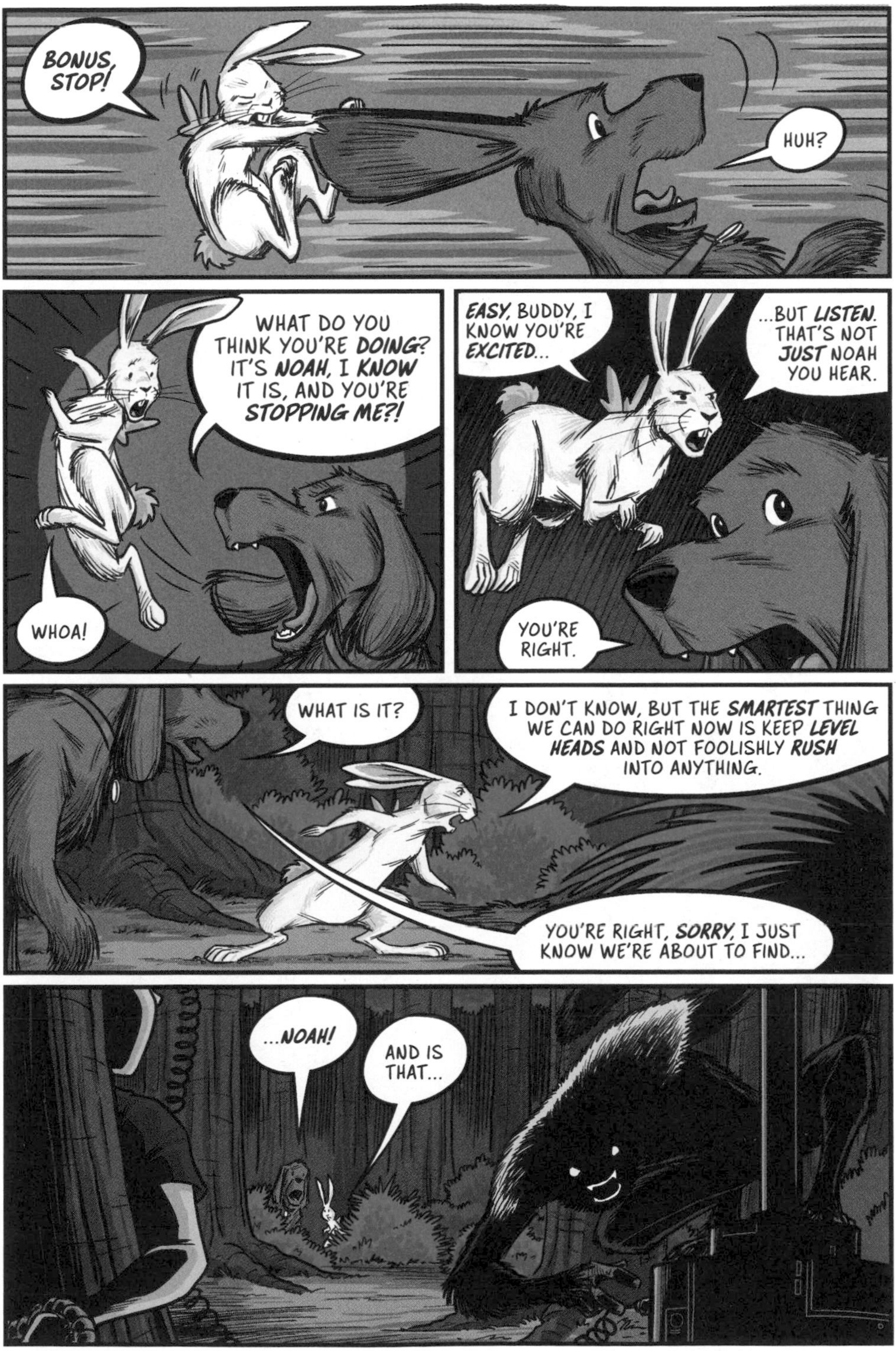
BONUS, STOP!
HUH?
WHAT DO YOU THINK YOU'RE DOING? IT'S NOAH, I KNOW IT IS, AND YOU'RE STOPPING ME?!
WHOA!
EASY, BUDDY, I KNOW YOU'RE EXCITED...
...BUT LISTEN. THAT'S NOT JUST NOAH YOU HEAR.
YOU'RE RIGHT.
WHAT IS IT?
I DON'T KNOW, BUT THE SMARTEST THING WE CAN DO RIGHT NOW IS KEEP LEVEL HEADS AND NOT FOOLISHLY RUSH INTO ANYTHING.
YOU'RE RIGHT, SORRY, I JUST KNOW WE'RE ABOUT TO FIND...
...NOAH!
AND IS THAT...

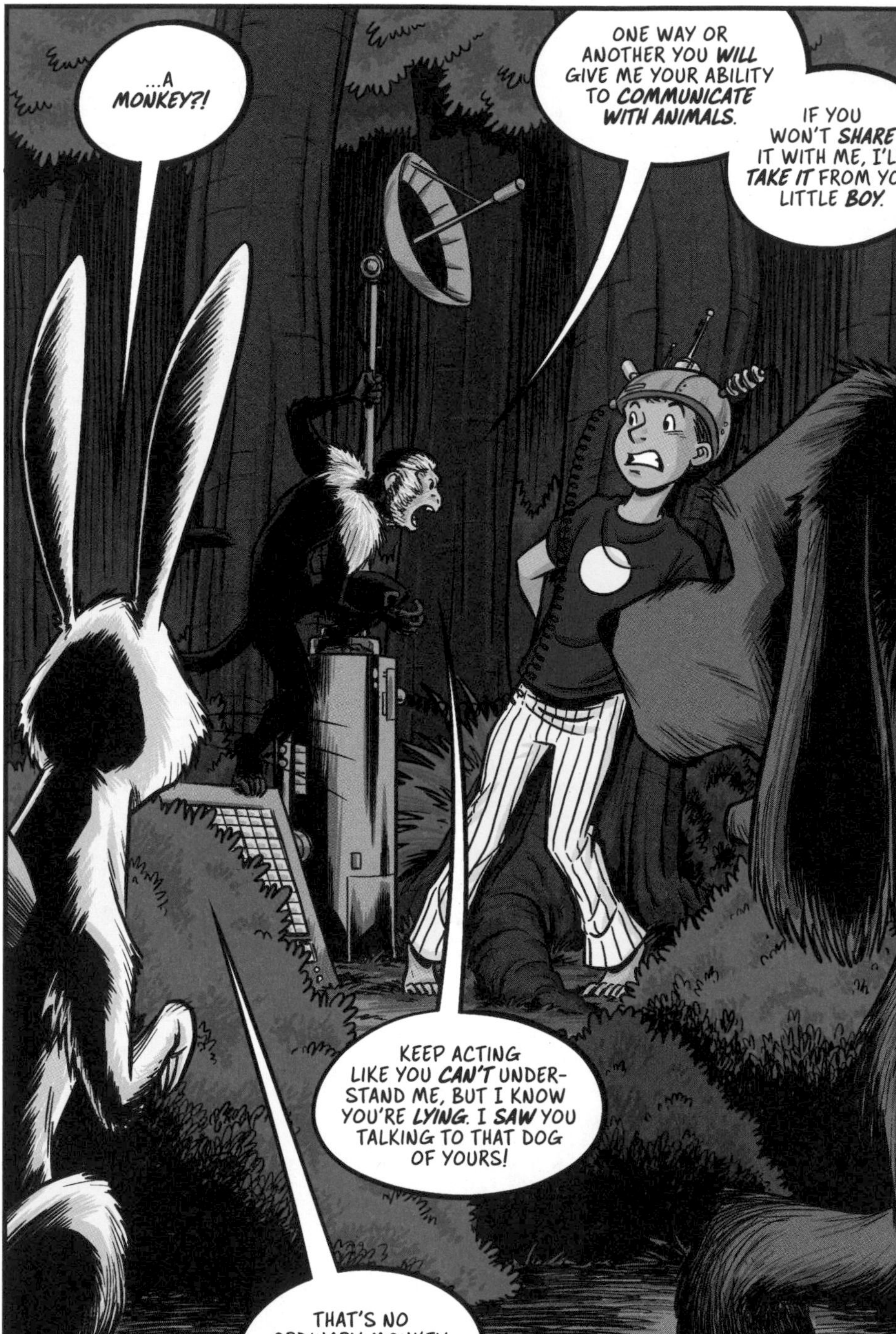
...A MONKEY?!
ONE WAY OR ANOTHER YOU WILL GIVE ME YOUR ABILITY TO COMMUNICATE WITH ANIMALS.
IF YOU WON'T SHARE IT WITH ME, I'LL TAKE IT FROM YOU, LITTLE BOY.
KEEP ACTING LIKE YOU CAN'T UNDER-STAND ME, BUT I KNOW YOU'RE LYING. I SAW YOU TALKING TO THAT DOG OF YOURS!
THAT'S NO ORDINARY MONKEY. THAT'S A CRAZY, EVIL MONKEY!!

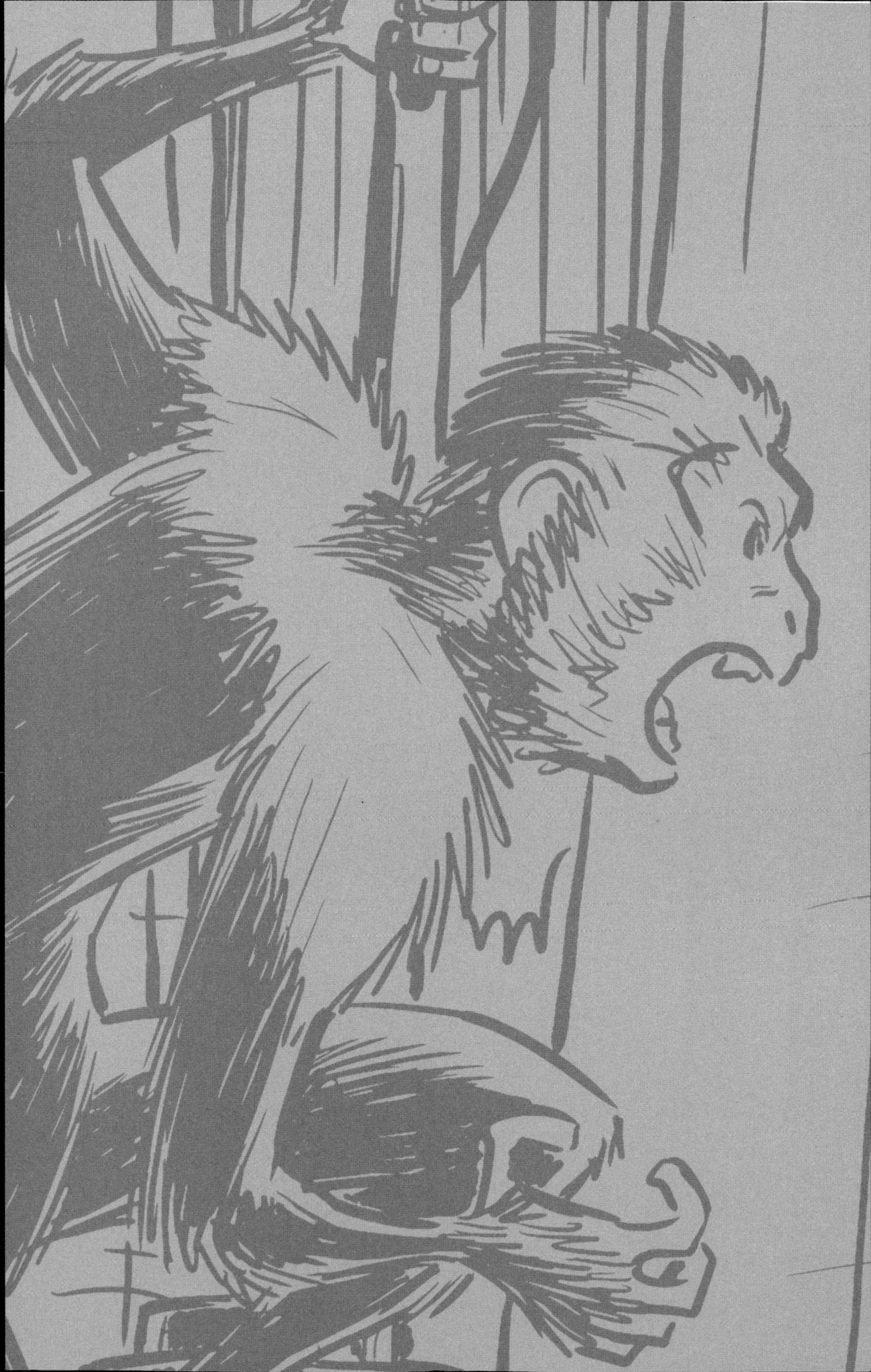

CHAPTER
FIVE

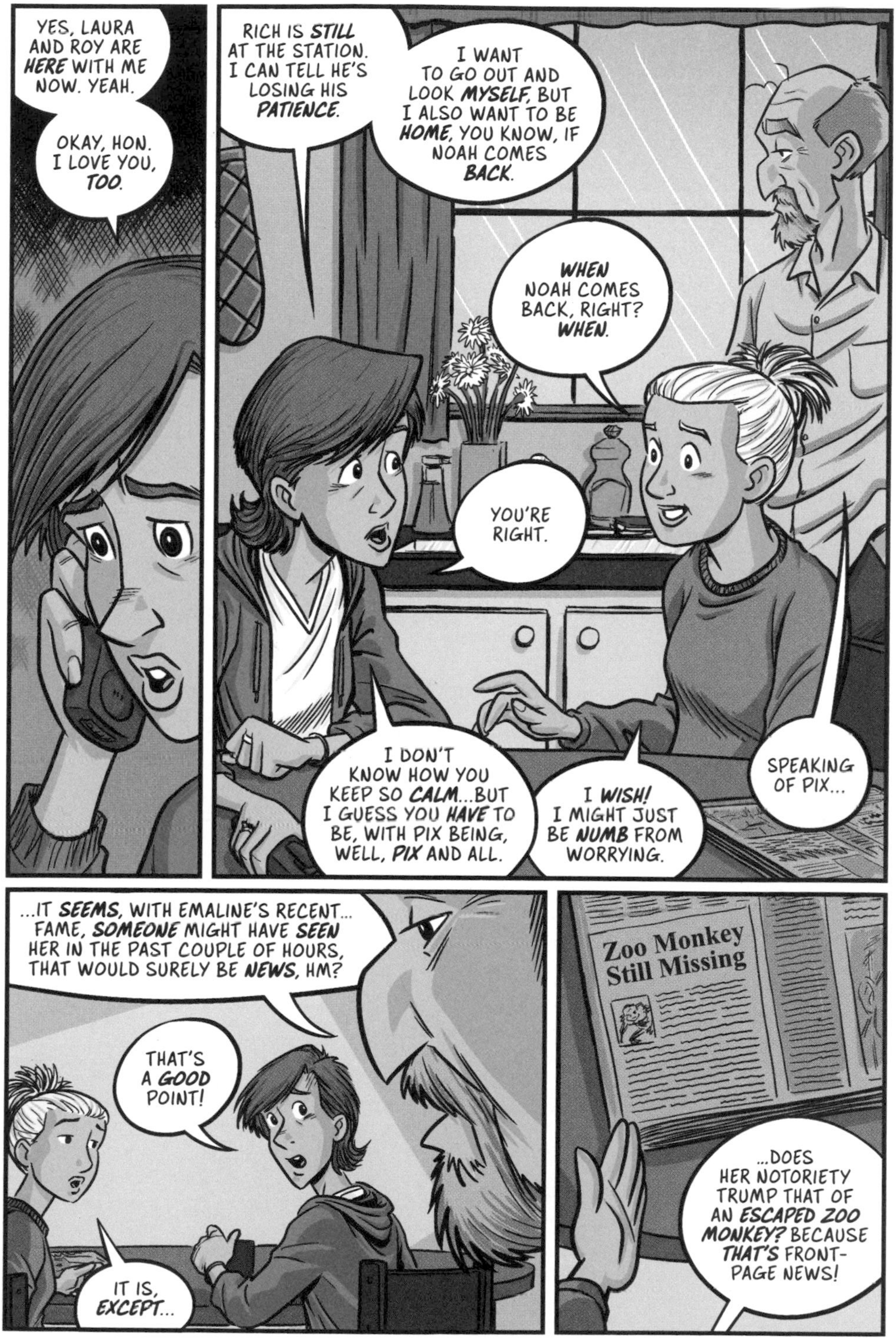
YES, LAURA AND ROY ARE HERE WITH ME NOW. YEAH.
OKAY, HON. I LOVE YOU, TOO.
RICH IS STILL AT THE STATION. I CAN TELL HE'S LOSING HIS PATIENCE.
I WANT TO GO OUT AND LOOK MYSELF, BUT I ALSO WANT TO BE HOME, YOU KNOW, IF NOAH COMES BACK.
WHEN NOAH COMES BACK, RIGHT? WHEN.
YOU'RE RIGHT.
I DON'T KNOW HOW YOU KEEP SO CALM...BUT I GUESS YOU HAVE TO BE, WITH PIX BEING, WELL, PIX AND ALL.
I WISH! I MIGHT JUST BE NUMB FROM WORRYING.
SPEAKING OF PIX...
...IT SEEMS, WITH EMALINE'S RECENT... FAME, SOMEONE MIGHT HAVE SEEN HER IN THE PAST COUPLE OF HOURS, THAT WOULD SURELY BE NEWS, HM?
THAT'S A GOOD POINT!
IT IS, EXCEPT...
Zoo Monkey Still Missing
...DOES HER NOTORIETY TRUMP THAT OF AN ESCAPED ZOO MONKEY? BECAUSE THAT'S FRONT-PAGE NEWS!

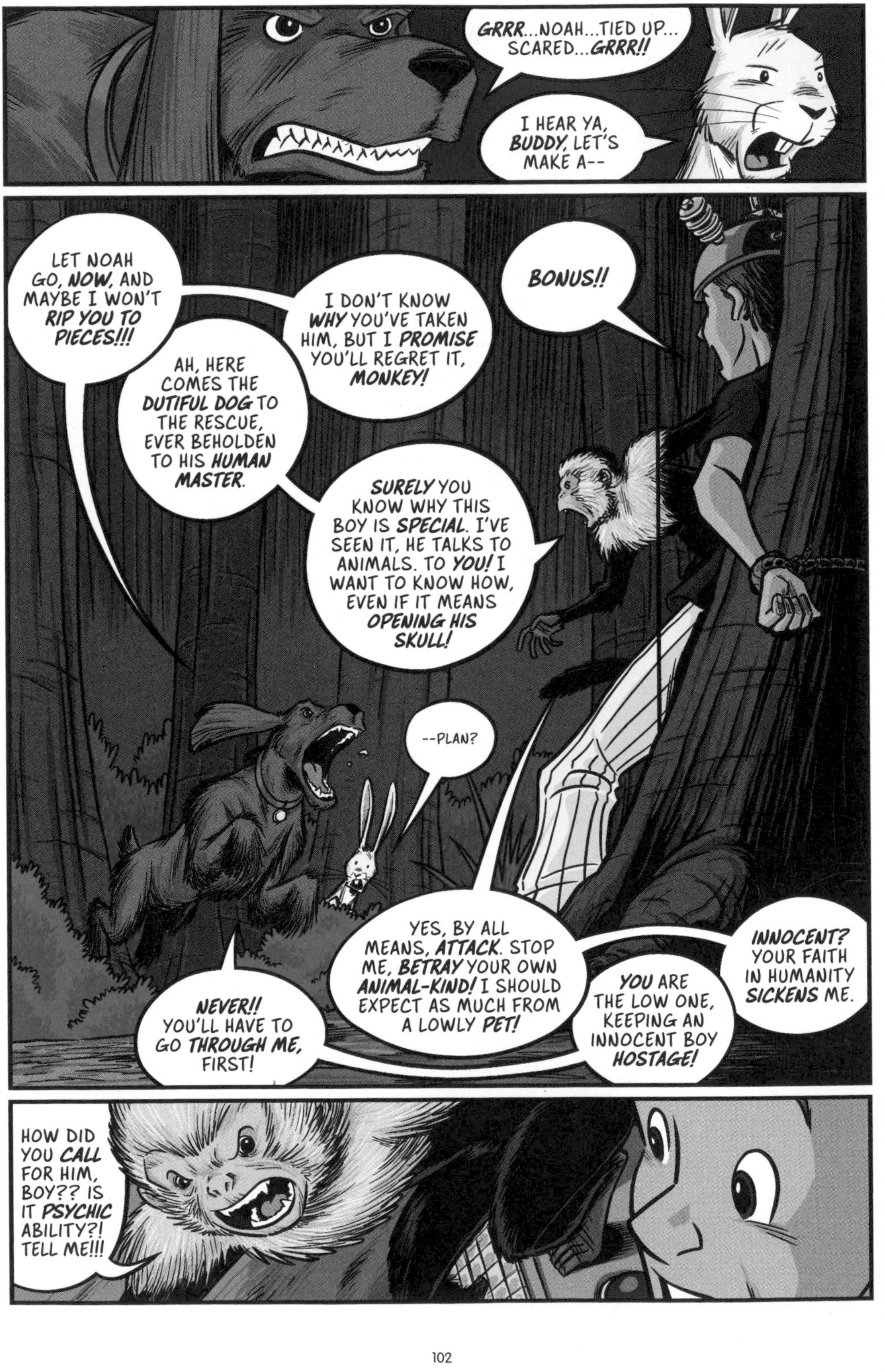
GRRR...NOAH...TIED UP... SCARED...GRRR!!
I HEAR YA, BUDDY, LET'S MAKE A--
LET NOAH GO, NOW, AND MAYBE I WON'T RIP YOU TO PIECES!!!
I DON'T KNOW WHY YOU'VE TAKEN HIM, BUT I PROMISE YOU'LL REGRET IT, MONKEY!
BONUS!!
AH, HERE COMES THE DUTIFUL DOG TO THE RESCUE, EVER BEHOLDEN TO HIS HUMAN MASTER.
SURELY YOU KNOW WHY THIS BOY IS SPECIAL. I'VE SEEN IT, HE TALKS TO ANIMALS. TO YOU! I WANT TO KNOW HOW, EVEN IF IT MEANS OPENING HIS SKULL!
--PLAN?
NEVER!! YOU'LL HAVE TO GO THROUGH ME, FIRST!
YES, BY ALL MEANS, ATTACK. STOP ME, BETRAY YOUR OWN ANIMAL-KIND! I SHOULD EXPECT AS MUCH FROM A LOWLY PET!
YOU ARE THE LOW ONE, KEEPING AN INNOCENT BOY HOSTAGE!
INNOCENT? YOUR FAITH IN HUMANITY SICKENS ME.
HOW DID YOU CALL FOR HIM, BOY?? IS IT PSYCHIC ABILITY?! TELL ME!!!

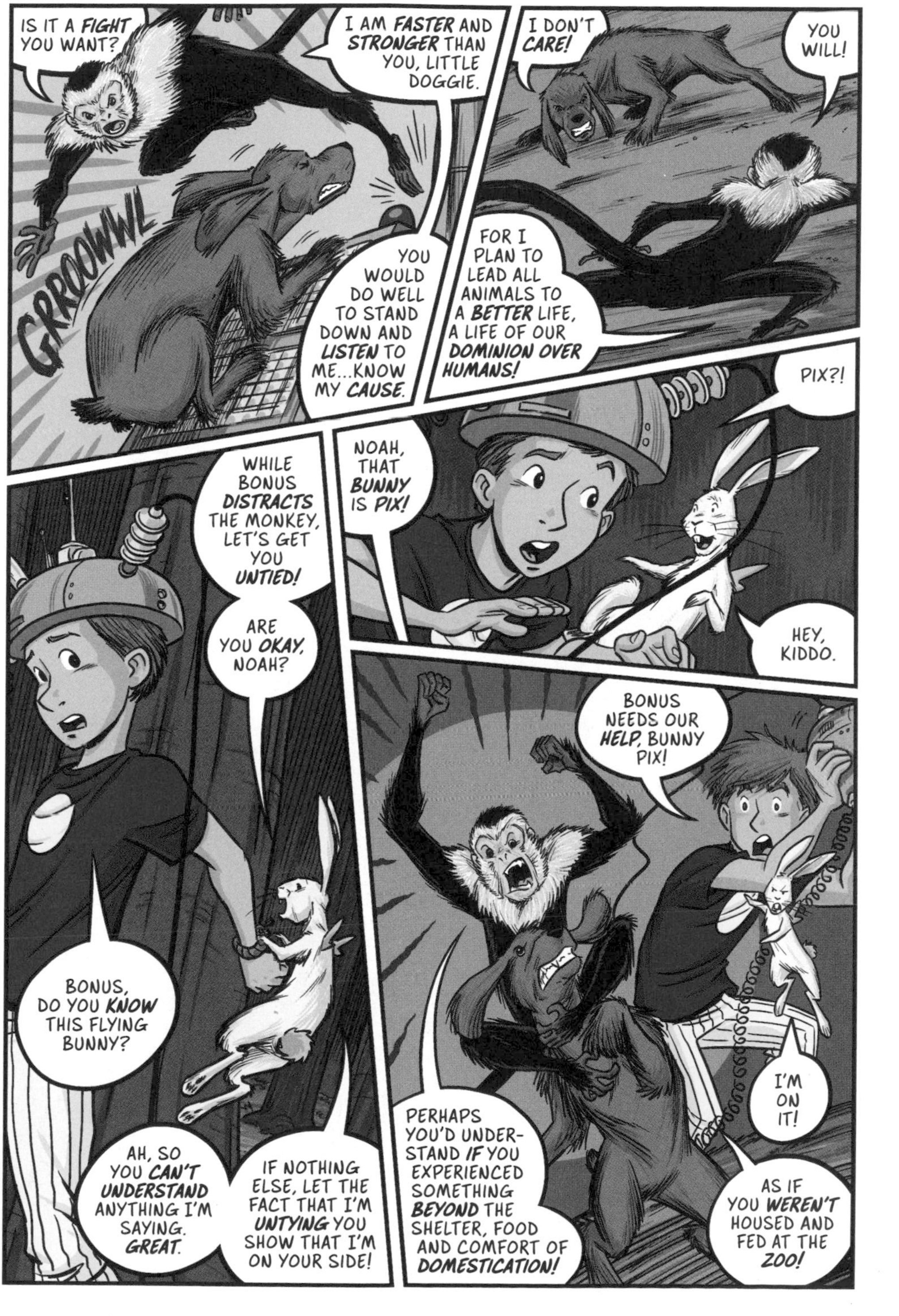

IS IT A FIGHT YOU WANT?
I AM FASTER AND STRONGER THAN YOU, LITTLE DOGGIE.
GRROWWL
YOU WOULD DO WELL TO STAND DOWN AND LISTEN TO ME...KNOW MY CAUSE.
I DON'T CARE!
YOU WILL!
FOR I PLAN TO LEAD ALL ANIMALS TO A BETTER LIFE, A LIFE OF OUR DOMINION OVER HUMANS!
WHILE BONUS DISTRACTS THE MONKEY, LET'S GET YOU UNTIED!
ARE YOU OKAY, NOAH?
BONUS, DO YOU KNOW THIS FLYING BUNNY?
AH, SO YOU CAN'T UNDERSTAND ANYTHING I'M SAYING. GREAT.
IF NOTHING ELSE, LET THE FACT THAT I'M UNTYING YOU SHOW THAT I'M ON YOUR SIDE!
PIX?!
NOAH, THAT BUNNY IS PIX!
HEY, KIDDO.
BONUS NEEDS OUR HELP, BUNNY PIX!
I'M ON IT!
PERHAPS YOU'D UNDERSTAND IF YOU EXPERIENCED SOMETHING BEYOND THE SHELTER, FOOD AND COMFORT OF DOMESTICATION!
AS IF YOU WEREN'T HOUSED AND FED AT THE ZOO!

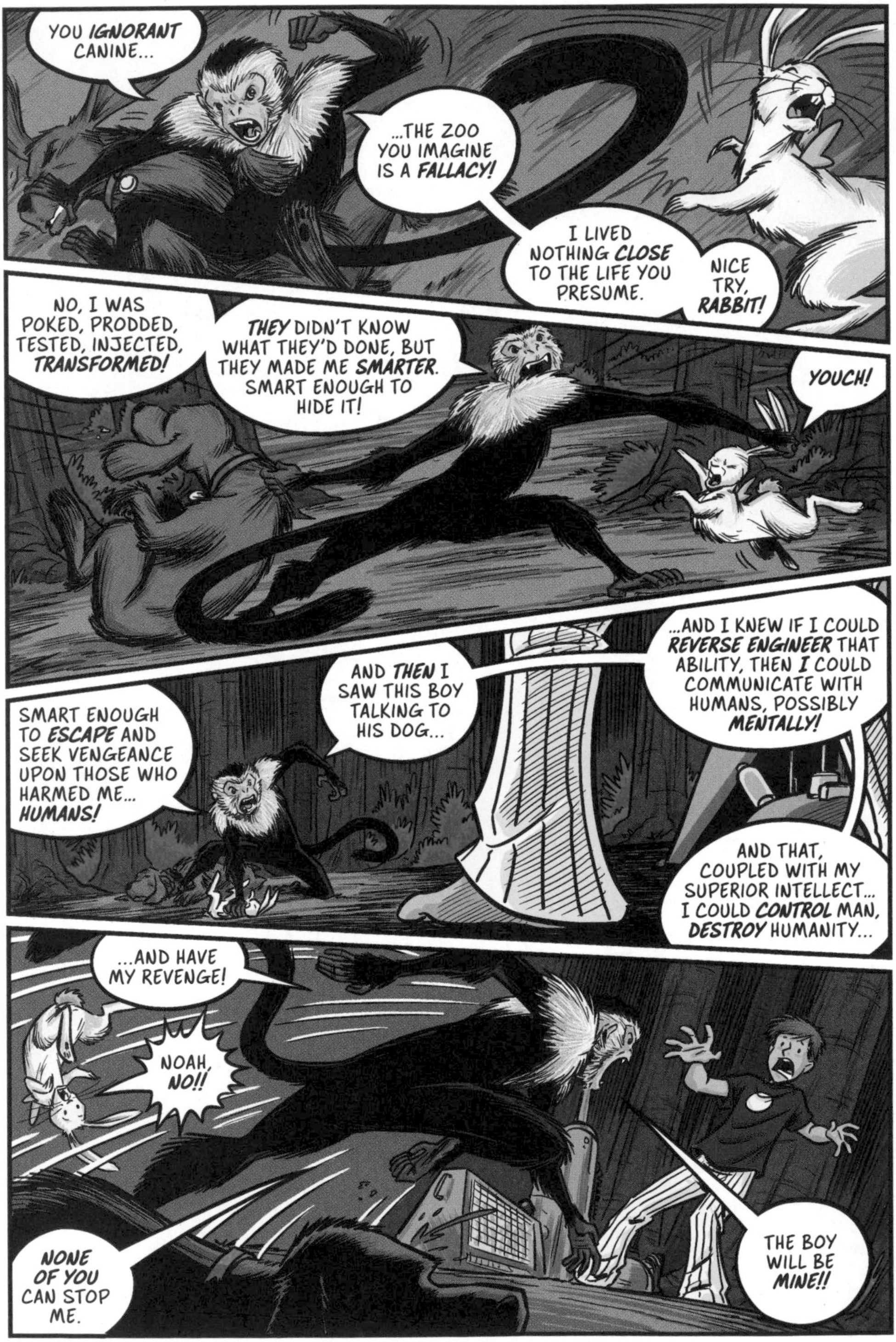
YOU IGNORANT CANINE...
...THE ZOO YOU IMAGINE IS A FALLACY!
I LIVED NOTHING CLOSE TO THE LIFE YOU PRESUME.
NICE TRY, RABBIT!
NO, I WAS POKED, PRODDED, TESTED, INJECTED, TRANSFORMED!
THEY DIDN'T KNOW WHAT THEY'D DONE, BUT THEY MADE ME SMARTER. SMART ENOUGH TO HIDE IT!
YOUCH!
SMART ENOUGH TO ESCAPE AND SEEK VENGEANCE UPON THOSE WHO HARMED ME... HUMANS!
AND THEN I SAW THIS BOY TALKING TO HIS DOG...
...AND I KNEW IF I COULD REVERSE ENGINEER THAT ABILITY, THEN I COULD COMMUNICATE WITH HUMANS, POSSIBLY MENTALLY!
AND THAT, COUPLED WITH MY SUPERIOR INTELLECT... I COULD CONTROL MAN, DESTROY HUMANITY...
...AND HAVE MY REVENGE!
NOAH, NO!!
NONE OF YOU CAN STOP ME.
THE BOY WILL BE MINE!!

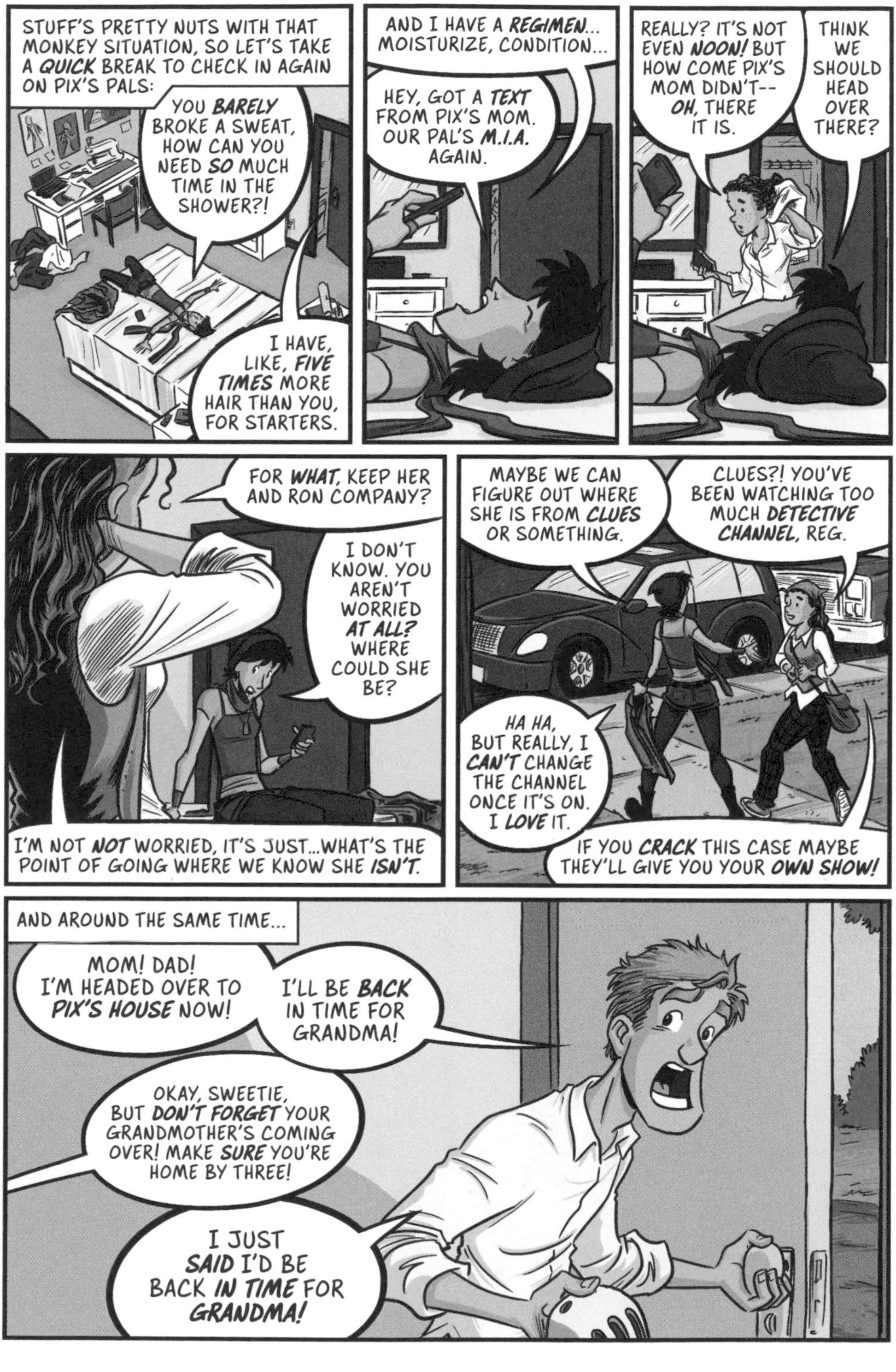
STUFF'S PRETTY NUTS WITH THAT MONKEY SITUATION, SO LET'S TAKE A QUICK BREAK TO CHECK IN AGAIN ON PIX'S PALS:
YOU BARELY BROKE A SWEAT, HOW CAN YOU NEED SO MUCH TIME IN THE SHOWER?!
I HAVE, LIKE, FIVE TIMES MORE HAIR THAN YOU, FOR STARTERS.
AND I HAVE A REGIMEN... MOISTURIZE, CONDITION...
HEY, GOT A TEXT FROM PIX'S MOM. OUR PAL'S M.I.A. AGAIN.
REALLY? IT'S NOT EVEN NOON! BUT HOW COME PIX'S MOM DIDN'T-- OH, THERE IT IS.
THINK WE SHOULD HEAD OVER THERE?
FOR WHAT, KEEP HER AND RON COMPANY?
I DON'T KNOW. YOU AREN'T WORRIED AT ALL? WHERE COULD SHE BE?
I'M NOT NOT WORRIED, IT'S JUST...WHAT'S THE POINT OF GOING WHERE WE KNOW SHE ISN'T.
MAYBE WE CAN FIGURE OUT WHERE SHE IS FROM CLUES OR SOMETHING.
CLUES?! YOU'VE BEEN WATCHING TOO MUCH DETECTIVE CHANNEL, REG.
HA HA, BUT REALLY, I CAN'T CHANGE THE CHANNEL ONCE IT'S ON. I LOVE IT.
IF YOU CRACK THIS CASE MAYBE THEY'LL GIVE YOU YOUR OWN SHOW!
AND AROUND THE SAME TIME...
MOM! DAD! I'M HEADED OVER TO PIX'S HOUSE NOW!
I'LL BE BACK IN TIME FOR GRANDMA!
OKAY, SWEETIE, BUT DON'T FORGET YOUR GRANDMOTHER'S COMING OVER! MAKE SURE YOU'RE HOME BY THREE!
I JUST SAID I'D BE BACK IN TIME FOR GRANDMA!

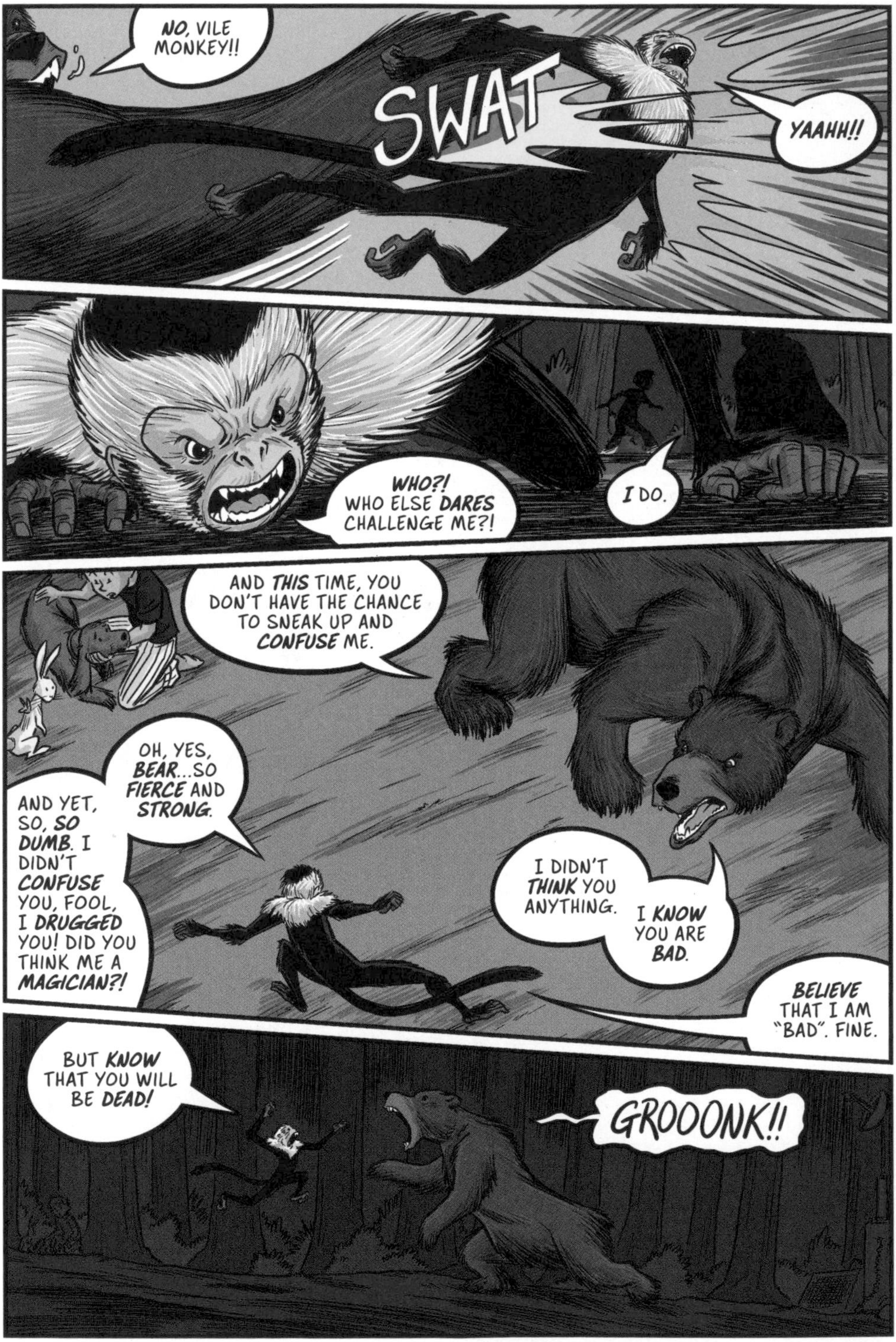
NO, VILE MONKEY!!
SWAT
YAAHH!!
WHO?! WHO ELSE DARES CHALLENGE ME?!
I DO.
AND THIS TIME, YOU DON'T HAVE THE CHANCE TO SNEAK UP AND CONFUSE ME.
OH, YES, BEAR...SO FIERCE AND STRONG.
AND YET, SO, SO DUMB. I DIDN'T CONFUSE YOU, FOOL, I DRUGGED YOU! DID YOU THINK ME A MAGICIAN?!
I DIDN'T THINK YOU ANYTHING.
I KNOW YOU ARE BAD.
BELIEVE THAT I AM "BAD". FINE.
BUT KNOW THAT YOU WILL BE DEAD!
GROOONK!!

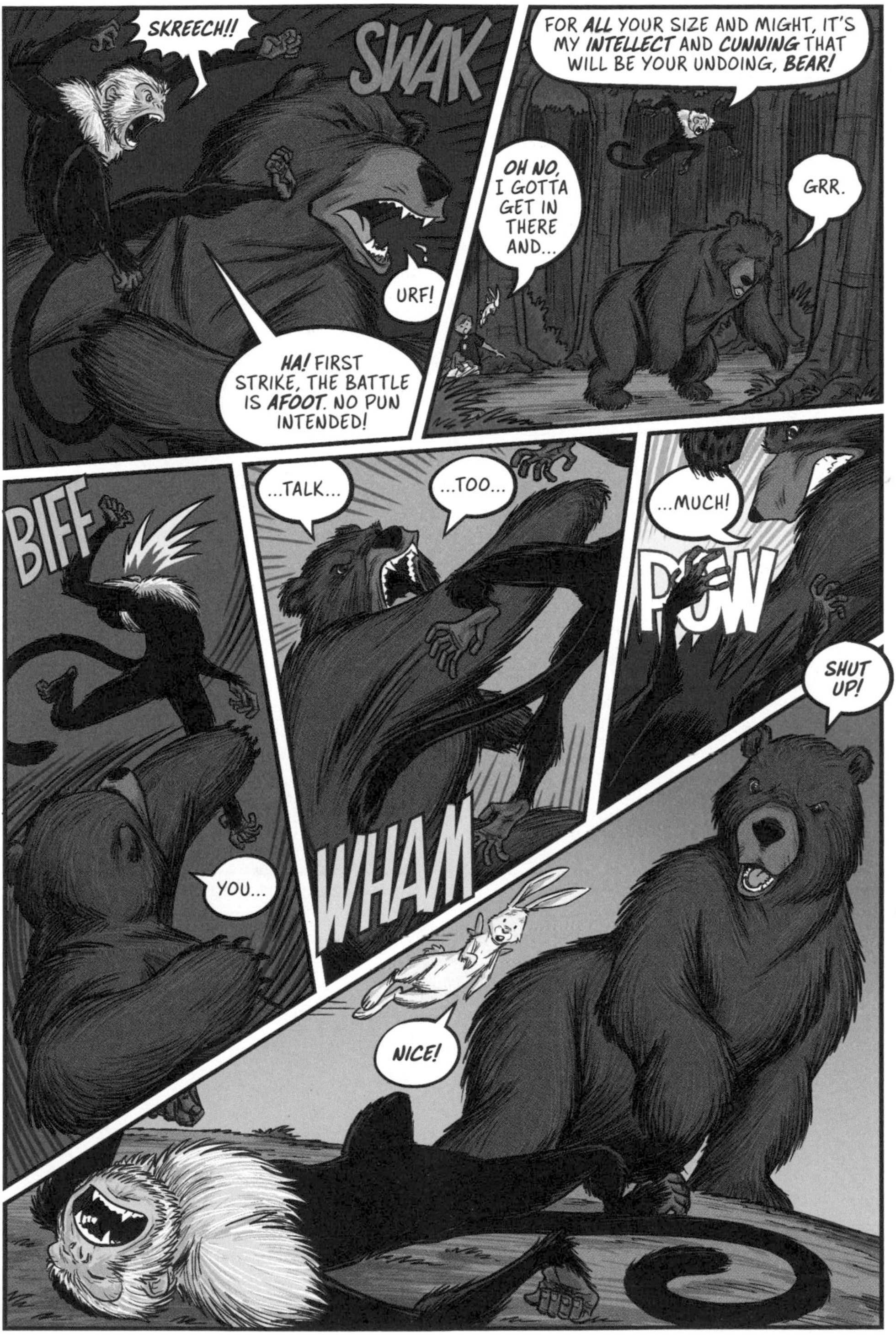
SKREECH!!
SWAK
URF!
HA! FIRST STRIKE, THE BATTLE IS AFOOT. NO PUN INTENDED!
FOR ALL YOUR SIZE AND MIGHT, IT'S MY INTELLECT AND CUNNING THAT WILL BE YOUR UNDOING, BEAR!
OH NO, I GOTTA GET IN THERE AND...
GRR.
BIFF
YOU...
...TALK...
...TOO...
WHAM
...MUCH!
POW
SHUT UP!
NICE!

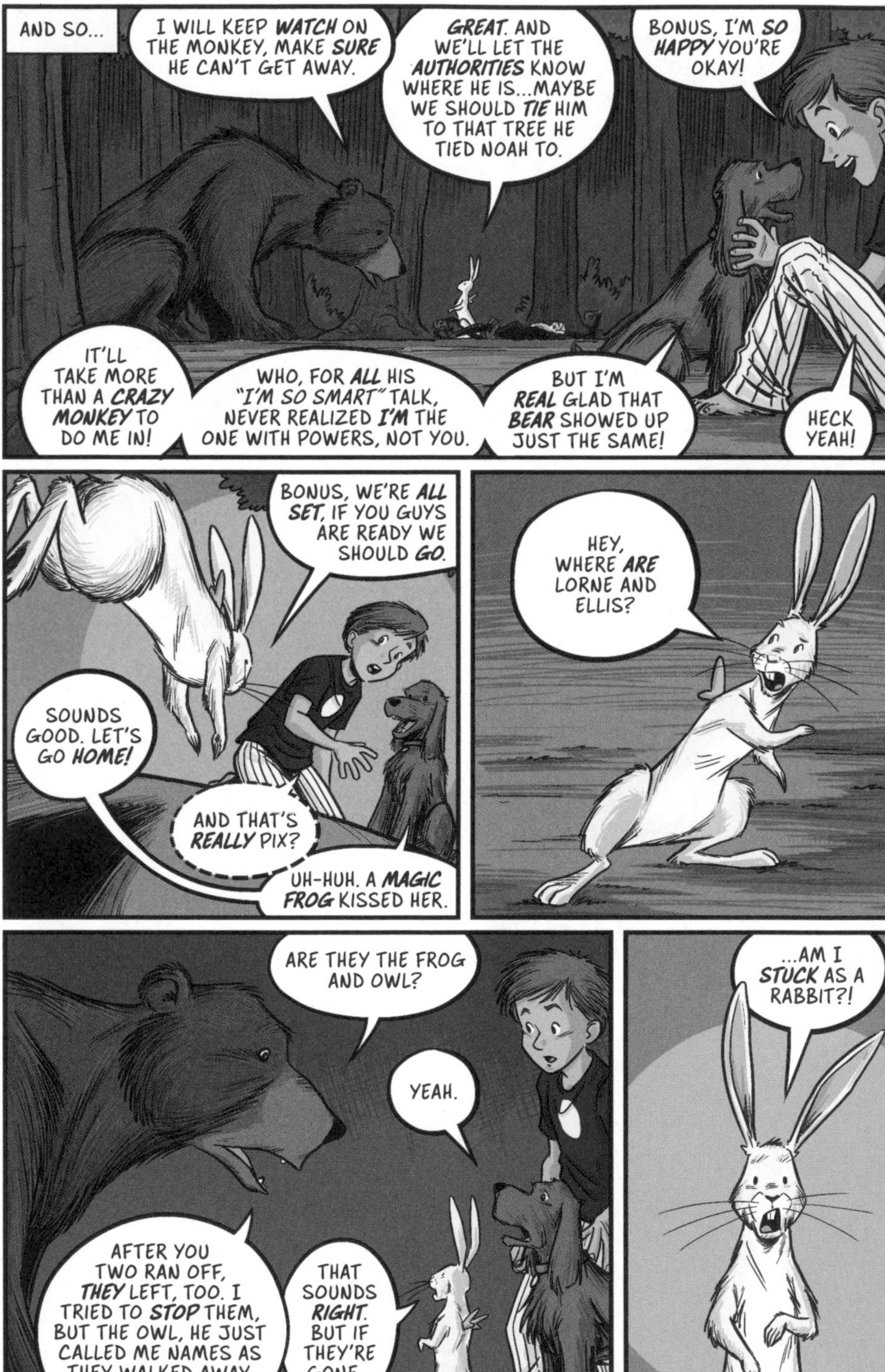
AND SO...
I WILL KEEP WATCH ON THE MONKEY, MAKE SURE HE CAN'T GET AWAY.
GREAT. AND WE'LL LET THE AUTHORITIES KNOW WHERE HE IS...MAYBE WE SHOULD TIE HIM TO THAT TREE HE TIED NOAH TO.
BONUS, I'M SO HAPPY YOU'RE OKAY!
IT'LL TAKE MORE THAN A CRAZY MONKEY TO DO ME IN!
WHO, FOR ALL HIS "I'M SO SMART" TALK, NEVER REALIZED I'M THE ONE WITH POWERS, NOT YOU.
BUT I'M REAL GLAD THAT BEAR SHOWED UP JUST THE SAME!
HECK YEAH!
BONUS, WE'RE ALL SET, IF YOU GUYS ARE READY WE SHOULD GO.
SOUNDS GOOD. LET'S GO HOME!
AND THAT'S REALLY PIX?
UH-HUH. A MAGIC FROG KISSED HER.
HEY, WHERE ARE LORNE AND ELLIS?
ARE THEY THE FROG AND OWL?
YEAH.
AFTER YOU TWO RAN OFF, THEY LEFT, TOO. I TRIED TO STOP THEM, BUT THE OWL, HE JUST CALLED ME NAMES AS THEY WALKED AWAY.
THAT SOUNDS RIGHT. BUT IF THEY'RE GONE...
...AM I STUCK AS A RABBIT?!

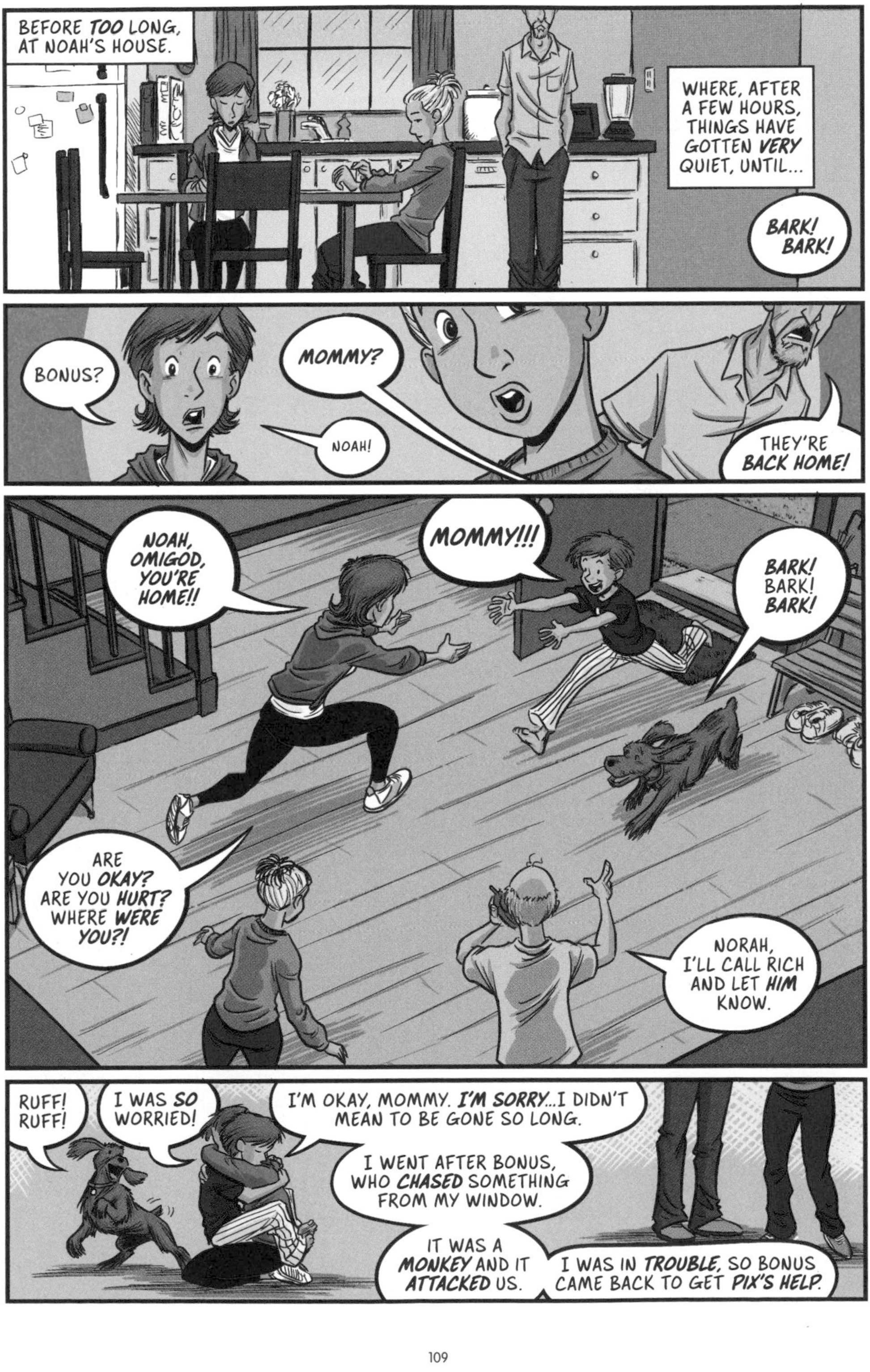
BEFORE TOO LONG, AT NOAH'S HOUSE.
WHERE, AFTER A FEW HOURS, THINGS HAVE GOTTEN VERY QUIET, UNTIL...
BARK! BARK!
BONUS?
MOMMY?
NOAH!
THEY'RE BACK HOME!
NOAH, OMIGOD, YOU'RE HOME!!
MOMMY!!!
BARK! BARK! BARK!
ARE YOU OKAY? ARE YOU HURT? WHERE WERE YOU?!
NORAH, I'LL CALL RICH AND LET HIM KNOW.
RUFF! RUFF!
I WAS SO WORRIED!
I'M OKAY, MOMMY. I'M SORRY...I DIDN'T MEAN TO BE GONE SO LONG.
I WENT AFTER BONUS, WHO CHASED SOMETHING FROM MY WINDOW.
IT WAS A MONKEY AND IT ATTACKED US.
I WAS IN TROUBLE, SO BONUS CAME BACK TO GET PIX'S HELP.

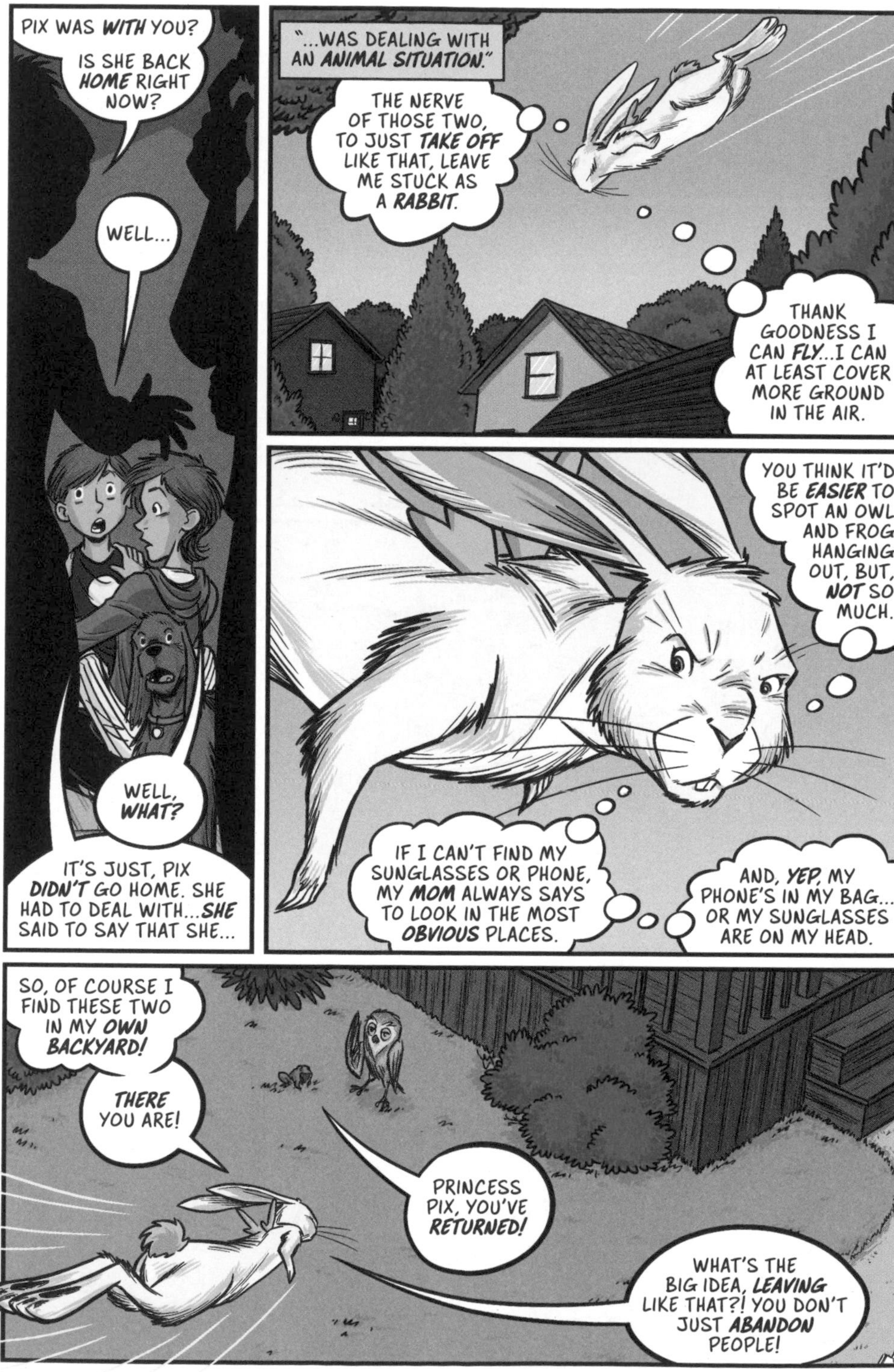
PIX WAS WITH YOU?
IS SHE BACK HOME RIGHT NOW?
WELL...
WELL, WHAT?
IT'S JUST, PIX DIDN'T GO HOME. SHE HAD TO DEAL WITH...SHE SAID TO SAY THAT SHE...
"...WAS DEALING WITH AN ANIMAL SITUATION."
THE NERVE OF THOSE TWO, TO JUST TAKE OFF LIKE THAT, LEAVE ME STUCK AS A RABBIT.
THANK GOODNESS I CAN FLY...I CAN AT LEAST COVER MORE GROUND IN THE AIR.
YOU THINK IT'D BE EASIER TO SPOT AN OWL AND FROG HANGING OUT, BUT, NOT SO MUCH.
IF I CAN'T FIND MY SUNGLASSES OR PHONE, MY MOM ALWAYS SAYS TO LOOK IN THE MOST OBVIOUS PLACES.
AND, YEP, MY PHONE'S IN MY BAG... OR MY SUNGLASSES ARE ON MY HEAD.
SO, OF COURSE I FIND THESE TWO IN MY OWN BACKYARD!
THERE YOU ARE!
PRINCESS PIX, YOU'VE RETURNED!
WHAT'S THE BIG IDEA, LEAVING LIKE THAT?! YOU DON'T JUST ABANDON PEOPLE!

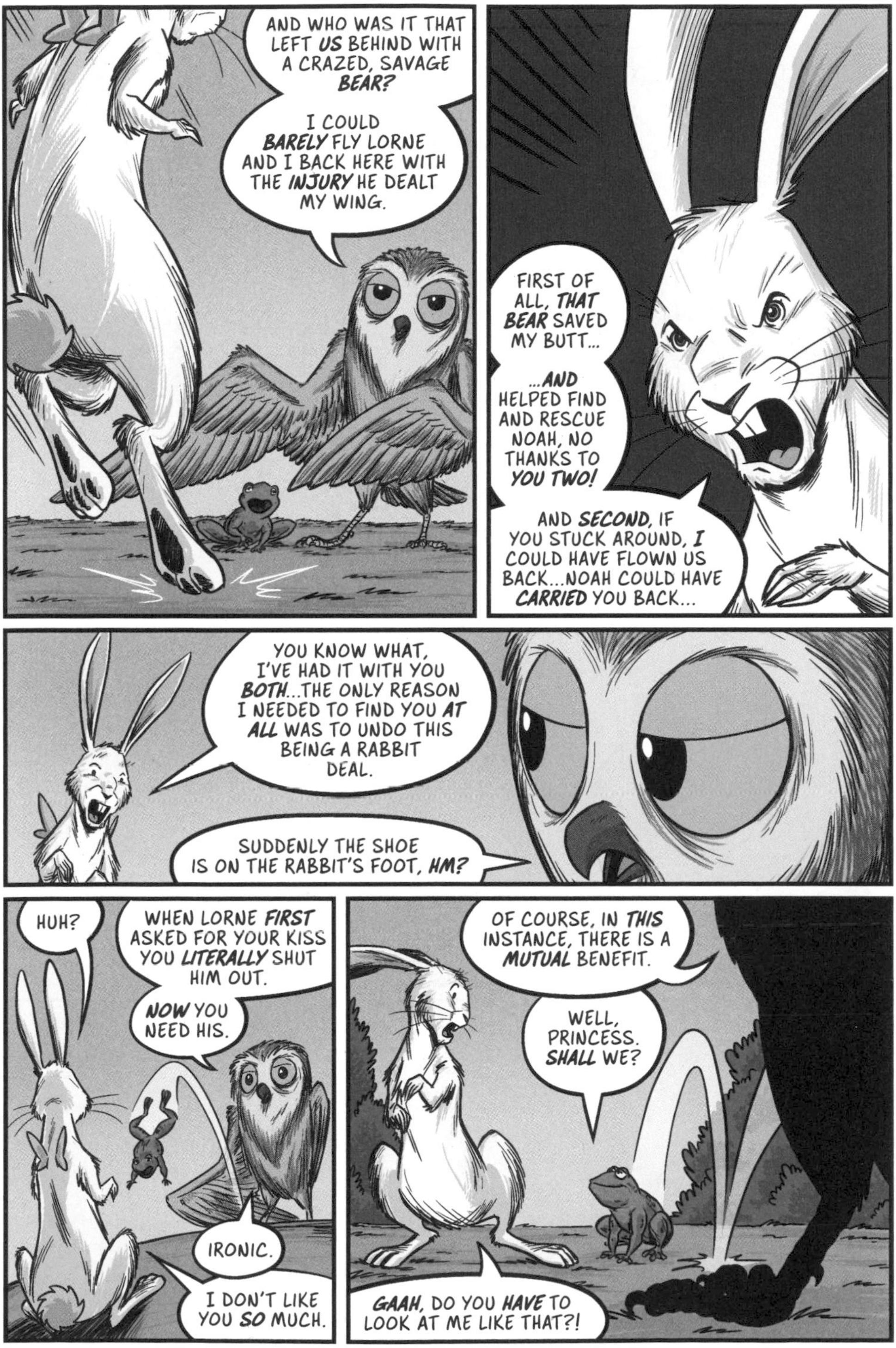
AND WHO WAS IT THAT LEFT US BEHIND WITH A CRAZED, SAVAGE BEAR?
I COULD BARELY FLY LORNE AND I BACK HERE WITH THE INJURY HE DEALT MY WING.
FIRST OF ALL, THAT BEAR SAVED MY BUTT...
...AND HELPED FIND AND RESCUE NOAH, NO THANKS TO YOU TWO!
AND SECOND, IF YOU STUCK AROUND, I COULD HAVE FLOWN US BACK...NOAH COULD HAVE CARRIED YOU BACK...
YOU KNOW WHAT, I'VE HAD IT WITH YOU BOTH...THE ONLY REASON I NEEDED TO FIND YOU AT ALL WAS TO UNDO THIS BEING A RABBIT DEAL.
SUDDENLY THE SHOE IS ON THE RABBIT'S FOOT, HM?
HUH?
WHEN LORNE FIRST ASKED FOR YOUR KISS YOU LITERALLY SHUT HIM OUT.
NOW YOU NEED HIS.
IRONIC.
I DON'T LIKE YOU SO MUCH.
OF COURSE, IN THIS INSTANCE, THERE IS A MUTUAL BENEFIT.
WELL, PRINCESS. SHALL WE?
GAAH, DO YOU HAVE TO LOOK AT ME LIKE THAT?!

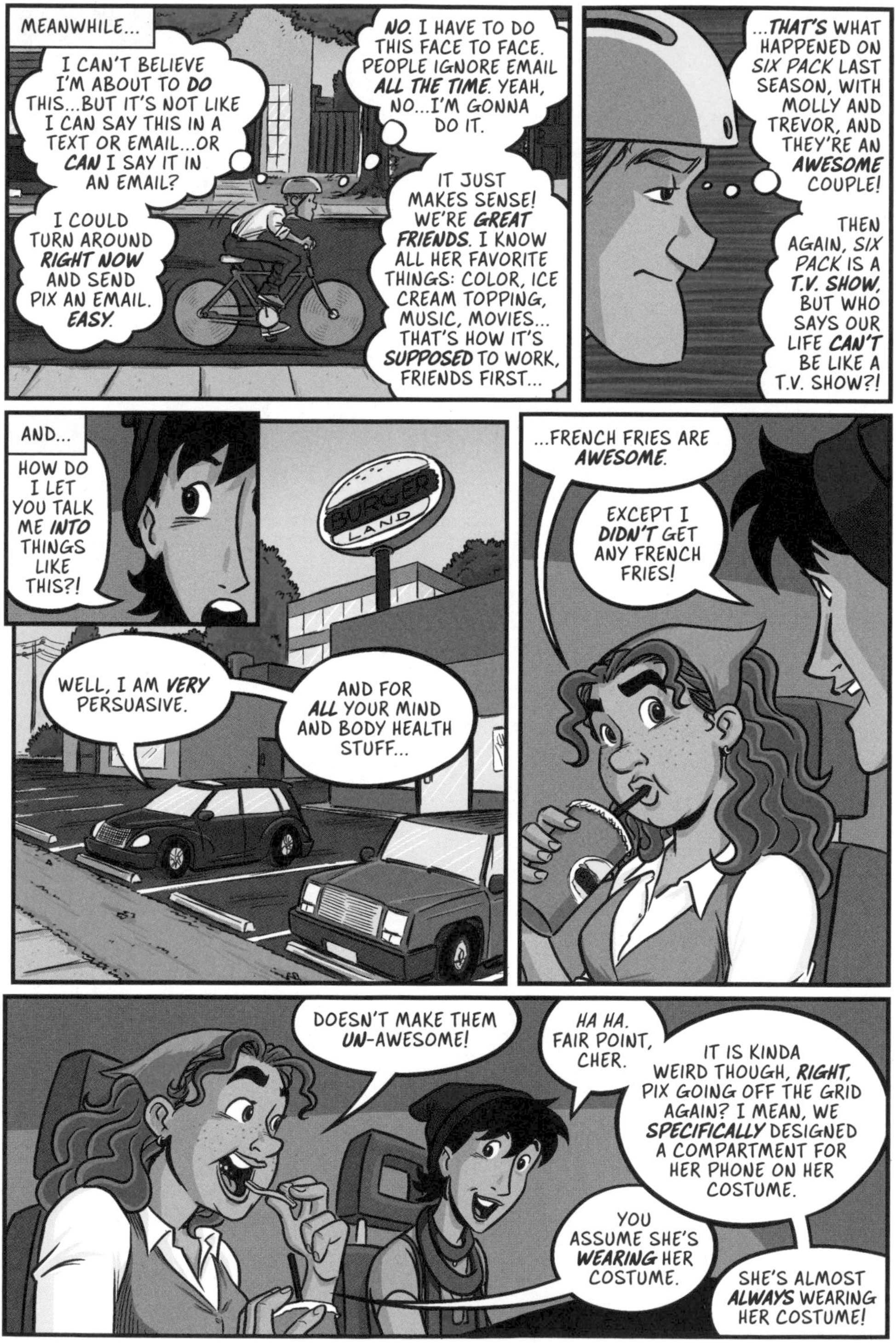
MEANWHILE...
I CAN'T BELIEVE I'M ABOUT TO DO THIS...BUT IT'S NOT LIKE I CAN SAY THIS IN A TEXT OR EMAIL...OR CAN I SAY IT IN AN EMAIL?
I COULD TURN AROUND RIGHT NOW AND SEND PIX AN EMAIL. EASY.
NO. I HAVE TO DO THIS FACE TO FACE. PEOPLE IGNORE EMAIL ALL THE TIME. YEAH, NO...I'M GONNA DO IT.
IT JUST MAKES SENSE! WE'RE GREAT FRIENDS. I KNOW ALL HER FAVORITE THINGS: COLOR, ICE CREAM TOPPING, MUSIC, MOVIES... THAT'S HOW IT'S SUPPOSED TO WORK, FRIENDS FIRST...
...THAT'S WHAT HAPPENED ON SIX PACK LAST SEASON, WITH MOLLY AND TREVOR, AND THEY'RE AN AWESOME COUPLE!
THEN AGAIN, SIX PACK IS A T.V. SHOW, BUT WHO SAYS OUR LIFE CAN'T BE LIKE A T.V. SHOW?!
AND...
HOW DO I LET YOU TALK ME INTO THINGS LIKE THIS?!
BURGER LAND
WELL, I AM VERY PERSUASIVE.
AND FOR ALL YOUR MIND AND BODY HEALTH STUFF...
...FRENCH FRIES ARE AWESOME.
EXCEPT I DIDN'T GET ANY FRENCH FRIES!
DOESN'T MAKE THEM UN-AWESOME!
HA HA. FAIR POINT, CHER.
IT IS KINDA WEIRD THOUGH, RIGHT, PIX GOING OFF THE GRID AGAIN? I MEAN, WE SPECIFICALLY DESIGNED A COMPARTMENT FOR HER PHONE ON HER COSTUME.
YOU ASSUME SHE'S WEARING HER COSTUME.
SHE'S ALMOST ALWAYS WEARING HER COSTUME!

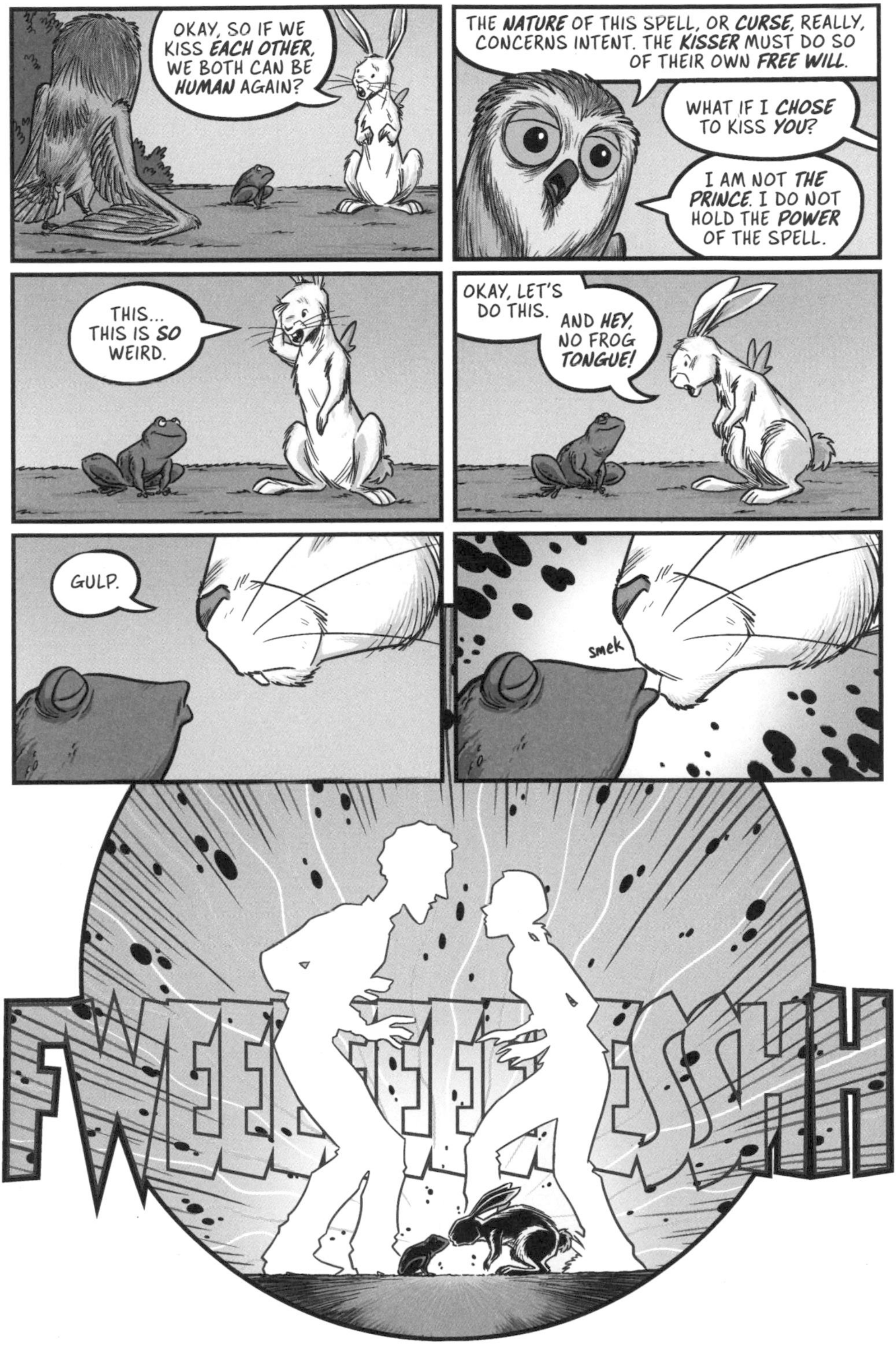
OKAY, SO IF WE KISS EACH OTHER, WE BOTH CAN BE HUMAN AGAIN?
THE NATURE OF THIS SPELL, OR CURSE, REALLY, CONCERNS INTENT. THE KISSER MUST DO SO OF THEIR OWN FREE WILL.
WHAT IF I CHOSE TO KISS YOU?
I AM NOT THE PRINCE. I DO NOT HOLD THE POWER OF THE SPELL.
THIS... THIS IS SO WEIRD.
OKAY, LET'S DO THIS.
AND HEY, NO FROG TONGUE!
GULP.
smek
FWEEEEEESSHH

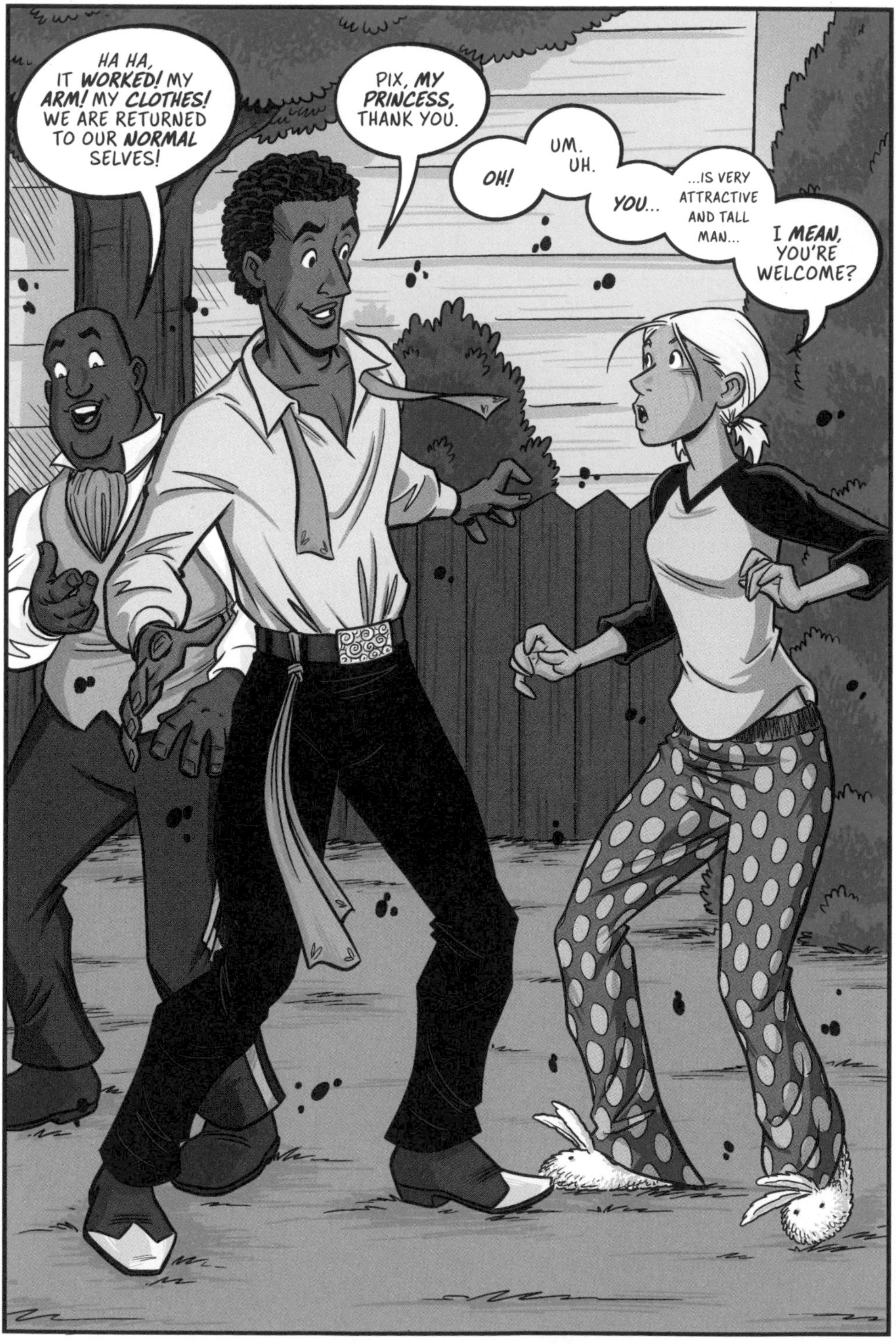
HA HA, IT WORKED! MY ARM! MY CLOTHES! WE ARE RETURNED TO OUR NORMAL SELVES!
PIX, MY PRINCESS, THANK YOU.
OH!
UM. UH.
YOU...
...IS VERY ATTRACTIVE AND TALL MAN...
I MEAN, YOU'RE WELCOME?

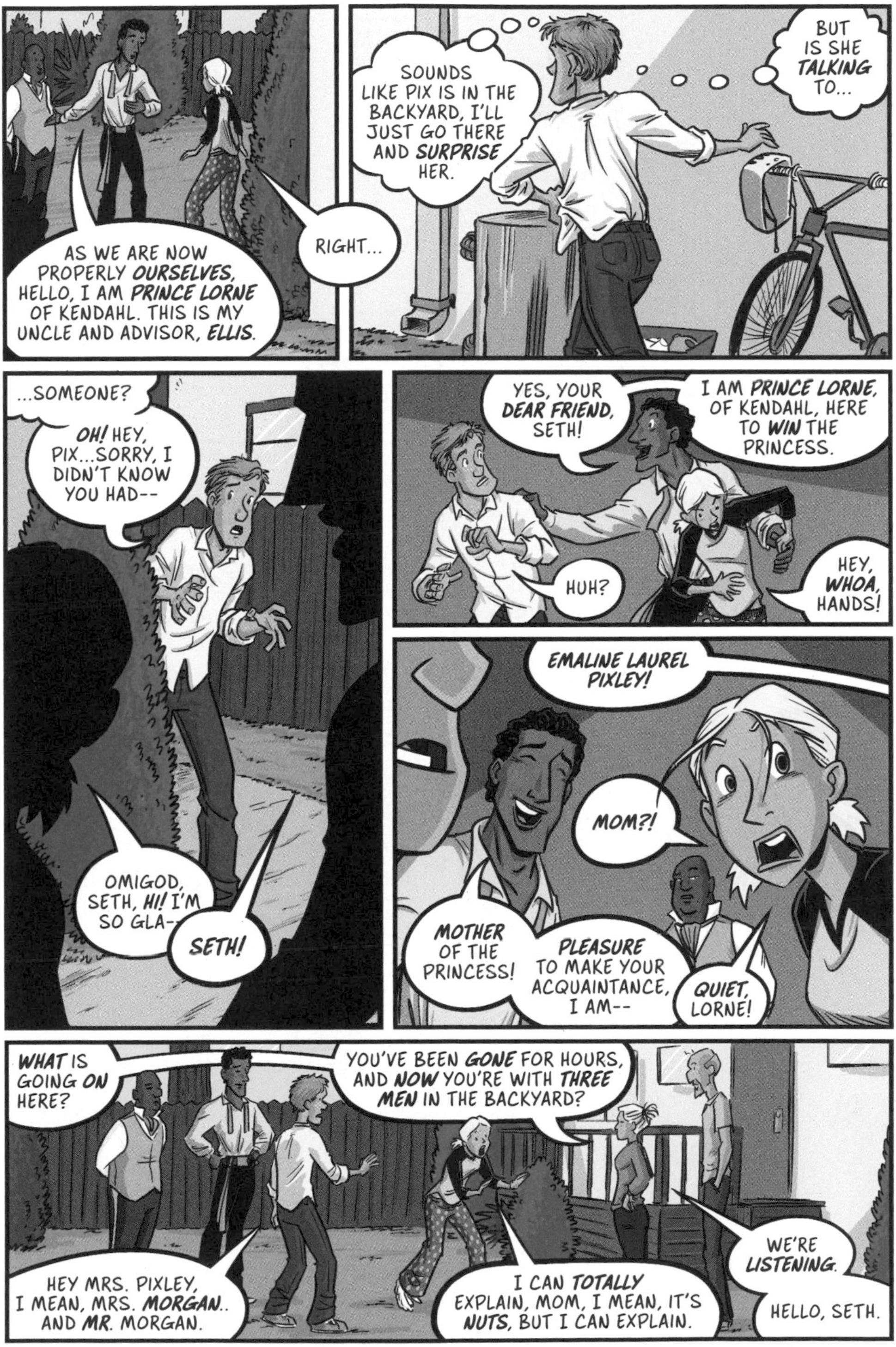
AS WE ARE NOW PROPERLY OURSELVES, HELLO, I AM PRINCE LORNE OF KENDAHL. THIS IS MY UNCLE AND ADVISOR, ELLIS.
RIGHT...
SOUNDS LIKE PIX IS IN THE BACKYARD, I'LL JUST GO THERE AND SURPRISE HER.
BUT IS SHE TALKING TO...
...SOMEONE?
OH! HEY, PIX...SORRY, I DIDN'T KNOW YOU HAD--
OMIGOD, SETH, HI! I'M SO GLA--
SETH!
YES, YOUR DEAR FRIEND, SETH!
I AM PRINCE LORNE, OF KENDAHL, HERE TO WIN THE PRINCESS.
HUH?
HEY, WHOA, HANDS!
EMALINE LAUREL PIXLEY!
MOM?!
MOTHER OF THE PRINCESS!
PLEASURE TO MAKE YOUR ACQUAINTANCE, I AM--
QUIET, LORNE!
WHAT IS GOING ON HERE?
YOU'VE BEEN GONE FOR HOURS, AND NOW YOU'RE WITH THREE MEN IN THE BACKYARD?
HEY MRS. PIXLEY, I MEAN, MRS. MORGAN.. AND MR. MORGAN.
I CAN TOTALLY EXPLAIN, MOM, I MEAN, IT'S NUTS, BUT I CAN EXPLAIN.
WE'RE LISTENING.
HELLO, SETH.

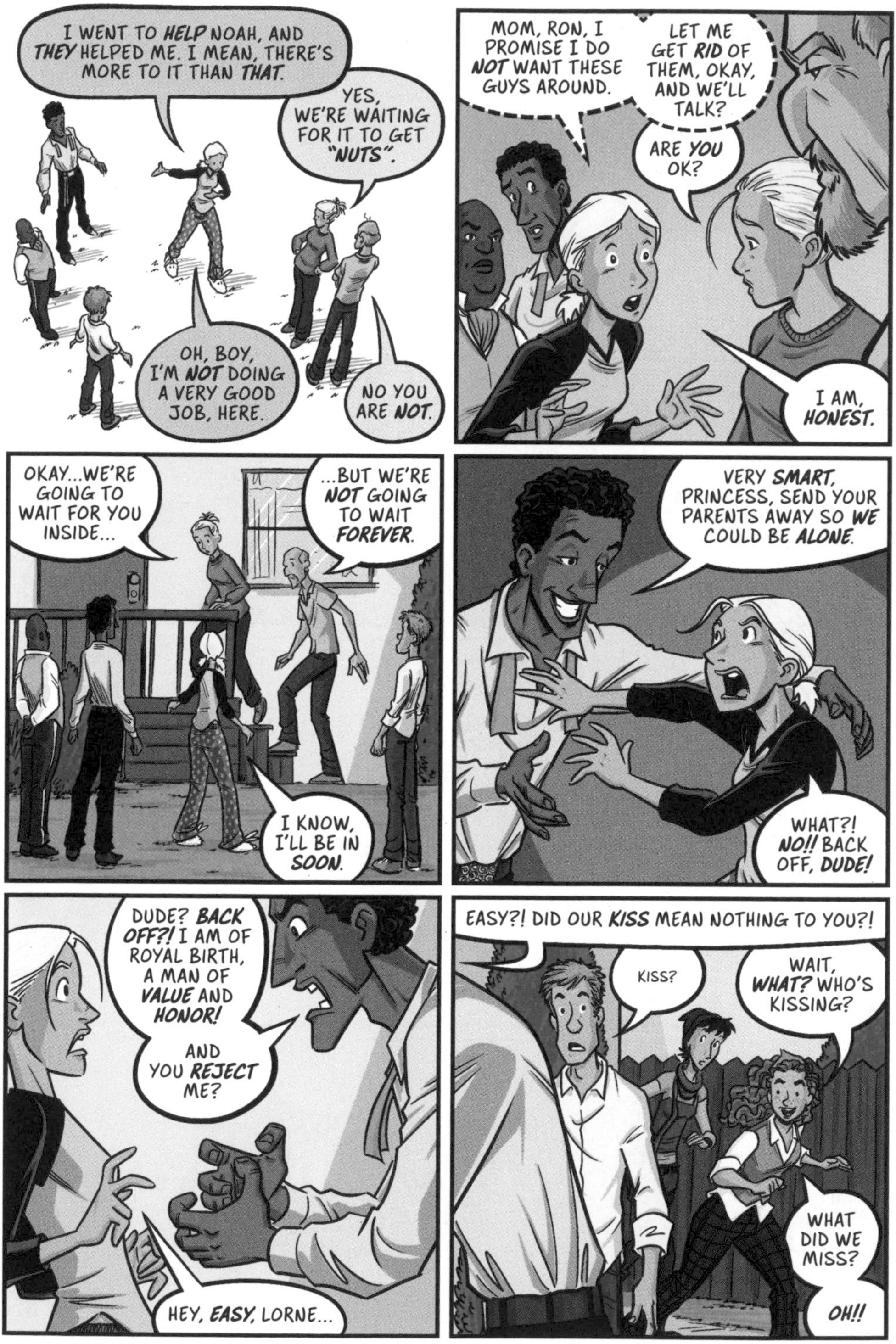
I WENT TO HELP NOAH, AND THEY HELPED ME. I MEAN, THERE'S MORE TO IT THAN THAT.
YES, WE'RE WAITING FOR IT TO GET "NUTS".
OH, BOY, I'M NOT DOING A VERY GOOD JOB, HERE.
NO YOU ARE NOT.
MOM, RON, I PROMISE I DO NOT WANT THESE GUYS AROUND.
LET ME GET RID OF THEM, OKAY, AND WE'LL TALK?
ARE YOU OK?
I AM, HONEST.
OKAY...WE'RE GOING TO WAIT FOR YOU INSIDE...
...BUT WE'RE NOT GOING TO WAIT FOREVER.
I KNOW, I'LL BE IN SOON.
VERY SMART, PRINCESS, SEND YOUR PARENTS AWAY SO WE COULD BE ALONE.
WHAT?! NO!! BACK OFF, DUDE!
DUDE? BACK OFF?! I AM OF ROYAL BIRTH, A MAN OF VALUE AND HONOR!
AND YOU REJECT ME?
HEY, EASY, LORNE...
EASY?! DID OUR KISS MEAN NOTHING TO YOU?!
KISS?
WAIT, WHAT? WHO'S KISSING?
WHAT DID WE MISS?
OH!!

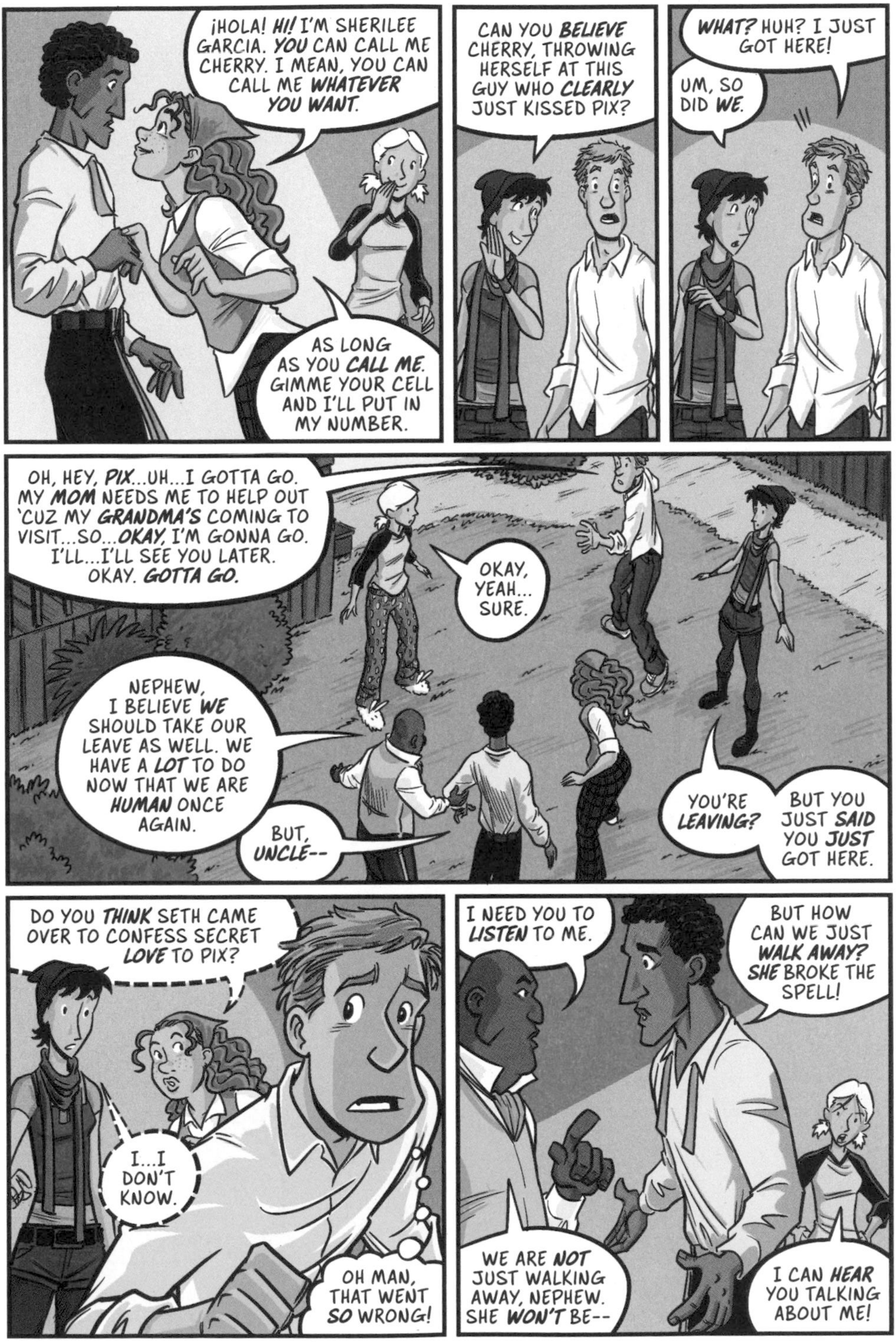
¡HOLA! HI! I'M SHERILEE GARCIA. YOU CAN CALL ME CHERRY. I MEAN, YOU CAN CALL ME WHATEVER YOU WANT.
AS LONG AS YOU CALL ME. GIMME YOUR CELL AND I'LL PUT IN MY NUMBER.
CAN YOU BELIEVE CHERRY, THROWING HERSELF AT THIS GUY WHO CLEARLY JUST KISSED PIX?
WHAT? HUH? I JUST GOT HERE!
UM, SO DID WE.
OH, HEY, PIX...UH...I GOTTA GO. MY MOM NEEDS ME TO HELP OUT 'CUZ MY GRANDMA'S COMING TO VISIT...SO...OKAY, I'M GONNA GO. I'LL...I'LL SEE YOU LATER. OKAY. GOTTA GO.
OKAY, YEAH... SURE.
NEPHEW, I BELIEVE WE SHOULD TAKE OUR LEAVE AS WELL. WE HAVE A LOT TO DO NOW THAT WE ARE HUMAN ONCE AGAIN.
BUT, UNCLE--
YOU'RE LEAVING?
BUT YOU JUST SAID YOU JUST GOT HERE.
DO YOU THINK SETH CAME OVER TO CONFESS SECRET LOVE TO PIX?
I...I DON'T KNOW.
OH MAN, THAT WENT SO WRONG!
I NEED YOU TO LISTEN TO ME.
BUT HOW CAN WE JUST WALK AWAY? SHE BROKE THE SPELL!
WE ARE NOT JUST WALKING AWAY, NEPHEW. SHE WON'T BE--
I CAN HEAR YOU TALKING ABOUT ME!

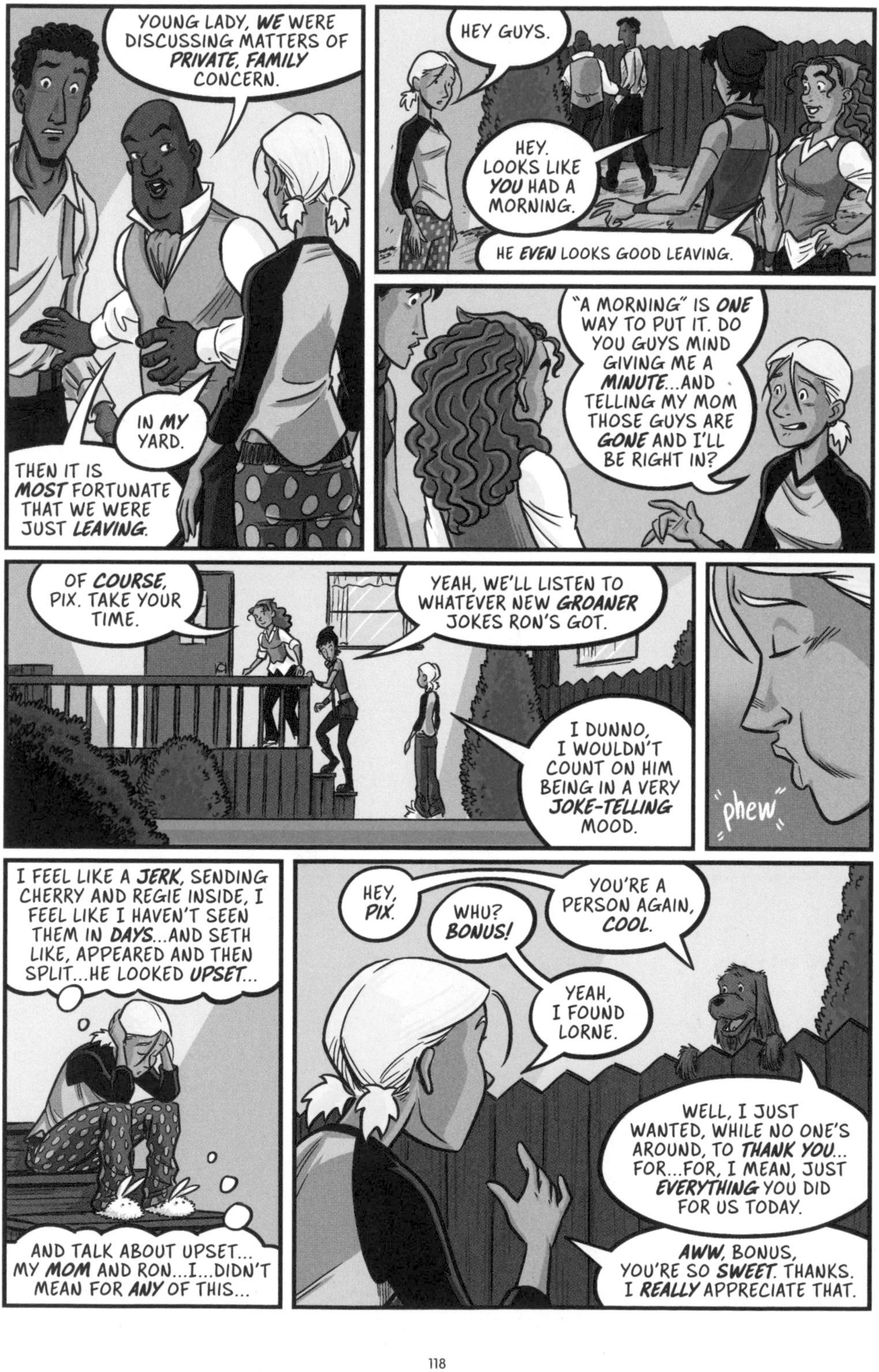
YOUNG LADY, WE WERE DISCUSSING MATTERS OF PRIVATE, FAMILY CONCERN.
IN MY YARD.
THEN IT IS MOST FORTUNATE THAT WE WERE JUST LEAVING.
HEY GUYS.
HEY. LOOKS LIKE YOU HAD A MORNING.
HE EVEN LOOKS GOOD LEAVING.
"A MORNING" IS ONE WAY TO PUT IT. DO YOU GUYS MIND GIVING ME A MINUTE...AND TELLING MY MOM THOSE GUYS ARE GONE AND I'LL BE RIGHT IN?
OF COURSE, PIX. TAKE YOUR TIME.
YEAH, WE'LL LISTEN TO WHATEVER NEW GROANER JOKES RON'S GOT.
I DUNNO, I WOULDN'T COUNT ON HIM BEING IN A VERY JOKE-TELLING MOOD.
phew
I FEEL LIKE A JERK, SENDING CHERRY AND REGIE INSIDE, I FEEL LIKE I HAVEN'T SEEN THEM IN DAYS...AND SETH LIKE, APPEARED AND THEN SPLIT...HE LOOKED UPSET...
AND TALK ABOUT UPSET... MY MOM AND RON...I...DIDN'T MEAN FOR ANY OF THIS...
HEY, PIX.
WHU? BONUS!
YOU'RE A PERSON AGAIN, COOL.
YEAH, I FOUND LORNE.
WELL, I JUST WANTED, WHILE NO ONE'S AROUND, TO THANK YOU... FOR...FOR, I MEAN, JUST EVERYTHING YOU DID FOR US TODAY.
AWW, BONUS, YOU'RE SO SWEET. THANKS. I REALLY APPRECIATE THAT.

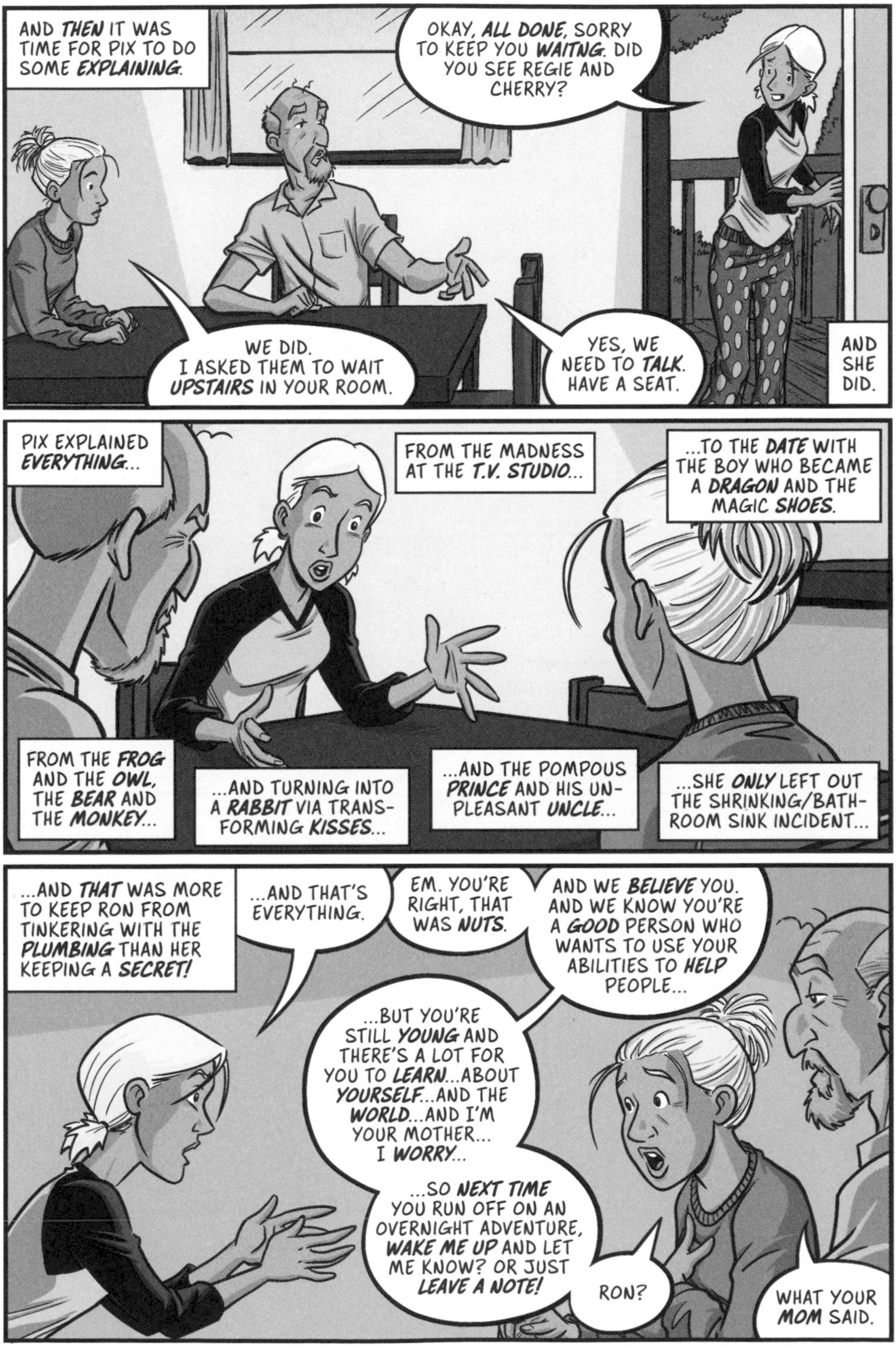
AND *THEN* IT WAS TIME FOR PIX TO DO SOME *EXPLAINING*.
OKAY, *ALL DONE*, SORRY TO KEEP YOU *WAITNG*. DID YOU SEE REGIE AND CHERRY?
WE DID. I ASKED THEM TO WAIT *UPSTAIRS* IN YOUR ROOM.
YES, WE NEED TO *TALK*. HAVE A SEAT.
AND SHE DID.
PIX EXPLAINED *EVERYTHING*...
FROM THE MADNESS AT THE *T.V. STUDIO*...
...TO THE *DATE* WITH THE BOY WHO BECAME A *DRAGON* AND THE MAGIC *SHOES*.
FROM THE *FROG* AND THE *OWL*, THE *BEAR* AND THE *MONKEY*...
...AND TURNING INTO A *RABBIT* VIA TRANSFORMING *KISSES*...
...AND THE POMPOUS *PRINCE* AND HIS UNPLEASANT *UNCLE*...
...SHE *ONLY* LEFT OUT THE SHRINKING/BATHROOM SINK INCIDENT...
...AND *THAT* WAS MORE TO KEEP RON FROM TINKERING WITH THE *PLUMBING* THAN HER KEEPING A *SECRET!*
...AND THAT'S EVERYTHING.
EM. YOU'RE RIGHT, THAT WAS *NUTS*.
AND WE *BELIEVE* YOU. AND WE KNOW YOU'RE A *GOOD* PERSON WHO WANTS TO USE YOUR ABILITIES TO *HELP* PEOPLE...
...BUT YOU'RE STILL *YOUNG* AND THERE'S A LOT FOR YOU TO *LEARN*...ABOUT *YOURSELF*...AND THE *WORLD*...AND I'M YOUR MOTHER... I *WORRY*...
...SO *NEXT TIME* YOU RUN OFF ON AN OVERNIGHT ADVENTURE, *WAKE ME UP* AND LET ME KNOW? OR JUST *LEAVE A NOTE!*
RON?
WHAT YOUR *MOM* SAID.

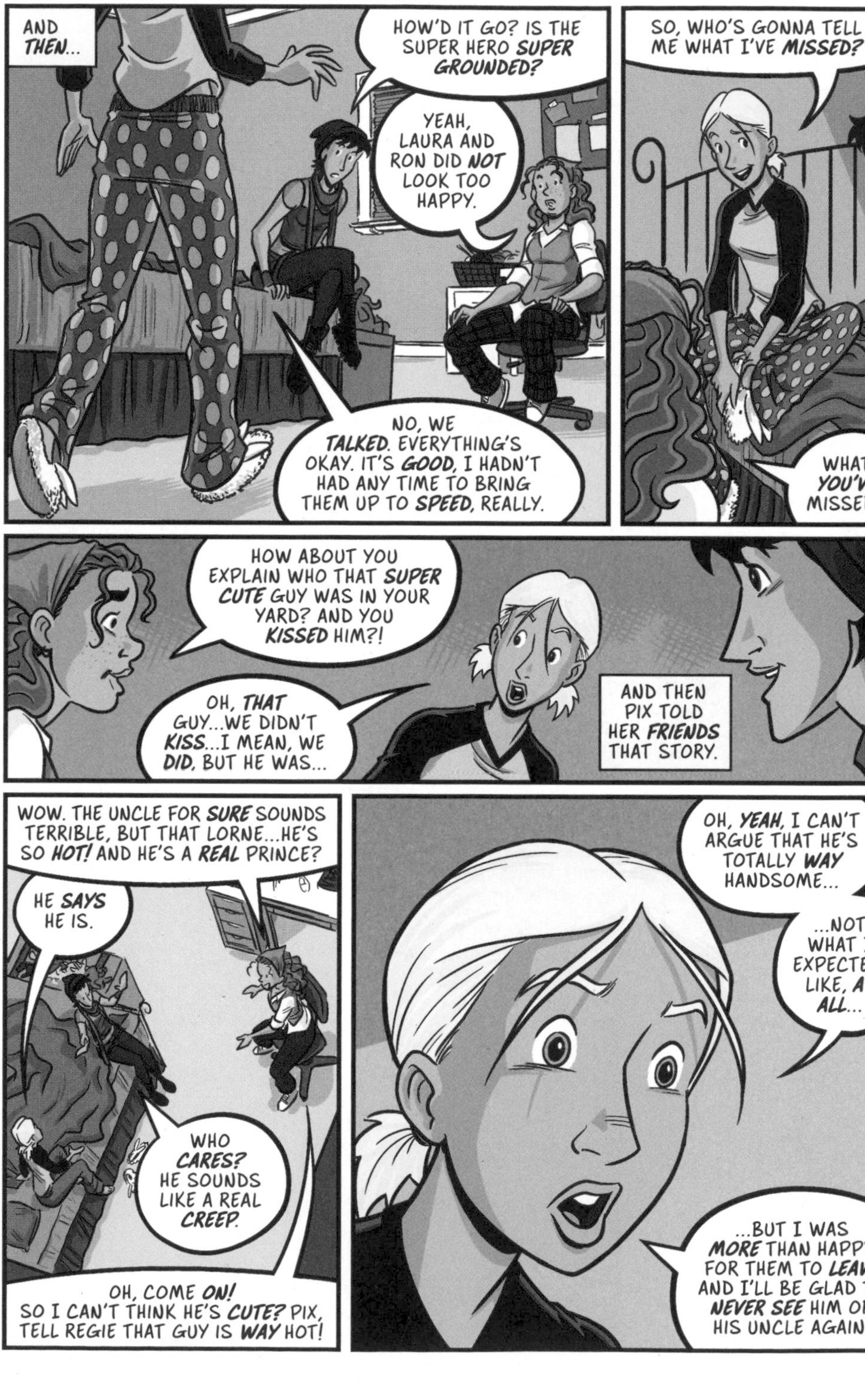
AND THEN...
HOW'D IT GO? IS THE SUPER HERO SUPER GROUNDED?
YEAH, LAURA AND RON DID NOT LOOK TOO HAPPY.
NO, WE TALKED. EVERYTHING'S OKAY. IT'S GOOD, I HADN'T HAD ANY TIME TO BRING THEM UP TO SPEED, REALLY.
SO, WHO'S GONNA TELL ME WHAT I'VE MISSED?
WHAT YOU'VE MISSED?
HOW ABOUT YOU EXPLAIN WHO THAT SUPER CUTE GUY WAS IN YOUR YARD? AND YOU KISSED HIM?!
OH, THAT GUY...WE DIDN'T KISS...I MEAN, WE DID, BUT HE WAS...
AND THEN PIX TOLD HER FRIENDS THAT STORY.
WOW. THE UNCLE FOR SURE SOUNDS TERRIBLE, BUT THAT LORNE...HE'S SO HOT! AND HE'S A REAL PRINCE?
HE SAYS HE IS.
WHO CARES? HE SOUNDS LIKE A REAL CREEP.
OH, COME ON! SO I CAN'T THINK HE'S CUTE? PIX, TELL REGIE THAT GUY IS WAY HOT!
OH, YEAH, I CAN'T ARGUE THAT HE'S TOTALLY WAY HANDSOME...
...NOT WHAT I EXPECTED, LIKE, AT ALL...
...BUT I WAS MORE THAN HAPPY FOR THEM TO LEAVE AND I'LL BE GLAD TO NEVER SEE HIM OR HIS UNCLE AGAIN.

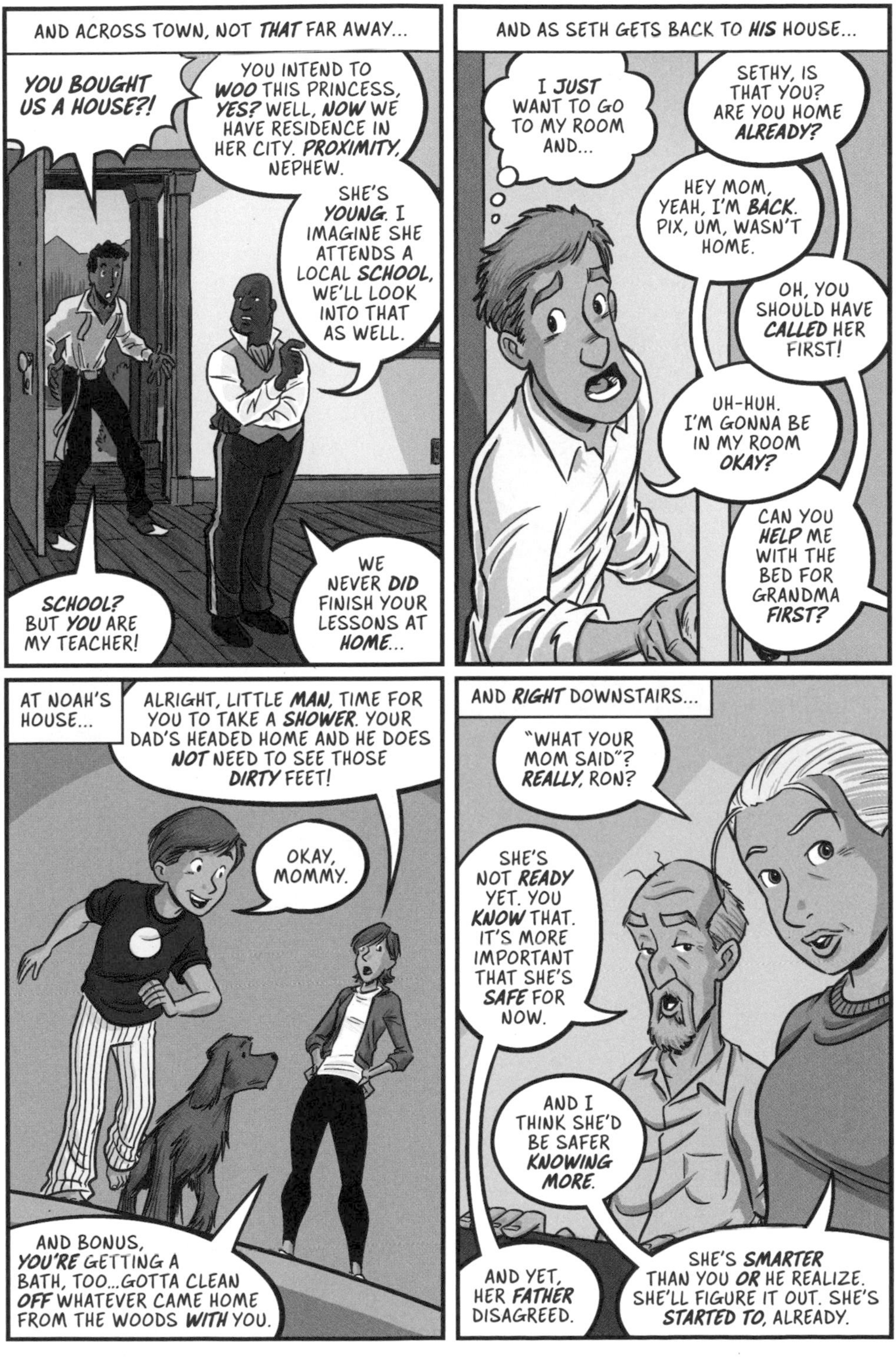
AND ACROSS TOWN, NOT THAT FAR AWAY...
YOU BOUGHT US A HOUSE?!
YOU INTEND TO WOO THIS PRINCESS, YES? WELL, NOW WE HAVE RESIDENCE IN HER CITY. PROXIMITY, NEPHEW.
SHE'S YOUNG. I IMAGINE SHE ATTENDS A LOCAL SCHOOL, WE'LL LOOK INTO THAT AS WELL.
SCHOOL? BUT YOU ARE MY TEACHER!
WE NEVER DID FINISH YOUR LESSONS AT HOME...
AND AS SETH GETS BACK TO HIS HOUSE...
I JUST WANT TO GO TO MY ROOM AND...
SETHY, IS THAT YOU? ARE YOU HOME ALREADY?
HEY MOM, YEAH, I'M BACK. PIX, UM, WASN'T HOME.
OH, YOU SHOULD HAVE CALLED HER FIRST!
UH-HUH. I'M GONNA BE IN MY ROOM OKAY?
CAN YOU HELP ME WITH THE BED FOR GRANDMA FIRST?
AT NOAH'S HOUSE...
ALRIGHT, LITTLE MAN, TIME FOR YOU TO TAKE A SHOWER. YOUR DAD'S HEADED HOME AND HE DOES NOT NEED TO SEE THOSE DIRTY FEET!
OKAY, MOMMY.
AND BONUS, YOU'RE GETTING A BATH, TOO...GOTTA CLEAN OFF WHATEVER CAME HOME FROM THE WOODS WITH YOU.
AND RIGHT DOWNSTAIRS...
"WHAT YOUR MOM SAID"? REALLY, RON?
SHE'S NOT READY YET. YOU KNOW THAT. IT'S MORE IMPORTANT THAT SHE'S SAFE FOR NOW.
AND I THINK SHE'D BE SAFER KNOWING MORE.
AND YET, HER FATHER DISAGREED.
SHE'S SMARTER THAN YOU OR HE REALIZE. SHE'LL FIGURE IT OUT. SHE'S STARTED TO, ALREADY.

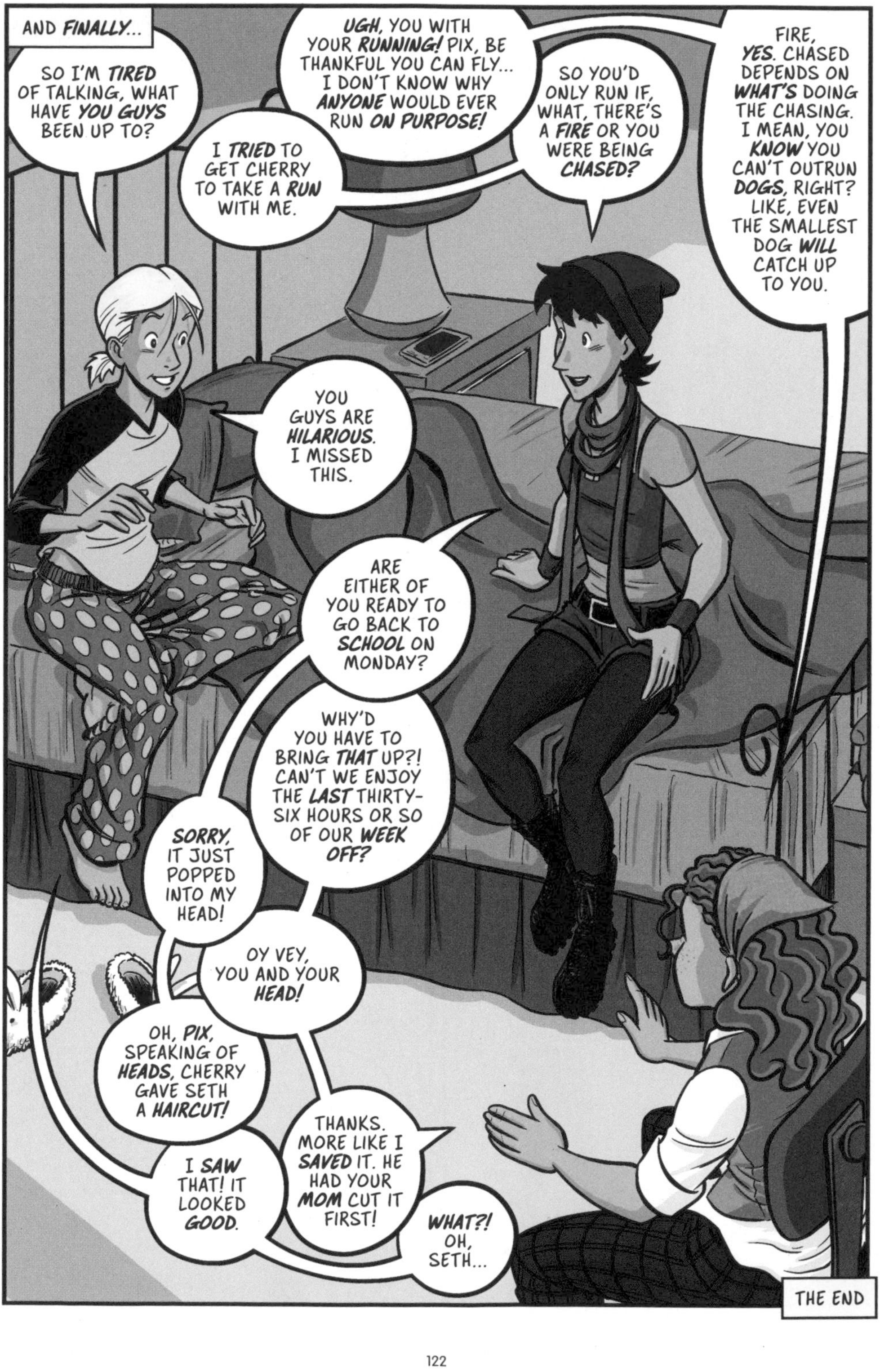
AND FINALLY...
SO I'M TIRED OF TALKING, WHAT HAVE YOU GUYS BEEN UP TO?
I TRIED TO GET CHERRY TO TAKE A RUN WITH ME.
UGH, YOU WITH YOUR RUNNING! PIX, BE THANKFUL YOU CAN FLY... I DON'T KNOW WHY ANYONE WOULD EVER RUN ON PURPOSE!
SO YOU'D ONLY RUN IF, WHAT, THERE'S A FIRE OR YOU WERE BEING CHASED?
FIRE, YES. CHASED DEPENDS ON WHAT'S DOING THE CHASING. I MEAN, YOU KNOW YOU CAN'T OUTRUN DOGS, RIGHT? LIKE, EVEN THE SMALLEST DOG WILL CATCH UP TO YOU.
YOU GUYS ARE HILARIOUS. I MISSED THIS.
ARE EITHER OF YOU READY TO GO BACK TO SCHOOL ON MONDAY?
WHY'D YOU HAVE TO BRING THAT UP?! CAN'T WE ENJOY THE LAST THIRTY-SIX HOURS OR SO OF OUR WEEK OFF?
SORRY, IT JUST POPPED INTO MY HEAD!
OY VEY, YOU AND YOUR HEAD!
OH, PIX, SPEAKING OF HEADS, CHERRY GAVE SETH A HAIRCUT!
I SAW THAT! IT LOOKED GOOD.
THANKS. MORE LIKE I SAVED IT. HE HAD YOUR MOM CUT IT FIRST!
WHAT?! OH, SETH...
THE END

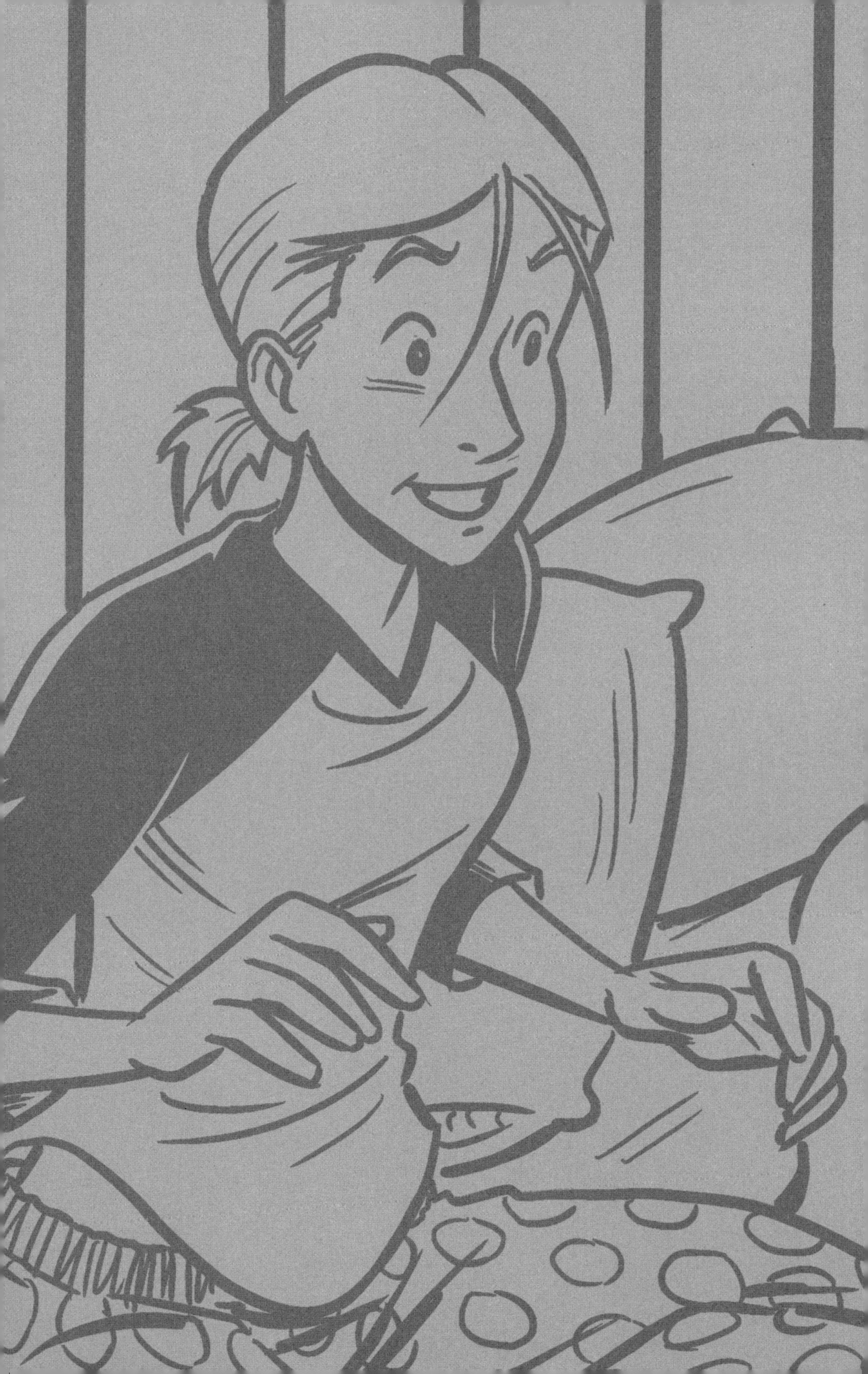

ORIGINS OF PIX

Figuring out what our hero would look like

Pix's desgn came from a lot of trial and error and sketching and doodling. Here are my early sketches trying out different looks for her costume, her fairy wing cape, hair styles, and more.

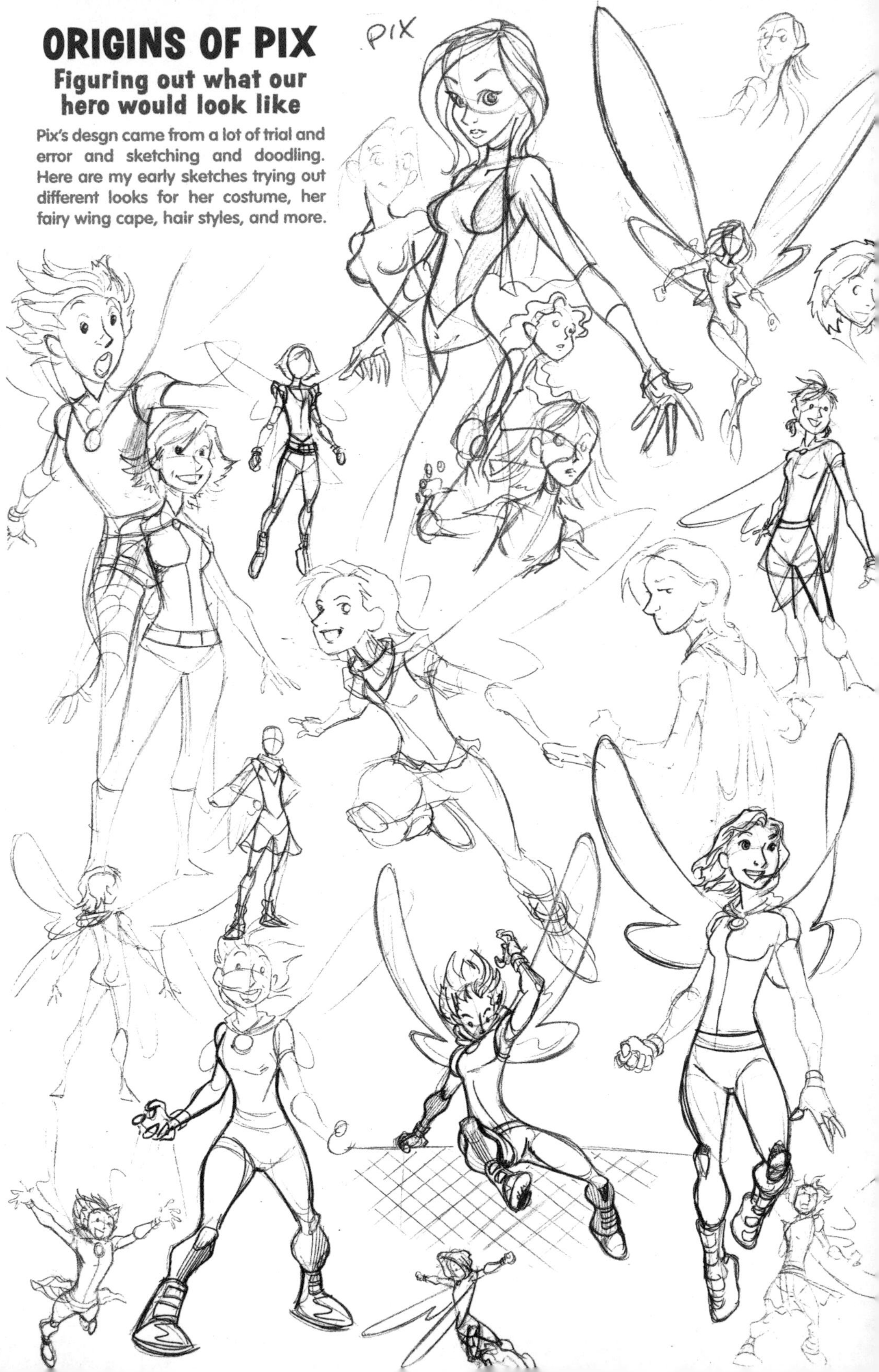
PIX

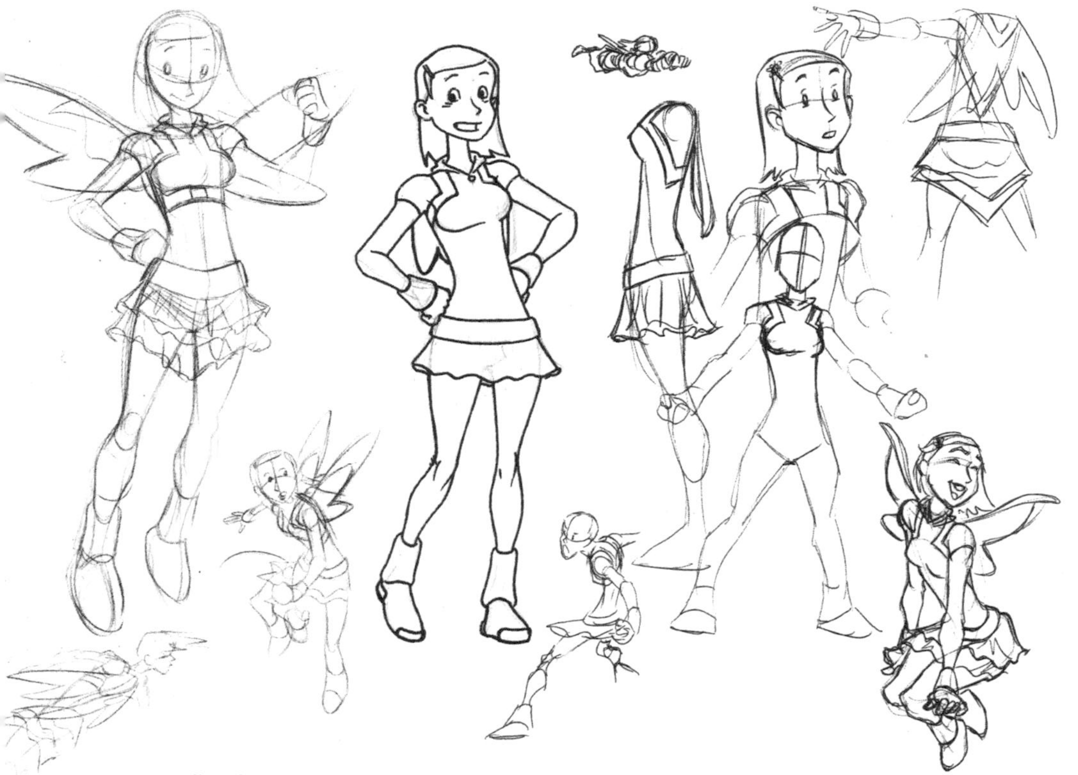

Eventually I found the right design for her, and THEN I had to select her costume colors. I tried a lot of different options, finally deciding on purple, yellow and white…

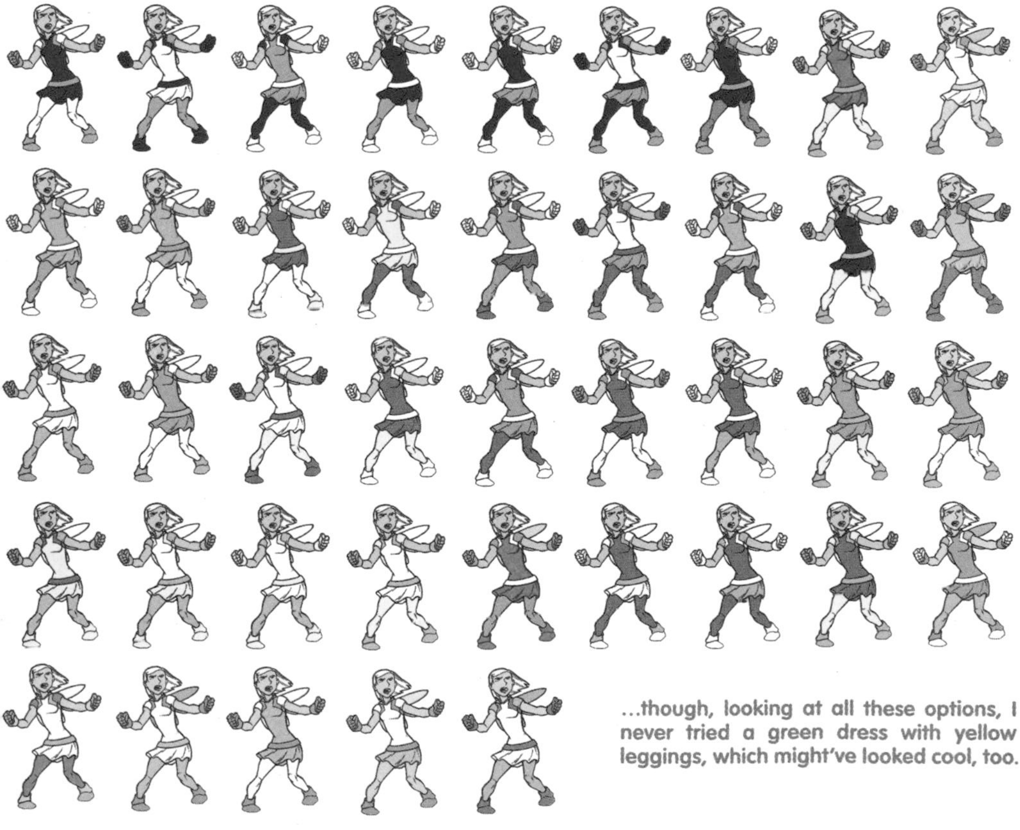

…though, looking at all these options, I never tried a green dress with yellow leggings, which might've looked cool, too.

PIX EXTRA!
a bonus Pix story (with Bonus!)

This short story originally appeared in a "kids and comics" themed anthology, the A2CAF Comics Showcase, a free giveaway at the 2016 Ann Arbor Comic Arts Festival (a2caf.com).

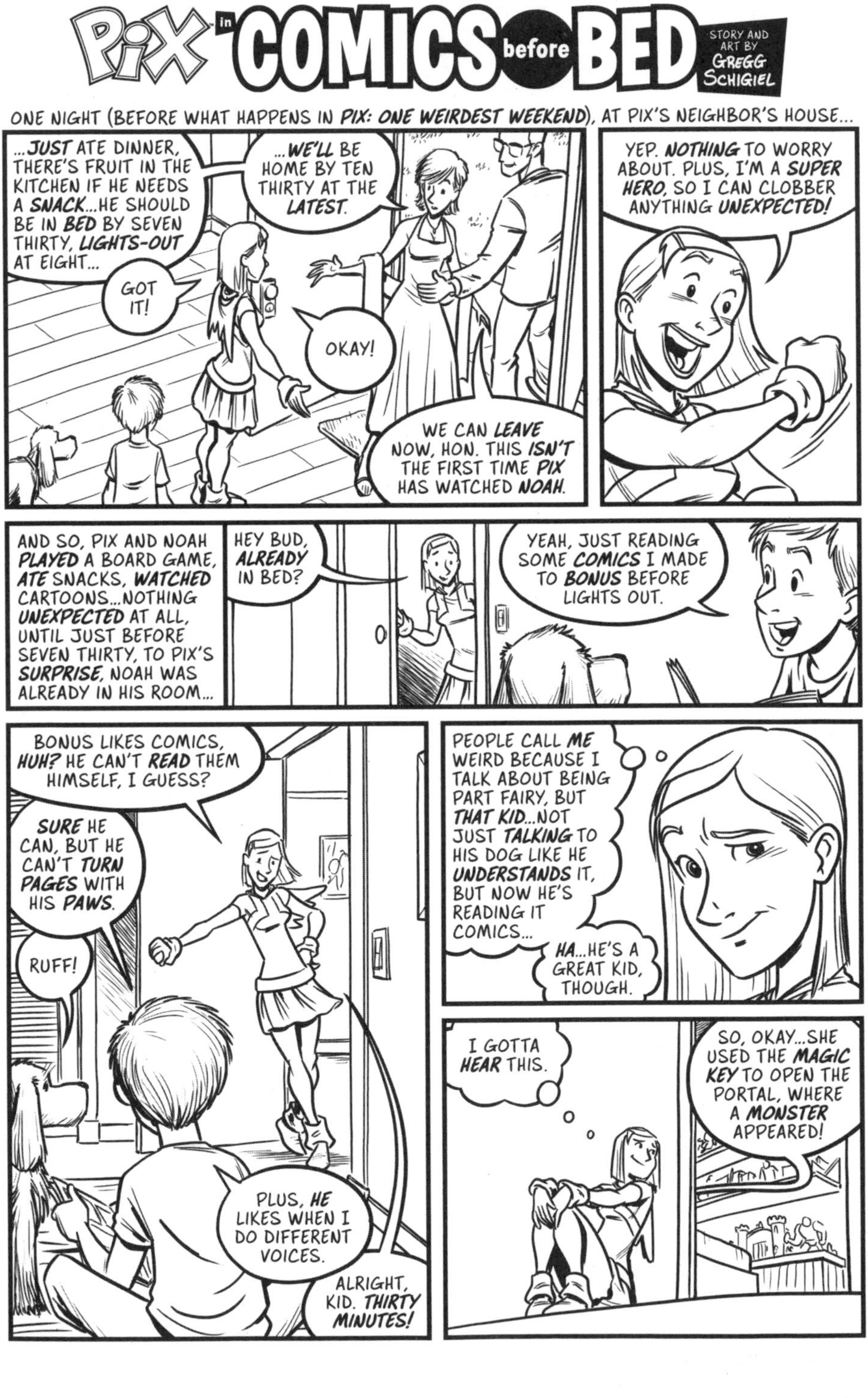

PIX in COMICS before BED
STORY AND ART BY GREGG SCHIGIEL
ONE NIGHT (BEFORE WHAT HAPPENS IN PIX: ONE WEIRDEST WEEKEND), AT PIX'S NEIGHBOR'S HOUSE...
...JUST ATE DINNER, THERE'S FRUIT IN THE KITCHEN IF HE NEEDS A SNACK...HE SHOULD BE IN BED BY SEVEN THIRTY, LIGHTS-OUT AT EIGHT...
GOT IT!
...WE'LL BE HOME BY TEN THIRTY AT THE LATEST.
OKAY!
WE CAN LEAVE NOW, HON. THIS ISN'T THE FIRST TIME PIX HAS WATCHED NOAH.
YEP. NOTHING TO WORRY ABOUT. PLUS, I'M A SUPER HERO, SO I CAN CLOBBER ANYTHING UNEXPECTED!
AND SO, PIX AND NOAH PLAYED A BOARD GAME, ATE SNACKS, WATCHED CARTOONS...NOTHING UNEXPECTED AT ALL, UNTIL JUST BEFORE SEVEN THIRTY, TO PIX'S SURPRISE, NOAH WAS ALREADY IN HIS ROOM...
HEY BUD, ALREADY IN BED?
YEAH, JUST READING SOME COMICS I MADE TO BONUS BEFORE LIGHTS OUT.
BONUS LIKES COMICS, HUH? HE CAN'T READ THEM HIMSELF, I GUESS?
SURE HE CAN, BUT HE CAN'T TURN PAGES WITH HIS PAWS.
RUFF!
PLUS, HE LIKES WHEN I DO DIFFERENT VOICES.
ALRIGHT, KID. THIRTY MINUTES!
PEOPLE CALL ME WEIRD BECAUSE I TALK ABOUT BEING PART FAIRY, BUT THAT KID...NOT JUST TALKING TO HIS DOG LIKE HE UNDERSTANDS IT, BUT NOW HE'S READING IT COMICS...
HA...HE'S A GREAT KID, THOUGH.
I GOTTA HEAR THIS.
SO, OKAY...SHE USED THE MAGIC KEY TO OPEN THE PORTAL, WHERE A MONSTER APPEARED!

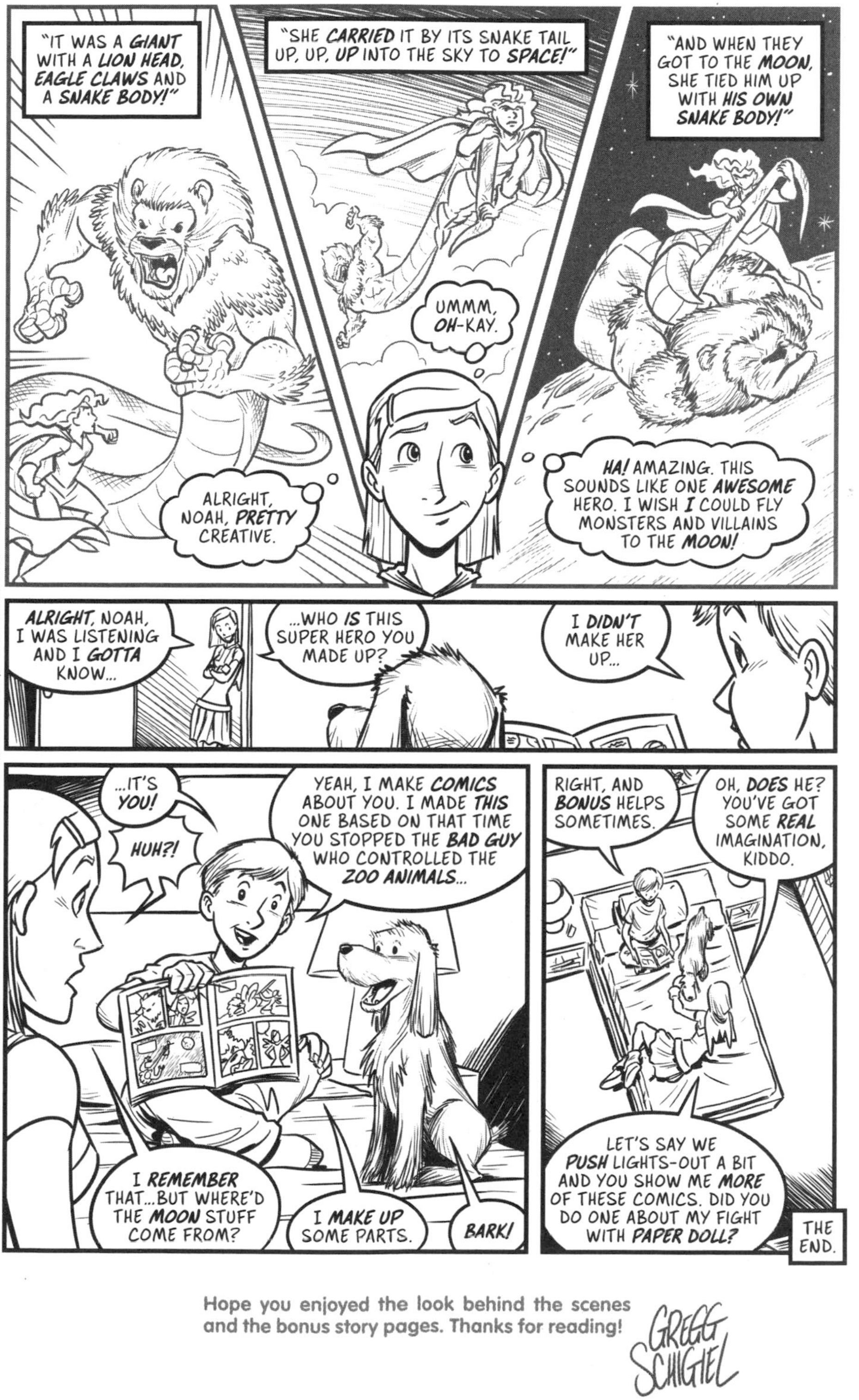
"IT WAS A GIANT WITH A LION HEAD, EAGLE CLAWS AND A SNAKE BODY!"
"SHE CARRIED IT BY ITS SNAKE TAIL UP, UP, UP INTO THE SKY TO SPACE!"
"AND WHEN THEY GOT TO THE MOON, SHE TIED HIM UP WITH HIS OWN SNAKE BODY!"
UMMM, OH-KAY.
ALRIGHT, NOAH, PRETTY CREATIVE.
HA! AMAZING. THIS SOUNDS LIKE ONE AWESOME HERO. I WISH I COULD FLY MONSTERS AND VILLAINS TO THE MOON!
ALRIGHT, NOAH, I WAS LISTENING AND I GOTTA KNOW...
...WHO IS THIS SUPER HERO YOU MADE UP?
I DIDN'T MAKE HER UP...
...IT'S YOU!
HUH?!
YEAH, I MAKE COMICS ABOUT YOU. I MADE THIS ONE BASED ON THAT TIME YOU STOPPED THE BAD GUY WHO CONTROLLED THE ZOO ANIMALS...
I REMEMBER THAT...BUT WHERE'D THE MOON STUFF COME FROM?
I MAKE UP SOME PARTS.
BARK!
RIGHT, AND BONUS HELPS SOMETIMES.
OH, DOES HE? YOU'VE GOT SOME REAL IMAGINATION, KIDDO.
LET'S SAY WE PUSH LIGHTS-OUT A BIT AND YOU SHOW ME MORE OF THESE COMICS. DID YOU DO ONE ABOUT MY FIGHT WITH PAPER DOLL?
THE END.

A2CAF Comics Showcase published May 2016 by Fifth Avenue Press, a production of the Ann Arbor District Library, 343 S. Fifth Avenue, Ann Arbor, MI 48104.

Hope you enjoyed the look behind the scenes and the bonus story pages. Thanks for reading!

GREGG SCHIGIEL

PIX'S SUBURBAN SUPERHERO ADVENTURE CONTINUES IN...

MAY 2017 from *image*®